Golden

Illuminati

Raymond Buckland

Golden

Illuminati

Raymond Buckland

PENDRAIG Publishing
Los Angeles, CA 91040

Golden Illuminati
By Raymond Buckland
First Edition © 2010
by PENDRAIG Publishing

Cover Design & Interior Images
Typeset & Layout by: Jo-Ann Byers Mierzwicki

Cover Art
(Traditional oil on canvas) by: Vladislav Pantic

PENDRAIG Publishing
Los Angeles, CA 91040
www.PendraigPublishing.com
Printed in the United States of America

ISBN: 978-0-9827263-8-9

Pre-Dawn

March 13, 1881 – Saint Petersburg, Russia

As on every Sunday for more than a score of years, Alexander Nikolaevich – Tsar Alexander II of Russia – went by closed carriage to Manege to review the Life Guards of the Reserve Infantry and of the Sapper Battalion regiments. Six Circassians accompanied him, trotting through the snow close beside the heavily-reinforced, imperial carriage. A seventh Cossack sat beside the coachman. Two sleighs followed, bearing the head of the tsar's guards and Police Chief Dvorzhitsky. The procession took its usual route along the Catherine Canal and then across the Pevchesky Bridge over the Moika River.

Alexander bent forward, pulling back the blind very slightly. He peered out through the narrow slit which then afforded him a limited view of the passing scenery. The elaborate, yellow-painted, iron railings of the bridge made him think, momentarily, of his father, who had been the first to pass over this structure some forty years before. The new bridge had replaced the old wooden one that had been located farther downstream. A smile briefly crossed his handsome face as he recalled his father's oft-repeated story of why the bridge had been placed where it now was.

"Yuri! Count Yuri Alexandrovich Golovkin! What a character! One day he was in so much of a hurry to see me that he stepped from his boat before it had come to rest. He fell into the Moyka and, I swear, if his companion had not acted quickly he would have drowned. When Stasov asked me where to locate the new bridge, I said 'Put it close to Yuri's home, so he doesn't keep falling into the river!'" Then he would laugh and laugh.

Alexander let the blind fall back into place. He felt good. That morning he had signed a document granting the first ever constitution to the Russian people. Count Loris-Melikoff had urged him not to review the parade that week; to allow some time for his actions to take effect. But Alexander was not one to break with tradition.

The imperial carriage continued on its way, now passing through narrow streets lined with cheering people. In the first of the following sleighs, Police Chief Dvorzhitsky's eyes swept back and forth, studying the crowd. He felt uneasy. The revolutionaries had been active of late and had previously tried to assassinate the tsar. They wouldn't give up. Suddenly he tensed.

A short young man in a heavy, black overcoat with a fur collar, pushed through the crowd toward the carriage. As the police chief opened his mouth to cry out, the man lunged between two onlookers and threw an object at the carriage. It hit one of the front wheels and bounced to the ground, exploding with a deafening roar. The young man, and those all around him, was knocked to the ground. The closest Cossack fell with his horse, both besmeared with blood. The driver of the carriage toppled to the ground, the Cossack beside him grabbing-up the reins and controlling the team.

Dvorzhitsky threw aside his fur travel rug and leapt to the ground, his feet slipping on the trodden snow. He lurched forward toward the carriage. Pushing his way between the distraught Circassians, he arrived at the carriage door as Alexander opened it and leaned out.

"Get back inside, Imperial Majesty! There may well be ..."

"No! I must see to my fallen Cossack."

Alexander descended from the carriage and moved across to the dying soldier, pushing past his chief of police. Dvorzhitsky noticed that four police officers had dragged the young man in the black coat to his feet and now held him firmly, awaiting orders. He turned back to the tsar.

"Majesty ..."

The young man being held, shook his head as though to clear it and then shouted something over his shoulder.

"Quickly!" Dvorzhitsky urged, taking the liberty of grasping the tsar's arm. At that moment another object landed at the tsar's feet, exploding on impact.

Later, Police Chief Dvorzhitsky was to say: "I was deafened by the new explosion, burned, wounded and thrown to the ground. Suddenly, amid the smoke and snowy fog, I heard His Majesty's weak voice cry 'Help!' Gathering what strength I had, I jumped up and rushed to the tsar. His Majesty was half-lying, half-sitting, leaning on his right arm. Thinking he was merely wounded heavily, I tried to lift him but the tsar's legs were shattered, and the blood poured out of them. Twenty people, with wounds of varying degree, lay on the sidewalk and on the street. Some managed to stand, others to crawl, still others tried to get out from beneath bodies that had fallen on them. Through the snow, debris, and blood you could see fragments of clothing, epaulets, sabers, and bloody chunks of human flesh."

The remaining loyal Cossacks got Alexander into one of the sleighs and he was rushed to the Winter Palace. A trail of blood marked where he was carried up the marble staircase to his study. There he was laid on a couch. Dr. Borkin had been summoned and was in attendance. Gravely he spoke to Princess Catherine[1] and the members of the Romanov family who had rushed to Alexander's side.

"His Imperial Majesty's legs are destroyed," he told them, "and he is bleeding to death. There is nothing that can be done for him. He has but fifteen minutes left, God rest his soul."

The tsar was given Communion and Extreme Unction. At 3:30pm the royal standard flying above the palace was finally lowered.

The thrower of the first bomb was found to be Nikolai Rysakov. That of the second, fatal, bomb was Ignacy Hryniewiecki. Had that second bomb failed, there was a third man, Emelianoff, who had a bomb wrapped in newspaper, under his arm. All three were members of a group of radicals calling themselves the *Nrodnaya Volya*, The People's Will.

---

1. *On July 6, 1880, within one month of the death of the Empress Maria on June 8, 1880, Alexander had married his long-time mistress Princess Catherine Dolgoruki, in a morganatic marriage.*

July 2, 1881 – Washington, D.C.

James Abram Garfield was pleased. He was about to take a train from the Baltimore and Potomac Railroad Depot, in Washington D.C., to visit Williams College, Massachusetts. He had graduated from Williams with distinction in 1856. Old memories played through his mind as he descended from the barouche and moved toward the railroad waiting room. It was nine o'clock in the morning. The train was due in fifteen minutes.

It was less than four months since Garfield's inauguration as the twentieth president of the United States, yet he looked forward to the break in his duties. After a successful military career, and at the urging of Abraham Lincoln, he had entered Congress at the age of thirty-two. In 1880, at age forty-nine, he was elected U.S. Senator for Ohio but became involved in the presidential campaign for John Sherman. However, through a series of unexpected events, he ended up being elected President himself.

Garfield had gone on to do battle with the powerful Senator Roscoe Conkling and had won, but it had been a hard battle of nerves. He desperately needed this break. Beside him strode his good friend James Gillespie Blaine, Secretary of State in Garfield's cabinet. Blaine was a tall, distinguished-looking man with a full head of hair and a white beard and mustache, in contrast to Garfield's receding hairline and dark beard.

"Not too long a wait," said Blaine, pulling out his gold pocket watch and studying it. "If the train is on time, that is." They both chuckled.

They passed through the barrier and moved on along the platform. Suddenly a figure burst out of the ticket office.

"Oh, no!" Garfield groaned. He immediately recognized the man as Charles Guiteau, a sometime lawyer who had been harassing the president for months, seeking an appointment as an overseas ambassador ... a position for which Garfield thought him entirely unsuited. After numerous demands – first for ambassadorship to Vienna and then to Paris – Blaine had told the man to leave and never to return.

"My God! ..." Blaine suddenly raised his arm and tried to move between Guiteau and the president.

"What ...?" Then Garfield saw what his friend had seen. Guiteau held a large service revolver in his hand – a Webley British Bulldog .44 – and swiftly raised it and pointed it at the president. Without a moment's pause, he twice pulled the trigger.

Bang! Bang!

Two shots rang out, not seconds apart. They were fired at point-blank range and there was no chance of them missing. Garfield felt a sharp pain in his arm and then an excruciating one in his stomach. He gasped "My God! What is this?" Then he fell to the ground.

Mortally wounded, Garfield remained fully conscious but in great pain. A railway guard grabbed the gunman and detained him until a policeman appeared to arrest him. Guiteau went without a struggle, apparently proud of what he had done. Blaine cried vainly for a doctor. Eventually one emerged from the waiting room. He administered brandy and spirits of ammonia, upon which the president vomited. Then, almost miraculously, a leading Washington doctor, D. Willard Bliss, appeared and took charge. However, it was a mixed blessing.

"We must locate the bullet," said Bliss. He rolled up his sleeves and produced a long, needle-like object from his bag. This he inserted in the president's stomach wound and started moving it around, Garfield crying out pitifully at every movement. Suddenly the probe became stuck between shattered fragments of the eleventh rib and Garfield screamed aloud. It took some time for Bliss to get the probe free and remove it. He then inserted his finger in the wound and moved it around, widening the opening.

Eventually Blaine was able to get the president moved to the White House, as he put it "Before the good doctor kills the man!"

Over the days and weeks that followed, as many as sixteen doctors examined President Garfield. Most of them probed with their fingers or with instruments that had never been sterilized. Indications were that the bullet had lodged close to the spine, though the general consensus of the doctors was that it was somewhere in the abdomen. As the summer wore on, the heat, humidity and insects did nothing to help Garfield's condition. He developed internal sores and the wound continuously oozed puss.

At one point the inventor Alexander Graham Bell visited the White House with a hastily constructed metal detector. Bell failed to locate the bullet and left frustrated, unaware that the president lay on a mattress containing the newly invented metal coil-springs.

It was decided to move President Garfield to the New Jersey shore, where a large house, known as the Francklyn Cottage, was made available for him. The railroad quickly laid track from the main line to the house and, on September 6, a special train of three railroad cars took him there. The president, a well-built man of six feet, initially weighing 210 pounds, now weighed only 130 pounds. Mrs. Garfield sat beside her husband for the railroad journey, trying to reassure him.

On the evening of September 16, Dr. Bliss was summoned by a servant to the bedside of the ailing man. Immediately, Bliss saw that President Garfield was dying. He summoned Mrs. Garfield, two other doctors – Agnew and Hamilton – and Colonel Rockwell. At 10:35pm James Garfield died.

Charles Guiteau never denied shooting the president, but always claimed that it was the doctors who killed him.

Guiteau, like his father Luther, followed the teachings of John H. Noyes. Noyes promoted communal living and multiple sex partners; anathema to most Victorians. In 1860, young Charles Guiteau had traveled to the Oneida, New York, community that was the hub of Noyes's cult, and took up residence. He had remained there for five years.

March 2, 1882 – London, England

It was true that the Queen's carriage on the Royal train had a lavatory, but that hardly made up for the jolting stops and starts, the noisy steam whistle, and the general dirt and dust of the long journey. So thought Queen Victoria, as she stepped down from the wooden carriage, thankful to be back at Windsor. The Taff Vale 4-4-2 tank locomotive, newly painted and boldly sporting the royal coat of arms, gave a final snort and blast of steam, as though bidding a fond farewell to its royal passenger. Victoria refrained from looking in its direction and, instead, forced a smile toward the gathered villagers of Windsor who crowded the platform. She could see that the crowd also stretched away down the road, leading from Windsor railway station toward the ever-present Windsor Castle.

The station master bowed the Queen toward her horse-drawn carriage, sweeping his top hat back and forth, as though clearing a path. She gave him a brief nod and allowed the footman to assist her into the carriage. A platoon of the Queen's Life Guards sat astride their horses in line behind the coach, the sun glinting off their helmets and breastplates.

Her majesty made herself comfortable in the brougham, permitting her youngest daughter and constant companion Beatrice to smooth down her skirt and adjust the tartan, woollen, knee-blanket. How refreshing, Victoria thought to herself, to be out of that smelly, jolting, railroad monster. The Royal railway carriage had been designed especially for her comfort, she knew, but it really did not compare to the horse-drawn variety. As the coachman cracked his whip and the pair of matched dapple grey mares moved out of the Windsor station yard, the queen peered out of the window and raised a tentatively acknowledging hand to the cheering throng that lined the street. It was but a short drive to the castle and, despite the chill in the air, the sun was shining and the sky was clear.

"Open the window, child."

"But – is it not too cold, mama?"

"Tsk! Open the window. We will not freeze to death on such a short journey. The air will do you good. Look at your pale face, will you?"

Dutifully, Beatrice reached across her mother and lowered the carriage window.

She had hardly settled back into her seat when she screamed.

On the crowded street, a tall, angular, young man in a bowler hat reached through the cheering onlookers on either side of him and raised a pistol to point at the Queen. Without a moment's pause, he pulled the trigger. Beatrice screamed again as the bullet flew into the carriage, narrowly missing the Queen, and tore through the wood and fabric of the back panel. Victoria, seemingly unmoved, watched as the crowd turned on the would-be assassin and disarmed him. He was dragged to the ground and would surely have been trampled had not the police, led by Superintendent Hayes of the Windsor Police, not grabbed him and hustled him away.

"Drive on!" Victoria commanded, raising her voice to the coachman, who had allowed the mares to pause. He jostled the reins and the brougham resumed its journey. Without asking permission, Beatrice leaned across and closed the window.

"It is worth being shot at ... to see how much one is loved."

Beatrice looked at the queen, eyes wide.

"You – you don't mind people shooting at you, mama?" she asked in a whisper.

"There have been six – make that now seven – attempts on our life." Her mouth set in a grim line. "Edward Oxford. John Francis. John William Bean. William Hamilton. Robert Pate. Arthur O'Connor. We remember them all."

The failed assassin was a young Scotsman named Roderick Maclean. He had previously sent a poem to the Queen, expressing his love and loyalty of the monarch. Unfortunately, it was some of the worst poetry that anyone had ever seen! It was roundly rejected. Maclean took the rejection very much to heart, seeing it as an affront to his artistic abilities. He determined to have his revenge.

Maclean was tried for high treason, found "not guilty but insane," and sent to an asylum. He had been a member of *Tobar nam Buadh*, The Spring of Virtues.

Daybreak

London, England – March, 1899

"*Y*ou are going to need money ... a great deal of money."

Mathers swallowed and let his eyes follow his visitor as the other man moved across to the sideboard where, uninvited, he poured himself another glass of whisky. He then moved to stand at the window. He left the whisky decanter open and Mathers unconsciously crossed the room to close it.

"Don't you think it cost a lot of money to start the French Revolution?" asked the figure at the window, gazing down at a passing hansom cab. Mathers could hear the clip-clop of its horse's hooves even though the window was closed. "And the assassination of the American presidents Lincoln and more recently – what was his name? – Garfield? The elimination of Russia's Alexander II? Do you not think these things cost money?"

Mathers knew these were rhetorical questions but he moved to stand beside the other man.

"Yes. You are going to need a *great* deal of money." He downed his whiskey, handed Mathers the glass, and then moved to the door where he pulled on his overcoat. "Think about it, Samuel. Let me know what ideas you come up with." He took up his top hat, gloves and cane and left the room.

Mathers gazed down into the empty glass in his hand and gnawed on his lip. Where was he going to get "a great deal of money"?

The rain came down steadily as Samuel Lidell MacGregor Mathers turned off Charing Cross Road into Denmark Place. He paused to glance back at the busy thoroughfare with its clatter of horsedrawn traffic and then, drawing his Inverness coat closer about him, turned back to study the small bookshop in the little alleyway.

Chambers
Antique and Collectible Books; Maps; Prints.
Printer ~ Fine Printing
Prop.: Alec Chambers, Esq.

Mathers had found old and interesting books here before and now made it a habit to drop by at least once a week, to check on any new stock. As he pushed open the door, a dull bell clattered its announcement of his arrival. He closed the door behind him and advanced into the cramped confines, slipping off his cape and shaking it vigorously. He hung it, with his hat, on the oak hall-rack positioned by the door.

"Ah, Mister Mathers," greeted an elderly clerk perched on a high stool behind the counter. His watery grey eyes peered over the wire rims of his spectacles. A hesitant smile attempted to play at the corners of his mouth. "We 'aven't seen you in a few days, sir. Narsty weather outside, I see."

Mathers nodded, wordlessly, and proceeded to the rear of the store where he knew the latest arrivals were shelved. He was a tall man with a military bearing, having served for a few years in the First Hampshire Infantry Volunteers. For a decade or more since then he had acknowledged no regular job but, instead, did odds and ends; dabbling in various professions. Now in his mid-forties, he had once been slim but had begun to exhibit considerable weight around his midsection. He had reddish hair, tinted with grey, and sported a military-style mustache but no beard. Dull yellow teeth gave testimony to years of addiction to a tobacco pipe, though he was now strongly opposed to such practice.

Against the back wall of the store stood a bank of ancient volumes, all leather-bound; many in distressed state. Mathers's eyes scanned across the titles. He was familiar with most. Twice his hand reached out and removed a volume. He examined each briefly and then replaced it.

"Not much new here," he observed.

"No, sir." Edward Merryfield, the dusty clerk who had been a part of the store since its founding almost fifty years before, laboriously climbed down from his stool and moved across to stand beside his regular customer. "Mister Chambers was saying only yesterday that the estate sales 'asn't been givin' up many good books of late."

"And where is Mister Chambers?"

"'E is at one of them sales even now, sir. Gentleman down in 'ampshire what got hisself shot at one of them 'unting parties. Viscount Something, I fink it was. Mister Chambers said as 'ow 'e 'ad a good library, sir."

"Hmm. All right. Tell him to keep aside anything he thinks will interest me. I will look back in a couple of days."

"Yes, sir. Very good, sir."

As Mathers turned to leave he noticed a flat wicker basket on the counter. It held a number of small, green, paper-bound books. He picked up one of them.

"What are these?"

"Oh, that is Mister Chambers's latest publication, sir. Just printed yesterday. 'E dropped 'em off as 'e was leaving this morning, sir."

"Did he though?" Mathers looked at the title. " *The Life and Times of Nicholas Flamel,* by Alec Chambers," he read. "I did not know Chambers was an expert on Flamel."

"Well, I don't know about that, sir," volunteered Merryfield. "But 'e's got what he says is one of the largest collections of books an' things on al – alchem ..."

"Alchemy."

"Yes, sir."

"Has he now? Hmm."

Mathers threw down a crown, took one of the books and, donning his hat and coat, left the shop.

Alec Chambers studied the rows of leather-bound books crammed into the shelves of the library. They were in no particular order and had apparently been placed according to size and color. Either the deceased had not been a true bibliophile or else he had left it to his wife or one of the servants to arrange the volumes. Alec sighed. This didn't make it easy to examine works by any particular author or on any particular subject. He would have to search through the entire library to find those that were related.

"Damned disgrace!" muttered a bespectacled, white-haired gentleman who walked with a limp. He seemed to be talking to himself, as he struggled past the shelves, but Alec replied to his comment anyway.

"No idea of categorizing," he said.

The older man stopped, surprised, and looked up at Alec. "You are that young Chambers fellow, are you not?" he demanded.

"I am indeed." Alec inclined his head. "And you are Mister Stephen Colleridge, if I am not mistaken." Colleridge, he knew, had been one of the major booksellers in the city for a great many years. Alec's father always spoke of him with respect.

"Hrmph! I see no point in denying it." The white-haired man ran his fingers along a line of books. "At least they seem to have been looked after. Dusted off, from time to time, I imagine. Could be worse."

"Indeed," Alec acquiesced. "But that does not help us find anything, does it?'

Colleridge grunted again and continued on around the shelves.

"What is your interest?"

Alec looked up to see an angular young man, in a well-worn tweed suit, descending the spiral staircase that rose to the upper shelves.

"Oh, a number of subjects," Alec replied. "Travel, folklore, occult, biog...."

"Occult?" The other man raised his eyebrows. "You have an interest in that?" He had by now reached the floor level and advanced on Alec. He held out his hand. "Bertram Spendright at your service, sir. Hmm! I suppose since those Cambridge men started their Society for Psychical Research there has been a revival of interest in all that arcane mumbo-jumbo." Alec said nothing. "Well, you may be in luck. I think I saw some obscure works up on the topmost shelf, to the extreme left. It looked like a set of two or three volumes devoted to one or more of those abstruse and recondite disciplines."

Alec thanked him and began the climb up the spiral staircase.

Alec Chambers inherited the book shop from his father, William Chambers, when the old man had died seven years before, in 1892. Alec added a small printing press to supplement the meager income that came from the sale of books. He mostly printed pamphlets, small posters, and slim booklets for individuals and organizations.

Alec – fair-haired and clean-shaven – was twenty-eight years of age, unmarried, and totally absorbed in his shop, his printing and, now, the publication of his first book. He wasn't expecting any great sales of it, especially since it was a biography of a little-known figure of the fourteenth century, but he did consider it a major accomplishment. He just hoped that there would be enough sales to cover the cost of producing the book.

It was late afternoon and Alec was busy sorting out the books he had acquired at the estate sale of the late Viscount Donnington, when the shop bell clattered and he looked up to see Samuel Mathers enter.

"Good afternoon, Mister Mathers." Alec stood up, hastily dusting-off his knees. Mathers had become a regular customer, interested in the occult books that Alec occasionally came across. Alec didn't know much about the man, other than that he was the leader of some sort of society which – according to Mathers – had a number of prominent people among its membership.

"Chambers! Good. I believe you have some new stock?" Mathers glanced around the shop.

"Yes. I have just been sorting it. Not much in your line though, I am afraid. Mainly old volumes on the inland waters of England, the joys of fly fishing, and the right way to hunt pheasant."

"That is all?"

"Oh, there are a number of others, but nothing to compare to the pheasant and pike volumes, I am afraid." He smiled. "I had thought I had stumbled onto something but it was just a three-volume edition of Cornelius Agrippa's *Occult Philosophy*, which I know you already have. However, there is a very promising sale coming up in a fortnight. Much more in line with your interests I think, Mister Mathers."

"Oh?"

"Personal library of a titled gentleman who was, among other things, a Freemason and a connoisseur of books on phrenology, cartomancy, and the Kabbalah."

"Ah! Good. Very good." Mathers again looked about him. "Oh, by the way. I picked up one of your slim volumes on Flamel, when I was in here the other day. Your man might have mentioned it."

"Yes. Yes, he did. Old Merryfield always gives a full report." Alec smiled. "My first book. Did ... did you care for it, I wonder, Mister Mathers?"

"It was ... interesting. I would have liked more detail, of course. But, considering the slimness of the volume, it certainly touched a number of fine points." He paused. "I had not realized that you were an expert on alchemy."

"Well, not really on alchemy, per se," said Alec. "And certainly no expert. But I have made Nicholas Flamel an especial subject of mine."

"And your research ...?"

Alec thought his customer seemed anxious to get details. "I do have something of a library myself, on that particular subject," he admitted.

"Yes. Yes, your man intimated as much."

Mathers moved across to a nearby set of shelves, but it seemed to Alec that he wasn't really interested in the books there.

"This 'library' of yours, Chambers. What sort of volumes does it contain?"

For some reason that he couldn't define, Alec wished that he could change the subject. "Oh, nothing special. Just a general cross-section."

"Are the books for sale?"

"No!" He answered quickly, and then felt that he had, perhaps, been too sharp. "No, I'm afraid they are just my own collection. Nothing too unusual. Nothing that I would place on the shelves here, for sale."

Mathers nodded, as though he totally understood. "Of course." He ran his hand along one of the shelves of books. "But they are all on alchemy, right?"

Alec suddenly felt uncomfortable.

"Have you seen these, that I got in last week?" he asked, moving quickly to another section of the shop and indicating a complete set of Daniel Defoe's works, all in soft leather bindings. "There is a first edition of *A System of Magick* here; 1727. Original calf. I understand it was Lord Palmeston's copy."

"Really?" Mathers crossed quickly to his side. "I had not noticed that." He carefully removed the indicated volume and gently opened it. Alec appreciated the man's care with the book.

"And what are you asking for this - this amusing little volume?"

"Two guineas, sir."

Mathers' eyebrows rose. "A tidy sum," he murmured.

"But not out of line, as I know you are aware, Mister Mathers." Alec kept his voice low and his eyes on the volume.

"Hmm. Yes." Mathers paused a moment before nodding. "All right. I will take it. Now, back to Monsieur Flamel."

Alec groaned inwardly, but congratulated himself on the sale of the Defoe book. "You have an interest in Flamel yourself?" he asked.

"Oh, no more than the next man, I am sure." Mathers pretended to lose himself in the slim, calf-bound book he held. "He was the most successful of the alchemists, was he not?"

"Oh, yes." Alec resigned himself to talking about alchemy. "Yes, he was the one 'philosopher' who has been well documented regarding his successes. As I am sure you know, he amassed a considerable fortune and subsequently gave generously to churches, hospitals, and charitable institutions."

"All gold he had manufactured from base metals."

"Indeed."

"And, according to your book, he kept records of all his experiments."

"He certainly did."

Mathers digested this information for a few moments. Suddenly he reached into his pocket and removed a piece of folded paper.

"Chambers, I have a small task for your printing establishment. My usual shop has regrettably gone out of business." He unfolded the paper. "In about ten days I shall be giving a lecture at Jackson Hall. I need a quantity of flyers that I may get someone to hand out; hopefully to bring an eager crowd. Here is what I need."

Alec took the paper and studied it.

Samuel Liddel MacGregor Mathers
acclaimed Occultist and
Chief of the Second Order of the
GOLDEN DAWN
will on Friday 14th of April 1899,
at 8:30 pm
at Jackson Hall Victoria Street
deliver a Free Lecture on
the History of that Order.
Questions will be entertained.

There was nothing untoward about it; a simple job. "May I ask the name of your previous printing establishment?" Alec asked.

"Wilkinsons. In the East End. Not the most elegant of shops, but they could get jobs done at short notice, which I often needed."

"They burned down, did they not?" said Alec.

"Yes. Regrettably. And very inconveniently."

"And, may I ask – what is the Golden Dawn? I have heard of it, in passing, but have no true awareness of its identity."

Mathers had started toward the door but now paused and looked back. "It was formed a decade or more ago. Today it has well over two hundred members, drawn from every class of society; from a simple watchmaker, living in Yorkshire, to such estimable persons as poets, scholars, accountants, physicians, and more. I should not give names, of course, but ..." Mathers dropped his voice to a whisper. Alec was obliged to move closer to hear. "Mister William Butler Yeats the poet and playwright who, earlier this year, founded the Irish Literary Theatre in Dublin, in association with Lady Augusta Gregory, is a prominent member, as is the actress Florence Farr. I myself have the honor of being the Chief of the Second Order of the Golden Dawn." Mathers moved to the door. "Modesty prevents me from enumerating my many contributions." He raised his voice again. "I would like two hundred of those announcements at your earliest, if you would." He placed the two guineas for the book on the counter and went out.

His departure left Alec feeling ill at ease, yet he could think of no good reason for that agitation. He looked again at the notice to be printed.

"Alchemy? Was that not all twaddle and balderdash?"

"No, it was not." Mathers was irritated, though he didn't know why since, until recently, he had held much the same opinion of what was termed 'the Hermetic Art'.

"Leastwise, it may have been in the majority of cases," he continued, "but not in all cases by any means." He poured sherry for himself and his guest.

"Oh?" The Reverend Monty Winters raised his bushy eyebrows, and accepted the proffered glass.

"As you know, The Hermetic Order of the Golden Dawn is just that – a 'Hermetic' Order; indirectly associated with so-called alchemy."

His guest nodded but concentrated on his drink.

"We are not so much into the 'base metals into gold' aspect," continued Mathers. "Leastwise, one or two of our members may have conducted the odd experiment, but the stated purpose of our society is 'to aid members to test, purify, and exalt the individual's *spiritual nature* so as to unify it with his or her Holy Guardian Angel.' As you know, Dr. Wescott had originally obtained MacKenzie's cipher manuscript and I

was myself instrumental in fleshing that out into workable rituals, which became the basis of the Golden Dawn."

"So your society is more a group of ritualists than scientists or chemists?"

"You could say that, I think." Mathers finished his drink and poured himself a second.

"You said that not all cases of alchemy were balderdash," persisted Winters.

"There were one or two of the old-time practitioners who seem to have been exceptionally skilled at it. One Nicholas Flamel is probably the best known. Born in Pontoise, France, in 1330, or thereabouts."

"But is that not all hearsay, Samuel?"

Mathers sipped his drink, sat down in the winged chair opposite his friend, and settled back. "On the contrary, Monty. All Flamel's work was extremely well documented. He produced gold enough not only for his own needs, but to finance various institutions and set up a number of charities."

"He actually produced gold?" Monty Winters had trouble crediting the idea.

"Yes." Mathers nodded.

"So, why have not others followed the path he trod?"

Mathers put down his glass and sat back, steepling his fingers. "That is why I asked you here, Monty. I would like to get your opinion."

"Of course, old boy. Always willing to help a chap put two and two together."

"I have told you how I need to get my hands on a large amount of money ... and soon."

The bushy eyebrows came together. "You never told me why."

"No." Mathers took up his glass and had another sip of the sherry. "No, and I have asked that you not press me on that point. Just trust me, based on our years of friendship. I need a very large sum of money in a very short amount of time."

"You have considered robbing a bank, of course?" Monty Winters laughed at his own joke, but quickly let it die when he saw that his friend was not amused. "No, of course not. Sorry. Poor sense of humor." He stroked his black, Mephistophelean beard.

"I was thinking about Flamel, and his secret to success." Mathers kept his eyes steadily on his friend's face.

Winters had grown serious. "You say you need this money in a short amount of time. Then would not pursuing alchemy defeat that object? Surely – from what I recall of what little I have read on the subject – those chaps spent years on their projects."

"Not Flamel. Oh, initially, yes. He spent perhaps half his life perfecting his process. But once it was perfected, then he was able to produce gold whenever it was called for. Others, before and after Flamel, followed the same route; spending many years – oftentimes a whole lifetime – trying to duplicate what Flamel achieved."

"I see." Winters took a long drink. He nodded his head slowly, absorbing all that Mathers had said.

"So you see, all I need is access to Flamel's notes; his laboratory records."

"That's all?" Winters gave a snort. "I would think that is a great deal. Surely, if this alchemist's notes were still in existence, the whole world would be chasing after them?"

"If they knew that they still existed, and exactly where to find them, I am sure they would," said Mathers. "But it is my belief that the notes are available but no one knows about them, or knows enough to search for them. Here – let me show you something."

Mathers got to his feet and walked over to a side table. He picked up a slim green volume and carried it over to his friend, opening the book and flicking through to an illustrated page.

"What's this?"

"This," said Mathers, "is the privately-printed work of a casual acquaintance. A young man named Alec Chambers. He is something of an authority on Flamel. Now, look at these illustrations."

Winters studied them, turning the pages to scan them all. "Fascinating, but I am afraid they don't mean anything to me. What are they?"

"According to what Chambers says, they are black and white reproductions of pages from Flamel's own notebook."

"Really?"

"Now, my thought is, where did Chambers get these illustrations?"

"And . . ?"

"The man has a collection. He refers to it as his 'library' though I have no idea of the actual size of it. Anyway, he has a collection of alchemical texts. What if he does, in fact, own the Flamel notebook?"

Winters set down his now-empty glass and tugged at his beard. "You think he might have?"

"I don't know. But it is a thought."

"Indeed it is." He tugged some more at his beard. "So why doesn't this chap make gold for himself, if he has the notebook?"

"He is a bibliophile. He is more interested in the book than in its contents . . . if he is even aware of the value of the contents."

The clergyman sat quietly thinking for a moment.

"Where does this person live, might one ask?"

"His bookshop is in a little alley off Charing Cross Road; Denmark Place. There is, I have noticed, a small set of rooms behind the shop. I imagine he lives there, surrounded by his books."

"Hmm."

"Another sherry, Monty?"

Alec was surprised to find the door to his shop standing open, on his arrival there at eight of the clock in the morning. Merryfield lived in a small flat at the back of the shop but did not usually unlock and open for business until nine in the morning; an hour after Alec's usual arrival time. It would be extremely unlike Merryfield to go out, for whatever reason, and leave the door open, thought Alec.

He stood for a moment just inside the doorway and looked about him. All seemed in order. He listened. All was quiet.

"Merryfield!" he called. "Mister Merryfield!"

It remained quiet. As Alec took a step forward, his foot kicked against something. Looking down, he saw that it was a large sliver of wood, apparently broken off from somewhere. Picking it up, Alec realized where it had come from. He swung about and examined the shop door. Sure enough, there was a large section missing from it; just below the lock. Indentations told him that someone had used a jemmy and forced the door.

Now troubled, Alec hurried forward and almost fell as he rounded the front bookcases. Dozens of books were strewn across the floor, obviously pulled from the rear cases. From where he now stood, Alec could see that the small door into Merryfield's flat was wide open. Again calling Merryfield's name, he cautiously moved forward.

Edward Merryfield lay face down on the rug in front of the now-cold fireplace. The back of his head had been smashed-in and blood covered the area. Alec moved swiftly forward and knelt to check his old employee. The figure was cold. Dead.

"Once again, if you would be so kind, Mister Chambers. You say that nothing is missing?"

Alec shook his head and let out a deep sigh. "No. Nothing, so far as I can see. Of course I will have to do a complete inventory check to be certain but, on the face of it, nothing has gone."

"Do you keep money here overnight?" The short, dark, police inspector's brown eyes bored into Alec's face. "Either in the shop or in this flat?"

Alec shook his head. "No. I always empty the drawer at the end of the day and then take it home with me, to add up and enter in the books."

"The deceased ..." he consulted his notebook, "Mister Edward Merryfield, didn't handle that?"

"No. Leastwise, not when I was in town, which is most of the time. On rare occasions, when I may be away, Mister Merryfield would maintain custody of the day's income."

"But this was not the case last night?"

"No."

Inspector Henry Kent pursed his lips and studied his notebook. He licked the tip of his stubby pencil and made a notation.

"You got along well with your employee, Mister Chambers?"

"What? Why yes, of course! He had been with the business for donkey's years. He worked for my father before me. What sort of a question is that?"

The policeman ignored him. "No property – books – missing?"

"Books? The shop is full of books, inspector! It is going to take a long time to determine whether or not they are all here. But so far as this little flat goes, no; I don't think anything was taken from here. Mister Merryfield was not himself much of a reader."

"I see." Another notation.

The door opened and a portly police constable stuck his head inside. "Take the body, sir?" he asked.

"What? Oh, yes. Yes, I think so."

The policeman came all the way in, accompanied by a second officer. They rolled Merryfield's body onto a stretcher, covered it with a dirty blanket, and carried him out. Alec couldn't watch and fixed his eyes on a small framed painting of London Bridge, hanging on the wall above the fireplace mantel.

"What – what exactly killed Merryfield?" Alec asked. "I know it was the blow to his head, but . ."

"He was hit with a life-preserver."

"A what?"

"Life-preserver. Many burglars carry them. The most popular type is a small ball, sometimes made of lead and attached to a piece of gut. The gut is fastened around the burglar's wrist. He can easily carry the ball in the palm of his hand and then, if he has to defend himself, or decides to attack someone, he can swing the ball on the length of gut and hit his target over the head. Usually it just knocks them out but occasionally – if it's a larger piece of lead or it's swung especially viciously – it can kill. As it did here."

"I see."

"What's this?" The inspector indicated a pile of pale blue papers resting on the corner of the wooden table near the door.

"Oh! Sorry." Alec moved to pick up the pile. "I was carrying these when I came in. I must have put them down there when I saw ... when I ..."

The inspector picked up the top sheet from the pile and read aloud what was on it.

"Samuel Liddel MacGregor Mathers, acclaimed Occultist and Chief of the Second Order of the Golden Dawn ..." He looked at Alec and raised his eyebrows in a question.

"A small printing order. I just ran them off last night and was bringing them in to pass on to Mister Mathers later this morning."

"You know this Samuel Mathers?"

"Well, yes. He gave me the order for the printing." Alec wondered what this could possibly have to do with the events of the morning.

"Samuel Liddel MacGregor Mathers." There was a note of contempt in the policeman's voice.

"You are familiar with him?" Alec asked.

There was a long silence. Then, "Oh, yes. Yes, we know our Mister Mathers."

"We?"

"Scotland Yard."

It was Alec's turn to raise his eyebrows.

"Oh, didn't I mention, sir, that I am from Scotland Yard? When the crime is such an obvious murder, we are always pulled in, you see."

"Oh, dear me!" Samuel Mathers paused in the doorway and looked hard and long at the abused shop door. "So this was the miscreants' means of entry."

"You have heard?" asked Alec.

"It was in *The Times*," said Mathers, coming into the shop. "A brief account on page five, with too few details. But is that not always the case? Your elderly employee was, as I understand it, bludgeoned to death, yet nothing was stolen from the shop. Is that not correct?"

"It seems that way. Poor Merryfield."

"Quite so."

Alec stood behind the counter. He straightened copies of the *Lamp of Thoth* magazine, on display there.

"Your precious alchemy collection? That is safe?"

"Oh, yes. Of course."

Mathers nodded. He seemed to consider for a moment. "You do not keep your alchemy books here, then, in your living quarters?"

Alec frowned. "My living quarters?"

"Is that not where your man was killed?"

"Ah!" Alec moved along the counter, busying himself with unnecessary adjustment of various books. "I'm afraid you are under a misapprehension, Mister Mathers. I do not live here myself, on the premises. It was Merryfield who resided in the back flat."

Mathers was obviously surprised. Alec noticed him look toward the rear door and then around at the book shelves.

"Oh! Oh, yes, of course. Of course." He flicked open the top copy of the closest *Lamp of Thoth* and ran his finger down the list of contents. "You live where, then, exactly, Mister Chambers?" he asked, casually.

For some reason Alec wished to avoid giving this man the details of his home address. "In the West End," he replied. "Not too great a distance. Was there something special I can do for you today, sir?"

There was a long silence, as though Mathers was running things through his mind. "I thank you again," he finally said, "for the expediency with which you produced those advertisements for my lecture. I do hope we may see you there? I think you will find it of immense interest and value."

"Oh! Why yes, Mister Mathers. I will certainly try to make it. I'd look forward to it."

You never know, Alec thought to himself. *It just might be of interest. And I have nothing else to do that evening anyway. It may take my mind of this unfortunate business. Yes. Yes, I might attend.*

"I didn't mean to kill the old fart! I didn't even know 'e was there. You said ..."

"Never mind what I said. The fact remains that you have killed a man."

"All right! All right! I know. Fing is, what do we do now?"

"What do we do now? I think the question is more 'What do you do now?'"

"'Ere! I was workin' for you, you know! And I can tell that to anyone as needs to know, if you foller me."

"I follow you only too well. In fact I am somewhat ahead of you."

"What d'ya mean?"

"You are due a holiday. A foreign holiday, I think."

"What? 'Ere, I don't want to be goin' to no foreign parts."

"Would you rather be going to the gallows? To be 'making the drop'? ... No, I thought not. Here. Here is more money than you deserve and instructions for your passage to the Continent. You must make your own way down to Gravesend. There is a boat – the *Magpie* – leaving on the morning tide. Do not miss it. The captain has further instructions for you. I trust we will not meet again."

The room was half empty; the audience scattered about the wooden chairs, most of them toward the rear of the room. Alec stood just inside the entrance, deciding where to sit. His eyes moved over the assembled few and noted that the men far outnumbered the women. There was a pall of cigar smoke hanging over all and a bitter, acrid smell hinting of urine. Alec noted two men sitting in a corner, passing a bottle back and forth. They seemed to have no interest whatsoever in the coming proceedings.

"Welcome!"

He turned to find a young woman, two or three inches shorter than himself, proffering a flat wicker basket in which rested a few pence.

Alec stuck his hand in his pocket and pulled out some change. He tossed a shilling into the receptacle.

"I thought it was free," he said.

She smiled. "Just donations."

He found her smile very pleasing. She looked to be in her early twenties and was smartly but not overly dressed in a green faille walking suit; the polonaise over the skirt draped back into a bustle. Her red hair

– generally termed "ginger" when he was in school – was piled up on top of her head. He found her green eyes captivating; hard to turn away from. They seemed to reflect the silken sheen of the dress fabric. Alec found himself wondering just who the young lady was and how she fitted-in with Samuel Mathers and his organization. His eyes remained fixed on her as she moved away toward other members of the audience.

Just then, two men – one of them Mathers; the other bald, mustachioed, and of ruddy complexion – came onto the stage from behind the side curtains and sat down at a table placed in the center.

The redhead came back past Alec. "Will you not take a seat?" she murmured. Then she disappeared through a door, presumably leading backstage, carrying her basket of meager contributions.

Alec took a seat in the back row, at the center aisle.

The bald man on the platform with Mathers stood and noisily cleared his throat. He tapped on the table with a gavel and slowly the buzz of conversation died down. The man scrutinized the audience, his dark eyes seeming to bore into everyone. He wore a brown, tweed, Norfolk suit with a yellow tie, and had a pair of gold-rimmed, pince-nez perched on his bulbous nose. He looked over the top of them as he addressed the crowd.

"We are honored, I think you will agree, to be addressed today by none other than Samuel Liddell MacGregor Mathers, the Count of Glenstrae and, most importantly for this evening's address, the Founder of the Second, or Inner, Order of the Hermetic Order of the Golden Dawn."

Alec noticed that the man doing the introduction kept glancing down, to read from a piece of paper.

"Mister Mathers will enlighten us on the origins of the Order and his part in that estimable history, through to the present day. You are encouraged to present any questions you may have, though please keep them until the end of the address. Thank you."

He sat down and Mathers got to his feet, to a smatter of applause. He wore a swallow-tailed frock coat over charcoal-grey trousers, and a dark blue waistcoat with a solid gold watch-chain draped across its front. His cravat was black with a diamond pin obvious at its center.

Mathers had a grim countenance as he, like the man who had introduced him, looked all around the hall, apparently making eye contact with every single person. His eye did not waver as it met Alec's but passed on, seemingly without recognition. Mathers wrinkled his nose in distaste of the cigar and cigarette smoke.

"Thank you, Colonel, for that introduction." He coughed as though to clear his throat. "One of the precursors of the Hermetic Order of the Golden Dawn," said Mathers, his voice penetrating dramatically to the far reaches of the hall, "was founded in Frankfurt in 1807. It was called 'Rising Dawn' – *Loge sur aufgehenden Morgenrothe.* It combined both the Kabbalah and alchemy in its work." Mather's eyes now locked on

Alec. "Another early order – *Chabrath Zerek Aour Bokher*, or the 'Society of Shining Light' – similarly included alchemy." He paused, and then turned his eyes to others in the audience. "The first of these organizations was brought to England by the Duke of Sussex, in 1817. The second actually preceded it, arriving here in 1810. Some twenty years or so later, Kenneth MacKenzie, an accomplished occult scholar, was initiated into the Order of the Gold and Rose Cross in France and then brought to England a manuscript of that Order's nine grades of attainment."

"'Ere! What's with all these 'Orders' then?" One of the two men with the bottle shouted out, getting to his feet. "What's this got to do with any gold dawn?"

"Right!" His companion agreed.

The man who had introduced Mathers tapped his gavel. "All questions at the end, if you would be so kind." The man sat down.

"All will be made clear as we progress," said Mathers, apparently unperturbed. "Now then. Try to follow me, if you would be so kind? Nearly forty years ago, in 1866, an occult group was formed that was heavily influenced by a man named Frederick Hockley. Regrettably he died nearly fifteen years ago. Hockley had a very large library of rare alchemical works. On his death, this library fell into the hands of Dr. William Wescott, a personal friend of mine. Wescott also acquired certain notes originated by Kenneth MacKenzie. These notes were in the form of a cipher manuscript."

"A what?" It was the same man who interrupted.

"A cipher manuscript. A text written in a secret code."

"Why is that then?"

The gavel banged again, and Mathers ignored the question.

"Dr. Wescott, knowing of my propensity with languages and with ciphers, and my knowledge of the Kabbalah, asked me to flesh-out MacKenzie's notes, to work on the secret manuscript, and to help construct a new magical order. This new order would be dedicated to practical magic and for it we chose the name The Hermetic Order of the Golden Dawn. Its stated purpose was to aid the members to test, purify and exalt the individual's spiritual nature so as to unify it with his – or her – Holy Guardian Angel. The code of the Cipher Manuscript I determined to be from a fifteenth century code originated by the Abbott Trithemius. The basis of what I uncovered was to become the foundation stone of our new Order."

The two men, their bottle apparently now empty, got up and noisily exited the hall. Alec was glad to see them go, for both his own sake and for the sake of Mathers.

"It was Dr. Wescott, along with Dr. William Robert Woodman, who commissioned me to make the first English translation of Knorr Von Rosenroth's classic *Kabbalah Denudata*." Mathers paused to allow the import of that to sink in. "Those two gentlemen were also instrumental in introducing me to the *Societas Rosicruciana in Angelia*, a singularly forward looking Rosicrucian society.

"I am sure that many of you are aware of, if not intimately familiar with, the Theosophical Society of our friend and colleague Madam Helena Blavatsky. The Esoteric Section of that society is – or attempts to be – on a par with our Golden Dawn. Yet for many the Theosophical Society is too … what shall I say? … too 'Oriental' for their tastes. What so many of us need is something essentially English; or at the very least, European."

There were a few murmurs of assent from the audience.

"For that very reason it seems that our Golden Dawn has drawn away many of that good lady's members." Alec couldn't help noticing a small smile of satisfaction on Mathers's face. The lecturer continued.

"Our society has grown to five temples in England, and has initiated some three hundred members. In the metropolis here we have the Isis-Irania temple. There are also temples across the Irish Sea in Dublin and across the Channel in Paris. Eight years ago Dr. Wescott founded the Wescott Hermetic Library as an alchemical resource for Golden Dawn members."

Mathers paused and deliberately poured himself a glass of water from a carafe standing on the table. He drank from the glass, his eyes roaming the hall. Alec couldn't help feeling that the man must be thinking that the audience was hanging on his every word.

"The late Dr. Anna Kingsford," Mathers finally continued, "the well-known warrior for women's rights was, I am proud to say, a great influence on my early life. It was she, who demanded that women should share equally in all matters of the Golden Dawn. Women and men on an equal footing."

There were murmurs from both the men and the women in the audience.

"We have never regretted that decision."

Out of the corner of his eye, Alec noticed a movement off to his right. He looked and saw the attractive redheaded young lady slip back into the hall and move to take a seat on the far end of the row where he sat. Their eyes met briefly and she gave him a quick smile before turning her head to listen attentively to Mathers.

Samuel Mathers went on to talk about his years in France, with his wife Moina. He claimed that he had been called there by the "Secret Chiefs". While there, he established a working temple which he dubbed the Temple Ahathoor. With Moina he created a ritual "*The Rites of Isis.*" Alec noted the heavy Egyptian influence in all of this. The Rites of Isis, Mathers explained, were public rites. Far from being secret rituals held away from prying eyes, these were public demonstrations of the fledgling Order designed to promote interest and to draw would-be initiates. He added that the annual subscription was twelve shillings and sixpence, though intimating that the following year it would be half a guinea together with an admission fee of one guinea.

Alec glanced briefly at the young lady, wondering if she ever played a part in such rituals. All this talk of secret magical orders was not entirely new to him, thanks to his reading and his personal interest in various aspects of the occult. His father had been a Freemason, as were the majority of prominent men in London, though Alec had eschewed such affiliation. He had to admit to himself that Mathers's talk had sparked some small interest; though perhaps curiosity was a better word.

Mathers continued speaking for another hour. A few of the audience slipped away in ones and twos but the majority heard him out. There was a smattering of questions, mainly about membership in the Order and what it actually entailed, and then the gentleman who had introduced Mathers banged his gavel and announced that tea and biscuits would be served at the back of the hall. Alec looked up to see that the young lady had left her seat. He quickly spotted her behind a long table, offering cups of tea to the members of the audience. He got up and headed her way.

Nursing his cup of tea, Alec stood where he could keep an eye on the young lady. She continued to refill cups and press biscuits on the group that hovered about the refreshment table.

"Ah, Chambers!" It was Samuel Mathers. The tall man strode purposefully through the group of people standing chatting together and paused beside Alec.

"A most interesting speech." Alec felt compelled to comment and compliment.

Mathers nodded, as though he expected no less. "Words that will come back to you time and again, Mister Chambers. Make note of them." He raised a hand to acknowledge a woman who waved to him from across the room. "By the way, you had spoken of an estate sale of occult books coming soon?"

"Yes." Alec nodded. "In three days. I will be going down to Kent. It's the gentleman who was a Freemason and had a most interesting personal library. I will be sure to keep you in mind, Mister Mathers."

"You do that. Yes. Excuse me." The tall man hurried off through the throng, in the direction of the woman who had acknowledged him.

Alec tried to turn his attention back to the refreshment table, but then got drawn into conversation with a middle-aged gentleman who, after remarking on Mathers's professed experiences in France, launched into his own views on the death of Prime Minister William Gladstone the previous year.

"You know, Gladstone was known by his nickname of 'the GOM,' standing for the 'Grand Old Man'," he said. "But Disraeli – who could not abide the man – said it stood for 'God's Only Mistake'!" He laughed at the time-worn joke. "Now, this current chap, the Marquess of Salisbury

34

- oh yes, he is well loved and this is his third time at PM, but still . . . he just does not have the character that old Gladstone had, would you not agree?" He bit into a digestive biscuit.

Alec nodded absently and again caught the eye of the redhead. He couldn't help noticing the color rise in her cheeks, but at the same time felt his own face flush. He gulped down the remaining drops of tea in his cup and excused himself from his boring companion. As the crowd finally began to thin, he walked up to the table to place his empty cup there. The young lady moved swiftly to take it, ignoring a number of other empty ones in doing so. Their eyes met yet again and this time Alec held the contact.

"That was awfully good tea," he said, somewhat lamely. "Miss ... Miss ...?"

"Wilde." She smiled and seemed pleased. "Not really the best place to judge, here with these massive, crowd-pleasing, institution teapots."

"No." *He had to linger; he had to prolong the contact.* "Er, would – would you care to go to an ABC or a Lyons teashop and compare beverages, Miss Chambers?" he asked. "There is a Lyons Corner House just along the road, on Victoria Street."

"Now?"

"Why not? Oh, unless you have to ... do you need to stay and clear up, or anything?"

She smiled and shook her head. "No." She untied the apron she'd been wearing over her dress, folded it, and set it on a chair. "Just give me a moment and I will be with you – Mister ... ?"

"Chambers."

They both smiled.

MacGregor Mathers stood at Speakers' Corner in Hyde Park and studied the passing carriages. He was just beginning to get anxious when he spotted what he was looking for; a deep maroon brougham pulled by a single all-black mare. There were no identifying armorial bearings on the door of the carriage; just a small monogram which could easily be overlooked unless one was looking for it.

The driver pulled up beside Mathers and reined-in the horse. With a quick glance to either side, Mathers opened the door and climbed in. He had hardly closed the door when the vehicle set off again at a brisk pace.

"So there were no books of interest in the private rooms behind the book shop?" The occupant of the brougham sat back in the shadows.

Mathers himself tried to sit as far back as possible in the seat, in case anyone should peer into the carriage and recognize him.

"No. No, it seems there was some sort of a misunderstanding and young Chambers lives elsewhere – with his library."

"A misunderstanding on whose part?"

Mathers ran a finger around his collar, which had seemed to grow tight about his neck. "It was a natural misunderstanding," he said. "I have since rectified it and now know just where Mister Alec Chambers dwells."

"I hope you are not planning any more foolish break-ins, and especially no more murders?"

"No! No, of course not." He swallowed. "And the death of the old man, of course, was not planned."

"It would be most unwise if there was a repeat, especially so soon after this botched affair." The speaker took out a silver cigar case and selected a smoke. He did not offer the case to Mathers, who slipped his handkerchief out of his pocket and held it over his nose as the carriage began to fill with smoke. The other man flapped his hand briefly, as though to dissipate the cloud. "Hrmph! You don't smoke, do you?"

"No. But that is quite all right, sir."

They drove on in silence for a while, making the circuit of Hyde Park. The man spoke again.

"From what you say, this Nicholas Flamel holds the secret to your need for money."

Mathers bit his tongue at the inference that it was he, personally, who needed money. The sum they sought was for the fulfillment of the plans approved by the organization. He, Mathers, was only an instrument; the one in the association who had been given the task of finding the necessary finances. He sighed. "I was wondering," he said, "exactly why there is no money available for this endeavor? I had always believed that the Illuminati was well financed."

His companion drew on his cigar before replying.

"'Well financed' is a relative description. There is any number of developments going on around the world at all times. Some of them require vast sums – I have mentioned the French Revolution before, to you, as an example from the past. The first and the upcoming Boer Wars are another example … taking a great deal of money. Others are not so demanding but need to be financed locally. This is one such project." He blew a smoke ring. "You agreed to take this matter on your shoulders, if I recall aright, Samuel. Is this a change of heart?"

"No! No, of course not!" Mathers was quick to put such fears to rest.

"I think your plan to embrace the supposed successes of this fifteenth century alchemist stand a slim chance … if indeed they *were* successes, and if you can find no other way."

36

"We stand in need of a sizeable sum," said Mathers. "We need to purchase the material, transport it here to this country, pay those involved, and bring together all the many elements of the plan."

"All before the beginning of November."

"Quite." Mathers tried to appear more confident than he felt. "That gives us almost five months."

"And if you do not succeed?"

"I will."

There was another long pause in the conversation.

"Leigh Cranwell has it on good authority that there is a supposedly 'unbreakable' cipher in the *Bibliotheque Nationale de France* which points to the true location of Flamel's tomb. I intend to decipher that text, locate the tomb, and uncover the missing papers which are said to be buried with his body," said Mathers.

"You say you have the proof of this alchemist's success."

Mathers reached into his waistcoat pocket and produced a coin, which he passed to his companion.

"And what is this?"

"It's a rose noble," said Mathers. "The second gold coin minted by Edward the Third. They were supposedly made for the king by alchemists; early ones by Raymond Lully but this later one by Nicholas Flamel himself, from alchemically-produced gold."

"And you believe this?" asked the smoker.

"I – I am not alone in that view, sir."

There followed a long pause, during which Mather's traveling companion turned the gold coin over and over in his hand. He finally slipped it into his own pocket. "It should not be too difficult for you to get the necessary information from this Chambers person, without going to extraordinary measures," he said. "Just remember that time is of the essence. We do have that timetable to which we must adhere."

"Of course." Mathers eased closer to the window. "Though I do find myself forced to point out that there can be no guarantees in this business. Flamel produced gold from base metals. *If* we can obtain his formulæ and if the process does indeed work, then we will be home free and clear." He paused. "But there are a lot of those 'ifs'."

"Which brings me back to asking, what if you don't succeed?"

"There is always next year." Mathers voice was low. He was grateful when his companion did not immediately respond.

"You think that this Chambers has the books and papers you need?"

"I think there is a very good chance," responded Mathers. "He has quite a collection, from what I understand. Though how detailed the information is, I don't know ... yet. But he recently published a book in which he included black and white facsimiles taken from rare Flamel material, which he must obviously have in his possession. I believe that material, together with any work notes that must assuredly be in Flamel's tomb, may be our answer."

His companion tossed the cigar butt from the carriage. "We all have every confidence in you, Samuel. You will not let us down, I know."

Mathers felt his collar tighten even more.

The other man raised his cane and banged it against the roof of the carriage. The coachman slowed the horse and brought it to a stop. Mathers opened the door and stepped down. Without any further exchange of words, the brougham drove away.

he late Sir John Bellamy had been an active member of the Order of Freemasons in east Kent County, and also had a lifelong interest in matters metaphysical. His library reflected his interests and Alec found that a large number of fellow Masons and occult collectors – the serious, the curious, and the dilettantes – were attending the estate sale of his lordship's magnificent library. He eased his way through the people crowded about the polished walnut bookcases and slowly started working his way along the shelves, appraising the leather-bound volumes.

He briefly exchanged pleasantries with other collectors and book-dealers he knew and encountered at such sales, including Stephen Colleridge and Bertram Spendright, whom he had met at the previous sale.

"A veritable feast for the bibliophile," commented Colleridge drily, not taking his eyes off the shelves of books.

"Magnificent library," agreed Alec.

Alec's funds were limited, though he was not averse to over-extending himself temporarily, knowing that he could make handsome profits on virtually anything he bought. He finally settled on William Blake's *The Book of Urizen*, a first edition of Michael Maier's 1618 *Atalanta fugiens*, Dionysos Andreas Freher's manuscript *Paradoxa Emblemata* made available sixty years ago, *The Red Tree of Gana*, and a superb edition of *Aurora consurgens* from the early sixteenth century. He also picked up a number of lesser works, a few prints and some early maps, including one drawn by Oronteus Fineus in 1531.

The sale took best part of the day and it was late when Alec finally got home, but he felt well satisfied with his purchases.

The hansom pulled up outside the white Georgian-style house on Westmoreland Terrace and Sarah Wilde descended. She paid the cab driver and, closing her reticule, turned toward the front door of the home. Sarah lifted the hem of her skirt and advanced up the steps to the door. Before she had a chance to ring the bell, the door opened. Alec stood there, smiling.

"Oh! Mister Chambers," she said.

"Sorry. Am I being too obvious? I didn't mean to startle you, Miss Wilde." Alec stepped to one side and ushered her in.

After she had removed her hat, gloves, Persian lamb capelet and matching muff, Sarah followed Alec down the wainscot-lined entrance hall and into the library. There she settled comfortably onto a leather-covered upholstered couch. She wore a black taffeta silk skirt with a flounce, the frills embroidered in lilac silk soutache. Her silk waist was of deep purple finished all over with clusters of fine tucks with contrasting hemstitching. Alec looked at her admiringly and then seated himself on an adjacent chair. He wore a deep burgundy, soft eiderdowned, house jacket over large-checkered, charcoal and black trousers.

"I cannot thank you enough for coming, Miss Wilde," he said. "And *sans* chaperone. Very 'modern', if I may say so?"

"It is I who should thank you for the invitation," she responded, with a smile. "And as for 'modern', this is almost the beginning of the twentieth century, I must remind you, sir." She looked about her. The walls were lined with floor-to-ceiling bookcases, all filled with leather-bound volumes. A large mahogany desk had papers strewn across its surface and a number of books and papers had overflowed onto a chair and an ottoman. She took in the globe of the world and the astrolabe on matching stands on either side of the heavily curtained window. A stone-faced fireplace stood opposite the window. Tastefully framed hunting prints were scattered on the available wall space.

"This is a cozy room," she said. "I would warrant you spend a great deal of your time here."

"Indeed I do. Probably far too much time," he said with a smile. Alec glanced around at the filled shelves. "This is my life, Miss Wilde. Books here and books at my shop. Books have always been a part of my life, thanks to my father."

"You told me about him," she said. "When we had tea together, that first time, in Lyons Corner House." She smiled. "I shall always remember that." She felt a blush brush her cheeks and hoped he didn't notice it.

"I'm glad," he murmured. "It was special for me, too."

There was a tap on the door and an elderly manservant entered. "You said you might care for some tea, sir," he said. He gave a slight bow of acknowledgement in Sarah's direction.

Alec came to his feet. "Excellent, Gordon." He turned to Sarah. "Tea, Miss Wilde? Though I don't know that it will be up to Lyons' standards."

She laughed. "I am quite sure it will be fine," she said. "Yes, please."

The servant turned and left the room.

Some time later, the two of them were sipping tea and nibbling on muffins and petit fours.

"You said that you had something you wanted to show me, Mister Chambers?" Sarah set down her cup and looked expectantly at him.

Alec set down his own cup and, rising, moved over to the well-covered desk. It took him only a moment to burrow amongst the papers and extract a green-covered book. He held it up. "Yes. This is my own book – the one I told you about. It's the story of Nicholas Flamel."

"The alchemist you talked about in the tea shop?"

He nodded. "Yes. The most successful of all the alchemists. As I told you, many of them, over the centuries, claimed to have managed to transmute base metals into gold, but only Flamel is on record as having truly achieved that."

"You said he gave lots of money to hospitals and charities."

"That is correct. He funded the construction of a number of Parisian poorhouses, donated large sums to numerous charities, founded free hospitals, financed cemeteries, and endowed churches. He restored the front of Sainte Genevieve des Argents and endowed the institution of the Quinze-Vingts. The blind inmates of that institution, in memory of him, gathered each year at the church of Saint Jacques la Boucherie to pray for Flamel. This they did every year through till about 1790. Flamel was even responsible for the alchemical figures to be seen in Notre Dame Cathedral." Alec spread his hands wide. "And all of his accomplishments are well documented," he said.

Sarah was impressed. "How was he able to make that change – that 'transmutation'?"

Alec sighed. "There is so much about science, and about this new branch of it – modern physics – which we do not yet understand, Miss Wilde. For example, without going into details, just a couple of years ago Joseph Thomson caused a sensation by discovering that cathode rays are composed of negatively charged particles which he calls 'corpuscles'. Don't ask me what that means, exactly, but it apparently caused quite a sensation in academic circles. They are now calling these corpuscles 'electrons'. Mister Tesla has been investigating what he calls x-rays. Sir William Ramsay, just last year, produced helium from radium. We might even say he 'transmuted' radium into helium, to use the alchemists' terms. In France, Pierre and Marie Curie are working with radioactivity ... please do not ask me to explain any of this! I am no scientist myself." He smiled broadly.

"So all of this means what, exactly?" Sarah asked. She tried to follow Alec's enthusiasm.

"It means that there is an on-going examination of things which, heretofore, have been taken for granted but which, on scientific investigation, have shown themselves to be ... different! It means that what Flamel did, might very well have been possible. It just was not – and perhaps still is not – entirely explainable ... but that does not make it any the less viable. It makes one almost believe that *anything* is possible and that transmuting base metals into gold – not unlike Ramsay's turning radium into helium – is ... well, if not child's play, at least far from impossible."

"At least for Nicholas Flamel."

"Precisely."

"So where does that leave us ... you, Mister Chambers?" she asked.

Alec thumbed through the book he had produced and, opening it to the first of a series of illustrations, carried it across to where Sarah sat. She took the book from him and examined the illustrated pages.

"What am I looking at?"

"Reproduced pages from Nicolas Flamel's working manuscript."

She studied them, and then looked up into his eyes. "Where on earth did you get these?" She found herself catching his excitement.

He turned away from her and moved toward the book shelves. "They are copies of the hand-colored originals," he said. He paused a moment, as if undecided whether or not to confide in her. Then he added "I have them."

Alec pulled a large leather-bound book from a shelf and came back to where she sat. He settled beside her on the couch and lovingly ran his hands over the volume he held. He was momentarily hesitant to carry on with what he had started but, making up his mind, he gave a sigh and continued.

"This is an old book that my father happened to get at an estate auction."

"'Happened' to get?"

He laughed. "Really! He was at an auction and bought a whole section of a library, sight unseen. It was not until he got the books home that he was able to go through them at his leisure and examine his purchase."

Sarah sat forward on the edge of the seat. "What did he find?"

"I have never shown it to anyone else, Miss Wilde. But, look at this." The book Alec held was a thick, leather-bound, gilt-edged volume the title of which had long since been worn away. He opened the front of it and turned the first few pages. Sarah gasped. Just a few leaves into the book the pages had their inner sections cut out, leaving an opening; a hidden well in the middle of the book. The inclusion it contained was a much smaller, ancient-looking book, hand-sewn, with irregular pages. The ragged edges were brown with age and looked to be extremely brittle.

"What is it?" Sarah found herself whispering.

"It is the notebook of Nicholas Flamel, the alchemist."

Sarah stared in disbelief.

42

"Please, Miss Wilde, promise me you will not tell anyone that I have this. There are people whom I believe would literally kill to possess it."

Her eyes grew big and round. Her hand went to her heart. "Believe me, Mister Chambers, I would never betray your trust. I am honored that you have shared this with me."

"In particular – and don't ask me why I feel so strongly about this – do not, whatever you do, let Mister Mathers know about this."

"I promise."

Alec closed the book and lay it down beside him.

Samuel Lidell MacGregor Mathers – *Frater S' Rhioghail Mo Dhream*, known to his fellow-initiates as "S.R.M.D." – sat up straight on his chair, in the position of the Chief Adept. His white cassock and red cloak were pristine; his yellow shoes peeping out from under the hem of the robe. Yellow and white nemyss; rose-cross on yellow collar; he held the scepter of five elemental colors surmounted by a pentagram. He sat behind the Veil in the East, symbolically in Tiphareth. Other officers were in their Sephirotic Stations – the Third Adept in the north-east, Second Adept in the south-east, Hiereus in the west, Hegemon east of the altar. Immediately before Mathers was the White Altar; beyond that, the temple filled with its banners and tablets. The hall was in darkness; the elemental lamps unlit, with no lights except those burning behind the veil and the shaded candles of the officers.

The Second Adept spoke. "Very honorable Fratres and Sorores, assist me to open the Portal of the Vault of the Adepti. Honorable Hiereus, see that the entrance is closed and guarded."

So began the Hermetic Order of the Golden Dawn Ritual of the Portal of the Vault of the Adepti. Mathers was in his element. He spoke his now familiar words in a strong voice that carried to the four corners of the temple.

"In and by the Word, I permit the Portal of the Vault of the Adepti to be opened. Let us establish the Dominion of the Mystic ETH over the four elements."

He turned to face the east. The others followed suit. Mathers moved to a position in front of the Air Tablet.

The ritual progressed for more than an hour. In the Portal Ritual, the aspirant is introduced to the fifth and final element of Spirit, thus completing the component parts of his or her elemental constitution. Arthur Machen, the author, was the aspirant concerned in this particular ceremony. Mathers had himself been giving Machen instruction and was well pleased with the man's progress.

After the ritual had ended, and the participants had left the temple room and returned to the lounge area, Mathers moved to offer his congratulations.

"I found the ceremony most moving, Frater SRMD," said Machen, with his lilting Welsh accent.

"I imagine these rituals give you background for your macabre tales." It was Edgar Jepson, a writer of crime novels who loved to denigrate Machen and his published horror stories.

"Not at all!" Machen did not easily accept Jepson's jibes. "My work ..."

"Gentlemen! Gentlemen." Mathers held up his hands. "This is no time for squabbling. Let us join in celebration of the advancement of one of our number. We are all one, here in the Fellowship of the Golden Dawn."

"Here, here!"

"Indeed."

Others who had gathered around, beamed at one another and slapped Machen on the back. Maude Gonne gave him a quick peck on the cheek. Her already low-cut robe seemed to have slipped to one side, exposing much of her left breast. Machen forgot all about Jepson as he struck up a conversation with her.

"It is interesting, is it not," said Aleister Crowley, appearing beside Mathers, "that the Portal ceremony, although not assigned to any sephirah, involves the alchemical process of analysis and dissolution; a kind of alchemical exorcism, as it were?"

Mathers turned his attention away from Maude Gonne and Machen. "What? Oh, yes, Frater Perdurabo. Of course. Purely alchemical, as is so much of this degree. Introspection and psychic balance is so much a part of the core work of our Order."

Aleister Crowley, at twenty-four little more than half Mathers' age, was a fast-rising star of the magical order. He and Allan Bennett had entered at about the same time and had vied with one another to advance more rapidly than had any one else since the founding of the group. Mathers had a grudging respect for Crowley, but did not entirely trust the man.

"I see Maude has latched onto our Welshman," continued Crowley. He chuckled. "Taffy will be disappointed there, I fear. She has been around."

"Frater Perdurabo!" Mathers spoke sternly. He did not care for Crowley's familiarity and his denigration of many of the women in the group. "Let us restrict ourselves to a spiritual focus, at least this evening."

A stocky man who wore a large mustache, and whose hair seemed to be prematurely receding, joined Mathers and Crowley.

"Ah, Frater Sacramentum Regis!" Mathers greeted him. "What did you think of our little ceremony, SR?"

The newcomer was Arthur Edward Waite, a scholarly mystic who wrote extensively on occult and esoteric matters. It was one of Waite's books that had indirectly led to Crowley joining the Golden Dawn.

44

"I could not help but note that Hegemon mumbled his words again. You really must speak to him about that. It quite throws off the balance of the whole thing."

"Hmm. You are right, of course," agree Mathers. "I will speak to him."

"There are several who could benefit by learning to project," said Crowley. "Frater Levavi Oculos in particular, I would say. I could give some direction there. Perhaps I shall offer some classes."

The evening wore on. The excitement of performing the ritual gave way to post-rite relaxation. Mathers, who was a non-smoker, did not allow cigarettes or cigars in the temple or the lounge, but did accept small libations on such occasions. The clink of glasses mingled with the slowly growing prattle of conversation. Then, in ones and twos, the participants excused themselves and went to the dressing rooms to change back into their street clothes before going home. Mathers, loathe to strip off the elegant trappings and accouterments of his office, was the last to go.

As Mathers came out into the hallway, on his way to the front door of the temple building, he encountered the red-headed secretary of the Order, Sarah Wilde. She had not been one of the celebrants that evening but had been working late in the office.

"Ah, Miss Wilde. You are working late, I see."

"Yes, sir. There were some accounts I wanted to bring up to date before the weekend. I thought I would take care of it while you were all in temple. Did your ritual go well?"

"It did indeed, young lady. I was well contented."

"Was Florence here tonight?"

Florence Beatrice Farr, the actress and musician, had taken the motto *Sapientia Sapienti Dono Data* ("Wisdom is a gift given to the wise"), when she was first initiated into the Isis-Urania Temple of the Esoteric Order of the Golden Dawn, in July of 1890. She had been a mistress of George Bernard Shaw – who disliked and mocked her interests in the occult – and, it was said, of a large number of other men. Her present interest seemed to be Aleister Crowley. A leading light in the Order, learned in its lore and rituals, Florence was the Golden Dawn's Chief Adept in Anglia. Sarah Wilde was one of her biggest fans.

"No, I am afraid Miss Farr had a theatrical engagement tonight."

"Oh." Sarah couldn't hide her disappointment. "Oh, well. Good night, Mister Mathers."

"Goodnight, Miss Wilde."

The curtains were partially drawn but sufficient light entered the room from outside for him to see what he was doing. He moved quickly over to the bookcases.

"Ah, our Mister Chambers is methodical to say the least." The man ran his gloved hand along the shelves and nodded his head in satisfaction.

"All the books arranged in subject order, and then by author. Very nice."

One section of the library was devoted to books on alchemy and associated subjects. He saw an early edition of John Baptista Porta's *Natural Magick*, Eliphas Levi's *Dogma and Ritual of Magic,* Arthur Edward Waite's relatively recently published *Lives of the Alchemystical Philosophers* and August Strindberg's even more recently published *Antibarbarus.* There was the seventeenth century *The Pansophy of Rudolph the Magus*, J. C. Barchusen's *Elementa chemicae* of 1718, and *Testament of Nicolas Flamel* - the J. and E. Hodson's publication of 1806. He was amazed at the variety – and the presumed value – of the collection. Not all were first editions, by any means, but a substantial number were either first or at the very least very early editions.

But he was on a mission. He had no time to admire particular titles; just to locate the manuscript of a particular philosopher. He moved on in his examination. He would occasionally remove a book to get a clearer picture of its title and contents, but did not spend a lot of time on any one.

He finished with the alchemical books and then spied a large volume on a nearby piece of furniture. He crossed the room and, opening the well-worn leather cover, gave the title and author a cursory glance. Just then there came a sound from the hallway. Quickly, he moved across to the window and slipped behind the heavy tapestry drape.

A young maid entered the room, holding a coal scuttle and the makings of a fire. She went directly to the fireplace and turned up the gaselier. Kneeling, she started humming to herself as she began laying the paper and kindling.

He peered out from the curtain and watched her intently. He then glanced down at the timepiece he partially withdrew from his waistcoat pocket. The hour was advancing; he needed to move on.

The maid had been singing quietly to herself but now paused as she applied lucifer to paper and leaned forward to gently blow on the kindling as it started to take hold. He saw that as she blew, she screwed up her eyes to keep the smoke from them. Now was his chance, he thought. Swiftly yet silently he slipped out from behind the curtain and moved across to the open library door. As he passed through it and hurried toward the main entranceway, he heard her start to sing again. He smiled to himself, hummed a little, and left the house.

It was early evening when Alec returned home from the book shop. He let himself into the house, hung up his coat and placed his top hat, gloves, and cane on the hall table. He headed toward the library, looking forward to an aperitif, a good meal, and then a relaxing evening at home. Gordon appeared at the head of the stairs to the lower quarters.

"You are ready for your brandy sour, sir?"

"Yes, please, Gordon. And then I will eat in the library, I think."

"Very good sir."

Alec let himself into his favorite room and noted, with satisfaction, that the fire had been made-up in time to warm the room for his arrival. The gas lamps cast a pleasant glow. He placed the two books he had brought home with him on an occasional table and settled into his favorite chair.

It was not until the old retainer had brought him his drink and then gone away again, to get Alec's dinner from Mrs. Jenkins, that Alec sensed that all was not as it should have been. There was nothing immediately striking, but he felt suddenly uneasy and looked about him. It didn't take long for him to realize what was amiss. Some one had been into the library and had interfered with the books.

He came to his feet, put down the glass, and moved swiftly to the bookcases. The majority of the volumes seemed undisturbed but it was obvious that someone had been rifling through the section on alchemy. Books were out of order, with many of them sticking out beyond the edges of the shelves and one even pushed in backwards.

The door opened and the old butler came in, bearing a tray.

"Gordon! What has been going on in here?"

The old man carefully lowered the tray onto a marble-topped occasional table beside Alec's chair and then turned to his employer. "Your pardon, sir?"

"What has been going on? Look at these books. Have you been routing around in the library?" Alec knew the answer before he even asked the question. Old Ian Gordon would no more think of disturbing Alec's library than he would of shouting out loud. The old man moved forward and peered at the indicated shelves.

"It does indeed appear that the normal order has been disturbed," he said.

"An understatement if ever there was one!" Alec was growing more and more dismayed. "Who was in here today, Gordon? Did Mrs. Jenkins have any reason to come up here?"

"No, sir. That I would swear to."

"Someone must have been here. What about Meg? She laid the fire and lit it, presumably?"

"Yes, sir, that she did. But that was but an hour before you came home and she spent no longer than usual at the job. Besides, sir, she would have no reason to look at your books; she can barely read."

Alec grunted.

"As you may recall, sir," continued Gordon, "you had me go out on an errand this forenoon. To the City. I did not return till after three of the clock, though Mrs. Jenkins made no mention of any visitors whilst I was gone, sir."

"You were gone what, then? Two-three hours?"

"Possibly closer to four, Mister Chambers. The cab on the way back seemed to take an eternity."

Alec pulled a coin out of his pocket and gave it to the old retainer. "Well, see if you can find a faster one. Get over to Scotland Yard and ask for an Inspector Henry Kent. Give him my name and ask him if he'd be so good as to get here as soon as possible."

"Is anything missing?" was the Inspector's first question, as Alec knew it would be.

"Strangely, perhaps, no." He had gone over all of the titles carefully while he waited for the policeman to arrive.

Alec had discovered one anomaly however, which he felt might go a long way to explaining the mysterious intrusion. The heavy book containing the Flamel notes had been left on the leather couch, where he and Sarah had sat studying it the previous evening (he chastised himself for neglecting to put it away in some secure place). It had been closed but now the front cover was open. The title page had been revealed to show the book to be – ostensibly – an encyclopedic treatise on astronomy. Such, Alec presumed, had been sufficient to deter the intruder from examining the volume further. The man – or woman – had obviously been interested only in books on alchemy. He had had no clue that the very book he discarded was the one containing what he most sought.

Inspector Kent examined the alchemy books, the shelves, the door to the library. He then went to look at the front door to the house; the one that opened on to the street. On his knees, he looked closely at the keyhole.

"Aha!"

"You have found something, Inspector?"

The short man's brown eyes gleamed. He came to his feet, pointing down at the keyhole. "See those scratches, sir? Just fine lines, they would appear to the untrained eye."

Alec leaned forward and looked. There certainly were some marks that should not have been on a well-polished door.

"Signs of a competent cracksman, Mister Chambers. Signs of the lock-picking tools of the professional. 'Betties,' or picklocks, sir. Seen such scratches a hundred times."

"But does it not take a long time . . . ?"

"Matter of less than a minute, Mister Chambers."

"In broad daylight?"

"In broad daylight." The Inspector seemed well pleased with himself. "Now, all we have to do is see if anyone noticed any stranger hovering about your door at any time around the noon hour."

In less than ten minutes the policeman had his answer.

"A crossing-sweeper, Mister Chambers. Down on the corner. Says he noticed a clergyman, if you can believe that. Fellow with big bushy eyebrows and a spiky beard, he says. This vicar was standing at your door one minute, and then had disappeared the next. Obviously opened the door and slipped inside, if you ask me."

"A clergyman?"

"Oh, don't take too much notice of that, sir. Some of these burglars will dress up in all kinds of disguises. Now," out came the notebook and the stubby pencil. He licked its tip and made a notation. "With the break-in at your shop, and the murder of your employee, and now this attempted burglary right at your residence, what exactly are we looking at, Mister Chambers?"

"What do you mean?"

"Oh, let us not be coy, sir. There's obviously something important that someone is after. And I will lay my reputation on the line that you know what it is. Right, Mister Chambers?"

"I thought we had an agreement that you would not break and enter his house?"

"No. We had no such agreement." The Reverend Winters avoided looking into Samuel Mathers' eyes. "You may – I say *may* – have had some sort of understanding in your mind, but we never actually spoke directly on that subject. And besides, I did not 'break' and enter; I simply entered."

Mathers stared hard at the bushy eye-browed clergyman for a very long time. Finally he shrugged and settled back in his corner chair at the Reform Club. He signaled a waiter for a whisky, which was brought to him on soundless feet through a maze of high-backed leather chairs, each supporting an elderly gentleman either sleeping or reading *The Times*.

Nothing further was said for some time. Eventually Mathers carefully looked around him and then leaned toward Winters.

"So you found nothing of interest at all?"

"Nothing. Oh, there were plenty of books on alchemy, as I told you. Many of them worth a pretty penny, I would say. But no sign of that Flamel notebook. Leastwise, not as you described it."

Mathers pursed his lips and nodded slowly. "Well, we may have to think further on that. Meanwhile, there is some other information that might be available."

"Oh?" Winters looked up sharply.

"Our delightful Society *Scriba*, Miss Wilde ..."

"The attractive red-haired young lady?"

"The very same. I had noted that she and our friend Alec Chambers have become occasional companions. I am not suggesting any improprieties, you understand," he said quickly, as Winters' eyes grew larger. "No. Simply that they have apparently found some sort of shared interests. They often take afternoon tea together at a nearby cornerhouse."

"And ... ?"

"And I had occasion to speak with Miss Wilde on this subject. She volunteered the information that she had indeed seen Mister Chambers's library, though she could not place the Flamel book, at least as I described it."

"So where does that leave you? I thought you needed that notebook to do your alchemical mumbo-jumbo?"

Mathers took another long sip of his whisky. He took his time putting down the glass, while his friend grew more and more impatient.

"Well?"

"Ssh! My dear Monty. Let us not draw attention to ourselves." Mathers signaled a refill and indicated another drink for his friend also. While awaiting the attendant, he reached into his pocket and pulled out a black-covered notebook. He opened it, studied it for a few moments and then, when the drinks had been brought and the waiter had retired, looked over at Winters.

"Miss Wilde, while speaking on another subject, happened to mention one of our members whom we have not seen in a while: Mister Leigh Cranwell."

"Cranwell?"

"An on-again/off-again member. His memory – or perhaps, to be fair, his total absorption in his own interests – frequently fails him when it comes to remembering to attend ritual. I made it a point to drop him a line and he visited the society offices just yesterday."

Winters' expressive eyebrows went up in question.

"He is one of those I mentioned as dabbling in the *chemistry* of alchemy. He has performed a number of experiments, though none of them with any great success I understand. He was describing to me a small booklet which he owns, on the life and death – presumed death – of our Nicholas Flamel. He promised that I might peruse it."

"Does not Chambers's book deal with all that?"

"Yes, and no. An unsatisfactory answer I know, dear friend. Alec Chambers does cover the details of Flamel's death but he does not go into the features of his burial in quite the same detail as does this monograph owned by Leigh Cranwell."

"So what does this one tell you, that the other does not?"

"The most important thing it tells is that Flamel's papers were all placed in his coffin at the time of his death, to be buried with him."

"What about this volume that Chambers possesses?"

Mathers shrugged. "I am not sure. There must be any number of ways in which he could have come by it; it has, after all, been in existence – in or out of the grave – for well over five hundred years. We may even have been attaching more importance to it than it warrants."

Winters sat forward in his chair. "And no one else has thought, before now, to follow-up on this idea of Flamel's works being buried with him?"

"Well, of course they have ... but to no avail." Mathers looked smug.

"What are you hiding, Samuel?"

"It seems to be firmly established that the papers – the very ones I need – were indeed buried with Flamel. They may or may not have included this booklet now owned by our Mister Chambers. But it also seems to be firmly established that no one knows exactly where Flamel's *body is buried*. His original grave was opened by a mob right after he was first laid to rest. The coffin was found to be empty! It was then believed that he had been spirited away to his wife's family farm, outside Paris, and quietly buried there. But again, they were wrong. All that was found there was a buried log!"

"Go on!" Winters' voice was hoarse.

"Theories have been that Flamel faked his own death, that his loyal assistant Agramant kept moving the body, that Flamel discovered the elixir of life and still lives … and so on."

"To go back to my original question, Samuel," said Winters. "Where does that leave you?"

Mathers again glanced down at his notebook, and then tucked it away in his frock coat pocket. He smiled. "There is the Flamel tomb at the Church of the Holy Innocents. There is another supposed tomb at the end of the nave of Saint Jacques la Boucherie. There are also other possible sites. As you know, Monty, my forte – or one of them – is cryptology and ciphers. Leigh Cranwell has it on good authority that there is a supposedly 'unbreakable' cipher in the *Bibliotheque Nationale de France* which points to the true location of Flamel's tomb. I intend to decipher that text, locate the tomb, and uncover the missing papers."

Monty Winters's eyebrows knit together like some huge caterpillar. He studied his drink and said nothing.

It was an unusually fine day in Hyde Park with the sun sporadically peeping through clouds despite a fine misty rain falling intermittently. A mass of people gathered about the orators at Speakers' Corner.

Mathers stood leaning on his polished ebony cane, wearing a plush beaver top hat, black frock coat and black-and-grey striped pants. His waistcoat was of grey silk with matching satin cravat. All was surmounted by a light, otter-collared overcoat. He ignored the shouted exhortations of the flat earth theorists, the fanatics prophesying the impending end of the world, and the many hecklers of the Marxists and other political proponents competing for attention.

He was relieved to see the carriage approaching and, briefly raising his cane in acknowledgement, stepped to the edge of the pavement. As it came to a halt he wasted no time in opening the door, climbing in, and closing the door behind him. As the brougham accelerated, a young woman in a dark brown taffeta walking suit, ornamented with frills, briefly turned and lowered her umbrella. As the vehicle started to speed past her, her eyes focused on the monogram on the door of the carriage. The sun shone on the red hair that escaped her bonnet.

"I understand we have a change of plan ... again?" The occupant of the carriage sat back and tapped the end of his cane rhythmically against a small wooden chest that rested on the seat opposite him.

"In effect, yes, sir," said Mathers. "Though it is really just a development of the original."

"*Tempus fugit*, Samuel. *Tempus fugit.*"

Mathers cleared his throat. "Oh, yes, sir. Yes, I am well aware of that. Believe me, I am keeping a very close eye on things."

"June draws on apace. July lies ahead."

"Indeed, sir. But in fact we are making tremendous progress."

"We are?" The cane stopped tapping. "How, pray?"

Mathers spoke quickly, trying to get it all out at once. "In two days I leave for France, where I have made arrangements to visit the *Bibliotheque Nationale*. I have a contact there who will allow me access to the rare documents division. The manuscript I seek is already set aside for my perusal. As you know, sir, I am at my best when working on a challenging project such as the Flamel Enigma. I believe I can break that cipher as easily as I did the MacKenzie one ..."

"It took you over a year to do that, as I recall."

"Indeed. However – in my own defense, if I need such – that was a most unusual work ..."

"And you think this Flamel puzzle will not be so?"

"I have the advantage of preparation, sir. As I understand it, Flamel's work is tied-in with *The Book of Abraham the Jew,* which was part in Latin, part in Hebrew and part in the unknown cipher. I am, as you know, familiar with Egyptian hieroglyphics, with ancient Greek, with Etruscan ..."

"Yes, yes! I am not here to challenge your credentials, Samuel. I would just like to see you moving on a trifle. To that end, I have here cut your journey a little shorter for you." He again tapped the top of the wooden chest on the carriage seat. "Open that and see what I have brought you."

Puzzled, and hesitant, Mathers leaned forward and fumbled with the catch. It came open and he threw back the lid. Although the brougham was a closed carriage, enough light streamed in the windows to show him what was there. Lying on the dark blue velvet of the box's lining, was an ancient manuscript. He went to lift it out.

"No! No, I would not try to take it out here," said his companion. "It is far too delicate."

"What – what is it?"

The other man chuckled. "It is the manuscript you were going to study at the *Bibliotheque Nationale*. I learned of your interest in it – do not, pray, ask me how – and I made arrangements to, shall we say, borrow it. You may take it with you and start your studies immediately. As I said, *Tempus fugit*, Samuel. *Tempus fugit*."

He hated to leave a job unfinished. He knew it was crazy to return to the scene of the crime and yet ... he had to do it! But to place the odds a little more on his side, this time he left it until well after midnight; two o'clock in the morning, to be exact.

Monty Winters was dressed all in black, with a black beret on his head. He walked to Westmoreland Terrace from Victoria Railway Station, passing few people along the way. From Buckingham Palace Road, he hurried across Ebury Bridge and turned onto the terrace. The house he wanted was just a few doors along on the right. With a quick glance up and down the deserted street, he stepped up to the front door, the betties already in his hand. Within two minutes he was once again standing in the hallway of Alec's home. He stood for a while letting his eyes adjust to the darkness.

"Now, Mister Chambers," he muttered to himself. "Let us see how smart you are. Not too smart, I warrant, since you have not changed your locks."

He moved silently forward and entered the library. He made sure the heavy drapes were closed and then struck a lucifer and lit one of the gas lamps beside the fireplace. He turned down the light to a very low illumination; just sufficient for him to make out the arrangement of books on the shelves.

It was something that Samuel Mathers had said that had brought about the desire to finish what had previously been unsuccessful.

"I know the book is there; it has to be. Do you think there's a safe in room?" he'd commented.

"Doubtful," the clergyman had responded. "He has a number of very rare, and valuable, books and none of them is locked away, so why would he place this one notebook in a safe?"

"Hmm." Mathers had nodded his head in agreement. "Yet I cannot help thinking that it is inside something; not out in the open where one might easily see it."

Inside something; not out in the open. Yes, thought Winters. That made sense. He would have seen the book if it had simply been standing on one of the book shelves, but he would swear it was not so placed. No, it had to be hidden in some way.

He once again slowly ran his hand along the shelves. Several of the titles now seemed almost familiar. He recognized the large gilt-edged volume that had previously been lying on the couch. *Astronomical Compendium and Star Delineator*. His hand moved on. And then it stopped.

"These are all well ordered, as I recall," he thought. "In subject order and then according to author ... yet, here we have a large astronomical tome in the middle of the alchemical books and tracts!"

He eased the large volume out from its place on the shelf and carried it over to a small marble-topped occasional table close to the fireplace. He turned up the gas lamp a fraction and studied the book. He opened the cover and turned to the title page.

ASTRONOMICAL COMPENDIUM AND STAR DELINEATOR
A STUDY OF THE NIGHT SKY
AND THE RELATIONSHIPS OF THE PLANETS AND STARS
THE NATURE OF THE ELEMENTS, STARS, SIGNS, &C.
BY SIR THEODORE RIVERS, K.H.
LL.D. F.R.S. V.P.R.S.E. &C. &C.
WITH NOTES ON:
THE MYTHOLOGICAL DEITIES ATTRIBUTED TO THE CONSTELLATIONS,
A KNOWLEDGE OF THE CELESTIAL INFLUENCES, AND
THE CONSTELLATORY PRACTICE OF TALISMANIC MAGIC

It looked to be a most interesting work but still, he mused, why was it out of place in the order of the library? He turned another page and saw the dedication and introductory notes. He was about to close the book but idly turned a few more pages.

"*Eureka!*"

There before his amazed eyes was a deep well, cut through the pages of the book, and nestling in the well rested a dark, leather-covered, ancient-looking volume. He noted that it was hand-sewn, with irregular pages. The ragged brown edges of the pages looked to be delicate and brittle. The back cover was missing but otherwise it seemed to be intact. Reverently Monty Winters lifted the book from its hiding place and carefully opened the front cover. The parchment revealed was covered with a graceful and elaborate handwriting, interspersed with brightly colored illustrations. In the top left corner he saw the name "Nicolas Flamel". He had found the book for which Mathers searched.

Leigh Cranwell had many times been described as having a face like a ferret. Aleister Crowley once said of him: "He reminds me of that character from Ben Jonson's *The Alchymist*. What was his name? Abel Drugger. Jonson said, 'He lives on cheese and has the worms.' I think our Mister Cranwell lives on cheese and has the worms!"

Cranwell invariably dressed in single-breasted sacque suits, with matching coat, waistcoat and trousers, eschewing the frock coats favored by the majority of the Golden Dawn gentlemen. He would also sport a bowler hat rather than a top hat. He affected a mustache that was waxed and turned up at the ends. His hair was heavily laced with macassa oil and plastered tightly across the top of his head, to hide – to his mind – the bald pate beneath it. Yet for all that, Cranwell exhibited an oftentimes brilliant and intelligent mind. He had a small, personal library which Mathers had referred to in the past and which he had now come to peruse, at Cranwell's rooms in Notting Hill.

"I would offer you tea, Mister Mathers, but I am sure you are here with a limited amount of time so I will forego that pleasantry."

"Er, yes. Quite. You had previously been kind enough to show me a small volume you possess that deals with the philosopher Flamel and his ending days."

"Oh yes, indeed." Cranwell obsequiously hurried forward to where Mathers sat and thrust forward a well-worn copy of a book in dark blue cloth binding. "This is the same. *Philosopher Flamel 1330-1410* by Jeremy Hummel. I believe it was privately printed. There is no date but my guess would be circa 1790." He peered over the top of his pince-nez.

Mathers took the proffered book and carefully turned the pages. He came to what he was looking for and started reading, completely ignoring his host. Cranwell hovered near Mathers for a while and then retired to a far corner of the room. He rearranged books and straightened bric-a-brac, from time to time looking toward his guest to see if there was anything he needed. Mathers remained immersed in the book.

1410: Paris.

From hiding, Nicolas Flamel, with his loyal assistant Agramant, witnessed his own funeral. He heard himself greatly honored, with speeches from the Mayor of Paris, from Cramoisi, a member of the king's Council of State, and many others. They all spoke of Flamel's generosity and his charity.

Flamel's eyes went to the marker alongside his own grave-site – that of his wife Perenelle who was buried two years prior. As the ceremony drew to a close, Agramant moved out and mingled with the mourners. After a few minutes, as the gathering began to break up, he returned to where Flamel was secluded and told of having overheard plans for a crowd to go to Flamel's house and break into it. The house was on rue de Marivaux. Flamel was amazed and urged his good friend to follow the crowd and later report back on what actions they performed.

The throng was led by many of the prominent officials; those who had praised Flamel at the graveside. Agramant followed but hung back and watched them enter the house where they began to systematically strip it of anything of value. They seemed especially concerned about searching for something and someone even broke through a wall that they thought might have been hollow. Events rapidly got out of hand and soon the whole house was destroyed . . . but nothing special was found. The priest, who was among the scavengers, quickly left.

Agramant later found Flamel in a stable, where he had been resting and waiting for darkness. Together, they went back to the grave-site only to find the priest there, holding up a lantern and directing the gravedigger to dig-up the freshly buried coffin. When it was brought up, the gravedigger hurried off and the priest broke open the lid, obviously looking for something. But inside, instead of Flamel's body, he found only a log.

Agramant moved forward and confronted the priest. There was a struggle and the priest slipped, falling and banging his head. As he fell back, his body rolled into the open coffin. Agramant, with Flamel's help, put the lid back on the coffin. Agramant then sent Flamel on his way, saying that he would rebury the coffin and

would rejoin Flamel later. As he left, Flamel remarked that he could hardly wait to be with Perenelle again.

Mathers sat back, the book still open on his knee. After a moment his eyes focused on Cranwell.

"I must take this book with me, to study," he said.

Cranwell's expression changed as he put down an ornament he had been holding and advanced on Mathers.

"No! No. I had told you before, Mister Mathers, I do not loan out my books. They are for my edification and must always be at my elbow. I thought I had made that clear? This is why you came here, to my flat, to read from this volume." He removed his pince-nez and agitatedly polished them with an off-white kerchief he had pulled from the pocket of his trousers.

Mathers rose to his feet. Standing tall, he looked down on the short figure of Leigh Cranwell. "Am I not the acknowledged Chief of the Second Order of the Golden Dawn, Mister Cranwell? Am I not the author, myself, of numerous important Golden Dawn teachings, books, and documents?"

Cranwell seemed unfazed. "Indeed, Mister Mathers; indeed. I cast no aspersions, believe me. This is simply a little, shall we say, idiosyncrasy of mine?" He pushed the handkerchief back into his pocket, replaced the pince-nez on his nose, and then reached out and delicately removed the book from Mathers's hands, firmly closing it. "I trust there is nothing further I can do for you, sir?"

As Mathers climbed into a hansom cab and left Notting Hill, he determined that Leigh Cranwell would feel the brunt of his displeasure. The man had hopes of advancing through the esoteric order and yet felt he could refuse the master of that order? There was obviously a lot that Mister Cranwell needed to learn, in that respect. Yet the man might have his uses.

The waitress moved off to fill their order and Sarah smiled at Alec. He didn't return the smile.

"What's wrong?" She was concerned.

"The Flamel book has been stolen."

"What? The old one you showed me, hidden inside the other book?"

He nodded, but then said nothing while the waitress returned with their tea and a double-tiered tray bearing cucumber sandwiches, biscuits, and petit fours. Sarah poured the tea, adding milk and sugar as she'd learned Alec liked. She looked up at him from the steaming tea pot.

"Tell me," she said.

He glanced about him and then leaned in slightly.

"This time it was done at night. I was a fool not to change the locks on the outside door after that earlier break-in, but I never for one moment thought that anyone would come back a second time."

"How did they find it, inside that big book?"

He shrugged, and accepted the tea cup. "I don't know. Perhaps they were there long enough to thoroughly examine all of the books. Perhaps they were just lucky. I don't know."

She nibbled on a digestive biscuit. "Did they take anything else?"

"No. No, it seems they knew what they were looking for. They were only interested in the Flamel."

"That would seem to point the finger of suspicion, wouldn't you say?" she asked.

Alec sighed. "You are right, Miss Wilde. I try not to judge without hard evidence, but I must face it – Samuel Mathers is the only person who has shown the remotest interest in Nicholas Flamel, and in my book in particular."

"Did you inform the police?"

"Oh, yes." He nodded. "The good Inspector Kent didn't seem too surprised, but did not hold out too much hope for getting back the volume. He made a note in his little notebook." He smiled wrily.

"Even though we know who stole it?"

"Proof, Sarah. Proof. That is what is needed, as he reminded me."

She was silent, sipping her tea and then selecting a cucumber sandwich. She was pleased that he had called her Sarah.

"It is more than probable that time will provide the proof," Alec went on. "I do not expect anything to become obvious immediately, but I would think that eventually he will let slip some word, some comment, that will be an indication of his guilt."

Sarah suddenly smiled at him over the rim of the tea cup.

"What?"

She chuckled. "Alec ... you have no objection to my using your first name?" He smiled and, reaching out, squeezed her hand. It was all the answer she needed. "I was just thinking," she continued, conscious of her flushed face, "that perhaps we should do the same thing. Perhaps we should break into Mister Mathers's house and steal back the book!"

He joined her in a quiet laugh.

"You know, Sarah, that might be the answer." He took a sandwich himself.

*S*amuel Mathers sat at his desk, poring over the manuscript from the *Bibliotheque Nationale.* It was written in French, and very fragile. The Reverend Montague Winters stood at his shoulder, leaning ever further forward, trying to see what Mathers was seeing.

"Where did you say you obtained this manuscript?" asked Winters.

"I did not," returned Mathers.

"So, what is it?"

"It is a manuscript from the year 1610, written by Henri IV's emissary the Abbé Johannes Pontoise."

"And he is ... was?"

"He traveled a great deal. He here records that he met with another traveler, a Turkish philosopher, at Limoges. Pontoise claimed that this man could speak any known language plus many of the dead languages."

"Quite an accomplishment ... if it be true."

"Indeed." Mathers studied a passage through a large magnifying glass. "This fellow traveler said that he was a member of a group of seven philosophers who explored the world seeking wisdom. They termed themselves The Brethren of Inner Truth. Every twenty years they would reunite in Limoge. These sages claimed to have the secret of the Philosopher's Stone and the Elixir of Life."

"Is not the Philosopher's Stone used for the transmutation of metal?"

Mathers nodded. "So they say."

"So just where does this fit-in with your search for Flamel?" asked Winters.

Mathers sat back and stretched. "If we are to believe Pontoise and his traveler acquaintance, Nicolas Flamel was once one of this group of seekers; these Brethren of Inner Truth. This man said that Flamel lived a great many years longer than his purported time of death. The philosopher also knew Flamel's loyal assistant, named Agramant."

Mathers reached for a nearby brandy snifter and sipped the golden liquid. "Now, Monty, here is the exciting part."

Winters drew closer and held his breath.

"It seems that when Flamel finally did die – whenever that actually occurred – Agramant buried him ... and he told Pontoise' philosopher friend where the body was hidden."

Monty Winters let out his breath in a loud gasp. "And the details are here – in this manuscript?" Mathers took another sip of brandy, annoying and tantalizing Winters. "Well?"

"Patience, Monty, patience. How many times have I said that you need to pace yourself?"

The clergyman swung away from the table and strode about the room, waving his clenched fists in the air. He finally came back to Mathers' side and slammed his palms down on the desk. He took two or three loud, deep breaths and then stood up straight. His voice, when he spoke, was controlled but strained.

"Look here, old chap. You have dragged me into this whole mess and got me not just interested in it but worked up enough that I have broken into a house and have even stolen property for you. Now ... don't you think that you owe me something? Don't you think that you can stop playing games and just give me the straight information? Is that too much to ask?"

Mathers took the decanter and topped-up his friend's glass, which he handed to Winters.

"Here, my old friend. Have a sip of this nectar; you will feel better."

Winters spoke through clenched teeth. "Are the details you – we – have been seeking, dealt with in this manuscript? A simple yes or no will suffice."

Mathers gave a very quick smile and a nod of his head. "They are indeed, Monty."

"Yes!" The clergyman took up his brandy glass and gulped a large measure.

"However ..."

"What?!"

"They are in cryptic form. Apparently Johannes Pontoise was unable to decipher much of what Agramant said but he did record it verbatim, leaving it for readers of this manuscript to decide for themselves."

"And you can translate it, right?" Winters peered at his friend over the rim of his brandy glass.

"I believe I can ... though it may take a little time."

"What is time? Though you may need even more of it, my friend, to work not only on this French manuscript but also ... on this!" With a flourish, Winters produced the Flamel booklet from the pocket of his frock coat and placed it on top of the manuscript, in front of Mathers. " *Voilà!*" he cried, triumphantly. "This time I found it!"

If he expected praise from Mathers, he was disappointed. The tall man took up the book and got to his feet. He stared down at it for a long time, his hands caressing the ages-old leather cover.

"You went back to Chambers's rooms and broke in a second time, despite my forbidding it?"

Winters stood with his mouth agape. "It – it is the book you have been yearning for these many weeks," he said. "It is what you said you earnestly desired, above all things."

Mathers continued to stare at the book. He slowly turned his back on his friend, eyes still fixed on the tome.

"Yes. Yes," he said quietly. "You are right, old friend. I should be giving you thanks."

Sarah Wilde pushed open the door and entered the ladies' retiring room at the Golden Dawn's Isis-Urania Temple on Victoria Street.

"Oh! I am sorry," she said, stopping short. "I did not know anyone was in here."

Moina Mathers and Florence Farr sat – Moina on a brocade slipper chair and Florence languidly reclining on the recamier – each smoking an Egyptian cigarette from an elegant long holder. Moina was encased in a pink and rose ensemble that had tiered lace flounces contrasting to the tight bodice, unadorned neckline, and the pale kid boots on her feet. Florence wore a Worth gown of robin's egg blue and navy striped silk, with a rosette-edged hem. Cream lace decorated the sleeves and the bodice. Her slippers were of matching light blue satin with tiny silver buckles. It seemed to Sarah to be more suited to the stage than to Victoria Street. In contrast, Sarah's own modest suit of green brocade edged in brown velvet seemed very subdued.

"Ah, Miss Wilde," said Moina, Samuel Mathers's wife. "Always busy, are you not? My husband speaks frequently of your attention to details and your awareness of duty."

Her companion gave a laugh. "That is not a description that could ever be applied to me," she said. "I flitter wherever fancy takes me!"

Sarah recalled that Florence's one-time lover, George Bernard Shaw, had said of her that "she reacts vehemently against Victorian sexual and domestic morality." Sarah knew that the actress publicly championed such unpopular movements as campaigning for the welfare of prostitutes and she very much admired the woman for advocating equality for women in politics, wages, employment, and elsewhere. With the resignation of William Wynn Westcott, one of the co-founders of the Order of the Golden Dawn, two years before, Florence Farr had replaced him as "Chief Adept in Anglica", becoming the female leader of the English lodges.

Sarah smiled at the actress. "And how fares *The Countess Cathleen*, Miss Farr?" She knew that in recent years the actress had left the bed of the playwright to cohabit with the poet Yeats, and had recently been playing the character Aleel, bard and seer, in Yeats's play at the Irish Literary Theatre. It had closed only months before, though was now giving a brief encore presentation for the London audience, at the Lyceum Theatre on the Strand.

" *The Countess* fares well, I thank you, Miss Wilde. Is there anything we can do for you? Were you looking for me, perchance?"

"No. No, thank you. I was simply passing through on my way to the ritual room, to make sure that things are in preparation for the next rite."

"Then, pray, ignore the two of us," said Moina. She turned back to Florence and continued in conversation, her voice lowered so that Sarah could not catch any of what was being said. Sarah continued on her way, out to the ritual hall. She did not completely close the door between the two rooms.

"But Samuel is most insistent."

Sarah couldn't help being drawn back by the remark. Moina, obviously thinking that Sarah had entirely left the room, spoke quietly but her voice carried through to the adjoining ritual room.

"You cannot dissuade him?" Florence's voice was searching.

"No. He is adamant. Of course, I would accompany him; along with whomever else he felt was necessary, though I think the number would be few."

Florence grunted noncommittally. Sarah edged back toward the door, ostensibly placing candles in holders but her ear straining to catch the conversation.

"He normally takes so long to reach a decision," said Florence.

"I know. But he is like that. Sometimes he will get an idea in his head and then decides that he must act on it right away. It does not make for ease in long term planning."

"You say that he speaks of a time limit?"

"Indeed. He said that he has to have 'everything in place' – whatever that may mean – by the end of October."

"He said as much?"

"Not directly," replied Moina. "He was more speaking to himself than to me; a habit he seems to be getting into."

There was the noise of a chair scraping as one of the ladies arose. Sarah quickly moved to the far side of the room and busied herself with a thurible.

"Thank you for coming down to Scotland Yard, Mister Chambers." Inspector Kent sat down at his desk, opposite Alec.

It was a large, well worn desk, bearing chips and scratches and piled high with assorted folders and loose papers. A framed daguerreotype of his deceased mother stood at one corner, matched at the opposite corner by a similarly framed, hand-drawn pencil-sketch of a sad looking terrier dog. A penholder and inkwell at the center were almost buried by the detritus of papers, handouts, brochures, and notices. The inspector moved a pile of folders to one side, the better to see his visitor.

"You said that it was a matter of some import," said Alec.

"Those were my words, sir. Yes, indeed. 'A matter of some import.' Yes."

"And that matter is ... ?"

The inspector got up again and ensured that his office door was closed. When he had reseated himself he slid open the middle drawer of the desk and brought out a bulky folder, which he placed in front of himself, on top of all the other papers there. He fixed his deep brown eyes on Alec.

"Have you any acquaintance with – or have you even heard of – an organization that goes by the name the *Illuminati?*" he asked.

Alec thought for a moment before replying. "Illuminati? From the Greek for *illumination* or *illuminated ones.* You can make that 'enlightened ones', if you like. Was there not a sect or cult of that name in the sixteenth century, in Spain? Is that to whom you refer, Inspector?"

"Bavaria, was the country given to me, sir."

"Ah! Yes, of course." Alec nodded, thoughtfully. "You are right. A slightly different group. Yes, the Spanish had the *Alumbrados,* whereas the Illuminati almost certainly did originate in Bavaria."

"You *have* heard of them then, sir?" Kent persisted.

"Oh, yes; now that I put my mind to it. The designation was first to be found in the fourteenth century, associated with the Brethren of the Free Spirit, in Bavaria. They have been known by various titles at various times, always incorporating the word 'Illuminati'. I think they've also been associated – though incorrectly, to my understanding – with the Freemasons."

"Excellent!" Kent rubbed his hands together and smiled at Alec.

"Excuse me?"

"Your knowledge, sir. Excellent. I was told that you would be the man to approach."

"I am really no expert on the Illuminati," Alec protested.

"More so than anyone else, I would hazard, Mister Chambers."

Inspector Kent opened the folder in front of him and turned a few papers.

"The Boer War," he said, looking at Alec through lowered eyebrows. "Both the First Boer War and this Second Boer War which seems about to start. Various assassinations, such as the American Presidents Lincoln and Garfield, Alexander II of Russia, Gladstone – yes, Mister Gladstone, believe it or not."

"I did not know he was assassinated," said Alec.

"No, sir. You would not." He returned his attention to the folder. "Events such as the French Revolution, the American Civil War, the two Boer Wars ..."

"What are you driving at, Inspector?" asked Alec. "Reading off these people and events; what has any if this to do with the Illuminati?"

"Exactly, sir! What does it have to do with them?"

"I don't follow you."

The inspector sat back and patted the thick folder in front of him. "This folder has been building over the years, Mister Chambers. It was started by my predecessor here at the Yard, and then taken up and added to by myself. Everything in it has been connected to this Illuminati. Every fact examined and double-checked. Every assassination, every outbreak of war, every change of government. The Illuminati proclaim themselves responsible and to be what they call 'Founders of the New World Order'."

"A new world order?"

"A new world order," repeated the inspector. "And in order to have a new world order, it is necessary *to remove the old one*, would you not say so, Mister Chambers?"

"Well, yes. I suppose so. But surely no one organization can operate around the world?"

Kent leaned forward again and read from his folder. "China: Emperor Kuang Hsu." He had trouble with the pronunciation. "Germany: Emperor Kaiser Wilhelm I. Russia: Tsar Alexander II. Austria: Crown Prince Rudolf. Just last year Empress Elisabeth of Austria herself was assassinated. America: Presidents Lincoln and Garfield, as I've mentioned. I also have it on good authority that there have been threats made to the current President McKinley and major threats against King Umberto of Italy. Two assassination attempts on Alfonso, King of Spain, before his death in 1885. King Zogolli of Albania: over fifty assassination attempts before his death just four years ago. In February of this year, just a few short months ago, French President Faure died suddenly and under unusual circumstances, in Paris at age fifty-seven."

"You have proof of these?" asked Alec.

The inspector patted the folder. "All the proof you could ask for, sir."

Alec was dumbfounded. He sat quietly for a moment. "I had heard rumors, I must admit," he said. "For several years, it seems, I have been reading in the newspapers of the rise of anarchist activities both abroad and even in this country."

"Indeed, sir. One of the earliest was the bomb assassination of the Russian Tsar Alexander. This seemed to inspire the anarchists to attack other rulers and the aristocracy. They became especially active in France from about five or six years ago, even bombing the Chamber of Deputies in Paris in December, 1893. When the perpetrator of that dastardly deed was executed, they struck back with a bomb in a Paris café." He waved a dismissive hand. "But anarchists are not our main concern here, Mister Chambers."

"They are not?"

"No sir. They are the proverbial drop in the bucket compared to this Illuminati group."

Alec nodded. "The name Illuminati has been bandied about for years, but no one – no one of any consequence, I think – has ever before really taken this seriously. You are now telling me that you do have proof of the Illuminati's connection to these events?"

"Not just connection to, but involvement in. Perpetrators, you might say, sir." Inspector Kent again patted the folder, and remained with his eyes fixed on Alec.

"All right." Alec sat back and returned Kent's stare. "So you have proof. So where does that lead us? What do you want from me?"

"Scotland Yard – the 'men at the top' if you follow me, sir ..." he laid his forefinger alongside his nose, "... have uncovered a plot to bring down our beloved queen. To *destroy the British monarchy.*"

Alec was surprised to notice a slight catch in the inspector's voice. A chord had been struck in the down-to-earth police inspector's gruff persona.

"They have discovered a plot to kill the queen? To what extent have you uncovered it?"

"We have just scratched the surface, it seems, sir." Kent looked down and unnecessarily straightened the file. "We know that this Illuminati has the intention and, based on their past successes, probably the means. We need to nip this in the bud, as it were."

"How can I help?"

Just then there came a knock on the door. The inspector grunted "Come!"

The door opened and Alec was surprised to see Sarah standing there.

"Sarah!" He came to his feet.

"Alec!" She turned to Kent. "So sorry, Inspector. I did not realize ..."

He waved a dismissive hand. "Come on in, Miss Wilde. Close the door, if you would be so kind, and take a seat."

Alec noticed that Sarah was dressed in a dark brown walking suit devoid of flounces, frills and other trim but with a matching bonnet. Her vibrant hair filled a net snood beneath the bonnet. She looked efficient yet extremely attractive, he thought. Inspector Kent indicated a chair next to Alec. She crossed to it and they both sat down.

"I believe you know Miss Wilde? She is a member of our female department here at New Scotland Yard. She was one of the type-writer girls here but I have had occasion to call upon her to work, through me, on this case."

Alec looked at Sarah as though seeing her for the first time. "You are a policeman?" he asked.

She smiled. "I think the designation would have to be changed, should it ever become official."

Kent rested his hands on the folder in front of him. "Never mind that for now," he said. "Miss Wilde displayed great ability and general knowledge above that of the majority of type-writer girls, drawing attention to herself. I felt, and my superiors agreed with me, that she might be more useful away from her machine. Just to let you know, Mister Chambers, Miss Wilde has infiltrated the Golden Dawn Magical Order to keep me apprised of the doings of our Mister Samuel Mathers and company."

"You are a spy?"

Sarah blushed. "No one has ever put it quite like that, Alec. But yes, I suppose that is what I am. Rather exciting when you think of it in those terms! Very 'modern', would you not say?"

"And dangerous!" Alec sounded concerned and not a little indignant. He turned back to the inspector. "These 'men at the top', as you described them, are comfortable placing a young woman in possible jeopardy, Inspector? They have no concern for what may transpire ..."

"I did volunteer," said Sarah.

"You did?"

She nodded, and smiled at him. "As you know, I just act as secretary for the Golden Dawn – or *Scriba* as they insist on terming it. All I have to do is keep my ears and eyes open and report back to the Inspector."

"Nothing too dangerous, sir, I can assure you," said Kent.

"Which brings me to why I am here." Sarah turned her attention to the man behind the desk. "It would seem that Mister Mathers is planning on setting off in three days time."

Kent spoke to Alec. "Our man is going on a sudden trip to the Continent, it seems. Very unexpected."

"Mister Mathers is usually very methodical and does a great deal of research and planning before such a move. A trip to France would normally take him at least a month to prepare," Sarah added.

"Wait a minute! You are saying that you think this may be tied-in, somehow, with the Illuminati?" asked Alec. "That MacGregor Mathers is an Illuminati member?"

The inspector nodded. "Yes, sir, we do. Though exactly how it is tied-in I don't pretend to know. But the Illuminati Director for the South of England gave him the order to go abroad."

Alec's eyebrows rose. "Mathers is not the main man, then?"

"Oh, he would like to be," said Kent. He chuckled humorlessly. "Yes, sir. That he would. Very much so. But right now he takes his orders from the top man."

"And that is?"

"Oh! Sorry, sir. That is Dr. William Westcott, the distinguished London coroner. He was one of the original founders of the Golden Dawn." The inspector riffled through papers till he found what he was looking for. He pulled a sheet from the file and read from it. "Dr. William Wynn Westcott was a Master Mason and Secretary General of the *Societas Rosicruciana* in Anglia. Along with our Mister Samuel Liddell MacGregor Mathers and Dr. William Robert Woodman – who deceased in 1891, incidentally – Dr. Westcott founded the Hermetic Order of the Golden Dawn in 1887."

"So Woodman died," said Alec. "What happened to Westcott?"

"Two years ago he withdrew from the Order," volunteered Sarah. "The reason was never fully explained to the membership. Mister Crowley insinuated that Mathers was behind his withdrawal, but I have learned that long after Dr. Westcott withdrew he was lending money to Mister Mathers so there was no ill will there."

"So why did he withdraw?" persisted Alec.

"It has been suggested that the good doctor's magical activities were at odds with his position as London coroner and that the medical 'powers that be' suggested he restrict the work he does beyond Harley Street," said the inspector.

"That could be, I suppose." Alec nodded.

"We are not certain, by any means, sir," said Kent. "My personal feeling is that Dr. Westcott found it more to his advantage to run Illuminati affairs from behind the scenes, and not to remain in the Golden Dawn spotlight."

"How do you know he still runs things?" asked Alec.

"Oh, Mister Mathers regularly meets with Dr. Westcott," said Sarah. "On several occasions I have witnessed him being picked up by the doctor's carriage. They drive around Hyde Park for a while and then Mister Mathers is dropped off again."

"Very interesting," said Alec. He was pensive for a moment. "It occurs to me that there is some connection between the two names: *Golden Dawn*, meaning growing illumination, and *Illuminati*, meaning Illuminated Ones."

"More than a coincidence, perhaps," agreed Kent.

"So just how many Golden Dawn members are also associates of the Illuminati?"

"That we cannot say, for certain, sir. Westcott and Mathers, yes. Possibly a Mister Leigh Cranwell, Mister Arthur Machen, Miss Annie Hornman. All possible associates; no positions of power in any way." He shrugged. "We just do not know at this point."

"Moina Mathers might also be one," added Sarah.

The inspector nodded. "Yes, of course. I had forgotten her."

"And what about the clergyman?"

"Clergyman?" Alec was interested.

"The Reverend Montague Winters," said Kent. "A close friend of Mathers. He is not a Golden Dawn member and we do not know whether he is of the Illuminati or not, but I strongly suspect that he may be. Oh, and

he is not – or no longer – a true cleric. He was defrocked – I think the term is 'laicized' – for 'conduct unbecoming holy orders' several years ago."

"Any connection to the clergyman who was seen entering my house, or suspected of the same?"

The inspector nodded slowly. "It seems very likely," he said. "Certainly his description matches that given to us by the crossing sweeper. We are still checking that."

"Would he, then, be the one responsible for the murder of my man Edward Merryfield?" Alec's voice was hard.

"No." Kent shook his head. "No, sir. We did look into that, so far as we were able, but it seems there was no connection. If, as we suspect, Mathers was behind the murder, then he used some other villain. Probably some nameless hired thug from the East End." He paused, then: "We have not given up on that, sir."

Alec nodded thoughtfully, his face grim.

Sarah stopped short as she entered MacGregor Mathers' office. Sitting behind the large mahogany desk, obviously making himself at home, was Aleister Crowley. He looked up and smiled at her.

"Were you looking for me, Miss Wilde?"

"No," she said. "Where is Mister Mathers? What are you doing here?"

"Mathers is not coming in today, did he not tell you? Apparently he leaves town tomorrow."

"I know. I have been told that I am to travel with his group. I wanted to discuss that with him."

"Indeed?" Crowley arched an eyebrow.

"Again, Mister Crowley, what are you doing in Mister Mathers's office?"

Crowley turned partially away from her and looked down at a book he had on the desk. "As it happens I am tutoring Allan Bennett. He should be along any minute."

"You are tutoring Mister Bennett?"

Crowley looked about him. "Is there an echo in here?" he said.

Sarah ignored his rudeness. "Does Mister Mathers know you are using his office?"

"As it happens I usually work with Allan at my rooms in Soho, but since good old SRMD is off to places unknown, I thought I would avail myself of more salubrious surroundings. Do you have a problem with that, Madam?"

"I hope you know what you are doing," Sarah said, and left the room.

It was after dark when Alec got home. He had taken Sarah out to dinner, before she left with the Golden Dawn group the following morning. It had been very pleasant, marred only by the thought of their separation. He was not pleased that she had to be a part of the Golden Dawn group but the Inspector had been pleased that she'd be along to see what was afoot. She would send back regular reports.

The servants had gone to bed, on Alec's earlier orders, and he entered his study and moved across toward the fireplace to turn-up the gaselier. As its warm glow illuminated the room, he turned and gasped. A grey-haired man sat in his favorite armchair, studying him.

"Who the devil are you and how did you get in here?" Alec demanded.

The man stood and inclined his head.

"My apologies for startling you." The voice was refined and educated, as befitted the expensive clothes of the visitor. Alec took in his perfectly groomed, steel-grey hair, his monocle, the gold watch chain, and the smart top hat, gloves and cane that lay on the floor beside the chair. "May I introduce myself? I am Lord Sunbury."

"You have not said how you got in here," snapped Alec, still recovering from his surprise at seeing the gentleman.

"Again, my apologies. My means of ingress are unimportant. May we be seated? There is much I would like to discuss with you and time is of the essence."

Grudgingly Alec advanced and took the chair opposite his own usual one, indicating for his visitor to resume his seat.

"May I get you some refreshment, my lord?"

Sunbury dismissed the offer with a gesture.

"I must ask you to treat as confidential this, our conversation here this evening."

"Of course." Despite himself, Alec was curious.

Lord Sunbury sat back more comfortably in the chair and crossed his legs. "You may be familiar with a segment of the Metropolitan Police known as the Criminal Investigation Department?" he said. Alec nodded. "You may not know, however, that about twenty years ago a Special Branch of that august group was formed, under Howard Vincent and William Melville."

Alec went to respond, but his visitor raised a hand.

"Just listen for the moment, if you would, Mister Chambers. This branch was originally known as the Special Irish Branch, since their *raison d'être* was to counter the Irish Republican Brotherhood. However, as time went on the 'Irish' appellation was dropped. Less than a decade ago Melville was assigned to protect the Shah of Persia on his state visit and it was just five years ago that he arrested the French anarchist Théodule Meunier less than a mile from where we sit, in Victoria Station.

Six years ago, in 1893, Melville became Superintendent of the SB. Today the focus of this Special Branch has become the protection of royalty and keeping track of the Fenians and political extremists."

"Like the Illuminati," Alec couldn't help interjecting.

Sunbury nodded. "I see you follow me, Mister Chambers. I was told that you were intelligent." He glanced about him. "You know, I think I might partake of a small sherry, if you have such?"

"Of course, my lord."

Alec got up and poured drinks for both of them, while his visitor continued.

"Today there are almost eight hundred members of the Special Branch; male and female. It is today headed by Colonel Sir Charles Vincent, recently knighted for his services, by the way. Ah, thank you." Sunbury took the proffered glass of sherry, sipped it, and then placed it carefully on a side table. "Vincent took the Parliamentary seat of Sheffield Central in '85, not that that has bearing on our present discussion. He speaks a number of foreign languages including German and Russian. I tell you this simply to give you an understanding of the caliber of the Special Branch's leadership."

"Am I to take it that you are a member of this group, Lord Sunbury?"

Another sip of sherry. "I have that honor, yes."

"So, why are you telling me all this?"

"There is often confusion, in the popular mind, between the Metropolitan Police Special Branch and the Intelligence Branch of the War Office. The latter, I am afraid, has a poor record and no great credibility, while the SB works – to my mind – many near-miracles."

"If I may ask," said Alec. "Where does Inspector Kent fit into this, if indeed he does?"

Lord Sunbury smiled, for the first time since he'd been there, Alec noted.

"The good Inspector is a valuable man. He has long since been deserving of promotion in his field, but both we – the SB – and he believe that he can best serve by remaining in the milieu in which he is now so firmly ensconced."

"Earlier today I was in the Inspector's office and he showed me a file – quite a bulky one, as it happens – detailing activities of the Illuminati."

Sunbury nodded. "Yes, we asked him to do that. It seems that, by your expertise in matters alchemical and metaphysical, you have been drawn into activities of great importance to the Special Branch. I would that we could protect you by disassociating you from our Mister Mathers and his merry band but, alas, it is too late." He paused and took another draught of the wine. "I am here, Mister Chambers, to advise you of the gravity of that in which you are now involved, and to plan how your involvement might benefit both your country and your monarch."

"I will be honored to do all that I am able," said Alec, sincerely.

Lord Sunbury nodded. "I gathered we would be able to count on you. Now! First things first. Tomorrow a small select group from the Golden Dawn leaves these shores for the Continent. Their mission, as we understand it, is to seek out the tomb of a medieval alchemist and to recover important manuscripts believed to lie within that tomb."

"Nicholas Flamel."

"Precisely." Lord Sunbury drained his sherry glass, put it down and came to his feet. He reached down and retrieved his hat, gloves and cane. "We would like you, Mister Chambers, to beat them to the punch; to locate and obtain those manuscripts before they fall into the wrong hands."

Alec rose himself. "Do you know why they so desperately seek them?"

"To learn the secret of turning base metals into gold."

"They want to make gold?" Alec sounded incredulous.

"Indeed. They have to finance their nefarious schemes; murders and revolutions do not come cheaply. Those manuscripts could be life blood to their cause."

"And you want me to go after them? But I do not even know their destination."

"Do not mistake the mission, Mister Chambers. You are not chasing after them; you are seeking that final goal yourself and going directly to it." He moved toward the door. "We have every confidence in you."

He went out the door and, before Alec could follow him, left the building. Alec stood still in shock and amazement. He had no idea where Flamel was buried.

*S*arah felt herself falling asleep; her eyelids were heavy and she was having trouble listening to what MacGregor Mathers was saying. The rhythmic clatter of the train's wheels and the rocking of the carriage added to the fact that she had slept badly the night before and had awoken early. She thought wistfully of her dinner with Alec the previous evening.

She glanced out of the window at the flowing green fields of East Kent sliding by as the dark green engine of the South Eastern & Chatham Railway bore their party toward Dover. They had made their last stop in Canterbury and were now heading to the end of the line, at the coast, where they would embark for France on a paddle-wheeled steam boat.

Sarah looked around at her traveling companions, squeezed together in the small First Class compartment. She sat next to the window. She was dressed for traveling, in a suit of camel's hair cheviot of light grey with a velvet collar. The suit was trimmed with braid and small gilt buttons. The panel skirt was lined with percaline and the coat with mercerized sateen. Her shoes were sensible Oxfords. Beside her was Moina Mathers, wearing a deep green, serge, traveling suit with white border stripes edging the sleeves, the bodice reveres, and the pleated flounce on the skirt's hem. Two-tone brown spectator shoes peaked out from beneath the hem. Her husband sat on her far side resplendent, as always, in his charcoal grey frock coat and grey pin-striped trousers. On the rack above his head, his plush beaver top hat rested beside Moina's trimmed straw walking bonnet.

Opposite Sarah sat Leigh Cranwell, engrossed in a book and completely ignoring Mathers' discourse. He wore the same brown, drab, single-breasted, sacque suit Sarah had seen him in on numerous occasions. His pince-nez balanced on the bridge of his nose and she could see the redness of the skin caused by the spring being too tight. Beside Cranwell was The Reverend Monty Winters in his usual somber clerical garb and beside him, opposite Mathers himself, sat Percy Purdy. Sarah

had not met Purdy before, and Mathers had failed to introduce the man to anyone. She looked at him now, trying to be inconspicuous. He was young and fresh-faced, seemingly very effeminate and emitting the faint smell of sweetened macassar oil. His black hair fell over his forehead contrasting with his almost white complexion. Deep brown eyes stared out, fixed on Mathers as he prattled on about his many achievements. A slight smile played on Percy's full mouth, though Sarah couldn't tell whether he was amused by Mathers or if that was simply his normal countenance. Like Cranwell, he wore a sacque suit but on him it looked tailored and smart. In the rack above rested a fur felt Fedora hat of the American influence.

Sarah noted that Moina's eyes were closed, though she didn't seem to be sleeping. Winters suddenly gave a snort, which she felt might have been a snore quickly turned into a cough. No one, she thought – with the possible exception of the newcomer Purdy – was paying any real attention to their professed leader.

From the engine came a loud whistle, which seemed to alert them all. There was a general movement of limbs, slight stretching, and a shifting in the seats. Mathers loudly cleared his throat and looked around at his companions.

"I know you are all anxious to hear the details of my plans," he said. "When we get established on the steam boat, at Dover, we will gather together and I will bring you all up-to-date on my findings and my intentions. Our immediate goal, as you know, is Paris."

Moina opened her eyes wide and smiled around at everyone. "Ah, Paris!" she said. "How I have missed it. It will be good to be back."

Mathers harrumphed and looked out of the window on his side of the carriage. "Yes. Well, we won't be there for the shopping nor for the food, I regret to say. We are there strictly on business."

"Since when has shopping not been business?" murmured his wife.

Mathers ignored her. Sarah chuckled inwardly.

"We will, of course, briefly visit our sister temple, the Temple of Ahathoor. It was there that Moina and I first created the Rites of Isis, if you recall."

Sarah and Monty, alone of the others, nodded their heads.

"Regrettably," continued Mathers, "we will not have time to spend there. We have other more important work to do."

"I can hardly wait to hear the details of that," said Winters, sighing and stretching his legs.

Sarah smiled out of her window at the passing fields, farms, and orchards.

Alec watched Ian Gordon load the trunk onto the carriage. In his mind he went over everything he had tried to do before leaving. Most importantly he had sent an urgent message to his old school chum, Jeremy Lowell, asking him to keep an eye on the shop. Jeremy was a gentleman farmer in Surrey who was always complaining that he was bored and that there was nothing to do. He would enjoy being a bookseller for a while, Alec knew. He had done so once before, when Alec had been ill, and had offered to fill-in any time in the future, if it was needed.

Alec had decided to go immediately to France and start his search there, rather than dig around in England and then have to cross the Channel. He was fluent in French, both reading and speaking the language, and was certain there would be far more clues in Flamel's homeland than might have been scattered about in England.

The train down to Dover was a local, stopping at all the stations along the way. Alec kept thinking of Sarah, who must have been on an earlier train. She might well reach France before he even left England. He sighed and brought his attention back to his book. It was his own volume on Flamel. He hoped that re-reading it might refresh his mind with the myriad of details concerning the alchemist. He wished now that he had made it a much larger appraisal of the man's life ... and death.

The train seemed to stand for an interminable length of time at Faversham station. Finally, with a whistle from the engine, it lurched forward and gradually resumed its steady pace toward the coast. Alec suddenly sat forward. He had turned a page and now looked at a print of the copiously decorated front of Flamel's supposed tomb, in the Church of the Holy Innocents, in Paris. He had forgotten about that. The front of the tomb was inscribed "*Nicolas Flamel et Perrennelle sa Femme*." Nicolas Flamel and Perenelle his wife. "Comment les inocens furent occis par le commandement du Roy Herodes." *How the Innocents were killed by the commandment of King Herod.* There were many figures and scenes depicted above and about the inscriptions. The majority were alchemical in nature, together with figures representing Flamel himself, at various stages in his life.

"The Church of the Holy Innocents," Alec murmured. He determined to start his quest there, though he knew that the original graveyard of that name – *Le Cimetière des Saints-innocents* – on the Grand Rue had been abandoned and cleared more than a hundred years ago, in 1786. But it was said that many of the more elaborate and decorative tombstones had been preserved. Surely, he thought, Flamel's would be among them.

The Golden Dawn group huddled around the tall figure of MagGregor Mathers as the paddle steamer the *PS Waverley* left the shelter of Dover harbor and headed out across the English Channel. A chill wind blowing off the surface of the choppy water caused them all to pull their overcoats tightly about them. They stood close to one another, partly to hear what Mathers had to say and partly for warmth. They were in the well of the passenger area, which was covered by a canvas awning but had open sides.

"I prevailed upon Mister Cranwell to accompany us," Mathers said, "because of his expertise in this area. He has studied Nicolas Flamel a little more than have I, and I believe he will be of great help in this our search for the alchemist's tomb." He then half-turned to indicate the dark-haired, bright-eyed newcomer to the group. "And I must introduce you all to Mister Percy Purdy."

Purdy said nothing but continuing to smile and inclined his head to each of them in turn.

"Mister Purdy volunteered his services when he heard of the object of my – our – search. He spent some time in France in his post-graduate years after leaving Oxford, actually researching Nicolas Flamel. He and I feel that he may well be able to abbreviate the time we spend searching, since he has already covered much of the ground."

"And what of your delving into those manuscripts you do possess?" asked Winters.

"Ah, yes," answered Mathers, enigmatically. He looked hard at the clergyman. "I did, I believe, at the time, give you an overview of the contents of the manuscript from the *Bibliotheque Nationale*." He went on to tell the others of the Brethren of Inner Truth and what the ancient Turkish philosopher told the Abbé Johannes Pontoise. "The promised details obtained from Agramant, regarding the location of the tomb, were disappointing, to say the least. I do not doubt that Pontoise had the information but he seemed unable to put Agramant's words into any order that made sense. There was talk of tombs – more than one – ancient churches and underground burials. Nothing specific, however; nothing on which we could follow-up with any certitude."

"And the Flamel notebook?" Winters persisted.

"You have the notebook?" asked Cranwell, suddenly alert. "Then what are we doing here in the middle of this wretched ocean?"

"It is not an ocean, Mister Cranwell," said Moina Mathers, acidly. "It is the English Channel."

He ignored her and stared hard at her husband. "Well?"

"We do indeed have a Flamel notebook," responded Mathers. "But my perusal of it – which involved not a little deciphering – indicates that it tells much of the history and philosophy of the alchemical art, together with a certain amount of information on the accumulation of ingredients for the great experiment, but it lacks the actual method of transmutation."

"May we see it?" Cranwell asked.

"Indeed ... if you feel you may be more capable than myself at its interpretation. However, I think you will agree that this is not the ideal place in which to bring out a rare fourteenth century manuscript!"

Cranwell grunted.

"When can we look at it?" asked Winters.

"When we get to Paris we will all be in need of rest and recuperation. After we have recovered and dined we will gather together and I will lead you through all that we have."

"I really don't know why he has to lock everything. It is as though he doesn't trust us."

For the tenth time Aleister Crowley tried to open the drawers of MacGregor Mathers's desk but without success. He smacked his hand down on the desk top and looked petulant. From across the room Charles Henry Allan Bennett watched him without comment.

"Really! Would you not consider it an insult?" Crowley asked.

Bennett shrugged, his dark eyes watching Crowley. "Did Mathers say you could use his office while he was away?" he asked.

It was Crowley's turn to shrug. "He is not using it ... obviously. Why should I not use it? It will be mine anyway, when our 'Great Leader' gives up the mantle."

Bennett moved over to the window and stood looking out at the gathering dusk. "Do you really think he will abandon the Golden Dawn?"

Crowley gave the desk top another thump with his fist and then walked over to stand beside Bennett. "Abandon? That's an interesting choice of words, Allan. Would you feel abandoned if he left?"

"He was one of the founders. He has done a great deal for the Order. Do not forget that."

Crowley turned away again and wandered over to the fireplace where he picked up and then replaced the various items decorating the mantel-piece. "Oh, I don't think SRMD will let any of us forget that. He is forever reminding us; me at least."

"Perhaps he feels that you need reminding."

"Oh, I am sure he does." He swung around to face Bennett. "But I have done my share, you know!" He spoke forcefully, through his teeth. Then he seemed to calm. He gave a dismissive wave of his arm. "Time will tell, my friend. Time will tell." He looked at the desk one more time before making for the door. "Perhaps I should call-in a locksmith." He laughed and went out.

Bennett stood thoughtfully for a moment before following him.

The Golden Dawn group gathered in the sitting room of the Mathers' suite at the Chopin Hôtel. They had all settled into their respective rooms and then had dined in the hotel dining room. Now they were eager to look at the Flamel notebook that Monty Winters had mentioned on the trip across the Channel.

Close to the rue Drouot and the rue Chauchat, the Chopin Hôtel was just off the Grands Boulevard, in the ninth arrondissement. It was reached through a narrow, glass-roofed pedestrian arcade. Just over fifty years old, the hotel had not weathered well, its purple velvet-covered couches and benches were faded and their corners showed wear. The gold of the tassels was tarnished and the gilt legs scratched. A bust of Chopin, its nose chipped, sat on an old upright piano in the hotel's lobby. The varnish on the parquet floors was worn. Each of the rooms was decorated with bouquets of tired, sad-looking tulips and hyacinths. But Mathers was willing to ignore the scrapes on the wallpaper and the stains in the corners for a few days; the price was right. In his checkered career he had stayed in far worse places than the Chopin Hôtel.

Percy Purdy and Monty Winters cleared the largest table in the room, setting the wilting flowers and dusty decorations on a smaller occasional table. Leigh Cranwell dragged two chairs across the room and Sarah and Moina sat on them. Purdy quickly dusted off the table's top surface with a hotel towel and then stood back to allow Mathers to lay down the manuscript.

"This is an actual notebook of Nicolas Flamel," said Mathers, carefully placing the small, leather-bound volume in the center of the table. "It has been, er, acquired from a young acquaintance of mine ... a young gentleman who runs a book shop. He can – he would – account for its authenticity."

"Would that be Mister Alec Chambers?" Sarah couldn't help asking, knowing well the truth of the answer.

Mathers ignored her. "Now I must ask you to treat this with respect, considering its age. As you see, it is already missing its back cover. Here ..." he opened the book at the first page. "Here you can see the signature of Flamel, with his notes and comments in the margins of the main work."

"Did he write the main work?" asked Cranwell.

"Undoubtedly. Though much of it would seem to be copied from somewhere else, and Flamel annotated it. He was, after all, a public scrivener for many years in his early days, earning money by copying and selling manuscripts."

Purdy leaned close over the parchment, studying everything.

"The illustrations are very colorful," said Moina.

"Strange alchemical symbols, I take it," said Sarah. "Do we know what they mean?" She looked up at Mathers.

He nodded. "Oh, yes. Well, in general we do, yes. There developed a 'tradition', we might term it, of symbolism in the ancient philosophy."

"And you have translated the Latin in the text?" Purdy asked, not looking up from the book.

"Yes. The Latin and the little Greek that I also found to be there." Mathers sounded pleased with himself.

"Yet it still does not give up the secret of transmutation?" Cranwell looked hard at Mathers.

"It does not. It is almost as though this was purely an introduction. Very disappointing. Flamel does not part with his secrets easily."

"May I see the last page?" asked Purdy, his eyes finally rising to lock onto those of MacGregor Mathers.

The taller man dutifully turned the pages to the last one in the book. Purdy's head went down again. His finger pointed to the lines of text and followed them down as he murmured to himself what they said.

"There is no clue there," said Mathers.

"You think not?"

"I know not, Percy." He sounded annoyed that his word was being questioned.

"It is Latin ..."

"I know it is Latin!"

Purdy remained calm. "It is Latin and it says Repente dives nemo factus est bonus et"

"And that means?" asked Winters. "My Latin is very rusty."

"'No one who is rich is made suddenly good, etc.'" said Mathers. "An aphorism of Publilius Syrus, I believe ..."

"Except," interrupted Purdy, "that it does not finish with etcetera."

"What do you mean?" snapped Mathers. "Of course it does. It is a neat closure to all that has gone before."

Leigh Cranwell pushed forward and looked over Percy's shoulder. He snorted.

"Purdy is right," he said. "It does not say etcetera, it says *et*."

"The same thing," growled Mathers.

"Not at all."

"What? What is going on?" Moina looked at each man in turn. "*Et. Etcetera*. What is the difference?"

Mathers said nothing for a moment, and then slowly nodded his head. "Yes," he said quietly. "Yes. Well done, Percy." He turned away from the table and walked over to the fireplace. The others watched him. He finally turned back to them. "I did not notice that," he said.

Sarah was amazed. She had never before heard Mathers admit to making an error or missing some small detail.

"Please explain," snapped his wife. "Are we to be left in suspense?"

"I saw the word *et* at the end of the aphorism," said Mathers, "and assumed it to be Flamel's slovenly writing of *etcetera* – I take it we all know what is meant by etcetera? 'And so on'?" The others nodded. "Well, as Mister Purdy has so admirably pointed out, it is most distinctly *et*, meaning 'and'."

"Go on." Moina still looked puzzled.

"'And' would mean that the sentence is not finished. In other words, there is a page or pages that follow on after those we see before us." He paused to let his words sink in. "This is not the complete notebook. There is more. No wonder the back cover is missing. Someone, at some time, found this portion but there is more that should be with it."

"And that 'more' would almost certainly contain what we seek – the methodology of the transubstantiation," finished Cranwell.

Alec studied his map of the city. The original *Cimetière des Innocents*, on the corner of rue Saint-Denis and rue Berger, now had a fountain at its center and had become a public square. The fountain had been designed by Pierre Lescot and sculpted by Jean Goujon and was moved to its present location when the cemetery was disbanded at the end of the 18th Century. The original cemetery was four times bigger than the present-day square and had been surrounded by a wall. Arched passageways had been progressively established and had attracted many business people who, in effect, set up shop at the cemetery. It was in the attics of these arcades that the bones exhumed from the communal graves were originally placed.

Alec knew that the professed "tombstone" of Nicolas Flamel had decorated the underside of the fourth arcade of the Charnier des Innocents. When the cemetery was cleared, this stone, among many others, was preserved. He aimed to study the decorations painted by Flamel to see if there were any clues left by the alchemist.

"And what is your interest in this obscure work?" The archivist peered at Alec over the top of his pince-nez.

"I am an English publisher," Alec responded. "I am working on a book about the ancient philosophers and, of course, wish to include Paris's most famous alchemist."

A smile briefly broke the granite surface of the archivist's face. "You English always make much of nothing, I think." He said the word *English* with some disdain. Alec remained calm and friendly. It would not pay to argue, even with such a petty official.

"Very well, Monsieur ..." he glanced at Alec's business card. "Monsieur Chambers. Proceed. But please – do not touch the surface of the memorial. It is old and delicate. *Bon jour.*" With a nod, he dismissed Alec and returned to his desk work.

Alec felt a thrill when he finally came to the Flamel stone. It was much larger than he had expected and in remarkably good condition. The panels seemed well preserved but a wooden barrier prevented him from getting close enough to examine it in as much detail as he wished. He pulled out his Flamel book and turned to the page with the illustration.

Michel and Babette Grenoble welcomed the English group and took obvious delight in giving them a tour of The Temple Ahathoor No. 7 of Paris. It was located at the villa d'Auteuil, at 87 avenue Mozart, in the suburbs soon to be a part of the 16th arrondissement. Mathers had originally chosen this particular villa because of it being well hidden from view, being in an inner courtyard with a few other houses. The entrance to its garden was located on avenue Mozart.

The doorway to the house was framed by two large stone griffons. The double main doors opened into a large vaulted hall which served as the main ritual room. At the rear, a curving flight of white marble stairs with a gilded bronze balustrade gave access to the upper floors. This grand staircase served as a dais for the throne used in many of the Golden Dawn rites.

Sarah followed the others as they traipsed after the Greenobles, admiring the ornate decorations, including four large painted panels depicting the Egyptian deities. It seemed obvious to her that the members of the Paris temple were of a more affluent stratum of society than their London brethren.

"Monsieur Mathers," breathed Madame Grenoble, gripping his arm and gazing into his eyes. "You must meet Mademoiselle Japhet. She is *formidable.*"

"And who, pray, is Mademoiselle Japhet?" asked Moina, icily.

"Moina!" murmured Mathers.

"Non." Babette Grenoble gave his arm a squeeze. She spoke to Moina but kept her eyes fixed on Mathers. "Celina Japhet is a famous medium."

"Her real name is Celina Bequet," interjected Michel Grenoble. "But she uses 'Japhet' for professional reasons."

"And she is a professional what?" asked Moina.

"As I have said, she is a medium," replied Babette, now turning to look at the stony-faced Moina Mathers. Babette was a few years younger than Moina and was obviously a devotee of France's premier actress Sarah Bernhardt. Babette had died her hair to match her idol's and wore copies of Bernhardt dresses.

"Not just any medium." Michel bubbled over with enthusiasm. "She was the personal medium for Allan Kardec. And she recently visited our dear temple."

"Kardec, the father of French Spiritism?" asked Monty Winters, suddenly interested.

"*Oui, Monsieur.*" Michel nodded his head. "He died almost exactly thirty years ago, but his movement, his beliefs and teachings, live on throughout France and, as I have heard, as far afield as South America and other countries." Michel had a long, thin mustache, curled upward in spikes at the ends. He habitually touched the ends as though to be sure they were still in place. His dark hair was parted in the center and ran outward toward his ears in large waves. It gleamed with Rowland's macassa oil.

Mathers nodded. "Yes, we are all familiar with Kardec, I would hazard. You say you are acquainted with the medium with whom he worked?"

The group gathered around the French couple. Sarah noticed that Purdy stood close behind Mathers, his face wearing a slight frown.

"*Mais oui, mes amis.*" Michel Grenoble was all smiles. "She was a brilliant young medium when she was introduced to Kardec ..."

"By Victorien Sardou," interjected Babette. "He is our famous dramatist. He wrote his play *Spiritisme* especially to honor Monsieur Kardec's work. He writes for our beautiful Sarah Bernhardt, I am sure you know?"

"Yes," said Mathers. "Our dear Florence Farr tells me that Mister Shaw refers to Monsieur Sardou's work as 'Sardoodledum'! Not very kindly, I believe."

Michel was not abashed. "No matter. It is Mademoiselle Japhet of whom we speak. She is an exceptional medium."

"Controlled by the spirit of her grandfather, you know," added Babette.

"Is the Temple of Ahathoor now a Spiritist habitat, then?" asked Leigh Cranwell.

"Oh, no. *Non, non, non!*" Michel and Babette spoke together.

"Not at all." Michel sought to calm them all. "*Non.* It is just that Mademoiselle Japhet gave our temple a demonstration of her ... abilities ... the other evening and we were all somewhat amazed by them."

"We thought you might like to sample her talents yourselves?" added Babette. "When you advised that you would be visiting, Frater S'

Rhioghail Mo Dhream," she used Mathers's ritual title as she again took his arm and gazed up at him, "we thought that it might be of especial interest to you. We would much have preferred to have performed *The Rites of Isis* for you, of course, but there was little time to prepare."

"I think not," said Monty Winters, in a low voice, stroking his beard.

"Of course!" Mathers contradicted his friend, smiling at Babette's earnest face and patted her hand. He then looked up and around at his small band of followers. "What say you, friends? Might this not be an education for us? Shall we enter the séance room of this Mademoiselle Japhet and see what she has to offer?"

Winters said nothing more, but kept his eyes cast down.

Sarah's heart seemed to skip a beat. She had seldom before thought about, nor studied, Spiritualism – or Spiritism, as the French version was termed – but was aware of various comments from others. She knew that Spiritualism was a large and ever growing movement, but apparently its format was such that it was not too difficult for the unscrupulous to fake the professed phenomena of the séance room. She did not doubt that there were genuine mediums, but they seemed to be in the minority. She wondered where this Celina Japhet fitted in the overall scene.

Alec looked up as he heard approaching footsteps.

"It should be just around the corner, Georgina," said a very English voice. "My *Baedeker* says it is still intact."

An elderly couple came into sight. The man had a walrus mustache and mutton-chop sideburns, both silvery-grey in color. He wore an Inverness coat with attached cape, which for a moment made Alec think of the fictitious Sherlock Holmes whose adventures were being so successfully serialized in *The Strand* magazine. Alec was somewhat relieved to see that the gentleman did not favor a deerstalker hat but rather a regular felt trilby. He swung a fine Malacca cane with an ivory handle.

The man's female companion wore a black wool crepon cape, edged with fur, over a dress of black and navy cheviot serge. Her hat was a sensible fur-felt walking hat with a drape of silk velvet on the brim. She wore fine gold-rimmed spectacles.

The two came to a halt when they saw Alec. He was crouched down, having been studying the lower illustrations on the tombstone. He now stood and raised his hat to the newcomers.

"A London accent, if I am not mistaken," he said. "May I present myself? Mister Alec Chambers, of Pimlico."

The man doffed his hat and indicated both himself and the lady by his side. "Professor Daniel Parmington and my wife Georgina," he said.

He smiled. "Yes, we are indeed fellow Londoners. So nice not to have to speak in my fractured French."

"What brings you to the tombstone of Nicholas Flamel, if I may ask?" said Alec.

The couple exchanged glances and then Parmington said, "I am an associate at the British Museum. Although we are on a short holiday, I never fail to take in any local items of especial interest. The concierge at our hotel mentioned this exhibit and we decided to visit it."

Alec turned back to the stone. "It is indeed unusual," he said. He pointed at the designs. "A number of alchemical scenes, as you can see."

"Yes, I do have some faint knowledge of the ancient alchemical philosophers," said Parmington, studying the memorial. "Though I am more aware of Paracelsus, Raymond Lully and Roger Bacon than I am of this Flamel fellow."

"Flamel was said to be one of the most successful, if not the most successful," said Alec.

"Indeed?"

"What does all this mean?" asked Parmington's wife, pointing to the different scenes on the tombstone.

"These – as I understand it – are scenes representative of various stages in the alchemical transubstantiation of metals," said the professor. He turned to Alec. "Am I correct?"

Alec nodded his head. "Indeed," he said. To Mrs. Parmington he added "There are many, many such traditional illustrations found in the copies we have of ancient alchemical texts. Why Flamel chose these specific ones, we do not know."

"And what do the little numbers mean?" asked the lady, leaning forward and peering through her spectacles.

"Numbers?" Both her husband and Alec now leaned forward beside her.

"Yes. See?" She pointed to two of the panels.

elina Japhet was an elderly spinster. She was short and portly –
five feet tall and almost as wide, thought Sarah – with a smooth,
round face smothered in fine white powder. There was no color on her
cheeks nor on her lips. Her near-white hair was drawn back in a severe
bun and held in a snood. Her black dress was of nun's veiling with lace
yoke; the trimming of satin bands. She had an imperious manner, as
though used to being waited upon.

"We have everything prepared for you, Madame," said Babette
Grenoble, fussing about the guest and leading her and the others into
the upstairs room. The large sitting room had been prepared for the
séance, with heavy drapes over the windows. A heavy round table sat in
the center of the room with nine ornate chairs drawn up to it.

MacGregor Mathers took the seat at one end, opposite the chair that
seated Madame Japhet. Moina sat to Mathers's right and the Reverend
Monty Winters to his left. Beside Moina was Percy Purdy with Leigh
Cranwell beside him. On the other side of the table Sarah sat between
Winters and Michel Grenoble, who was on the medium's right. Babette
was on Madame Japhet's left, next to Leigh Cranwell.

A large séance trumpet sat upright in the center of the table; the only
noticeable object in the room. Typically there were bands of luminous
paint around both the small and large openings of the aluminum cone,
to allow the sitters to see its progress should it move in the dark.

Sarah was not happy about being at the table. From Monty Winters's
dour expression, she was not alone. Sarah had never before attended a
séance and wasn't sure about the protocol. Babette must have noticed
her puzzled expression because, once the medium was seated, she
smiled brightly around at everyone.

"Welcome all, in love and goodness," she said. She inclined her head
toward the medium, who sat with her eyes half closed and breathed

loudly from the effort of climbing the flight of stairs to the upper room. "And especial welcome and thanks to the one and only Mademoiselle Celina Japhet, our distinguished visitor."

The medium stifled a belch and did not acknowledge the welcome.

"For those of you who are new to Spiritism," continued Babette, "we are about to hold a séance, which simply means a 'sitting'. Such a sitting necessitates a medium who is the contact; the 'conduit', Michel likes to say ..." Michel smiled at her and nodded his head. "She is able to make the connection between this our physical plane and the world of spirit."

"Because of the sensitivities of the medium," said Michel, "the séance is held in complete darkness. This aids the spirits in their attendance. By virtue of the lack of light, there is a strong possibility that the spirits may even make themselves known by appearing to us."

"How can they appear if it is all dark?" Leigh Cranwell sounded suspicious.

"Ssh!" hissed Mathers.

"No, that is quite all right," said Babette brightly. She addressed Cranwell. "The spirits appear in a form that materializes from the medium utilizing what is known as ectoplasm. This is a white substance of some esoteric sort that exudes from the medium's body. The spirits drape their forms with the ectoplasm so that they are covered. It is a luminous substance, enabling us to then see them in the low light."

"Are we ready?" interjected Celina Japhet.

"Er, yes. Yes, I think we are," responded Babette. She glanced quickly around at the others. "Perhaps you would keep any further questions until after the séance? All please join hands around the table. Michel ... the light."

Michel stood, reached up to the chains dangling from the four-branch gaselier above the table, and turned it down until there was no visible flame. Sarah reached out and took the hands of Montague Winters and Michel, as soon as he was reseated. She did not care to be in such darkness but realized there was nothing she could do about it. She couldn't help noticing that Winters's hand was ice cold.

"A prayer," mumbled their medium. She spoke with a heavy regional accent which Mathers had earlier placed as being from Bayonne. She quickly mumbled some words which no one else recognized nor joined her in saying. She then lifted her head and started to sing. Babette and Michel Grenoble joined her. It was an old French hymn which none of the English group seemed to recognize. After two or three verses, Celina Japhet's voice faded away and Sarah guessed that she had passed into a trance, as Babette had warned them she would do. The ragged voices of Babette and Michel faded away and there was silence.

"*Bon jour*!" A loud male voice suddenly came from somewhere near the gaselier on the ceiling, so far as Sarah could tell. She jumped at the sound and noticed that both Monty's and Michel's hands gave hers a momentary squeeze.

"*Anglais, s'il vous plait,*" said Babette, who seemed unperturbed by the unknown voice.

"Who is that?" hissed Winters, *soto voce.*

"Please! No talking," muttered Babette. She did, however, give a quick whispered answer. "It is Monsieur Bequet, Madame's grandfather, who is her spirit guide. He always comes through first."

Sarah was amazed at the volume of the spirit voice and the fact that it was so obviously male. There was no similarity whatsoever to the normal voice of the medium.

"Of course," responded the voice, cheerfully, this time emanating from a far corner of the room, again seemingly at ceiling level. "Welcome to our guests."

"And welcome to you, Monsieur Bequet," replied Babette. "What messages do you have for us this evening?"

"I have someone here who bids welcome to DDCF."

"Good god!" Sarah heard Mathers mutter. There was a sharp intake of breath from Moina.

"Still holding them together, I see, DDCF." A totally different voice, with a British accent, came from the opposite end of the room, from down close to the floor, so far as Sarah could tell.

"Good god!" said Mathers again. "Is – is that you William?"

The voice chuckled. "Yes it is. *Magna est Veritas et Praelavebit* what? 'Great is the Truth and it shall Prevail'. Thought I would come through and surprise you."

"Who is it?" hissed Winters.

"My old friend Doctor William Woodman. He, Doctor Wynn Westcott and myself were the founders of the Hermetic order of the Golden Dawn. DDCF is for my secondary motto in the Order: *Deo Duce Comite Ferro,* or 'God is my guide; my companion a sword.'" He paused. "William died over seven years ago. I'd recognize his voice anywhere."

Alec spoke from his position on his knees in front of the Flamel tombstone. He had his head stuck under the wooden barrier, the better to see the alchemical illustrations.

"Three of the lower panels have the number 50 on them. The last one seems to have a letter E. And I think the second one has a number 1, though it is not clear."

"What about these upper panels?" Professor Parmington hung over the top bar of the barrier and pointed his cane at the larger illustrations. "I see a 100 and a 51 to start with, but I am not sure about after that."

"There is a 10 at the end here," called Georgina Parmington, peering through her spectacles. "And before that is what looks like a backward 2."

"One moment," said Alec. He pulled his Flamel book out of his overcoat pocket and thumbed through it to the illustration of the tombstone. With a pencil he wrote down the numbers as they were called out. "Anything on the big central figure?" he asked.

Parmington and his wife both studied it.

"Nothing."

"No."

"And how about the very top panels; the five across the top and the two down each side?"

All of their eyes searched the illustrations. They could see nothing at any of those.

"What d'you make of 'em, Chambers?" asked the professor.

"They obviously have significance," replied Alec, thoughtfully. "They are not an intrinsic part of the alchemical designs, yet they have obviously been included for a reason."

"How exciting," murmured Georgina. "Quite a mystery."

"I have never seen any reference to these numbers in any of the literature," continued Alec. "Probably because no one was ever able to attach any meaning to them."

"Perhaps there is no meaning," mused the professor. "Just random numbers."

"Random? I really don't think so," said Alec.

"No. Neither do I," the professor agreed. "They must have been put there for a reason." He paused, then said "Where are you staying, old boy, if you don't mind my asking?"

"Not at all," said Alec. "I am at the Hôtel Sainte-Marie on the rue de Rivoli. And your good selves?"

"Not so far away. We are at the Hôtel du Quai-Voltaire, near the Pont des Saints-Pères. We wanted to be close to the Louvre, of course. What say we have dinner together, if I'm not being too forward?"

"An excellent idea." Alec was delighted. "Perhaps we can fathom out the meaning of this enigma over the poached salmon!"

"My thinking exactly. Please be our guest."

Sarah was listening, fascinated, to the exchange between MacGregor Mathers and the spirit of William Woodman. They spoke like two friends meeting at their club; exchanging news and views as though both were in the flesh. It took a moment for her to realize that there was another, very soft and quiet, voice speaking at the same time. It came from beside her left ear. She knew that Michel Grenoble sat to her left and she could feel his hand holding hers. She turned her head and almost cried out.

A vague luminous band floated in the air beside her head. She realized it was the band around the end of the spirit trumpet. The whispered voice she heard was coming from within the instrument which was apparently floating in the air.

Her immediate thought was that someone was manipulating the trumpet under the cover of the darkness. She squeezed Michel's hand to reassure herself that he was seated where he was supposed to be. She then carefully turned slightly in her chair and slid one foot back behind her, to sweep around on the carpet in case someone stood there. She failed to contact anything.

"*C'est moi, mademoiselle*," said the voice. "*Me comprenez-vous? Entendez-vous?*"

"*Je – je ne parle pas Français*," Sarah whispered, recalling her school days' lessons. "I do not understand French."

"*J'ai besoin de lui parler.* I must speak with you."

"Who are you?" Sarah asked. She was aware of Mathers and Woodman still conversing.

"My name is Perenelle." Came the soft response.

The name sounded vaguely familiar to Sarah but she couldn't place it. "Do I know you ... did I know you?" she asked.

"*Non.* No."

"The trumpet is floating!" It was Percy Purdy. He was usually so quiet Sarah was doubly surprised to hear him speak up.

"Ssh!" from Babette.

"It is floating," Purdy repeated, his voice now lowered. "The trumpet thing is floating."

Mathers stopped talking to his spirit friend.

"Purdy is right," said Monty Winters. "Look at the damned thing!"

"What is going on?" demanded Mathers.

"Ssh! Quiet, all of you!" hissed Babette.

"You must not wake the medium," added her husband.

Mathers lowered his voice but was equally demanding. "What is this, Madame Grenoble? What does this mean?"

"It means we are being blessed with a visit from another spirit," replied Babette. "It must be someone from many years ago, who needs the trumpet to amplify the voice."

"What does it say?" asked Moina.

As if in reply, the trumpet – its progress apparent from the movement of the luminous bands – swept up and down the length of the table and then all around the perimeter. It finally came to rest close to the ceiling but pointing down toward Mathers. A voice issued from it; the same woman's voice that had been speaking to Sarah. Now it was much stronger and able to be heard by all of them.

"I am Perenelle. You have knowledge of me."

"Perenelle?" repeated Mathers. "Perenelle?"

"Perenelle Flamel," said Leigh Cranwell. "Flamel's wife,"

"*Oui*, Monsieur. Look for me in Roubaix."

"This is ridiculous!" exclaimed Winters. "It is a fake; a fraud!" Sarah heard his chair being pushed back so forcefully that it tipped over. He pulled his hand away from hers. The next moment the room was flooded with light and she saw that Winters had reached across her to the gaselier and turned up the jets as high as they would go.

"Oh, no!" cried Babette.

The trumpet fell to the surface of the table with a clatter and then rolled off onto the floor at Monty's feet. He immediately stamped on it, flattening the end.

Celina Japhet gave a short sharp cry and her head fell rearward onto the chair back. Her hands fell to her sides.

"*Mon Dieu!*" Michel Grenoble took up one of the medium's hands and feverishly patted it.

"Monty! What the devil have you done?" cried Mathers.

"This is evil work," responded the clergyman. "It is the blackest of the black to which we have been exposed!"

Aleister Crowley steepled his fingers and lowered his head to glower at the woman sitting in the chair facing his desk. The desk – for long the pride of Samuel Liddell MacGregor Mathers – now bore upon its surface a disorderly pile of books (pulled from Mathers' bookshelves and not replaced), a bowl of peppermint sweets, a large magnifying glass, a stuffed lizard, an enormous crystal ball, and a photograph of Crowley dressed in the outfit of a Scottish chieftain. This latter was in an overlarge, ornate, silver frame. Crowley's recently affected meerschaum pipe lay in an ashtray close to his hand; a smattering of ashes around the receptacle.

The lady who was the object of Crowley's stare was Florence Farr who was, in fact, fifteen years Crowley's senior.

"I will ask you again, are you in contact with our 'beloved chief'?" Crowley asked.

"And I will once again reply that it is none of your business," snapped Florence.

Crowley snorted. "Well, if you are, you can tell him from me that the Order is running very nicely, thank you very much ... no thanks to him for going off and abandoning it."

"He did not abandon it, as well you know. He went on the trail of what could well bring a large amount of money to the Golden Dawn, as I understand it."

"Aha!" Crowley perked up and sat back in his chair. He wagged a finger at Florence. "So that's it!"

"What?" She looked puzzled.

"You are planning on how his money – if he ever gets any – will help you and your career."

"Nonsense." She got up and turned toward the door. "I had not even thought about myself. I was just happy that Samuel might be able to improve this magical order and possibly ..." she looked around the room and then directly at Crowley. "Possibly induce a better class of membership." She went out.

Crowley threw back his head and laughed.

It had not been poached salmon but Chateaubriand Beauveranaise that was the main course of the dinner at Véfour Jeune, an excellent restaurant at the fashionable Palais-Royal. Alec enjoyed it. The fish course had been Dover Sole, served with celery, preceded by French onion soup. The chateaubriand was served with mushrooms, carrots Vichy, chicken livers on brochettes, chestnuts, and asparagus. Dessert was apricot tart, with a savory of angels on horseback. Sherry, claret, and liqueurs had been on hand. An assortment of French cheeses led to coffee.

As the waiter cleared away the last of the dishes, leaving their coffee cups and the coffee pot, Alec brought out the Flamel book and opened it to the picture of the tombstone. Daniel and Georgina Parmington leaned forward to study it.

"I see you have written-in the numbers we found underneath the appropriate tablets," observed Daniel.

"Yes. I thought we might puzzle over them here in comfort."

"It is strange, is it not, that there were no numbers on some of the panels?" asked Georgina.

"I don't know," said Alec. "It may actually be significant."

"Or *none* of the numbers may be significant," added Daniel.

They studied the drawing for a while in silence.

"Would you not have thought that the numbers would be in Roman numerals?" asked Georgina. She laughed. "I suppose it doesn't matter but somehow – to me at least – it would seem more appropriate on such a large tombstone."

"Hmm," mused Alec. "That is an interesting point. I had not even considered it."

"Well done, my dear," murmured Daniel.

Alec drew a pencil from his pocket and wrote-in new numbers alongside the ones he'd already added.

"One hundred is 'C', as we know," he said. "Fifty-one would be 'LI.' Then over here we have our backward 2, so I don't know about that. Then a ten, which is 'X'.

"The bottom line is three fifties, or 'L's, with a one and the letter 'E' at the end."

Again their heads came together as they looked at the new additions.

"Good God!" exclaimed the professor.

"What?" Alec and Georgina spoke together.

"Look at the bottom line. Fifty; One; Fifty; Fifty; letter E. That's L.I.L.L.E. which spells Lille; the town north of here, almost on the Belgium border!"

"Well, I ..! I think you are right, Daniel," cried Alec. "So what do we get, following that reasoning, with the panels above those?"

"C.L.I. ..," called out Georgina, her spectacles down on the end of her nose. Her voice trailed off. "Then the backward 2 and an X. What does that mean?"

"It is as though there are letters missing. At least, if we are to follow this same reasoning that is the way it looks," said Alec.

"Let me see." Daniel pulled the book closer and leaned over it.

Alec sat back and sipped some coffee. He glanced back at the book. Suddenly he put down his cup. "Wait a minute, wait a minute!" His put out his hand and pointed at the figure they'd all been wondering about. "That is not a backward 2! From where I am sitting I can see it clearly. It is an upside-down five!"

"I say! You are right, Alec. I see it now," enthused Daniel. "Here – lend me your pencil." He took it and wrote-in a 'V'."

"No, write it upside-down," said his wife. He did so.

"It still does not make any sense," he said at last.

"I think we need to make another visit to the stone itself," suggested Alec. "There may be something we missed. Now that we know – or *think* we know – that there is some message hidden here, it may be easier to see."

"Agreed," said Daniel. "I would like to take another good look at that central figure; the one that did not seem to have any number by it."

"Right."

"I have an appointment at the Louvre tomorrow morning," continued the professor, "but we could meet at the tombstone again after lunch, if that would be convenient?"

"Most convenient," said Alec. "As it happens, I have thought of some other research I might do myself."

The Reverend Montague Winters stood with his back to the fireplace and his hands clasped behind him. Mathers strode up and down in front of Winters.

"How could you do that, Monty? It was totally uncalled for. It made fools of us all."

Winters was unrepentant. "Oh, I don't think so, Samuel. And I am still certain that it was all a big show; a sham."

"I *know* that I was talking to my old friend Dr. William Woodman! I know his voice. It is very distinctive. I would know it anywhere."

"And you believe that, even though he has been dead these many years?"

Mathers stopped pacing and moved to pour himself a drink. "This is Spiritualism, Monty. You do not understand it."

"Is this a part of your beloved Golden Dawn?"

"No! No, it is not." Mathers sipped his drink. "But through the rituals of the G.D. one becomes inured to things which others might find incredible. Oh yes, I know there is fraud – and a lot of it – found in Spiritualism. It is a practice, a religion, a philosophy that is wide open to charlatans. Yet that doesn't mean that *all* who profess such talents are fakers."

Winters grunted and moved, uninvited, to pour himself a drink.

"There are many excellent mediums, many who have been examined time and again by such distinguished scientists as Sir William Crookes, Dr. Richard Hodgson, Henry Sidgwick, and others," continued Mathers. "I believe this Mademoiselle Celina Japhet is one of those dedicated persons. She was, after all, medium to the distinguished Allan Kardec."

"And you truly believe that that trumpet object floated up in the air of its own accord?" Winters sounded incredulous.

Mathers smiled knowingly. "'There are more things in heaven and earth, Horatio, than are dreamt of in your philosophy'."

Winters again snorted. "Don't go quoting the Bard to me, Samuel."

There came a tap at the door.

"We will say no more about it," said Mathers, and then called out "Enter."

Leigh Cranwell came around the door. "Not to interrupt anything," he said, "But we were wondering where we might be going from here?"

"Oh, come in. Come in." Mathers put down his glass on an occasional table and moved to hold the door wide.

Cranwell entered, followed by Sarah Wilde and Percy Purdy. They seated themselves.

Mathers looked out into the empty hotel corridor and then closed the door.

"Where is Moina?" he asked.

"She said she had some shopping to do," said Sarah.

Mathers said nothing but moved to stand in front of the fireplace, where he could look at the assembled group. Purdy was the first to speak.

"You had asked me about Flamel's known activities in Paris," he said. "His habitual haunts, as it were."

"Yes. And?"

"I checked – thoroughly – all of those a year or more ago. I studied the most notable sites: his old house at 51 rue de Montmorency, the portal of Sainte Genevieve des Argents, the church of Saint Jacques la Boucherie, even his painted tombstone."

"And you found nothing? No clues to his final resting place?"

"None at all."

"Well at least that saves us from having to go over all that ground again," said Cranwell.

"Precisely," agreed Mathers. "And by that alone Mister Purdy has earned his place in this distinguished assembly." He inclined his head to the younger man, who remained with his eyes fixed on Mathers, his expression unchanging.

"Where, then, do we go from here?" asked Monty Winters, who had seated himself at the back of the room, behind the others.

Leigh Cranwell turned toward him. "Happily we were able to glean some small clue from our séance last evening. And we might well have obtained more details if you had not been so hysterical ..."

"Enough!" Mathers held up his hand. "I have reviewed last evening's performance with the Reverend Winters, Mister Cranwell, and we are now moving on from there."

"Moving on exactly to where?" came Cranwell's retort.

Mathers walked up and down in front of his small audience, giving them time to settle down after the brief exchange. He eventually stropped on front of Sarah.

"You have your notes from last evening, Miss Wilde?" he asked.

Sarah opened a notebook she had with her. "Right here, Mister Mathers."

"Good. Now, there was a brief mention given by the spirit professing to be Flamel's wife, if I recall."

"Indeed," said Sarah. She read from the notebook. "She – the spirit, that is – said 'I am Perenelle. You have knowledge of me.' Then she went on to say 'Look for me in Roubaix.' And that was all. That was when ..."

"Yes. Quite," said Mathers. "Hmm. 'Look for me in Roubaix'. What is Roubaix? Does anyone know?" He looked around the room.

"It sounds like a place," said Purdy. "Does anyone have a map?"

"I do." Sarah dug into her reticule and pulled out a Baedeker. She opened the red cover and unfolded the tissue-paper-thin map of Northern France. The others got up and gathered round her.

"Where are we looking?" asked Cranwell.

"Good question." Mathers peered at the detailed, small scale map. "It could be anywhere."

"Does Baedeker refer to it?" asked Purdy.

A look in the index at the back of the book revealed that all the information on Roubaix was on page 88. Sarah turned to it.

"'An important manufacturing town', she read. "'connected with the Scheldt and the lower Deûle by means of a canal'." She referred to the map for that area. "It is not far from Lille, it seems."

"Lille is near the Belgium border," said Winters.

"Is there a hotel?" asked Mathers.

"Yes." Sarah nodded. "The Ferraille, on rue Nain, near the Place de la Mairie."

"Ladies and gentlemen – *lady* and gentlemen," Mathers corrected himself. "We will be leaving for Roubaix first thing tomorrow morning. Miss Wilde, kindle advice my wife when she returns."

"I have spent much of the morning at the *Bibliotheque Nationale de France*," announced Alec, when he met the Parmingtons at the site of the tombstone. "There I was able to locate a copy of Flamel's own exposition of these alchemical figures."

"Oh?" The professor was immediately interested.

"Yes," continued Alec. "I had a vague remembrance of such a book existing but have never before been encouraged to seek it out. Happily the archivist at the bibliotheque knew immediately what I needed and was able to present it for my study."

"And it is about these mysterious figures?" asked Georgina.

Alec nodded. "Oh, yes. Flamel describes each in detail. He says that they are copied from the old book – a *grimoire* – that he obtained for the sum of two florins."

"Two florins?" queried Georgina.

"Don't forget that this was back in the year 1350 or thereabouts," said Daniel.

Alec nodded. "Yes. He called it *The Book of Abraham the Jew* and said it was recorded on leaves of bark written on with a steel pen."

"So what did he say about the numbers?"

"He didn't," said Alec. "He did say that the central figure represents the Saviour coming to judge the world. Also, apparently all of the colors used were representative of the alchemical process, as are the figures themselves. For example, the background of that central figure, as you see, is green. This is because . . ." and here Alec looked down at his notebook. "As he said 'in this decoction the confections become green and keep this color longer than any other after the black'."

"But he says nothing about the numbers?" persisted the professor.

"Nothing."

"So perhaps it was not Flamel himself who placed them there."

"I tend to think that," agreed Alec.

"Then who would have?" asked Georgina. She and the professor both looked at Alec.

He thought for a moment. "I have been pondering that," he said. "The only person I can credit with adding them is Flamel's old assistant, Agramant. We know he was witness to the supposed burial of Flamel."

"Supposed?" asked Georgina.

"Yes. It turned out Flamel's body was not in the coffin," explained Alec. "When opened, it contained a piece of a tree trunk."

"Good lord!" exclaimed Daniel.

"So this brings me to an interesting possibility," said Alec. "Could it be that, as I have said, Agramant later added these numbers to the tombstone as a *clue to where Flamel really is buried*?"

Daniel could only repeat "Good lord!"

"How exciting," said Georgina. "Do you really think that is possible?"

"Possible, yes," said Alec. "Probable, I don't know."

The three of them moved back to the surface of the tombstone.

"I still fail to see any number on that main figure," said the professor, kneeling down to study it. "I think there is none." He looked at all details of the figure. "No. Nothing."

His wife helped him up again from his knees, and brushed off his trousers.

"There may not be anything," agreed Alec. "But since we are here, let us also take a good hard look at all of those top panels; the five across the top and the ones down the upper sides."

For the next half hour the three of them peered closely at every inch of the Flamel tombstone. They were about to give up and acknowledge there was nothing more to be seen, when Georgina let out a cry.

"I think I've found something!"

The two men sprang to her side. With trembling finger, she pointed to the large central Saviour figure.

"Look! In very small writing on the band that goes around the orb that he holds. Is that not something?"

Both men leaned forward.

"Difficult to say . . ." said Daniel.

"No! I think Georgina is right," cried Alec. "Yes. It is old and worn but yes, I think there is a very small '1,000' written there."

"One thousand. That is an M, is it not?"

Alec smiled. "I think I can see where this is taking us," he said. "Come." He led the way through to a nearby grass area and a wooden bench. The three of them sank down onto it. Alec pulled out his notebook and his pencil.

"Observe," he said. He wrote out the numbers. "In Latin numerals we have C, L, I, M, our upside-down V, and X."

He wrote them down.

C   L   I   M   Λ   X

"If that up-ended five had a small crosspiece to it, it would be an A, would it not?" he asked.

"Of course!"

"Climax," read Georgina. "Why climax?"

"Why, and what it all means, I don't know," said Alec. "Climax is an English word. The French word would be *apogée*. But I am willing to wager that this is the message hidden on the Flamel tombstone."

"So this is where the real detective work begins," said Professor Parmington.

Belgravia is bounded by Hyde Park, the Green Park, Sloane Street, and Pimlico. It consisted of a number of attractive streets and squares, including Belgrave Square, all of which had sprung up over the first quarter of the nineteenth century. Belgrave Square, in the center, rapidly became one of the most fashionable quarters of London. There were four large mansions in Belgrave Square; one at each of its corners. Each of these houses included a stable-yard, coach house, groom's quarters, and an octagonal clock tower. There was a *porte-cochere* at the side of each of the houses.

The deep maroon brougham of Dr. William Westcott pulled up to one of the corner mansions. A hansom cab drove off as the carriage arrived. Westcott descended from the carriage and approached the main entrance. As he reached the door it opened, seemingly of its own accord, and he went inside.

A stooped, white-haired butler led Westcott through the wainscoted hallway, past a green onyx marble staircase, toward the morning room. Westcott glanced up at the circular lantern light above the Hall, noticing the *caiyatydes*, the female figures used as pillars. The columns were all of matching green onyx. There were large sculptural groups over the door through which Westcott had entered, and there were bronzes on the stairs.

The room to which the butler led the guest had a coffered, painted-timber, gilded ceiling and polished walnut paneled walls. There was a large, white marble fireplace. A thick Turkey carpet covered the floor so that no footsteps could be heard. On one wall was a huge painted fresco of the sinking of the Spanish Armada in 1588 and on the wall opposite it hung an ancient tapestry of a medieval woodland scene. Over the fireplace hung an oil portrait of Sir Francis Drake, in an ornate, heavy, gilt frame.

Dark green leather wing chairs formed a circle around the room, facing inward. Many of these were occupied when Westcott entered. In a quick glance around he counted nine people. With himself as the tenth,

he knew there were three more to arrive. He moved forward and, with a brief nod to each of the others, took one of the empty chairs. Beside each chair stood a small occasional table on which rested a decanter of brandy, one of sherry, and one of water, together with glasses. Each table also held a box of cigarettes, one of cigars, matches, a cigar cutter, and an ash tray. The cigars were fine Havannahs.

No one spoke but waited patiently for the rest of the number to arrive. This did not take long; two gentlemen arriving together, shortly followed by the third. They took their seats.

A tall man in a black frock coat, grey waistcoat and trousers, who was sitting close to the fireplace, came to his feet. The sartorial monochrome was relieved by a dark blue cravat bearing a diamond stud which winked in the light from the chandelier. He had a full mustache which swept outward to mingle with mutton-chop sideburns. All this was topped by bushy eyebrows and a sweep of full hair, grey turning to white. He had a high-nosed aristocratic face. A monocle gleamed in his right eye. He stood straight-backed, his gimlet gaze moving rapidly but smoothly around the room to study each attendee in turn.

"Welcome, gentlemen, to a meeting of the governing body of the West European Arm of The Ancient Illuminati. We have a lot to cover today. I have your reports, for which I thank you, and on your side tables you will find a copy of the agenda for this meeting."

There was a brief rustle as people took up the sheets of paper and looked at them.

"Italy, I especially noted your report on Signor Guglielmo Marconi's invention of what is termed wireless telegraphy. I would ask you to keep on top of this development. It could well prove valuable to our organization."

A distinguished-looking, black haired figure in a dark green frock coat smiled and raised his arm in an ephemeral wave of acknowledgment.

"Germany, I note that Count Ferdinand von Zeppelin has received a patent in the United States, for his rigid airship. I believe it was only four years ago that he received the German patent, was it not?"

A rotund gentleman with a red face, bald head and waxed mustache struggled to his feet. He bowed his head and clicked his heels. "*Jawohl,* Alpha. That is correct. As I said in my report, the good Count's designs are in fact based on ideas originally conceived by one David Schwartz, a Croatian aviator. I attempted contact with that gentleman but, regrettably, he is now deceased."

"What is this new Zionist movement?" asked the tall figure addressed as Alpha.

"It is led by a man named Theodor Herzl," replied the German. "He was recently received by the German Emperor and also by the Ottoman Emperor in Jerusalem. He received a positive reception at the Hague Peace Conference just a week ago, I understand. We have him in view, Alpha, and will continue our reports." He clicked his heels again and sat.

"Good." The tall man removed his monocle, polished it with a fine kerchief he withdrew from his trouser pocket, and then replaced the lens in his eye. "Spain. Would you care to expand on your report?"

"*Sí,* Alpha. I would be happy to do so." An olive-skinned gentleman whose jet black, well-oiled hair was brushed tightly back on his head, rose casually to his feet. He had been the last to arrive. His face was gaunt, with prominent cheekbones. His nose was large and hooked, making Westcott think of a bird of prey. His dazzlingly white shirt had a line of decorative frills that ran around its meeting with the red and gold waistcoat. The black cravat was pinned with a ruby surrounded by diamonds. The dark grey frock coat he wore looked somber in comparison. A thick gold watch chain was matched by a number of large gold rings on his fingers. They flashed as he gestured with his words. He smiled around at the other seated members.

"England! Is it always this cold?"

The others chuckled. He continued. "*¡Perdoné!* To business. As you all know, in April of last year hostilities broke out between Spain and the United States of America. They escalated. We had Captain-General of Cuba, Ramón Blanco y Erenas, working to persuade Máximo Gómez to join with Spain against the Americans. However, hostilities halted in late August and by the end of the year the Treaty of Paris was signed. The war became known in Spain as *El Desastre,* 'The Disaster.' We then used that disaster to give impetus to *Generación de 1898* – a group of active and influential poets, novelists, philosophers, etc. Mainly through them we were able to suppress the restoration of the monarchy."

"You have your finger on the pulse?"

"Indeed we have, Alpha." He smiled confidently and then sat down. The German grunted and lit up a cigar.

Alpha consulted a sheet of paper before continuing. "Our England representative reports that he was instrumental in encouraging the dowager Chinese empress to give substance to the secret society called *I Ho Ch'uan,* known generally as 'The Boxers'. They have rapidly gained in power and we understand that some sort of rebellion is about to take place but, of course, that is now outside the jurisdiction of the members of this particular meeting. England, do you have anything to add?"

Westcott, himself as straight-backed as the leader Alpha, stood and cleared his throat. He addressed himself as much to the others in the room as to the leader.

"As you all know, there have been various attempts on the life of Her Majesty over the years. She is the final monarch in the House of Hanover. As we determined at our last meeting, it would seem prudent to accelerate the end of this monarchy, which has become rather static, since such action would usher in Albert Edward as sovereign. Edward is much more malleable than his mother and could be a most valuable instrument to the Illuminati."

"How do your plans progress, for this action?"

Westcott hesitated for only a beat. "They progress well, Alpha. The overall plan is somewhat complicated but I have given full details in my report."

"Yes. I have it."

"Much hinges on the financing of this project, as with so many of our active arms, but I feel the man I have at the helm is thoroughly competent and will bring the project through to a most successful conclusion." He bowed his head and then sat down.

The man who had been addressed as Alpha at the assembly stood bidding farewell to the Illuminati members. Dr. William Westcott was the last to leave. Alpha took his arm and led him to a small alcove where the elderly butler, patiently holding Westcott's coat, hat, gloves and cane, could not overhear them.

"You expressed confidence in your man, William. We have been friends for many years now. You may have fooled the others of the assembly, but did I not detect a slight hesitation in your avowal?"

Westcott allowed a small smile. "You were never inattentive, Alpha." He sighed. "Yes, I admit the slight reservation ... though I would emphasize *slight*."

Alpha spread his hands and inclined his head, questioningly.

"My man Mathers is enthusiastic," continued Westcott. "He would dearly love to climb the ladder in our organization and to that end is dedicated. I do not doubt his sincerity. However ... his abilities, I fear, do not match his desires."

"Will he come through? I need hardly remind you of the importance of this project."

"Oh, he will come through," Westcott assured him. "It is the time element that troubles me. Mathers can be exceedingly ... ponderous. He tends to think too much, to the detriment of his actions."

"But he will come through?"

"Yes." Westcott nodded his head. "Yes, I believe he will."

Sarah looked around at the group in the compartment of the train going to Lille. She was reminded of their initial rail trip to Dover, on the South East & Chatham Railway. She felt a pang of home-sickness and wondered how Alec was, where he was, and what he was doing.

They were in a first class carriage. Sarah had been surprised that Mathers would pay the first class fare but Leigh Cranwell explained to her that the second class carriages were often poor and on the Nord and Ouest lines were rarely furnished with cushioned seats.

MacGregor Mathers was again holding forth, telling the ever-rapt Percy Purdy about his and Moina's previous time in France, a number of years before. Sarah couldn't determine the relationship between Mathers and the intense Purdy. She had several times encountered them with their heads close together, talking animatedly but falling silent when they saw her nearby.

Monty Winters seemed to grow more morose by the day; his beady eyes peering out darkly from beneath his bushy eyebrows. He kept looking at her and Sarah felt uncomfortable with his attention. Leigh Cranwell, as usual, kept his own counsel, seemingly lost in his own little world. Moina said little, which Sarah thought was unusual for her. She glanced at Mathers' wife now. Moina sat with her back straight, her head up and level, her eyes closed. But Sarah knew that she was not asleep; she was listening to her husband prattle on to the doe-eyed Purdy.

"So what is our plan of action?" asked Winters, suddenly raising his head to stare at Mathers. He tugged at his Mephisthophelean beard.

Moina opened her eyes and came alert. "Yes," she said. "Just exactly what do you have in mind, Samuel?"

Mathers drew back from where he had been leaning forward slightly toward Purdy. He seemed surprised at the sudden focus of the others.

"Our first stop, naturally, will be the hotel," he said. "Miss Wilde?"

"The Ferraille, on rue Nain," she said. "I posted a request for reservations yesterday. They should have rooms ready for us when we arrive."

"And then?" persisted Winters.

Mathers did not answer immediately. Finally he said "As you all know, the only clue we have is from our sitting with Mademoiselle Japhet, directing us to Roubaix. The spirit – yes 'spirit', Monty – of Flamel's wife told us to go there. Had that sitting not been interrupted we may have obtained more detailed instructions. However ... we must do what we can. It may well be that we will receive further direction when we arrive. There must be some good reason for Madame Flamel to have given that initial clue. I believe that she will follow through on that and direct our steps from there."

"So our path is laid out for us by a dead spirit?"

"You have a better plan?" asked Mathers, sternly.

The clergyman shrugged. "This is all a wild goose chase anyway," he said. "Why should not a ghost become our leader?"

Mathers did not respond.

"How long until we arrive at Lille, Miss Wilde?" asked Leigh Cranwell.

"That last stop was Busigny. This train arrives in Lille at 2:14 p.m.," replied Sarah. "We then take a local train to Roubaix, though we do have to wait for almost an hour for the connection."

"Oh, no!" exclaimed Moina. "Not sitting in one of those dreadful, dusty waiting rooms? They won't even admit one onto the platform until the train is ready to receive one. There is no breath of air in those rooms."

"But Roubaix is not far from Lille?" Cranwell asked Sarah, ignoring Moina's complaint.

"Not far at all. Fifteen kilometers, it says."

"Hmm. That is approximately ten miles. Can you tell us anything more about the place?"

Sarah pulled out her Baedeker and turned to page 88.

"'Lille is situated on the Deûle River,'" she read. "Near France's border with Belgium. It is the capital of the Nord-Pas de Calais region and the *préfecture* of the Nord department." She turned a page or two. "Alas, that would seem to be all. Nothing on Roubaix itself."

Cranwell grunted and returned to the book he was reading.

Alec and the Parmingtons sat at a *terrasse* café and sipped their drinks. It was a balmy day with a weak sun peeping through scattered clouds. For a while they sat and silently observed the passers-by.

"Our holiday is passing much more pleasantly than expected," observed Daniel.

"We still have a week or so," added Georgina. "Are we going to follow-up on these exciting clues?"

Daniel laughed. "You have really caught the spirit of the chase, my dear," he said. He turned to Alec. "Well, my friend? What is the next move?"

"I don't want to interfere any more with your holiday," Alec replied. "But the next move – for me at least – is to travel to Lille and there see if there is any clue that connects to the word 'climax' or *apogée*, a name, perhaps."

Daniel glanced at his wife, and then returned his attention to Alec. "Would it be in the cards for us to come along?" he asked. "We don't want to be a nuisance, of course, but ..."

"My dear fellow," said Alec, enthusiastically, "I would be delighted. It would seem a suddenly lonely pursuit without the two of you."

They all laughed, and clinked their glasses of tea in a wordless toast.

"To Lille, you say?"

"Yes," said Alec.

The Ferraille Hôtel was small but comfortable, Sarah found. There were few other guests besides the Golden Dawn group. Roubaix was close enough to the border that Belgium was the final destination for most travelers; only those with specific business in Roubaix itself tarried there. There was no restaurant at the hotel but there were a number of *estaminets* in the town at which it was possible to get beer and wine and a modest repast. They settled on the Pagant Deloose, a short walk from the hotel.

"My senses tell me that we should start our enquiries at the church," said Mathers, when they had all eaten and were sitting back relaxing.

"There are two main ones," said Sarah. "There is a French Protestant church right here in Roubaix and there is what they refer to as an English church outside town on the road to Lille."

"My money is on the French church," said Winters. Cranwell nodded.

"It would seem the most logical," said Purdy.

"It is a very old church," said Sarah, "while the other is relatively modern, I think dating from the late seventeen hundreds."

"Very well." Mathers nodded his head. "We will start by studying the gravestones in the churchyard; see if there is any mention of Perenelle Flamel anywhere."

"You mean we are to go scrambling about a churchyard looking at gravestones?" asked Moina, in a querulous voice.

"It would seem to be the best way to locate what we seek," said Percy Purdy, glancing at Mathers for approval.

"Yes, but ... scrambling about a churchyard ..." Moina's voice trailed off.

"There are no fancy shops here, Moina," said Mathers sternly. "You knew before we came that we had a job to do. You agreed to be a part of it."

"How long is this going to take?" she asked.

"We don't know."

"Until we find the gravestone for Perenelle Flamel," said Winters, forcibly. He had long since wearied of Moina's manner.

Leigh Cranwell took no notice of Mathers's wife. "I suggest we break up the site into segments, each of us taking one," he said. "That way there will be no duplication and we can get the job done quickly."

"Agreed," said Mathers.

"And if there is no Perenelle Flamel gravestone?" asked Winters.

There was silence for a moment.

"We will face that when we come to it," said Mathers finally.

"Perhaps we should conduct a séance on a tombstone," Winters continued. "Get in touch with our ghost!"

"I have been studying the map of the area around Lille," said Georgina. "I cannot see anything labeled Climax or *Apogée*."

Daniel had been dozing in a corner of the carriage, as the train slowly chugged along the track toward Lille. He now looked up.

Alec set aside the Flamel book he had once again been studying. "How far out from the city have you looked?" he asked.

"According to the scale on the map, about twenty miles," replied the professor's wife. Her spectacles were down on the end of her nose and she now peered over the rims at Alec and her husband.

"That should be far enough, I would think," said Daniel.

"I agree," said Alec. "Perhaps it's not a place; not a town or small village."

"What do you mean?"

"Perhaps it is just a local point of interest, like a particular hill or a woods, or something."

"That is going to make it difficult," said Georgina.

"Yes." Alec stood up and braced himself against the side of the compartment, stretching. He looked out at the farms moving past the train. "Or perhaps it is the name of a farm. Who knows? It could be anything." He sighed and then sat down again.

"You know, you have not told us exactly why this is so important to you," said Daniel. "Oh, I can see the fascination of chasing something from history – believe me, working at the British Museum that is a lot of what I do every day. But, if I may say so, you seem to have more of a dedication to this hunt."

Alec made up his mind. He liked the Parmingtons and enjoyed their company. He decided to let them in on the purpose of his quest. He started at the beginning, with his encounter with Samuel MacGregor Mathers, and told them everything that had happened, right up to his briefing from Inspector Henry Kent and his meeting with Lord Sunbury.

"The Illuminati?" asked Daniel incredulously.

"You have heard of it?"

"Oh, yes. Yes, the name has cropped up from time to time. Never in a very favorable light, I might add."

"And where is this delightful sounding Miss Wilde?" Georgina asked. "Not in any danger, I hope."

"I sincerely hope not," said Alec, with feeling. "She is a very brave woman. But no, she should be safe. She is merely traveling with the Golden Dawn group to keep an eye on their progress. Apparently she will try to post reports to the Inspector on a regular basis. If anything should happen to her, I am sure the Inspector would let me know right away."

"So what is our plan of campaign?" asked Daniel. "What do we do when we get to Lille?"

"I have thought of some possibilities," said Alec. "We need to speak to the local people and see if anyone recognizes the name or term Climax or *Apogée*. We must check with hotels, restaurants, local merchants. We need to ask and keep asking."

"Anything else?"

"Yes. I intend to go to the local newspaper office, *La Vérité de Lille*. I hope to be able to dig back into their archives and see if I can find any reference to what we seek."

"Good. Then Daniel and I will do the foot-work and the enquiring," said Georgina.

"If my poor French is up to it," added Daniel.

"We should stay in the very center of the town, I would think," said Georgina. "So that we can move out in any direction when necessary. Do we know what hotels there are?"

"That is something I have been checking," said Daniel. "There are not a great number but I would suggest the Grand-Hôtel de Lyons, on rue du Priez and rue Faidherbe. It seems to be reasonably priced but well regarded."

"Fine," said Alec. "We will go there straight from the station."

"The problem, of course," said Daniel, "is that we are dealing with something that happened over four hundred years ago."

The hotel dining room was half empty, with couples and individuals scattered at tables about the room. Small potted palm trees were the main theme with a number of healthy-looking aspidistras on tall stands spaced between the palms. In a corner near the kitchen a thin-faced, balding pianist played soft classical music while the two waiters scurried back and forth, bearing platters to the diners.

The walls of the dining room were Pompeian red with dado and frieze in old gold and moss-green. Dark wainscoting was on the walls and ceiling. The thick curtains were of Pompeian red and soft olive.

"It seems a long time ago," agreed Alec, "but in rural France things move very slowly. Just look at the buildings in Lille. Many of them date from the time of Flamel. Why, in Paris, if you recall, Flamel's old house is still standing and is today a restaurant."

"That is very true," said Georgina. "Not too different from parts of England, if it comes to that."

The waiter arrived with their order and they spent some time eating the soup; a very fine cream of asparagus, which was followed by Parisian salad with cheese fingers, and then baked salmon with sauce hollandaise. The main entrée was roast chicken with potato balls, ham timbales, cucumber sauce, and green peas. Dessert was mousse au chocolat, assorted pastries, meringues, and lemon sherbet. Eventually, after the crackers and cheese, they all settled back with their coffee and liqueur.

"I approached the local newspaper," said Alec. "They are quite amenable to my digging through their archives. In fact, when I mentioned what I was looking for they suggested I call upon an old retired editor who, I was assured, had a memory that is remarkable. If anyone would have heard of *Apogée*, they say, it would surely be he."

"Wonderful," said Daniel. "Because all the people we spoke to today looked at us as though we were, well ... tourists!" They all laughed.

"Well, it has been a long day," said Georgina. "I think – if you gentlemen will excuse me – I will retire so that I may start afresh tomorrow morning."

Both men stood as she got up and left the dining room. They then reseated themselves and lit up cigars. Daniel called for brandies, which were quickly brought.

"I must thank you again, Alec," said Daniel. "You have really brought an excitement into what had promised to be a very mundane holiday."

"Not too much excitement yet," responded Alec. "But with any luck, there will be some very soon."

Dr. William Westcott's secretary ushered in three visitors.

"Thank you, Ferguson. That will be all for this evening."

"Sir?" The secretary seemed surprised.

"I said that will be all," responded Westcott. "You may leave. Go home. You are done for the day."

"Yes, sir." Ferguson didn't argue. It was most unusual for him to be told to leave, especially when he had just brought in visitors, but he didn't question it. He returned to the outer office, picked up his coat and hat, and left.

Dr. Westcott waited until he heard the front door of the building close before turning to the two men and one woman.

"Welcome," he said. "Won't you please be seated." He studied his visitors.

The two men, Konrad Krüger and Franz von Knigge, were as different in physical appearance as it was possible to be. Krüger was short and rotund; his waistcoat, seen beneath his black frock coat, obviously straining at its buttons. His hair was cropped so short that he might as well have shaved his head, thought Westcott. A full mustache flowing into bushy sideboards, together with fierce hirsute eyebrows, made up for the lack of cranial hair. A monocle was clenched in his right eye. An obvious dueling scar on his left cheek attested to the fact that he was, or had once been, more athletic than his current figure suggested.

Franz von Knigge was tall and painfully thin. His grey frock coat hung on him apparently without touching his body below the shoulders. His hair was black and parted on the right, gleaming from the oil which plastered it down to his head and forehead. A small black mustache with waxed, upturned ends, drew attention away from his pale watery eyes. His color was pallid, in contrast to his companion's ruddy glow. His striped trousers were too short, Westcott noticed, displaying a pair of grey spats.

Both men clicked their heels in military fashion before seating themselves.

The woman allowed her sealskin fur coat to slide off her shoulders onto the back of a chair. She was tall, with blonde hair and – to Dr. Westcott's mind – an overly painted face. She sat and crossed her legs, revealing an extended slit in her dark blue Worth gown that allowed her ankles to be boldly displayed. The moiré gown was cut low, a style Westcott attributed to the Continent, and was decorated with black ribbons and numerous contrasting mother-of-pearl buttons. Her bonnet was of matching blue with an upstanding peacock feather. She produced a cigarette holder from her reticule and loaded it with a pale mauve Egyptian cigarette. Von Knigge, closest to her, produced a box of safety matches and struck one, leaning forward to light the lady's cigarette. She drew on it, blowing clouds of light blue smoke about the room.

"You arrived promptly," said Westcott. "I was not expecting you until tomorrow."

"We were informed that time was of the essence, Herr Doctor," said Krüger.

"And so it is. So it is." Westcott got to his feet and poured sherry into glasses on his side table. He passed one to each of his visitors, taking one for himself.

"I take it that our business, Herr Doctor, is an illuminating one," continued Krüger. The pale man nodded emphatically.

Westcott pursed his lips. "An illuminating one indeed." He repeated. "*Ja, mein Herr.*"

"This is not an unusual request for us," said the blonde woman, looking around with obvious disdain at the stark furnishings of Dr. Westcott's office. "It will be executed promptly."

"I would none-the-less appreciate some details of what services you perform," said Westcott, seating himself at his desk and opening a box of Havannah cigars. He offered them to the male visitors, who each took one. "You come highly recommended but I am personally unacquainted with your expertise."

Krüger used the cigar cutter and then passed it on to his companion. "Our expertise, Herr Doctor, is in discovering hard to find articles; acquiring them; and placing them in the hands of those most desirous of owning them."

"All for a pre-determined fee, of course," said the woman. Her name, Westcott learned, was Rikka Arndt.

"And that fee ... ?"

"A percentage is absorbed by us, of course," said Krüger. "There are, after all, various expenses that must be covered. The balance ..."

"And the main reason for the exercise, of course," put in Rikka.

"Goes to the cause of our beloved Illuminati," concluded Krüger.

Westcott drew on his cigar and nodded.

So the trio sought out objects desired by various collectors and, in whatever manner they deemed most fitting, obtained those objects and offered them for sale, sometimes to the highest bidder. That many of the objects that changed hands in this way were illegally obtained was obvious to Westcott.

"I have a man presently in southern France," he said. "He believes that he can discover an ancient manuscript – one of the fifteenth century – and, following directions contained in that document, can produce enough gold to meet a certain need."

"The manuscript in question is, then, alchemical." It was more a statement than a question from Rikka.

Westcott nodded.

"So why are our services required?" asked Krüger, blowing out clouds of smoke as he bit savagely into the end of his cigar.

Westcott sighed. He rose to his feet and, cigar in one hand and sherry glass in the other, walked about the room as he spoke. "There are a number of 'ifs' in his course of action. Firstly, he needs to discover that which he seeks. Secondly, it needs to fulfill his expectations regarding the alchemical instructions. Thirdly, his associate needs to be able to follow those instructions and produce what is desired. And fourthly – and most importantly – all of this needs to be accomplished by the beginning of October at the very latest."

"*Sprechen Sie lauter.*" The thinner of the two gentlemen spoke for the first time. His voice was high and seemed, thought Westcott, to admirably

113

suit his body. "If I may ask, Herr Doctor? If you have all of this 'in hand', as one says, then why do you need our services?"

"Are you familiar with the expression 'to hedge one's bet', Herr von Knigge?" The thin man nodded. "Then you must appreciate that if you are able to acquire this manuscript, its value – to some collector of such ancient documents – may well be greater than the *possibility* of my man's alchemical experimentation."

"Is there not something about a bird in the hand applicable here?" asked von Knigge. Westcott acquiesced.

"*Sehr gut.*" Krüger put down his wine glass. "Do we wait upon your man to find this object or do we proceed on our own and, probably, find it before him?"

"Since time is of the essence, then I encourage you to proceed at your own pace, even if it means intruding upon my man's search. Acquisition of the object is the first order of business."

The trio looked at one another and gave the briefest of nods.

"Disposition of the manuscript can also be left to you, I presume?" continued Westcott.

"I already have, in my mind, two gentlemen – one here in England and the other in Italy – who would pay handsomely for such a manuscript," said the blonde. "They have no interest in the contents of the volume, only in its age and condition."

"Excellent!" Westcott refilled all their wine glasses. "I will give you details of the whereabouts of my man and you may proceed immediately. But first, a toast!"

They all raised their glasses.

"It took me several days of digging through a lot of dusty files," said Alec. "In fact it was in an old copy of the newspaper more than a hundred years old that I found it."

"How did you do that?" asked Georgina.

"I told you about the old retired editor they turned me onto?" Daniel and Georgina both nodded. "Well, he suggested that I concentrate on land transfers. He said that they rarely occurred around here but when they did, there would be details of the name of the farms and of their owners. He said that if that failed I might look through obituaries, though that would take much longer."

"And what did you find?" asked Daniel.

"In July of 1784 there was a land sale of two hectares – that is about two hundred acres – that constituted a farm named *Apogée de Vie.*"

"'Life's climax'," murmured Daniel.

"Yes." Alec nodded. "And in a couple of places in the report it had just been shortened to *Apogée* ... our Climax."

"Oh, well done Alec," said Georgina, smiling at both men.

"Where is this special farm?" asked Daniel.

"It is between here and a small town called Roubaix, to the north-west of Lille. It is only about five miles away."

"Well, what are we waiting for?"

The carriage they had rented deposited the three of them at the entrance to a nondescript farm in the middle of gently rolling hills. Full hedgerows sectioned off rectangles of land so that the whole area looked like a gigantic patchwork quilt. Cows were to be seen in some pastures and sheep in others, but mainly the land had been tilled. Lille was situated in a well irrigated and fertile plain on the Deûle River, with Roubaix on its outskirts. Products of the area included linen and woolen goods, cotton, cloth, oil, machinery, sugar and chemicals. "Lisle thread" was world famous.

"Let us hope the farmer is friendly" said Georgina, as Daniel handed her down from the carriage.

Alec asked the driver to wait for them and then led the way up to the front door of the farmhouse. It was an old, stone-built house, with a red tile roof. Most of the windows had worn, wooden shutters, though some sagged on their hinges. One or two shutters were missing. A chimney at the end of the building emitted a plume of fragrant wood smoke.

"It looks old, but not five hundred years," commented Daniel, studying the lines of the building.

"Look at the rear," said Alec. "It looks as though there has been a newer front section built onto an ancient rear."

"Hmm. You may be right."

"The woodwork could certainly do with a coat of paint," said Georgina.

A plump, middle-aged woman in a worn and stained dress and apron answered their knock at the front door and stood wiping her hands on her apron. She seemed surprised to see visitors, and not a little suspicious. Alec, in his flawless French, assured her that they meant well and would just like to have a few words with the man of the house.

"He is in the cowshed," the woman replied. She pointed a bony finger in the direction of a sadly neglected barn. The three of them thanked her and moved off toward it.

A gaunt, unshaven man, with his trousers stuffed into rubber boots and a hat of indeterminate shape perched on his head, emerged from the dark interior as they drew near. He came to a halt when he saw them and eyed them warily.

"*Messieur? Et madame?*" he added. "*Qu'est-ce qui se passe? Qu'est-ce qu'il y a?*"

Alec introduced himself and the Parmingtons and, as briefly as he could, explained that they were looking for an old grave for Perenelle Flamel, and that they had been led to believe that it might be on the farm property.

The farmer removed his hat, scratched his head, and then replaced the covering.

"What do you want with this old grave?" he asked.

"Then it is here?" asked Alec eagerly.

The farmer shrugged. "I don't know." He pointed off across the fields. "There is an old family graveyard – not my family, you understand – but one with a number of very old stones in it. It might have the one you are looking for. I would not know."

"May we go and look?" persisted Alec.

Again he shrugged. "I suppose so. But you mind, now, that you close all gates after you!" He looked hard at them, one by one. "I do not want none of my animals wandering off."

Alec assured him they would take every precaution. He got exact directions and then led the Parmingtons out of the farm yard.

The graveyard was larger than they had expected; almost a quarter of an acre in size. It was surrounded by a low, dry-stone wall, some sections of which had fallen away. The more recent graves – those from 1800 on – were in rows but the older ones were scattered in no special order. Many of these older markers were broken or chipped and most were so badly worn that it was impossible to read what was written on them.

"I don't know that we have gained anything," said Daniel, trying to read one of the stones. "It looks as though they go back to the right time period, but it is not possible to read any details."

"Here! Here's something," called Georgina. She was at the far corner of the graveyard. As the two men joined her she pointed to a flat stone that had been broken off at its base. It lay face down, sunk so deep into the ground that its surface was barely visible. "If it has been there for a while, maybe it has been protected from the weather," she said.

"Good thinking," said Daniel.

The stone had obviously been lying flat for many years; possibly centuries. Alec looked around and found some broken tree limbs. He and Daniel worked at clearing the stone. It took them half an hour to get to the point where they could dig branches into the ground to pry up the slab. Using two limbs as levers, he and Daniel slowly raised the stone and turned it over.

"Goodness!" exclaimed Georgina.

"Upon my word!" said Daniel.

"Good lord!" was Alec's comment.

The face of the gravestone was clear and little worn. The engraving was relatively easy to make out. It read:

PERENELLE FLAMEL
B. 1340   D.1416
WIFE OF NICOLAS FLAMEL
+

REDEMPTOR INVICTUS SANCTIFICARE ANGELICUS PATEFACTUM
CONCEDERE MERUM GAUDIUM CONIUNCTIM-SANCTUM

"Very impressive," murmured Daniel.

"What does the Latin mean?" asked Georgina.

"I have no idea."

"My Latin is very rusty," said Alec. "I wish it were otherwise. I keep meaning to work at it but ..."

"I know what you mean," said Daniel.

"So, where do we go from here?"

Georgina took out a notebook and copied down what was on the gravestone.

"The grave of Perenelle Flamel?" asked the white-haired sexton, pulling his threadbare coat more tightly about him. "No, you will not find that here."

"You are sure?" demanded Mathers.

"*Oui, Monsieur.* No question," he said. "You are not the first to come looking."

"There have been others? Recently?"

He laughed and, straining to lift his head, looked up at the dull grey sky. "All of the time. Over the years. Some years we will have a whole lot of people while others it is only a few. But it seems the stories never go away." He looked down again at the ground.

"Stories?" demanded Moina. "What stories?"

"Why, of gold tombstones, and coffins filled with riches. Of the elixir of life, yours for the taking. Of ancient recipes for producing untold wealth without lifting a finger." He laughed, without humor. "Hah! Fools! No one appreciates what our dear ancestor Nicholas achieved."

"He was your ancestor?" asked Mathers, incredulously.

"He was the ancestor to *all* of us," came the reply. "He was the true father of France. But was he appreciated? *Non.* He was not. Such is always the way, is it not?"

"Come on, Samuel," said Winters. "This old fool is not going to be of any help."

"I agree," said Cranwell. "Let us get on. We will do better by ourselves."

"Wait," said Mathers. He turned to the stooped figure. "If Perenelle Flamel is not here, do you know where she is?"

The old man's rheumy eyes looked up at the tall figure before him. He had to fight to press back his head from its natural downcast position. He did not maintain it for long, but let his face return instead to studying their shoes and boots. "She is at rest, God mind her."

"Where?" Mathers voice was sharp and commanding.

"With her family." The old man turned and shuffled away.

"Wait!" cried Mathers.

"Oh, let him go," said Winters. "He is rambling"

"I don't know so much." Mathers was thoughtful as he watched the frail figure return into the old church from which he had earlier emerged. "I do not know so much."

They had had no success finding a Flamel gravestone in the churchyard. Yet the old sexton was obviously familiar with that which they sought, Mathers reasoned. He sensed that the old man knew more than he was saying. Winters was obviously thinking the same thing.

"Well, Samuel? Would you like me to have a little 'private conversation' with our elderly friend?"

Mathers was torn. He well knew what any 'private conversation' would entail and did not enjoy contemplating the actions that the clergyman would take. Yet, time was of the essence. *Tempus fugit, Samuel. Tempus fugit.* He could hear the tone in Dr. Westcott's voice even now. Slightly mocking, as though he expected Mathers to fail. Mathers gave a barely perceptible nod to Winters and then turned to the others, urging them away from the church.

"Come! Let us find somewhere warm and out of this wind. I think I saw a café just down the road."

Behind them, Winters went into the church.

"The old sexton remembered what we needed to know," said Winters, when he rejoined Mathers and the group, relaxing at the café. His eyes did not meet with any of the others as he slipped into a seat beside Mathers.

"Oh?"

"Yes. Apparently there is an old family graveyard – Perenelle's family – and she is buried there, though her husband Nicholas is not."

"Well done, Monty," murmured Mathers. "Where is it?"

"About five miles or so from here, at the family farm ... or what once was the family farm. It has changed hands a number of times since then, it would seem."

"Let us proceed."

The old farmer was surprised to have a second group of strangers come to his farm. He didn't normally see anyone – not even neighbors – for days at a time.

Mathers found the man taciturn and uncooperative.

"I am not running a tourist attraction here," the farmer said. "I have got my work to do. I cannot keep breaking off to direct people to the old family plot. And I don't want hordes of people tramping across my fields and frightening my animals."

"I assure you, my good sir," said Mathers, "that we will take all due precaution and disturb your beasts not at all. Simply point the direction we must take and we will bother you no more."

"Hrmph!" The farmer snorted and, lifting his hat, scratched his head. "Well, I don't like it," he said. "Now you be sure to close all gates after you, understand?"

"Yes indeed. We understand that. We will be most attentive to these matters."

With a final grunt, the farmer pointed across the fields. "There is a small copse and then a low stone wall about the place," he said. "You will either find it or you will not." And with that he turned away and plodded off toward his barns.

"Damned foreigners!" snorted Winters.

Leigh Cranwell laughed; unusual for him. "In actual fact it is we who are the foreigners here," he said.

"Come! Let us find this graveyard." Mathers strode off across the farm yard and opened the gate into the field beyond. The others followed after him.

"There are plenty of old markers here, certainly," said Mathers, peering at a worn gravestone that leaned at a sharp angle. "But the more ancient ones are so worn it is hard to make any sense of them."

"The older ones seem to be over in this section," called Sarah, indicating the area closest to the far stone wall. The others moved to join her.

"This looks to be yet another waste of time," grumbled Cranwell, rubbing lichen from the face of a stone.

"Patience, Leigh, patience," urged Mathers.

Moina perched herself on a solid section of the wall and watched the others. "Is it not almost luncheon time?" she asked, of no one in particular. "Where will we eat? Not that atrocious little café, I hope."

No one paid any attention to her, as they moved slowly about the grave site, trying to read the inscriptions.

"I see some of them have fallen over," continued Moina, after a while. "Do you not need to pick up all of them and see what they say?"

Mathers straightened up and looked about him. "You know, my dear, you are right. An excellent observation."

She preened herself but Sarah noticed that she made no move to join the others at their labors.

"Cranwell! Monty! Purdy! Perhaps we should concentrate for a while on lifting the fallen stones?" Mathers moved to one of them. He attempted to lift it and, after straining for a moment, managed to turn it over. "Hmm. Early sixteen hundreds for this one. Not old enough." He moved on, looking for another fallen marker. When he came to one he had to call on Winters to help him turn it. "Still not old enough!"

"Here is one," called Cranwell. "It looks as though it was dug up and then fell back down again. Purdy! Give me a hand."

Percy Purdy moved to help Cranwell lift the stone and turn it.

"*Eureka*!" Purdy pointed to the inscription. "Just look! It is very little worn considering its age. But here it is ... Perenelle Flamel. We have found her."

They all excitedly gathered around the gravestone. Even Moina came down off her wall, Sarah noticed.

"'Perenelle Flamel, 1340 to 1416'," read Mathers. "And see – 'Wife of Nicolas Flamel'!"

"What is the inscription underneath?" asked Winters, peering down at it.

"Redemptor invictus sanctificare ..."

"Yes, yes! We can all read the words," snorted Winters. "But what does it mean?"

Mathers sighed. "Let me see. *Redemptor* – well, that is a buyer or contractor. There is really not a good translation. Then we have *Invictus* which is 'invincible' or 'unconquered'. *Sanctificare* is 'sanctifying'. *Angelicus* is 'angels' and *Patefactum* means 'manifests'. 'Contractor invincible sanctifying angels manifests.' Hmm. That does not seem to make too much sense."

"Are you sure about these translations?" asked Winters.

"He is right," said Purdy. "Basically. I would suggest perhaps, 'Invincible contractor manifests sanctifying angels'. But, as Samuel says, it does not make a lot of sense."

"What's that next line?" Winters asked suspiciously.

"At least it has a little more meaning," said Mathers. "It reads 'Give pure joy together with saints.' I suppose that is a little more significant."

"Write it all down," said Winters. He turned to Sarah. "You have a notebook, Miss Winters?" She nodded. "Then copy down this inscription together with Mister Mathers's translation."

Sarah looked to Mathers, who nodded his head. She took out her notebook and did as she was bid.

Then "You have it?" asked Winters.

"Yes." She showed him the notebook.

"Good." The clergyman bent down and lifted a large stone that had tumbled from the stone wall. He hefted it above his head and then let it fall on the gravestone. The ancient marker shattered into several pieces.

"What are you doing?" shouted Cranwell.

"Making sure that no one else can use this," replied Winters. He picked up pieces of the broken marker and threw them randomly about the overgrown graveyard.

"Sacrilege," murmured Cranwell.

"But, I think a wise move," said Mathers. "Come. Our job here is done. Let us repair to some place warmer and more salubrious. Miss Wilde ... I will take charge of that page from your notebook."

Alec and the Parmingtons returned to Paris, all three of them lodging at the Hôtel Sainte-Marie, on the rue de Rivoli.

"I am afraid it is time for Georgina and me to return to the old country," said Daniel that evening. They were sitting in the hotel lounge enjoying a cognac. "Our holiday time is almost over."

"I shall be sorry to see you go," said Alec. "You have both been a tremendous help, not to mention jolly fine company."

"But where does this leave you, Alec?" asked Mrs. Parmington. "We found the Perenelle grave but you still need to discover Nicholas's resting place and, hopefully, his notebook."

"I have been looking at what we found," said Alec. He opened his large notebook and displayed the drawing he had made of the Perenelle gravestone. "This inscription is a clue, I am sure."

"My thinking exactly," murmured Daniel.

"Whoever was responsible for erecting Perenelle's grave marker was also responsible for the inscription."

"Agramant, you think?"

Alec nodded. "Who else? Yes, I would bet on it."

"So this inscription could be a clue he left as to where Nicholas is to be found?" said Georgina.

"I am certain. So first of all we must translate it."

"That should not be too difficult," said Daniel. "There must be scholars here who would be happy to do it for you."

"Oh, I am sure," agreed Alec. "But I think there is more to it than that."

They both looked at him enquiringly.

"Agramant would not simply spell out where Nicolas was buried, on this gravestone," Alec continued. "It has to be cryptic ... everything so far has been needing interpretation."

"So what do you propose?"

"I will work on it here," said Alec, "but I would like to ask you to do me a favor."

"Anything, old boy."

"I have a very good friend minding my bookstore back home. Jeremy Lowell. I would like you – if you would – to take a copy of this to him and fill him in on what we know so far. He is a genius when it comes to codes and ciphers. See if he has any suggestions. Would you do that for me?"

"Of course we will." Georgina beamed.

Alec smiled as he noted that she was including herself in on the project. "Many thanks," he said.

"You think Crowley would do that?" Leigh Cranwell sounded doubtful.

"His Latin is fine," responded Mathers.

"It is not that I am questioning," said Cranwell. "I don't think it is any secret that he is jealous of your position as head of the Golden Dawn."

Mathers snorted and waved an unconcerned hand.

"No, this is serious," said Cranwell. "He can be very childish and petty at times. I cannot see him lifting a finger to help you in anything, especially when you are on the other side of the Channel."

"Is there no loyalty with your members?" asked Winters, settling himself into a winged armchair in the Mathers's suite at the Chopin Hôtel, in Paris. The Golden Dawn group had returned there after tracking down the grave of Perenelle Flamel.

"Of course there is." Mathers was defensive. "There is an oath that is taken at initiation, apart from anything else. Crowley would not flout that, I'm sure."

"Well, I am not so sure," said Cranwell.

"Never the less," continued Mathers. "I have posted to Aleister a copy of what we found and have asked him to apply his talents – and he does have considerable talents – to deciphering what we discovered. I am certain that there is a clue embedded in that gravestone inscription."

"Oh, I agree," said Cranwell. "But whether or not Crowley will uncover it is another story."

Sarah knew that just to walk through the Louvre without even stopping to look at the treasures would take all of two hours, it was so large. All of the buildings together constituted the largest palace in the world; about forty-five acres or three times the size of the Vatican including St. Peter's. For this reason, if no other, she knew that she had to focus on just one area for her first visit. Sarah had slipped away from the rest of the Golden Dawn group, had posted her latest report to Inspector Kent, and was now determined to see at least one of the highlights of Paris. Always fascinated by ancient Egypt, she headed for the Musée des Antiquités Egyptiennes, off from the Cour du Louvre.

At the entrance to the first room she entered, the Salle Henri Quatre, was a large sphinx in pink granite. This room contained the largest objects of the collection. Along with a number of sphinxes were monuments commemorating special events; steles; votive stones; statues from tombs and temples; bas reliefs and sarcophagi. She spent a pleasant hour studying the objects and reading the explanatory labels.

The Louvre always quickly filled with visitors. Sarah was looking down at the guide – which she was pleased to find was printed in both French and English – when she rounded a large statue of Bes and bumped into someone.

"Good Lord! ... Sarah!"

She almost dropped the guide booklet when she found herself face to face with Alec.

"Alec!" Without stopping to think, she rushed forward into his arms. He gave her a long, warm hug before stepping back and, as though suddenly remembering himself and where they were, raising his hat in greeting. She was pleased to see that his face was flushed.

"Sarah! How wonderful! What are you doing here?"

"I might ask you the same."

"I saw some friends off at the Gare du Nord and, on an impulse, decided to look in at the Louvre."

"What a wonderful, delightful coincidence."

He looked around. "I doubt very much that there is a Lyons Corner House or an ABC tea room anywhere around?"

She laughed, and felt good. "Can we go somewhere?" she asked.

"Anywhere. Come on ... we can visit the Louvre anytime. Let us get out of here, find a café, and catch up on things."

They spent almost an hour together at a café on the rue de Rivoli. The beverage, even though it was presented as Earl Grey tea, was served in a glass and did not compare, they decided, to that of their favorite Lyons tea shop. But they drank it and ordered more.

"So the GD group found the Perenelle stone?" said Alec.

Sarah nodded. "Yes. And smashed it!"

"Barbarians!"

"It was that dreadful Montague Winters. I don't know what Mister Mathers sees in the man, though I understand they went to school together, or something."

"And what do they plan to do now? Where do you go from here?"

Sarah shook her head. "That I don't know. They all seemed to think that what was written on the gravestone was some sort of secret code. They sent it back to Aleister Crowley, though I thought Mister Mathers was the one who was the expert in codes and ciphers."

"I am sure they are right about it being a coded message," said Alec. "I had reached that conclusion myself ... What a good job we found the stone before Winters smashed it."

"Do you know what it means?"

"Not yet. I, too, have sent it back to London. The Parmingtons are going to drop it off to my friend Jeremy."

"The Parmingtons sound like a delightful couple."

Alec smiled. "They are indeed. They were good company and made it a whole lot less lonely, I can tell you."

"I hope I meet them sometime."

"I am sure you will."

"So do you just sit and wait, now?"

Alec drained his tea and put down the glass. "That's about all I can do. Lord Sunbury urged me to get to the Flamel grave before Mathers and his people. But I cannot do that till I know where it is. I am hoping that gravestone message will tell me."

"And before Mathers deciphers it." Sarah looked down at the locket-watch fastened to her lapel. "Oh, my! I must be getting back to the hotel. They will be wondering where I am."

"But I cannot lose you. I mean ... at which hotel are you staying?"

Sarah smiled to herself. She felt warm and wanted. "We are at the Hôtel Chopin," she said. "And you?"

"The Hôtel Sainte-Marie, right here on the rue de Rivoli. Can we meet at the Louvre again tomorrow?"

"I will try," she said. "If I can get away unnoticed I will be there – in the Egyptian room again – at about two o'clock." She got up and extended her hand. "So very wonderful to see you again, Alec."

He took her hand and held it for a long moment before releasing it. "And you, Sarah. Please take care of yourself."

As Sarah entered the hotel she saw Percy Purdy sitting in the lobby. He got up as soon as he saw her.

"Mister Mathers would like to see you immediately, in his suite," he said. Sarah thought he seemed very smug.

"Very well," she replied, and turned to the ancient lift at the rear of the lobby.

"Suite" was an over-elaborate name for the rooms of Samuel and Moina Mathers, she thought. There were two bedrooms – the Mathers always slept apart, she had learned – and a small sitting room where the group would gather for their meetings. *I wonder what he wants*, she thought as the lift attendant pulled back the concertina metal gate and let her out at their floor. She soon found out.

Samuel and Moina sat stiffly on the settee and Montague Winters lounged at the fireplace. Sarah glanced at the clergyman and moved into the room.

"Please take a seat," said Mathers, with no greeting of any sort.

126

Sarah sat down on a straight-backed chair.

"My wife and I had taken a carriage ride along the Champs Elysée," said Mathers. "As you may well know, at the Place de la Concorde the thoroughfare branches off into the rue de Rivoli."

Sarah's heart seemed to miss a beat.

"The rue de Rivoli," repeated Mathers. "I know you know that road well for did we not, but a short while ago, espy you sitting in a café there?"

"You – you may have done," said Sarah in a quiet voice.

"With a certain gentleman."

She said nothing.

"I think you know to whom I refer, Miss Wilde. It was, was it not, Mister Alec Chambers?"

Sarah sat up straighter and looked Mathers in the eye. "Yes," she said. "It was Mister Chambers. Is there a problem with that?"

Moina gasped and Winters snorted.

"What, precisely, is Mister Chambers doing here in Paris, Miss Wilde?"

"I – I believe he is on a short holiday," she said, hoping that it was not a total untruth.

Winters again snorted. Mathers came to his feet and began pacing the room. He stopped in front of Sarah and looked down at her.

"Be so good as to think carefully before you answer me, Miss Wilde. Is Mister Chambers's presence in Paris in any way connected with our quest for the grave of Nicholas Flamel?"

Sarah took a deep breath and then rose to her feet. She looked up into Mathers's eyes. "To the best of my knowledge, Mister Mathers, Alec's – Mister Chambers's – presence here in this city has no direct connection to your search." She was being truthful but hoped she wasn't stretching that truth too far. "And I must say that I am not used to having my whereabouts nor my acquaintances questioned. I may be in your employ as a secretary, Mister Mathers, but that is the extent of it. I bid you good afternoon." She turned and walked out of the room, her heart beating in her chest so loudly she thought they must all hear it.

"Well I'll be damned!" exclaimed Winters.

"Monty!" Moina remonstrated.

"Yes, you probably will be damned," muttered Mathers. He crossed to stand beside his friend. "I must admit, I did not expect her to openly defy me. I would have liked to have learned more about our friend Chambers and what he is doing here."

"It certainly seems too much of a coincidence," said Moina.

"Would you like me to 'enquire further'?" asked Winters.

"What do you mean?"

"Oh, just go and talk to her. You know – one to one, as it were."

Mathers hesitated. He looked at his wife.

"Don't ask me," she said. "I want nothing to do with it. I never liked the girl, as well you know. Far too self-assured. It is this modern generation!"

"Yes. Well. She is an exceptionally efficient secretary, for all that." He looked at Winters. "You would not ... do anything ... untoward?" he asked.

Winters laughed and moved away, toward the door. "Oh you know me, Samuel. Of course not. Just a little tête-a-tête, that is all."

"Yes. I do know you, Monty," Mathers muttered as the clergyman left the room.

Sarah heard the tap on her door but before she could respond the door was opened and Monty Winters came in. He closed the door behind him and strode across the room to stand facing her. She had been beside the dressing-table and rose to her feet.

"Mister Winters! How dare you come into my room unbidden! What ..."

"Be quiet!" He spoke through tight lips, his voice low and menacing. "You may think you can toy with Samuel but it is going to be a different tale with me, young lady."

"W-what do you mean?"

She had half raised her hand as though to defend herself. He reached out and grasped her wrist.

"Oh! Let go of me. You are hurting me."

"Perhaps you need to be hurt." His face was now close to hers. She could smell garlic on his breath, presumably from his luncheon. She wrinkled her nose in disdain.

"Let go of me and leave my room," she hissed, meeting his gaze with unblinking eyes of her own.

"I will leave when I am ready to go," he said. "I have to teach you ... certain things, it seems. You must learn to respect your betters."

"You are certainly not my better!" she snapped. Her heart was racing and where he grasped her wrist was intensely painful, though she refused to let him see that.

He pulled her closer and, with his free hand, reached up and squeezed her breast.

Sarah had reached behind her and now her hand closed around a pair of scissors that lay beside needle and thread on the dressing-table. The scissors were small but they were the only weapon she could think of. As Winters pulled her to him she swung her arm around and down, stabbing him in the hand that groped at her body. He swore in a most unclergyman-like manner and let go of her, pulling the scissors from his hand.

Sarah ducked under his arm and ran to the door. Scooping up her reticule, she flung open the door and raced as fast as she was able down the corridor. She pushed through the door leading to the stairs and continued running down them as hard as she was able. She heard no sound of pursuit from behind.

Florence Farr burst into Mathers's office without bothering to knock. Crowley and Allan Bennett were sitting at a small gaming table next to the desk, playing a game of chess. Florence held up an envelope and then dropped it onto the desk.

"Here, Mister Crowley. By the second post ... a letter from Samuel."

Crowley didn't look up but studied the chess board. "So! Our fearless leader has deemed to report back to us, has he?"

"Don't you want to read it?"

"Not really, no." But Crowley eventually moved away from the chess game and leaned over the desk. He considered the envelope without touching it, like a scientist studying a newly acquired specimen.

"Hmm. The old rapscallion is living it up in Paris, I see." He returned to his seat opposite Bennett.

"Should you not read it?" insisted Florence.

"You would think," said Crowley, as though to himself, "that such an important organization as the Hermetic Order of the Golden Dawn would have installed one of these new-fangled telephones, wouldn't you? Everyone – and I do mean everyone – is getting them these days."

"I hear the United Telephone Company charges twenty pounds per annum for the privilege," said Bennett. "And that has to be within a five mile radius of the General Post Office."

Crowley waved a dismissive hand at Florence and, with his eyes on the board, addressed his opponent. "Now that is very odd, Allan."

"What is that?"

"Why my queen sitting where I now see her. Surely but a moment ago she was on the knight's square not the bishop's?"

"What are you saying, Aleister?"

"I am merely noting ..." he took a deep breath. "Hmm. Perhaps she moved herself. Let me see, my last move was to take your bishop on his own square so ... ah! Your last move opened the way for my queen to check your king, if I am not mistaken. I am going to mate you in two moves."

"What?"

"Aha!"

Florence threw up her hands in despair and left the room.

"I have no sympathy," said Moina.

Winters stood nursing his hand, a blood-stained kerchief wrapped around it.

"You did bring this on yourself," said Mathers, pouring himself a brandy and one for Winters. He passed the glass to the clergyman, who managed to take it despite his injured hand. "You assured me that you would do nothing untoward."

"I did not get a chance to do anything, untoward or not," snapped Winters, and took a long gulp of the liquor.

"From what you say, you certainly made a start," said Moina.

"Oh, I was just relaxing her. Taking her mind off things so that I could find out what needed to be found out."

"Well, you have lost all chance of that now. I imagine we will not see Miss Wilde again."

"You think she has gone running back to England?" asked Moina.

"More likely to that Alec Chambers," retorted her husband. "This was probably all some disgusting lovers' tryst. She may well have been planning on deserting us in any event."

131

"I don't know so much," muttered Winters, and took another swallow of brandy.

There was a tap at the door and Percy Purdy put his head around it.

"May we enter?" he asked.

Mathers waved his hand graciously and moved off to sit in the larger of the two winged arm chairs. Purdy came in, followed by Leigh Cranwell. They took seats on the settee.

"So what is the schedule?" asked Cranwell.

"What happened?" Purdy asked of Winters, indicating the injury. The clergyman stuffed the bandaged hand into his pocket and ignored the question.

"Our schedule is currently in abeyance," said Mathers. "We must, I'm afraid, wait on Crowley's reply. He will get onto it right away, I am sure. I will myself, of course, work on this conundrum and will probably solve it before he does, but he has access to all my volumes on ciphers while I must rely solely on my memory."

"My money is on you, sir," said Purdy.

"This is not a race," said Cranwell. "We just seem to have gone around in a circle. We are right back where we started."

"Not exactly," said Mathers. "We do have the lines from the Perenelle gravestone. They are our next clue. They will direct us to our goal." He looked around the room. "Take a day or two to relax. Moina I know will be going shopping ..." She smiled and nodded. "Take in some of the sights of Paris, gentlemen. Visit the Louvre; the Cathedral of Notre Dame; the Seine; Mister Gustav Eiffel's remarkable tower. It will not take Aleister and myself long to point us to the next clue."

Lord Sunbury's office was in direct contrast to Inspector Kent's. There was a large, polished, mahogany desk with its top surface mostly clear of paperwork. A Turkey carpet covered the floor and comfortable chairs stood ready for visitors. Inspector Kent sat on one of these; perched on the edge with his feet tidily together, as though ready to spring up at any moment.

Covering one wall was a large map of the world. On another wall was an ornately-framed oil portrait of Queen Victoria. Behind where Lord Sunbury sat at the desk, hung a number of photographs of his lordship with the queen, with various members of the House of Lords, and with distinguished men and women from all walks of life.

Two large ferns flourished in matching decorative vases, perched on tall stands on either side of the window. A small tray sat on a corner of the desk, holding a half-drunk cup of tea and an ignored ginger biscuit. Inspector Kent eyed the tray a number of times.

Lord Sunbury was looking through a fat folder which the policeman had brought to him. "This is all very interesting, Inspector. Your Miss Wilde has done a good job of keeping you apprised of the situation over in France."

"Yes, your lordship," murmured Kent. "But I regret to say that her last missive advised that she had been forced to leave the Golden Dawn group. Apparently the Winters character made inappropriate advances to her."

"Oh, dear!" Lord Sunbury shook his head. "Well, she knew his background when she volunteered. Still, it is unfortunate. Hopefully she came to no harm?"

"No, sir. She apparently caused *him* some small harm." The inspector couldn't help chuckling. Lord Sunbury joined him.

"Yes. I see here, in your report. That should teach the blighter!" Lord Sunbury's face grew serious again. "But one of the reasons I called you here is to let you know that the Illuminati's West European section held a meeting in Belgrave Square a few days ago. I am happy to say that we have been privy to what took place there. Our Dr. Westcott reported to the group that MacGregor Mathers was proceeding with his plans, but did not enlarge on what those plans happen to be. We had hoped to learn more of the nature of this threat to Her Majesty, of course."

"Do we at least have a time frame for the threat, your lordship?" asked Kent.

"All we know is that it is likely to be in late October or early November. Not too precise, I am afraid."

"And not too far away," added Kent. "Let us hope it is not another Jubilee Plot."

"Indeed."

Just over ten years before, in 1887, the British Empire had celebrated Queen Victoria's Golden Jubilee; the fiftieth anniversary of her accession to the throne. Fifty European kings and princes had been invited. A plan was uncovered - ostensibly by Irish anarchists - to blow up Westminster Abbey and half the British cabinet while the Queen attended a service of thanksgiving.

"How is our boy Chambers proceeding?" asked Lord Sunbury.

"Miss Wilde happened to encounter him, quite by chance, just a few days ago," replied Kent. "Very fortuitous, as it turned out, since it gave her somewhere to go when things got out of hand with the Mathers' group."

"Indeed. And Chambers is ... ?"

"As you'll see in my report, sir, Mister Chambers did manage to have access to the encrypted gravestone before it was destroyed. He feels that this does indeed hold the clue to the location of the Flamel grave. He is in the process of deciphering what was written on it."

"Any indication as to when he will complete that?"

"These things do take time, your lordship, as you well know. I am confident that Mister Chambers will proceed at all speed."

"Of course. I was not implying otherwise. Very well, Inspector," he closed the folder and handed it back to Kent, who came quickly to his feet. "Keep me up to date with any new developments."

"Of course, your lordship." Inspector Kent half backed to the door, not quite sure whether or not he should bow. He gave a quick inclination of his head and went out.

"I would say that each word represents either another word, a group of letters, or even just a single letter," said Jeremy, studying the page of writing that Daniel Parmington had brought to him.

"How on earth would we find which word or letter it is, given so few?" asked Daniel. "There are only five words on each line."

"Yes," agreed Jeremy. "In longer pieces you can look for repeat letters or words, which tie-in to things like double-e, double-s or double-t, for example. That at least gives you a start. But no chance of that with this short piece."

The two men pored over the paper on which Alec had written the gravestone inscription. They were in Alec's library. Alec had invited his friend Jeremy to stay at Westmoreland Terrace for the duration of his absence. Jeremy was a short, dark, mop-haired young man with a well-trimmed beard that followed his chin line. This was matched by a narrow mustache. Hair and beard were dark brown; the hair parted on Jeremy's left side with the resultant cow-lick constantly falling over his forehead when Jeremy leaned forward. He wore steel-rimmed spectacles and had a habit of taking them off and putting them on again. He now removed them as he sat back in his chair, brushing his hair out of his eyes.

"There has to be something obvious," he said, thinking aloud. "Some key hidden in it."

"Would any of Alec's books help?"

"I am sure they would, if we knew what we were looking for." Jeremy replaced his spectacles. "Let us see what he has." He got up and the two of them moved over to the bookshelves. They quickly found the small section on codes and ciphers.

"Just what exactly is the difference between a code and a cipher?" asked Daniel.

"A code uses symbols or groups of letters to represent words or phrases, while a cipher is much simpler with just one letter replacing another," explained Jeremy. "Ciphers have been in use since Roman times. Julius Caesar developed a simple substitute one."

They looked along the book shelf.

"There is *The Adams Cable Codex*, published just five years ago. Edward Alexander's *Telegraphic Cipher Code*, James Alexander's *Telegraphic Code*, and Luther Allen's *Commercial Telegraphic Code System*."

"What are all those about?"

"It is this new electromagnetic telegraph that some people are using," explained Jeremy. "It was developed in America by Mister Samuel Morse. Apparently it is very expensive to use, with the company charging by the word for messages sent. Consequently codes have been developed that represent a number of words or phrases. These books detail them.

"There are a large number of unsolved codes that we know about," continued Jeremy. "There is the infamous Voynich manuscript; the Beale ciphers over in America, from about fifteen years ago; the Phaistos Disk from Crete; the Indus script; the Rongorongo script of Easter island, to name just a few. All codes that have never been broken."

"That does not give us much hope for our problem," said Daniel glumly.

"Never say die," muttered Jeremy.

They spent nearly an hour looking through Alec's books. Jeremy finally sat back and took off his spectacles.

"If I didn't know any better I would say that this is from the Trithemius code."

"What is that?" asked Daniel.

"Johannes Trithemius, or Johann Heidenberg as he was born, lived in Trithemius – that is on the banks of the Mosel River in Germany. He was born in 1462. He became an abbot at the Benedictine abbey of Sponheim and amassed a huge library there. But in 1506 he left Sponheim and became Abbot of the Monastery of St. Jacob in Wurzburg."

"You seem to know all about him."

"He was a major figure in the rise of the occult movement in the sixteenth century. He was quite prolific, authoring a number of books. But what is of especial interest to us, Daniel, is that during the sixteenth century cryptography became very fashionable and Trithemius became an expert at it."

"Wonderful!" exclaimed Daniel. "Then you think this is a code that he produced?"

"That was my first thought ... until I realized that Trimethius was not born until fifty years after Flamel died, so there is no way Flamel could have used the Trimethius code!"

They sat in silence for long moments. Then, suddenly, Daniel sat up straight. "Wait a minute! Wait a minute," he said.

"What is it?"

"I don't know much about Flamel but, as I told Alec when I first met him, I do know a little of some of the other alchemists. People like Paracelsus, Roger Bacon and ... Raymond Lully."

Jeremy pulled off his spectacles. "Raymond Lully?"

"Aha!" Daniel grinned. "I think you know where my thoughts are heading. Was not he involved with codes, in some way?"

"Yes! Yes indeed. Lully was born a good hundred years before Flamel. Wait! Let us check." Jeremy jumped up and moved across once more to Alec's bookshelves. It didn't take him long to find what he was looking for.

"Here we are. *Biographies of Occult and Alchemical Figures* by Gregory Ames." He pulled out the book and sat down again, flipping through the pages. When he found what he was looking for he started to read. "*Ramon Llull (1232-1315) – sometimes Raymond Lully, Raymond Lull or Raimundo Lulio. A philosopher born into a wealthy family in Palma, Majorca, in the Balearic Islands; part of the Crown of Aragon. Llull invented a number of machines. One of these had two discs of paper that rotated individually to give a combination of letters, symbols, and attributes. This machine was purported to show all possible truths about any subject. The idea was further developed in the sixteenth century by Giordano Bruno and in the seventeenth century by Gottfried Leibniz.* Now wait a minute ..." Jeremy ran his finger down the page, muttering to himself. "*Here we are. Ramon Llull invented a number of codes and ciphers, one of which was later further developed by the German Abbot Johann Heidenberg also known as Johannes Trithemius.*" He looked up, a big smile on his face. "You know what this means?"

"Yes." Daniel nodded. "It means that your hunch may be correct; the inscription on the grave marker may be based on a code that was known to Flamel ... the code that *later* became known as the Trithemius Code. Am I right?"

"Absolutely," said Jeremy. "Of course, we are not out of the woods yet. We have still got to dig out that code and see how it might differ from Lully's original and then translate the engraving. But I think we are getting somewhere!"

"I am sure you will be pleased to know that we have finally got an answer from Aleister," said Moina Mathers, throwing open the door of her husband's bedroom and walking in. She stopped in her tracks.

There were two figures in the bed. One was Samuel MacGregor Mathers, the other was Percy Purdy. Purdy gave a squeal and leapt out of the bed, grabbing up his clothes from a nearby chair and rushing naked out of the room, pushing past Moina.

Mathers himself seemed unperturbed. He sat up in the bed and rubbed his eyes. "Really, Moina," he said. "You must knock before you enter a room."

For a moment Moina was speechless, and then she exploded. "Samuel! How could you? How long has this been going on?"

"Oh, come now, my dear. We were simply going through the ritual relationship of the thirteenth degree which, as you well know, is a sacred union ..."

"Don't give me that shit!" she retorted. "Ritual union is sacred and is performed in a consecrated circle, not in a bed of tangled, sweaty sheets! This is not the first time, Samuel, but it must surely be the last!"

With that she threw down the letter she had been carrying and stormed out of the room, slamming the door behind her.

"Oh, dear," murmured Mathers.

Afternoon

athers and Winters stood side by side at the window of the sitting room looking out at the excitement on the street below, where a brewer's dray had locked wheels with those of a hansom cab.

"You can hardly blame her for getting upset," said Winters.

"Oh, she should know me by now," responded Mathers. "After all these years we have never actually consummated our married state. I do not flaunt these things in her face but, dammit, she should have knocked before she entered my room."

"Ah, yes. There is that."

They stood in silence for a while.

"Moina ran out of here, you know," said the clergyman.

"She will have gone to the Ahathooor Temple and the Grenobles," said Mathers. "She will come to no harm there. Perhaps she can calm herself by meditating in the ritual room."

"What on earth possessed her to walk into your room anyway?"

"Oh, Lord yes!" Mathers turned away from the window and moved to the small escritoire at the side of the room. From the surface of the desk he picked up an envelope and turned to Winters with it.

"It seems we have finally heard from Aleister Crowley."

"Not before time."

"Indeed." Mathers took up a letter-opener and slit the envelope. He pulled out the letter and studied it.

"What does he say?" asked Winters.

Mathers re-read the letter before answering. "In effect he says that the code would seem to be one from Trithemius but that, if it is, it is not old enough. Failing that, the gravestone is a fake."

"What do you mean, not old enough?"

141

"Trimethius came on the scene long after Flamel had died and been buried, so Flamel, or even Agramant, could not have used that code."

"What else does he say?"

Mathers turned the paper to see if anything was written on the back.

"Nothing. That is it! Aleister has managed to tell us what it is not, but not what it is!"

"The man's a fool!" said Winters.

"Actually I suspect he is a genius, though don't let anyone know I said that," replied Mathers. "No, he is lazy. Just plain lazy. He thought it might be Trithemius – as did I, as a matter of fact – but then could not be bothered to look any farther."

"So where do we go from here?"

Mathers sighed. "I truly do not know why I entrusted this to Aleister in the first place. We have wasted valuable time. I see I am going to have to follow up on it myself, which is what I should have done right from the start. How would you like to go with me to the *Bibliotheque Nationale de France*, Monty?"

"By all means, old boy. Just don't expect me to read anything written in French."

Percy Purdy looked again. Yes, he was certain it was Miss Sarah Wilde; he would recognize that red hair anywhere. She was with a fair-haired young man. He guessed that to be the Alec Chambers that Samuel had talked about. The couple was hurrying across the road to the *Gare du Quai-d'Orsay* railway station.

Purdy had taken a carriage ride, to clear his head and to come to terms with Moina Mathers's untoward and decidedly inopportune discovery of the assignation between her husband and himself. He had almost determined that he should resign his position with the group – however vaguely sanctified it had ever been – and should return to London. But here was information he could give to Samuel that must surely be valuable. He had just crossed the Pont d'Austerlitz. He got the cab driver to pull over to the curb and let him alight. At a discreet distance, Percy followed the young couple into the big station.

The enormous building had only recently been completed, taking the place of the old Cour des Comptes which had been burned down by the Communards in 1871. There was a handsome new restaurant on the first floor, reached from the café below. Much of the vast structure was the Palais d'Orsay hotel.

Percy was pleased to see that Chambers seated Miss Wilde at a table in the café before leaving her and heading toward the booking office. Alec Chambers had never met Percy so Percy felt safe getting fairly close. When Chambers went to the booking window, Percy hovered near by, pretending to be studying the timetable. Percy's French was good and he had no difficulty hearing Alec ask for two first class tickets to Périgueux.

"Where the devil is Périgueux and why would Chambers be going there?" Samuel MacGregor Mathers had spent a long and frustrating day at the *Bibliotheque Nationale* and felt that he didn't need any further puzzles. "I thank you for your quick thinking, Percy," he said to the fawning Purdy. "It was indeed fortuitous that you spotted our Miss Wilde and her paramour and it was quick thinking to determine their proposed destination."

"Always glad to be of service," said Percy, his face glowing with the praise.

"I have borrowed a Baedeker's for Southern France, from the Concierge," said Leigh Cranwell. "It lists Périgueux on page thirty-nine. It even has a map of the place."

"What does it tell us?"

"Well, firstly it is anywhere from three to five hours by train from Bordeaux to the town."

"And Bordeaux is about three hundred miles from Paris, as the crow flies," said Winters. "All told, it would be a *very* long train journey."

"There does not seem to be anything special about Périgueux, according to Baedeker's," said Cranwell. "It is the capitol of the department of the Dordogne and is also listed as the ancient *Vesuna*, whatever that may have been."

"That was the old Roman town," said Percy.

"There is a cathedral there," continued Cranwell. "The Cathedral of St. Front. Hmm. Nothing special ... there is what is described as 'a curious tower', the oldest in France, that rises to 197 ft. and is part of a basilica of the sixth century."

"Anything else?"

"One moment ... There is a Freemason's Lodge, but that is listed as a modern edifice ... A museum; another cathedral – the Cathedral of St. Etienne – and ... no, nothing else that seems remotely of interest."

Monty Winters took the book from Cranwell and studied it.

"We have not yet solved our first mystery," said Mathers, "and here we have a second."

"Could it be that this is nothing to do with Flamel and his tomb?" said Percy. "It might just be the two lovers running away."

"Running away from what ... or whom?" asked Cranwell. Percy shrugged.

Mathers moved across to the fireplace and stood with his hands behind his back, studying the faces of his followers. "We need to determine," he said, "which is the more important, to work on the

translation of the gravestone legend or to chase after Chambers and Wilde, presuming that they have already rendered that text legible."

"How did your work at the Bibliotheque go today?" asked Cranwell.

"We ... we made a certain amount of progress," said Mathers stiffly.

"Ah! No luck eh?"

Mathers did not reply.

"We – that is to say, Samuel – did determine the type of code that it was," said Winters defensively.

"Yes." Mathers nodded. "Thank you, Monty. Yes, we did. It is indeed the same *form* of code that was used by Trithemius, as Crowley said. That is to say, each word on the engraving represents a single letter. Yet the time frame remains a mystery."

"So, using the Trithemius Code," said Cranwell, "What does the inscription say?"

"It just makes no sense," said Mathers, shaking his head. "The first line is some name or word I do not recognize, and I regret that we did not have time to get to the second line, though that is almost certain to be equally obtuse."

"What was the word?" asked Percy.

Mathers looked to Winters, who pulled a piece of paper from his pocket and looked at it. "It was 'Gurat', G.U.R.A.T," he spelled it out.

Leigh Cranwell picked up the Baedeker's and looked through the index. "Not a place listed here," he said, and put the book down again.

"It could be somebody's name," suggested Percy.

"Not Latin for anything, is it?" asked Winters. Mathers shook his head.

Alec was very conscious of Sarah's presence, as they sat together in the first class compartment of the train pulling out of Paris's Orléans station. They passed under the Ligne de Ceinture and past the large Hospital for Incurables. Near Choisy the line returned to the banks of the Seine.

Sarah sat beside him in the corner. Opposite them, with his back to the engine, sat an elderly curé, apparently absorbed in a book. In the far corner of the compartment was a fat, bald gentleman, in a dark brown sacque suit that seemed too small for him, peering through pince-nez spectacles at the fine print of a German newspaper. They faced a four hour journey to Orléans and then, on from there, another three hours to Limoge. It seemed a very long way yet Alec was somewhat consoled in having got them on an express train, since the journey by the local would have taken as long as twelve hours, depending upon the stops made.

"When do we get to where we are going?" asked Sarah. "And where are we going anyway?" She looked at Alec, her big green eyes wide, causing Alec's heart to miss a beat.

144

"We go to Limoge by way of Orléans, where we have to change trains," he said. "We change trains again when we get to Limoge, where we will have to stay overnight since it will be late when we arrive. Tomorrow morning, from Limoge we continue to Périgueux."

"Ah! You good people are traveling to Orléans?" exclaimed the cleric, lowering his book. "*Bonjour Monsieur, Madame.* Forgive me, but I could not help overhearing. And you must be English, are you not? I do speak a little of that language. I, too, am on my way to Orléans. I also change trains there. I am actually on my way to take up a new position at the little town of Varennes. You may or may not have heard of it?"

Alec sighed inwardly but smiled at the curé.

"I hope we are doing the right thing," said Mathers, his brow furrowed. He looked out of the window of the wagonette as it conveyed the small group over the cobblestone road toward the railway station. He would have preferred to have taken one of the less expensive, public, horse-drawn omnibuses but, with all of their luggage, it was impractical. He had reluctantly hired the hotel's carriage.

"You can still work on the code as we travel," said Cranwell. "I understand it is a very long journey so you will have plenty of time."

"Thank you, Leigh," said Mathers, with heavy sarcasm.

"No, you are doing the right thing, Samuel," said Winters. "Better the devil you know, and all that rot. We could spend a week or more here while you work on deciphering the thing, but my bet is that Chambers has already done so and we need to get on his tail."

"I do have to agree with the Reverend Winters," added Percy Purdy.

"Well, thank you all for your support ... I think!" said Mathers. "Monty, when we get to the station, you go ahead and get the tickets. Cranwell and Purdy can supervise the luggage."

"And you will be ..?" Winters's bushy eyebrows rose in question.

"I have to plan our itinerary," responded Mathers. He nodded acknowledgement to a party of three Germans who had recently booked into the Chopin Hôtel. Apparently they too were now departing Paris, he thought.

Almost an hour later the Golden Dawn party was safely ensconced in a first class carriage, bidding farewell to the environs of Paris. The train chugged slowly through the suburbs and out toward the more open countryside.

"It is obvious – presuming that Chambers has deciphered the message correctly – that Flamel's last resting place is, then, southwest of Paris," mused Mathers. "If I am finally able to read clearly what was written on Perenelle Flamel's grave marker, then we will proceed

directly to the place. If, for whatever reason, I am unable to, then we will pick up on Chambers and our renegade *Scriba* and allow them to lead us to the location."

"Will we be able to find Chambers?" asked Cranwell. "He is some hours ahead of us, and we only know that he is going to this Périgueux place. That could be a very extensive town."

"The Baedeker's says 29,611 inhabitants," interjected Percy.

"Yes." Mathers nodded. "But only four hotels. We can easily check on those, I think."

The conversation subsided. Winters opened an English newspaper he had found at the railway station and Cranwell became absorbed in a book he had brought with him. Percy sat looking out of the window at the passing scenery. Mathers drew out a pencil and notebook and started working on deciphering possibilities. It was more than an hour before anyone spoke.

"Do we have to change trains, Reverend Winters?" asked Percy.

Winters lowered his newspaper. "Three times," he said. "First time at Orléans, then at Tours, then not till Bordeaux."

Percy grunted and settled back in his seat, closing his eyes. He did not open them again until the train crossed the Loire, giving a good view of Orléans ahead on the right.

"Are we staying the night here?" Cranwell asked. "It is already late."

"No we are not," said Mathers firmly.

Winters opened his eyes wide. "We are not?" he repeated.

"There is a connecting train that leaves here at a little after four of the clock in the morning," said Mathers. "We will rest as best we can in the railway waiting room so that we are here ready to take that train."

No one commented.

"I shall miss the curé," said Sarah, smiling. "I think he thought we were husband and wife; he kept calling me Madame."

A smile hovered around Alec's mouth.

"He hardly stopped talking the whole time," continued Sarah. "Thank goodness he was continuing on a different line."

Since the French railways cooped up travelers in the waiting rooms, and did not allow them on the platforms until the train was ready to receive them, Alec and Sarah spent most of their waiting time between trains outside the Orléans station, stretching their legs. They walked along the rue de la République as far as the Place du Martroi, and then hailed a cab to take them back to the station. Eventually they were able to climb up into a carriage for the next leg of their journey to Limoge.

They had the compartment to themselves and looked out at the pleasant fields and farmsteads, until they passed through St. Cyr-en-Val, where the tracks entered the sterile marshy plateau of the Sologne.

"All right, Alec," said Sarah, turning to him with a smile. "Now that we're alone, tell me all about this mysterious code and how you deciphered it."

"It was not really me," he replied. "I got Daniel Parmington to take back to London with him a copy of what was on the gravestone, and to pass it on to my friend Jeremy Lowell. Apparently they worked on it together and came up with the answer."

"Wonderful," Sarah enthused.

"The stumbling block was the fact that it seemed to be a code invented by a man who was not even born when Flamel died."

"So how could Flamel, or his friend, have used it on Perenelle's gravestone?"

"Exactly. They could not have," said Alec. "But the answer turned out to be that the code had actually been invented by another alchemist named Raymond Lully, a hundred years before Flamel. The later supposed inventor, a German named Trithemius, had simply reworked the Lully code ... though not by much; it was still basically as Lully had devised it."

"Can you explain it to me?"

Alec was pleased that Sarah seemed so interested. "I will certainly try," he said, with a smile. He dug into his pocket and pulled out a notebook and a pencil.

"The code is based on a long list of words, each word representing a letter. There are words for every letter of the alphabet, going through the alphabet fourteen times, so there will be no duplication. When the words are put together they seem, at casual glance, to be sentences; though not all of them read as well as others. They seem, especially on such as a grave marker, to be simple religious aphorisms. But what gave the clue that it was a code was the fact that the words were Latin but didn't read as Latin sentences are constructed. That is what made Daniel and Jeremy think that they might simply be individual words strung together."

Sarah's brow wrinkled. "Can you give me an example, Alec?" she asked. "I think I see what you are saying but I'm not quite sure."

"Of course," he said. "Here. We will use the actual inscription." He wrote on a blank page of the notebook. "Here is the first line of the engraving: *Redemptor Invictus Sanctificare Angelicus Patefactum.* Roughly translated that means 'Redemptor Invincible Sanctifying Ages Manifests'. Now, if we go to the code words listed, we see that in the position of the first letter – the first list of equivalents - Redemptor is the equivalent of the letter G. In the position of the second letter, Invictus is the equivalent of the letter U. Similarly, Sanciticare is R, Angelicus is A and Patefactum is T. That spells Gurat. With five letters, it meant going through the alphabet five times."

"What is Gurat?"

"It turns out to be a small, rather remote village just north of a Roman road running between the towns of Périgueux and Saintes."

"How on earth did you find it?"

"Again friend Daniel is to be thanked," said Alec. "As I have mentioned, he is employed at the British Museum. Apparently this gave him access to some monstrous gazetteer that included even the smallest of villages. He traced the only Gurat in France."

Sarah sat forward. "This is fascinating, Alec. Now what about the second line?"

"Ah! Now that is even more interesting," said Alec. "It reads *Concedere Merum Gaudium Coniunctim-Sanctum*, which in English is 'Grant pure joyousness together with His Saints'."

"That sounds all right. As you say, a religious aphorism."

"Yes. But in fact once again each word represents a letter. Notice that *Coniunctim-Sanctum* is hyphenated. It translates as 'together with all His Saints'. And that phrase comes down to just one letter – the letter A."

"And the others?"

"It spells ARCA."

"Is that another little village?" asked Sarah.

"No."

She thought that Alec seemed pleased with himself.

"No," he continued. "*Arca* is Latin for 'coffin'. In fact for a coffin, chest, or box; especially *one that might contain some sort of treasure*!"

he Café de la Boule d'Or adjoined the hotel of the same name, where Alec and Sarah were staying the night in Limoge. It was a distance from the railway station but had been highly recommended by the station master. Alec guessed that the gentleman in question received a certain recompense from the hotel for making such recommendations to passengers, but was content to acquiesce.

The food at the café-restaurant was certainly excellent and they were glad to be able to relax after being cooped up in the train compartment for so many hours. It was late when they got to the hotel but the evening was warm and pleasant and, sitting on the *terrasse*, they sipped their coffee and watched the world go by.

"What time do we have to leave tomorrow, Alec?" asked Sarah.

"Not too early, I'm glad to say. The train departs at 9:38 a.m., according to the timetable."

"And what time do we get to Périgueux?"

"We should be there by early afternoon, I believe. I would like to push on from there for Gurat as soon as possible, though we may have to make an early start the next morning. That would then leave us plenty of time to find reasonable accommodation when we do get to Gurat. I doubt there are any hotels as such in the village, but I am sure there will be an inn or other place not too uncomfortable."

"I'm not worried," said Sarah. "I know how important this is to you, and to Inspector Kent, but I am almost feeling as though I am on holiday!" She smiled at him over the rim of her coffee cup. Then she became serious. "I have to keep reminding myself that this is all to do with a plot to kill the queen, not to mention the intentions of this Illuminati to take over the world."

"Indeed." Alec nodded his head, equally serious.

"When we get to Périgueux I will take the opportunity to write to Inspector Kent," continued Sarah. "I need to send a lengthy communication to bring him up to date, so far as I am able. I can then post it in Périgueux."

"Yes," said Alec. "The post offices in Paris were open until 9 p.m. I don't know if that will be the case in a small town but since we get there at noon there should be no problem." He put down his empty coffee cup. "I must send in my own report to the good Inspector." He looked across toward the clock on the Church of St. Pierre. "Perhaps we should be getting back to the hotel so that we can start on our reports?"

"The second line of our cryptogram seems almost as obscure as the first," said Mathers, sitting back in the railway compartment and stretching. "It reads *arca.*"

"Which is?" asked the Reverend Winters.

"It is Latin for 'coffin'," Mathers replied. "That would seem to be a good indication that we are on the right lines, though it does not help with the previous *gurat.*"

"I still think that must be Latin for something," said Winters.

"Not that I am aware."

"And you know all possible words in Latin?"

Mathers looked hard at the clergyman. "Sufficient, I would say."

"So what does it *mean*?" asked Winters. "It is one thing to have a translation of what was on the marker, but what does that translation mean? Where does it lead us?"

"So far it leads to Bordeaux," said Percy. "Look, we are coming into the Gare de Paris; the main station. I can see the river Garonne."

"I have been studying the map," said Leigh Cranwell, in a tone that seemed to the others to be one of disgust. "It seems to me that we have come the long way around. Are we not trying to get to Périgueux?"

"Yes. Of course," said Mathers. His brow furrowed. "What are you saying?"

Cranwell unwound one of the maps in the Baedeker's. "According to my calculations, we should have taken a more easterly branch line out of Orléans, which would have brought us down directly to Périgueux. I do not see that we needed to have come to Bordeaux at all."

There was a silence and they all looked toward Montague Winters.

"I – I ... You know my French is not good," he said. "Someone had talked about Bordeaux." He looked around, accusingly, at each of them. "They *are* tickets to Périgueux ... I was not sure what the ticket clerk in Paris was saying." He pulled out the railway tickets and looked at them. "They *are* to Périgueux. See?" He proffered them to Mathers, who did not look at them.

"Yes, they are," said Cranwell. "But by way of Bordeaux. We now have to make a connection to go north again."

"*Tempus fugit,*" muttered Mathers. "*Tempus fugit.*"

The Reading Room at the British Museum housed copies of all the many books ever published in England. Its huge dome had been built, forty years before, in what had been the central courtyard of the museum building. The design was by Sydney Smirke, brother of Sir Robert Smirke who built the main museum building. The famous round room was made of cast iron, concrete and glass, and incorporated the latest heating and ventilation systems. It was a masterpiece of mid-nineteenth century technology. The bookstacks surrounding it were also made of iron to take the great weight of the books and protect them against fire. In all they contained three miles of bookcases and twenty-five miles of shelves.

Daniel Parmington and his wife Georgina knew the Reading Room well, each having held a reader's ticket for many years and having spent unknown numbers of hours there. In fact, it was in the British Museum Reading Room that the Parmingtons had first met.

Daniel now bent over a large encyclopedia while, at his side, Georgina ran her finger down the lines of a gazetteer.

"You are right about Gurat," said Georgina, her gold-rimmed spectacles having settled on the end of her nose. "It is in Charente, which is one of the original eighty-three departments created in western France during the French Revolution. It says it is named after the Charente River."

Daniel nodded. "Pretty much what the encyclopedia says, my dear. But here is something of interest. It says that calcareous rock is predominant throughout the whole area."

Georgina looked away from her volume and stared at her husband. "What, pray, does the type of rock in the area have to do with anything?" she asked.

"Oh, sorry. It refers to 'its porous qualities and the relative facility with which it may be worked.' Apparently the whole area is full of caves, grottoes, subterranean passages and the like. It says that many have been inhabited by Man since prehistoric times."

Georgina leaned over and studied the book with her husband. "Look!" she pointed. "There are small and large subterranean churches there, and at Aubeterre and St. Emilion. They are 'considerably larger than the rock-hewn chapels at Bellevau, Brantome, Codon, Giget par Voeuil, Lyon and Mortagne.' How fascinating."

"'Rock-hewn chapels'," repeated Daniel. "Look - the Gurat Church is one of the subterranean ones. It is smaller than others but apparently in wonderful condition."

"There is a Romanesque parish church called Notre Dame only some 100 yards distant from the Gurat cave church. It was referred to in the thirteenth century."

"That is when Nicolas Flamel was around," said Daniel. Their eyes met.

Alec and Sarah spent much of the train journey simply staring at the puzzle

GURAT
———
ARCA

"Do you think the fact that Gurat is underlined is significant?" asked Sarah. "Or is it just a dividing line for the two Latin aphorisms?"

"With this sort of puzzle, I think *everything* is significant," said Alec, his eyes boring into the two simple words.

"Well, we know that Gurat is a village, and we know that Arca is a coffin or chest of some type." Sarah was thinking out loud.

"It makes me think of that children's riddle."

"Which one is that?"

Alec took his pencil and wrote in the note book. "It looks like this," he said.

NEATH = ON TOP
—————
NOT

Sarah studied it. "I don't get it," she finally said. "And this is a *children's* riddle?"

Alec laughed. "Well, it is the sort of children's riddle that I enjoyed as a child. Look, it actually reads: 'Not underneath is on top'. See?"

"Not *under*neath! Oh, I get it." Sarah laughed. "So simple when you know it."

Alec pointed at the original puzzle. "So I was wondering if that line meant that it should read 'Arca under Gurat'. What do you think?"

"Arca under Gurat. Hmm. So does that mean that the coffin is underneath the village? I suppose it has to be under something, but a whole village?"

"I know. It does not make sense and yet, in a weird way, it does."

Twenty minutes later the train was approaching Périgueux. Out of one side of the carriage was a magnificent view of the Cité, or medieval town. On the other side, somewhat higher in elevation, was the more modern town. Alec and Sarah gathered up their belongings.

"This place is steeped in history," said Alec. "I was reading about it. There are Roman fortifications and ruins of all sorts, châteaux from the tenth to the twelfth centuries, and there is the ancient Cathedral of St. Etienne ..."

"Where would be best to enquire about Gurat, do you think?" Sarah asked.

152

"Yes. That must be our priority," said Alec. "I would suggest first of all the stationmaster then, if he cannot help, perhaps we should proceed to the cathedral. What do you think?"

The stationmaster seemed to be willing to share only information on train times, destinations and fares, so the two of them left the railway station and took a horse-drawn omnibus over the cobblestone streets to the cathedral in the Cité.

"Gurat?" said the woman in response to their question. She was a sharp-faced, angular woman in charge of the souvenirs and informational leaflets at the cathedral. Her thin hair was pulled back in a bun and covered with a snood. Her plain black cheviot serge skirt was topped by a pale yellow percale shirt waist. Sensible black lace-up boots protruded from the hem of her skirt. "It is a bit early in the season for Gurat visitors, is it not?"

"Is it?" asked Alec, uncertainly.

"Oh, they are open all year 'round, mind you," she continued. "But the most people seem to come in late July and August, or so it seems to me."

"Might you tell us a little more about Gurat?" asked Sarah, smiling at the woman.

"What is to tell?" she said, busying herself with placing cathedral leaflets in racks and not returning the smile. "'Tis a church built down in the caves - S. George. Dates from the tenth century, they say. Not used much any more, though. They do have a regular Matins through the summer months, but there is no resident curé."

"Did you say, a church built down in the caves?" Alec's eyes grew large.

"Well, over at Dordogne is where most of 'em goes," she continued. "At Caudon the old parish church is deep down in the rock. That was originally a parish, was that. But then with the devastations of the companies all the inhabitants fled to Spain. Then there is the church of Our Lady of the Angels, at Mimet, which has got stalactites," she pronounce the word carefully, "coming down from the ceiling. And the church of S. Christophe at Peyre is all dug out of rock, they say."

"Is that all?" asked Sarah.

"Bless you, no. But I could spend all day listing of them." She rifled through the leaflets she had put out on display and pulled out one which she offered to Sarah.

"Thank you."

"To come back to Gurat?" urged Alec. "That is not, then, a village?"

"A village? Not that you would know," she said. "There is only a few houses nearby now, and a farm of sorts, but nothing of any consequence, to my mind."

"Oh." Sarah sounded deflated. "We were hoping to find an inn, or somewhere to stay."

"At Gurat? Bless you, no. Mind you, the farmhouse might be able to find you a bed for a night or two, though they don't make a habit of it, if you know what I mean."

They thanked the woman, bought a small souvenir of the cathedral, and then followed her directions toward a stable where she assured them they'd be able to hire a carriage to take them to Gurat.

"What were the 'devastations of the companies', she referred to?" asked Sarah, once they were out of earshot.

"I believe it took place in the middle of the fourteenth century," said Alec. "Not that I know much about it. But is it not interesting that we seem to keep coming back to that time period when Nicolas Flamel was alive?"

Sarah looked through the leaflet the woman had given her.

"It says 'The cave church at Gurat (Charente) adjoins a complex of grottoes in southwestern France. It is smaller than the enormous subterranean churches at St. Emilion and Aubeterre, but it is considerably larger than the rock-hewn chapels at Bellevau, Brantome, Codon, Giget par Voeuil, Lyon and Mortagne. The area abounds in grottoes and caves formed by water erosion, many of which have been inhabited by man since prehistoric times.' Oh, and here it says 'The village lies just north of the Roman road running between Périgueux and Saintes, and was on the pilgrimage route between Charroux and La Réole'."

They turned a corner onto a cobbled street that ended in a large wooden building outside of which stood a variety of horses, carts and carriages. Alec noted barouches, phaetons, broughams, dumpcarts, growlers, a baker's cart and a hearse, among others. A hand-painted sign on the front of the building proclaimed that horses could be rented for riding, carriages could be rented with or without a driver, and that all smithy services were available on the premises. The steady clanging of hammer against metal and the intensely smoking chimney attested to the latter. The pungent odor of horse droppings attested to the animals.

"These people should never have been allowed to contribute to the workings of the Illuminati."

Konrad Krüger, Franz von Knigge and Rikka Arndt stood behind a station hand-cart piled high with luggage, watching the Golden Dawn group as they in turn studied the list of train departures posted outside the booking office. "They have obviously allowed themselves to be misdirected and are even now arguing over the best course of action," said Krüger.

Indeed, the Reverend Montague Winters was gesticulating first at the departure board and then at the railway tracks, while Percy Purdy was stabbing a finger at the *Indicateur des Chemins de Fer,* which was published weekly by the various stations. Leigh Cranwell had invested in the rather more bulky *Livrets Chaix* for the Orléans line. He had his head down studying that, ignoring the others. Samuel MacGregor Mathers stood a little way distant from the others, his brows knit, his dark eyes flashing angrily.

The station master approached the group and managed to shepherd them into the waiting room, where they would be detained until the next train's imminent departure. The German group moved off and out of the Bordeaux station entrance, before they could be locked in with the others.

"Here is an interesting thing," said Winters, as the four of them settled into the carriage, ready for their three and a half hour journey to Périgueux.

"I have no interest in hearing it," said Mathers, snapping open a copy of the newspaper he had purchased at the station kiosk. "Kindly remain quiet and let us all meditate on what lesson we have learned from this fiasco."

"I say! Come on now, Samuel," remonstrated Winters.

"Ah! Ssh!" Mathers put his forefinger to his lips in a sign of silence. "Let us meditate."

Rather than meditate himself, Mathers buried himself in the newspaper and ignored his fellow travelers.

Percy looked out at the many picturesque castles along the banks of the Dordogne. They were reminders of the fact that they were retracing the route they had traveled coming into Bordeaux. The line moved north, through Libourne to Coutras, where it then parted company with the main branch and directed itself toward Périgueux.

It was almost an hour later when Leigh Cranwell looked up from his ever-present book and asked Winters "What was that interesting thing you remarked upon?"

Mathers grunted and rustled his newspaper. No one took any notice.

"Interesting thing?" said the clergyman, looking mystified. Then his face cleared. "Oh, yes. Right. Yes, I noticed that German group – the ones who were originally at our remarkable Hôtel Chopin for a day or so, back in Paris. You know, the two men and the blonde woman? They have, in fact, traveled the same route that we have taken ... even our little, er, detour through Bordeaux."

Mathers's newspaper dropped to his lap. "What? Are you sure about that, Monty?"

Winters nodded earnestly. "Oh, yes. Could not help but notice. Striking woman that."

"What is it, Samuel?" asked Percy.

Mathers folded his arms, and then lifted one hand to cup his chin. He didn't speak for a moment. Finally he gave a slight shake of his head. "No. Nothing. Probably pure coincidence. Never mind." But Percy thought he looked very uneasy.

Little was said for the rest of the journey.

Inspector Henry (Harry) Kent lived with his dog in a small semi-detached house off the Old Brompton Road, near Walham Green. His wife had been dead for a little over five years, passing from the consumption. They had had many happy years in the little house, with its white-painted picket fence – now very much in need of repainting – and its rose bushes around the front door. Harry Kent had adjusted to life alone, although he still greatly missed Nellie. Sometimes in the night, when he awoke and could not get back to sleep, he thought he could hear her hollow cough as she had lain in the second bedroom, her emaciated body sweating profusely with the intermittent fevers. Kent had been told that the best way to a cure was a sea voyage in a warm climate, with pure air and the most nutritious food. But that had been beyond his means.

He managed to keep a presentable home. Not that he often received visitors, for he had few close friends. His work had become his life and he kept himself busy to the extent of frequently carrying files home from the office, to work on in the evenings and at weekends.

Kent's mongrel terrier dog was named Gladstone, after the late Liberal Prime Minister. He had been found and adopted by the inspector ten years before, during Gladstone's third ministry. The two of them – Kent and Gladstone (the dog) – were a great comfort to each other.

"Gladstone, old man, I wish you could help me with this. There is a plot against Her Majesty and we just cannot determine when or how it will take place."

Gladstone listened attentively and wagged his tail thrice.

Kent spread out papers across the dining-room table. "We know who is the ringleader – our friend Dr. William Wynn Westcott – and we know who is doing his dirty work – Samuel Liddel MacGregor Mathers and company. But we have to wait for them to make some definite move, and I fear that that may not leave us time to re-act."

Gladstone's eyes did not leave his master's face.

"Pray God that Miss Sarah Wilde and Mister Alec Chambers can successfully discover the details of the plot and provide the information that will lead to its failure."

He moved papers around and Gladstone, feeling that his part in the proceedings was now over, lowered his head onto his front paws and closed his eyes.

Arthur Edward Waite had been born in the United States. His father had died when Arthur was young and his widowed mother then returned, with her son and a daughter, to her native England. At the age of sixteen, Arthur left school and became a clerk. With the death of his sister, in 1874, he found himself drawn to psychic research and by the time he was twenty-one he was studying various branches of the esoteric sciences at the Library of the British Museum. He was to become a prolific author. When he was nearly thirty he married Ada Lakeman – known as "Lucasta" – and in January of 1891 joined the Hermetic Order of the Golden Dawn. His writings were instrumental in encouraging a number of people to become Golden Dawn members, not least of them being Aleister Crowley.

"Ah! Here's Sacramentum Regis," said Maude Gomme, as Waite entered the ritual room. She drew on a cigarette that protruded from the end of an exceptionally long cigarette holder.

"Smoking in the ritual room?" asked Waite, looking about him to see that Maude was not the only one blowing smoke.

"Well, old boy, the ritual has not yet started you know," said Gustav Meyrick.

"I know." Waite wore a frown. "But smoking in the ritual room? Our esteemed leader ..."

"Our esteemed leader is nowhere near!" Aleister Crowley sauntered across the room to clap Waite on the shoulder, a gesture that did not sit well with the older man. "So I said, 'Let them smoke!' After all, if God hadn't wanted us to smoke he would never have produced tobacco, what?" He looked around, grinning. Several of those nearby chuckled at his joke.

"Even so ..."

"I would let it go, SR," said Arthur Machen, softly. "Crowley has not only taken the reins, he is turning the G.D. chariot in a new direction ... for good or ill."

"Frater Perdurabo!" John William Brodie-Innes, a leading member of the Hermetic Order of the Golden Dawn's Amen-Ra Temple in Edinburgh, who was visiting the London temple, called out to Crowley. "What will you do when Samuel returns?"

Crowley gave a careless wave of his hand and turned his back on Brodie-Innes. "You mean *if* he returns. We are not all the sheep that you and some others I could name seem to be. If SRMD wants loyalty from me, he first needs to show it *to* me. He cannot go waltzing off halfway around the world ..."

"The man has only gone across the channel, for pity's sake," interjected Waite.

"It is the same principle," snapped Crowley. "He has abandoned his duties and I have taken over. There has to be someone at the rudder, you know!"

There were murmurs from the members, who seemed almost equally split in their loyalties, thought Waite. He wrinkled his nose at the cigarette smoke.

White's Club, at 38 St. James's Street, was neither the most exclusive nor the most popular of gentlemen's clubs. Its membership, however, was restricted to those admitted by ballot. Candidates might be rejected by a small number of "black balls" or dissentient votes. Its entry fee and annual subscription were substantial; its cuisine attained a pitch of excellence unequalled by the most elaborate and expensive restaurants.

The three gentlemen at Lord Sunbury's table were all members of White's. They had dined well, in a private room, and now sat back with brandies at their elbows, passing the cigars.

"What is the word from the Foreign Office, Robert?" asked Sunbury, blowing a grey-blue smoke-ring into the air above the table and attempting to blow a second one through it.

Robert Cecil, Third Marquess of Salisbury, clipped the end of his cigar and lit it from the candelabra on the table. He was an expert in foreign affairs and in addition to being Prime Minister was also Secretary of State. He was going bald but recompensed himself with a large, bushy beard and mustache.

"All damned quiet at the moment, old boy. Very unsettling. Like waiting for the other shoe to drop, don't you know?"

The third member of the party was Herbrand Arthur Russell, 11th Duke of Bedford; a red-haired man with a large mustache and a smattering of freckles across the bridge of his nose. He held the office of Lord Lieutenant of Middlesex and was also President of the Zoological Society. He had been described as "a selfish, forbidding man with a highly developed sense of public duty and ducal responsibility." He lived a cold, aloof existence, isolated from the outside world by a mass of servants, sycophants, and an eleven mile wall around his estate.

"You have got to watch the Kaiser," he said, enigmatically, and lit his own cigar. "And don't forget the Anarchists!"

"I think we can all agree on that." Salisbury nodded.

"Anything going on that might be attributed to our friends the Illuminati?" asked Sunbury.

Salisbury snorted. "Rumors! Rumors and more rumors, Chetwynd. I would that our damned British government was half as well organized as are they."

Bedford studied the end of his cigar and said nothing.

"Let me throw out a name," persisted Sunbury. "Westcott. Dr. William Wynn Westcott."

"Is he not something in North East London?" asked Bedford.

Sunbury nodded. "The coroner for that district. Has an excellent medical reputation."

"Is he not tied-up with some Masonic group or something?"

"Not Masonic specifically," said Sunbury. "Though I don't doubt he is one of that fraternity. But his more serious connections are with the society known as the Hermetic Order of the Golden Dawn."

"I have heard of them," said Bedford. "Someone at the Zoological Society is a member. Run by some scoundrel who proclaims himself Count MacGregor of Glenstrae, or some such nonsense. Damned upstart!" He stroked his mustache. "Is not that actress of Bernard Shaw's a member?" he added.

"Florence Farr? Yes, I believe so," Salisbury replied.

"But this Dr. Westcott," persisted Sunbury. "Has his name come up in connection with anything ... untoward, Robert?"

"Untoward?" Salisbury sipped at his brandy. "Would you care to elaborate a little more, old boy? God knows, we all can act a little 'untoward' when in our cups, I would say." He laughed at his own humor.

"No." Sunbury shook his head and picked up his own brandy glass. "Never mind. You would know to what I alluded if, indeed, there were anything there." He looked at both men. "But do, I urge both of you, keep an eye open. I have reason to believe that Westcott is affiliated with the Illuminati and it is my belief that we are shortly to hear the most disturbing news where our beloved queen is concerned."

"A plot against Her Majesty?" Bedford's eyes opened wide.

"You might say, *another* plot against Her Majesty," said Salisbury. "Her Majesty has been inordinately blessed in her escapes to date. Are you saying that someone else is going to try to shoot her, Chetwynd?"

"The method I cannot say," answered Sunbury. "But yes, we have evidence that suggests a major plot is brewing that is centered on assassinating Her Majesty."

"Good Lord!" Bedford took a gulp of brandy.

"Care to elaborate, old man?" asked Salisbury.

"We have been watching our friend Westcott for some considerable time ..."

"Who is the 'we'?" interjected Bedford.

"Scotland Yard or, more specifically, the Special Branch of that establishment."

"Go on."

Sunbury drew on his cigar before continuing. "Westcott has been attending secret meetings at a house in Belgrave Square; a house known to be owned by a member of the Illuminati. Westcott's was a position of authority with this Golden Dawn but he withdrew, ostensibly because his occult studies interfered with his duties as coroner."

"You do not think that was actually the case?" asked Salisbury.

"No, we do not. We believe he withdrew because he needed to devote more time to the development of this plot against our sovereign. He has a keen 'second lieutenant' in this MacGregor Mathers, to whom he can leave the more mundane tasks while he concentrates on the necessary connections with higher authorities."

"How can we help?" Salisbury leaned forward, ignoring the growing ash on his cigar.

"I was hoping that perhaps you could especially, Robert," said Sunbury. "With the reach of the Foreign Office, we need to start connecting the dots of the Illuminati and pinpointing those overseas operatives working with the ones in the British Isles."

"Who is this Belgrave Square fella?" demanded Bedford.

Sunbury paused while the waiter refilled their brandy glasses and then retired. "It is Sir Charles Ridley."

"Good Lord! I have played cards with the man!" Salisbury ran a hand over his scalp.

"I have never spoken to him," said Bedford, "but did have a box next to his at last year's Ascot."

"Ridley has been making a number of excursions across the Channel, mainly to France, Germany, and Switzerland," Sunbury continued. "We need to know to whom he went – exact names and addresses if possible – and for how long he stayed. Can you provide that information, Robert?"

Salisbury pulled a small notebook and a silver pencil from the jacket of his evening dress suit. The ash from his cigar fell onto the tablecloth and he brushed it away. "I think we can manage that, Chetwynd," he said. "I will get on it right away."

"You might also pass-on the information to Jean-Paul Mignet of *La Sûreté Nationale*."

"The French?" Bedford seemed surprised.

"As a matter of fact," said Sunbury, "France's *La Sûreté Nationale* was founded in 1812 and was the inspiration for our own Scotland Yard.

Now our Colonel Jean-Paul Mignet is very much on top of things in his country, and is more than familiar with the actions of the Illuminati. He is part of the famed *Deuxième Bureau*."

Salisbury wrote down the name.

"I have it," he said.

Dr. William Wynn Westcott was not happy. He had been summoned to a meeting with the man known as Alpha. Alpha, together with a lady and two other gentlemen "of authority" in the Illuminati, sat at a large walnut library table, in an upstairs room of the house in Belgrave Square where Westcott had previously attended a meeting. Wine-red brocade covered the seats and backs of the chairs at the table. He was shown into the room by the white-haired butler, who then retired closing the heavy doors behind him. Westcott was not introduced to the other three but neither did he expect to be.

The doctor looked around. The room reflected the luxury of the rest of the house. It had a groin-vaulted ceiling and dark wainscoting paneled the walls to three-quarters of their height. Above that the white plaster was adorned with a multitude of coats of arms, stretching around the room. Westcott recognized them as belonging to the major figures of the Knights Templar. In the center of one wall was an Adams fireplace above which hung the seal of the Knights Templar: two armored figures astride a single horse, bearing red-crossed shields, with the motto *Sigillum Militum Xpisti* followed by a cross, in Latin and Greek characters. On the opposite wall to the fireplace was a large Diocletian window, heavily framed with deep green velvet draperies and a matching valance. It was a sunny day outside but it seemed to Westcott that little light came in through that window.

The four figures sat at one end of the table; a solitary chair was at the opposite end. With a glance at the figures, Westcott strode to the chair, uninvited, and sat down. Facing him, Alpha was to his left, with the woman beside him. Both Alpha and the man next to the woman were conservatively dressed in black cut-away frock coats, unobtrusive waistcoats and black cravats. The man at the extreme right, however, was more noticeable. He wore a silk-lined, charcoal grey, morning coat of finest twilled cashmere. His waistcoat was a golden satin brocade with black jet buttons, and his trousers black and grey fine-striped worsted. Westcott immediately recognized him as Sir Alfred Bowness, an industrialist from the north of England who was newly seated in the House of Lords. The man and woman in the center he did not recognize.

"We are delighted that you were able to join us, William," said Alpha. The others remained silent, studying him. Alpha glanced briefly toward the window. "Such a beautiful sunny day you have brought with you. We are indebted."

"What is it you want?" asked Westcott. He had up to now enjoyed a comfortable relationship with Alpha, even though the man was very much his superior in the hierarchy of the organization they both served. But now he sensed a change of attitude. He didn't understand why.

"The fine weather is almost certainly due to the fact that we are now entering June, the mid-year month, are we not?"

So that was it, thought Westcott. *They were concerned that the year was progressing without any sign of success on his part regarding the acquisition of the Flamel material. He would not be bullied,* he decided.

"Indeed," he said, nodding his head and, in turn, looking toward the window. "A good month to be in France, I would say." He casually crossed his legs.

"What do you mean?" The woman spoke with a French accent. She was blonde haired, dressed in an expensive princess-style polonaise gown of deep green, exposing a full yellow faille skirt decorated with pearls in a scallop design. Her bodice was of brown lace surmounted by a triple-stringed choker of pearls. Her brimmed brown velvet hat was trimmed in yellow lace, to match the skirt, with dyed yellow and brown ostrich plumes. Despite a veil, Westcott could see the steel-grey eyes boring into him and appraising him.

"I allude to the fact that my people are in that particular country at this very moment," said Westcott. "As you well know, Alpha." He looked hard at the leader.

Alpha nodded, thoughtfully. "Indeed I do, William. But the question might be, for how much longer will they remain there? Have they yet achieved that which they set out to do? These are the matters that concern us."

Bowness sat forward. The large and, Westcott considered, ostentatious diamond pin in his dark grey cravat flashed as it caught the light.

"Let us cut to the chase, as they say," he said. "Time is passing and we need the brass to set the wheels a-turning and get this show on the road."

In his turn, Westcott sat forward and looked directly at the Yorkshireman. "No one is more aware of the passing of time than am I," he said. "We are here dealing with an object that has been missing for nigh on five hundred years. In all that time many people have searched for it."

"So what makes you think that *you* can find it?" interjected the man seated next to the French woman. He had said nothing up till now but fixed his small, beady brown eyes on Westcott like a fox considering a rabbit before jumping upon it.

"Because we have a clue to which others were not privy," he said, staring down the man. "It was a clue that was in code and my man Mathers has broken that code and is even now in the act of accessing that which *we all*..." and here he looked hard at every one of his accusers "... which we all seek."

There was silence for several minutes. It was broken by Alpha asking "Have you confirmation that they have acquired it?"

163

Westcott thought that Alpha sounded a little more conciliatory.

"I expect that confirmation momentarily," he said, not meeting the other's eyes.

"Ah!" The woman expelled the breath she had been holding. "Then we still do not, in fact, have it?"

Westcott was steadfast. "I expect that confirmation momentarily," he repeated.

The four of them looked at him for what seemed to the doctor to be a very long time. Then Alpha stood up.

"Thank you for coming, William," he said, extending his hand in the direction of the door. "To expatiate more on this subject would be superfluous. You can see yourself out I am sure."

Westcott took his time standing and walking to the door. As he opened it and passed through it, he heard Alpha call after him.

"You will, of course, keep me apprised of the situation, will you not?"

He went out into the June sunshine and, eschewing a cab, decided to walk for a while.

*E*arly the next morning Alec hired a peddler's wagon – black, finely trimmed with yellow – into the rear of which he put their luggage. The seat was comfortable enough and the well-worn hood seemed serviceable. Alec's only concern was the right rear wheel which seemed to be slightly bent, however the farrier assured him that it would cause no trouble. The horse was an old but still lively blue roan mare.

Following the directions given to him at the smithy, Alec set out for Gurat, much of the way following the Isle River. The river was deeply entrenched and in many places they could see the walls of white limestone and crystalline rock glistening in the morning sunshine. The bent wheel gave the carriage an unusual swaying motion but they quickly got used to it and laughed about it.

The land was sparsely covered with trees; mainly oak woods – the source of the truffles for which the area was becoming famous. Pig rearing was one of the major industries, together with a variety of other livestock such as cattle, sheep and poultry.

They enjoyed a light lunch at Le Prieure Inn, just outside Chenehutte-Les-Tuffeaux, before pressing on toward Gurat, near the River Lizonne. It was already beginning to get dark when they eventually arrived there. Alec was tired but relieved as he turned the wagon into a bare square, at what he hoped was their destination.

There was a small, stone-built construction with a long hitching rail in front of it and a bell-cote at the far end. Two or three cottages stood independently farther along the road, and a larger farmhouse and barn set back a little from the road. Sarah pointed to it.

"That must be the place where we might be able to get lodging for the night," she said.

Alec indicated the small building in front of them. "And this must be the entrance to the church."

There was an old, much dilapidated, wooden sign on the side of the building, its writing scarcely discernable:

S. GEORGE
DIMANCHE MATINS
JUILLET, AOÛT, SEPTEMBRE

"Not very big," said Sarah.

"Don't forget that the church itself is underground," reminded Alec. "This must just be the entranceway."

"Do you think it may be locked?"

"We'll soon find out."

Alec jumped down and tied the horse to the hitching rail. He then handed down Sarah from the conveyance and together they made their way to the old wooden door. It was unlocked but stiff on its large iron hinges. Alec had to get his shoulder to the door before he could push it back far enough for Sarah to enter. She pulled in her crinoline skirts and thrust her way through.

It was dark inside and Alec spent some time searching around for some form of illumination. He eventually discovered a tall cupboard housing a multitude of paraffin oil lamps. None of them had much fuel but by repeatedly pouring from one into another, he eventually achieved one with a full reservoir. He was able to do this twice, so that each of them could have a lamp.

With the oil lamps lit and held aloft, Alec and Sarah looked around. There was a small and extremely dusty museum of sorts, with hand-written labels on the few exhibits. These all felt gritty when touched. Alec noted a pile of bones marked *ursus spelæus*, which the sign said had been found in a neighboring cave centuries before. The sign stated that it was a species of bear which lived in Europe during the Pleistocene age and became extinct at the beginning of the Last Glacial Maximum. There were also various ancient implements used in everyday life that had been found in the caves. Gurat had been used as a gunpowder plant during the French Revolution and, for a short time, as a foundry. There was another faded, hand-painted sign that claimed Gurat to be the smallest of the subterranean churches to be found in France. The community around the church had been at its height in the twelfth, thirteenth and fourteenth centuries but disappeared shortly afterward.

"Into the time of Nicholas Flamel," Alec remarked.

"Over there," said Sarah, pointing toward the top of a flight of wooden steps that descended into the clay-colored earth.

Alec led the way, pausing at the top of the steps which had a red silk rope tied across to prevent access.

"The hour is late," he said. "I think it might be best if we approach the farmhouse and see if we can, indeed, get lodging for the night. We can then

166

explore this to our heart's content in the morning ... and perhaps in better light. What do you think, Sarah?"

She smiled. "It is tantalizing to have finally got here but to run out of time to fully explore," she said. "But yes, you are right. We need to see about lodging."

"It is probably quite sturdy," Alec said the next morning, untying the red rope and testing the top wooden step with his foot. "For at least three months of the year it seems that they have regular visitors, so the steps should be sound. Nonetheless, I shall go first and we will proceed with caution."

It took them several minutes to descend the steps. Part of the way down the wooden stairs gave way to steps cut into the rock, which continued descending but curved to the left hugging the rough stone wall. They finally opened out into an oval area little more than ten feet square. The walls and floor were rough and it was difficult to tell whether they had been formed naturally or had been worked.

"Is this the bottom?" asked Sarah. She wrinkled her nose. The air smelled damp and musty.

"I presume so." Alec looked about him. "Look, there is an opening in the wall over there. Let's see where that leads."

They crossed to the doorless opening and peered through, shining their lanterns.

"Ah! The church proper," said Alec. "This, presumably, is at the rear of the nave."

"I don't see any seats for the congregation."

"In many of the older churches, the people stood throughout the ceremony," said Alec. "Though it may be that the chairs or pews are stored away for the winter months and only brought out for the three months they are open."

They advanced slowly through the area, across the uneven floor. Large support pillars had been carved to form a nave, chancel and apse. Sarah looked up toward the ceiling.

"The roof is very low," she said. "And it looks as though it has blackened from years of the burning of candles and lamps."

They came to a raised segment of the floor, with three steps up.

"This must be the chancel, or sanctuary," said Alec.

They stood at the foot of the steps and looked about them. The walls on either side had curved inward so that the area in front of them was narrower than that behind them. There were two vertical blocks of stone at the edge of the top steps; one on each side. Alec indicated them.

"I would guess that one is the pulpit and the other the lectern," he said.

Ahead was another rough step up, with a large horizontal block across behind it.

"The altar?" Sarah wondered aloud.

Alec nodded his head. "I would imagine so, yes," he said.

Beyond that, the ceiling sloped down sharply with the walls finally coming together, like the inside of the prow of a ship. They mounted the three steps and advanced toward the altar. Everything – steps, pulpit, lectern, and altar – seemed to have been carved out of the rock itself. The ceiling and walls may well have been naturally formed, thought Alec, but the rest of it had been fashioned with tools many centuries ago.

Sarah looked about her. "If this treasure-bearing coffin is *under* this church, does that mean we must dig up the floor?" she asked.

"A good question." He looked down. "But somehow I doubt it. It seems far too solid."

"Then where is it? There are very few places here for it to be."

"Just what I was thinking." Alec walked back and forth across the chancel. "Perhaps we were mistaken."

"Do you really think so?" she asked.

He shook his head. "No. I don't. It all seemed to fit together so well. I would swear that what we came up with was the only – or certainly the most likely – answer."

"What about the altar?" Sarah asked.

Alec moved forward and, going down on one knee, held the lantern close.

"It seems to be one solid block. Look. It has been decorated with fleurs-de-lis and oak leaves around the rim, with a verse between them."

"What does it say? Perhaps it's another clue."

They knelt side by side.

"*Ab ovo usque ad mala*," read Sarah. "What does that mean?"

"Now that is something I remember from my schooldays," Alec replied, with a smile. "It means 'From beginning to end,' as I recall."

They moved on to examine the pulpit, which had more fleurs-de-lis but no motto, and then the lectern. Here was another verse.

"*In hoc signo vinces.*" Sarah looked enquiringly at Alec.

"'By this sign you will conquer'" he said.

She was impressed. "You must have been a good little scholar."

He laughed. "Not really. It's just that certain things are drummed into your head and you never forget them."

Sarah returned to the altar and worked slowly along the front of it, closely examining the decorations. She continued along the side and then eased herself around the back.

"Alec! Look here!"

He sprang up from the lectern and rushed over to where she was holding up her lantern behind the altar. What he saw surprised him.

"I would suppose we do not need to try to dig up the floor after all," Sarah said.

There, against the back wall, where the sloping side walls came together, was a hole which obviously led to a lower level. The top rungs of a ladder protruded from the hole.

Sarah set down her lamp and, sitting on the ground, swung her legs over the edge.

"Wait a minute!" Alec cried. "We don't know what may be down there."

"Which is why I am going down the ladder," said Sarah. "The only way to find out what is down there is to go and look, would you not say?"

She smiled sweetly at him and he couldn't help but smile back.

"Well at least let me test the ladder first," he said.

"No problem. I can do that as I go down." And without waiting for his reply, Sarah put her foot on a rung and slowly started downward. She reached out and took the lantern with her as she disappeared below the floor level.

Alec hung out over the opening, his arm hanging down with his lantern, to try to give Sarah more light. She arrived at the bottom of the ladder and moved slightly away from it.

"What do you see?"

"Not too much," she called up after a pause. "It looks as though there is a small center area, with a long seat or some such, and then four doorways, or openings, to little rooms off this center section. It is really not at all spacious down here."

"Hold on. I'm coming down."

Alec's curiosity got the better of him and he followed Sarah down to the lower level. Stepping away from the ladder, he held up his lantern and looked around. It was as Sarah had described it. Together they moved into the rooms. Each of them was extremely small.

"I would guess that these were once cells for monks," said Alec.

"And what of the centre-piece?"

In the small area in the middle of the circle of cells was a stone bench. It was long and narrow; less than two feet in height. Like everything else, it seemed to be carved out of the rock itself.

"Probably where they sat to meditate, or whatever they did here," said Alec.

"Much too small to be a coffin."

"Agreed. No I think if we are to discover Monsieur Flamel's resting place it will have to be in the altar up above. Let's go back and have another look at that."

After a final look around, they ascended the ladder and returned to studying the large block that was the altar, and the other two blocks. They were absorbed in this when they were startled to hear a voice.

"So this is where all those clever clues have led us!"

Alec and Sarah looked up. Standing just inside the nave was Samuel MacGregor Mathers. Close behind him followed the Reverend Montague Winters, Leigh Cranwell, and Percy Purdy. Mathers was the only one holding a lantern.

Mathers looked about him. "Very cozy," he said. "How on earth did our erstwhile philosopher and alchemist find the place, I wonder?"

"No matter how he found it," growled Winters. "Where is his body?"

"And his papers," added Cranwell.

Alec got over his surprise at seeing the Golden Dawn group in the church. He stood up from where he was kneeling beside the lectern.

"I might have guessed that you would manifest yourself in this sanctuary, Mister Mathers." He waved his hand to indicate the small area. "However, as you may observe, there is precious little here to be discovered. It seems that our Nicholas Flamel has the last laugh."

"Surely not," exclaimed Cranwell.

"Have you discovered nothing?" Mathers demanded.

"You are too early, Mister Mathers," said Sarah. "We have not been here long ourselves."

"We stayed over-night in some atrocious little village ..." began Winters.

"La Chapelle-Grésignac," said Percy. "Actually quite a picturesque little place."

"Monty is right. It was atrocious!" snapped Mathers. "There was no inn and we had to sleep in some farmer's barn!"

"My sympathies," said Alec, with a smile. "No wonder you were up early."

"Well, we are here now," said Winters, advancing toward where Alec and Sarah stood. "I will take that lantern, Miss Wilde." He reached out his hand for it.

She pulled back. "I think not."

There was a click and a long-bladed knife appeared in the clergyman's hand. "And I think so," he said.

"Let him have it, Sarah," said Alec, moving close beside her.

Mathers and the others advanced to the chancel and then moved carefully between the altar, pulpit and lectern, looking closely at each.

"The altar must be the sarcophagus," determined Mathers.

"But there is no obvious lid," said Winters.

"'Obvious' is the operative word, I think." Mathers bent to peer more closely at the top edge.

Despite herself, Sarah leaned in also. "There is just the decoration around the top," she said.

Alec joined her. He still had his lantern, which he held close to the stonework.

"Here!" Winters thrust his lantern into the hands of Leigh Cranwell and began scraping at the top edge of the altar with the blade of his knife, which he still had in his hand. "This has a small chip out of it; enough to show that there is a separate top to the block."

They all gathered close. The clergyman ran his knife blade back and forth until they were able to see that he was correct; there was a crack that ran evenly along the front edge, blending in well with the decorations of the fleurs-de-lis carvings.

"It is a lid!" cried Cranwell.

"Then let us open it," said Mathers.

They all gathered along the front of the block and tried pushing at the top section. Nothing happened.

"It has been centuries," said Alec.

"Centuries indeed," agreed Mathers. "Try again."

Once more they pushed at the top of the slab.

"Keep up the pressure," grunted Winters. "I think I can feel it moving."

Suddenly, as though giving up the challenge, the top of the altar did start to slide, very slowly, toward the rear. Inch by inch it moved.

"Keep going!" Cranwell spoke through clenched teeth.

The more it moved, the easier it seemed to slide. The lid moved back until a sizeable hole was revealed. All three lanterns were swung over the top of the opening and all six pairs of eyes peered downward.

Chapter Sixteen

Sarah was surprised that there was only a slight musty odor that escaped the sarcophagus – for now she so thought of it, rather than as an altar. It was obviously a body that was inside, albeit an ancient skeleton with its flesh and much of its clothing turned to dust. What remained of its garments seemed to be a woollen *houppelande* with a once-fur collar. At one time the over-covering must have been a dark blue and she could see a fine silver thread in its weave. Short-toed black *poulaine-de-varlet* shoes were still in evidence, as was a time-ravaged, black, roundlet chaperon hat, which obscured the skull.

Sarah's eyes were drawn to the hands crossed on the chest. Two large rings were in evidence on the bones that had been fingers. Both rings were gold; one with a rich ruby set in its center and the other with a small circle of emeralds around a tiny pearl. About the figure's neck and resting on the chest was a heavy gold chain bearing a pendant with an intricate design on its face.

Montague Winters reached out and removed both rings, turning them over and over in his hands as he examined them.

"Monty, remove that pendant and pass it to me. It is of far more importance than some paltry gold rings," Mathers commanded.

The clergyman did as he was bid and then moved off to look again at the rings. Mathers, in his turn, studied the design on the pendant.

"What else is in there?" demanded Cranwell, his pince-nez quivering on his nose. "Are the papers there; the book?"

Mathers quickly returned his attention to the open coffin. "Indeed. Let us see, Leigh. Reach in and feel about."

"What?"

"Reach in and feel about. There is nothing obvious resting on, or lying alongside, the body. So reach down and feel underneath."

"Yes. Go on, Cranwell," added Winters.

"You do it," said the ferret-faced man in the cheap suit. "I am not digging about in the rotted flesh of a decaying corpse."

"It is five hundred year old detritus," snapped Mathers. "It is not going to bite you!"

"So why don't you do it?"

Mathers turned to Purdy. "Percy?"

Sarah thought that the young man's pale face turned even paler in the lantern light. He pushed back a lock of black hair from his forehead and looked quickly from side to side, as though seeking escape. His deep brown eyes were wide and he repeatedly licked his full lips.

"Er, me, Mister Mathers? . . . Samuel?"

Mathers caught the pleading look in his eyes.

"Oh, never mind! Monty, you do it."

"What?!"

"You do seem to fancy those rings, Monty, if I am not mistaken."

"Damn you!" The clergyman marched over to the stone sarcophagus and thrust his hands down inside. With his eyes screwed up, he seemed to grope around for a while before standing again and dusting dark grey powder from his hands.

"Nothing," he said.

There was a long silence.

"No – no papers? No book?" asked Cranwell, in a querulous voice.

"But there has to be," said Mathers, moving to look down again into the interior.

Alec laughed. "It seems you have all been on a wild goose chase," he said. "Nicholas Flamel has certainly led you on a merry dance across Europe."

"Who was it who said that the book would be in his grave?" asked Sarah.

"What? Why – why it is common knowledge," protested Mathers.

"Common knowledge, or just a rumor?" Alec persisted.

"Everything I have seen – everything I have read – has pointed to this."

Sarah felt sympathetic, despite all that they had been through. "Perhaps it, too, has fallen to ashes," she said.

Mathers and Alec both shook their heads.

"No," said Mathers. "A parchment book would not have completely disintegrated in just a few centuries, locked in a stone container such as this."

"And there would have been other material too," said Cranwell. "All on vellum. All should have survived."

"Well, at least you have found something," said Alec to Mathers. "May I have a look at the pendant?"

Mathers handed it to him and turned away. "Let me think," he said.

"What is this?" Percy let out a shout. He had been hanging back, toward the rear wall. He pointed excitedly down at the ground behind the altar. "Look! There is a ladder down to another level."

Alec and Sarah both spoke together. "Yes. We have been down there."

Mathers moved to Percy's side, looked at the protruding end of the ladder, and then turned to Alec. "You have been down there? And you did not think to mention it?"

Alec laughed. "Your arrival was not exactly a neighborly visit, Mathers."

"Far from it," added Sarah.

"What is down there?"

"Actually," said Alec, "there is nothing of interest. Much like this coffin here. There are four bare cells, apparently once used by monks. That is all."

Mathers pointed to Purdy. "Percy, you and Leigh go down and see. Look very carefully. Do not miss anything."

With a sigh, Purdy took one of the lanterns and, with Cranwell close behind him, started down the ladder.

While they waited, Alec and Sarah studied the pendant before handing it back to Mathers. "Interesting symbols," was Alec's only comment. Mathers did not respond.

Some minutes later Purdy and Cranwell climbed back out of the hole.

"Just as Chambers said," mumbled Cranwell. "Empty cells set around in a circle."

"Nothing else?" asked Mathers. "Did you look carefully?"

"Yes, we did," Purdy replied. "As Mister Cranwell just said, empty cells set around a central bench; probably for meditation or prayer, or some such. I have read of other such retreats in caves in this area. I do not think it is anything special."

"Hrmph! So our whole expedition has been for nought." Mathers brow knitted.

Sarah heard him mutter "Now what am I to tell him?" She wondered to whom he referred.

Mathers stood deep in thought for several minutes before turning to Winters.

"Monty. Be so good as to quickly descend that ladder and verify that indeed there is nothing of note below us."

The clergyman seemed about to protest, Sarah thought, but decided to do as instructed. He took the lantern from Purdy and climbed down the ladder. Everyone stood and waited until he returned. He said nothing; merely nodded to Mathers.

"Very well. Mister Chambers; Miss Wilde, I must ask you now to descend the ladder."

"What?" Alec was puzzled. "Why? You have just had three of your group verify that nothing is down there."

"Exactly," said Mathers. "Nothing is down there so you can interfere with nothing. Now, please descend the ladder."

Winters, sensing what his leader had in mind, once again flicked open his long-bladed knife and waved it in the air in the direction of the two. With his head high, Alec led Sarah to the ladder and gave her a lantern. He then followed her as she moved down to the cave below. Once on the ground, they looked up at the faces peering down at them.

"Now kindly move away from the ladder," commanded Mathers.

Even as they did as he bid, Winters and Cranwell pulled up the ladder out of the hole, leaving them without a means to get out again.

"Hey! Wait! What are you doing?" Alec cried, though he knew exactly what Mathers had in mind.

"You can make use of that meditation bench," came Mathers's voice. "You will have plenty of time to think about how you have interfered once too often with the affairs of the Hermetic Order of the Golden Dawn. I bid you farewell."

Alec and Sarah heard the four men move off, away from the entry hole and, presumably, out of the cave church.

The Reverend Montague Winters led the way up the steps, carrying one of the lanterns. Leigh Cranwell was behind him, followed by Percy Purdy. MacGregor Mathers brought up the rear, carrying the other lantern. Suddenly the group came to a halt, causing Mathers almost to run into Percy's back.

"What is the delay?" Mathers called. "Monty! Why have you stopped?"

"*Ich bin erfreut Sie zu sehen, Herr Mathers. Erinnern Sie sich meiner?*"

"What the ..!"

"Do not say that you do not remember us."

Mathers saw, looking down at him over the top railing, the large round face of one of the Germans who had been staying at the Hôtel Chopin and who, according to Monty, had been traveling across France in concert with his own group.

"Who are you? What do you want?" Mathers demanded.

"*Sehr verbunden.* May I present myself – formally? I am Konrad Krüger. My associate here ..." A thin, pale face peered momentarily over the top of the railing and then disappeared again. "This is Herr Franz von Knigge." A woman's face came into view and looked down at him, disdainfully, before also disappearing. "And our associate Madame Rikka Arndt. I believe we know all of your group."

"So I repeat," said Mathers. "What do you want?"

"Want? Why the same as your good self, V. H. Frater S' Rhioghail Mo Dhream." He used Mathers's magical motto. "Have you in fact retrieved the little book of Nicholas Flamel? Was it, indeed, in the coffin underneath Gurat?"

Mathers was unsettled. How did this obnoxious little German know all these facts? "Let us proceed up to your level, where we can talk," he said. His arm was beginning to tire, holding up the lantern.

"*Nein.* I think not. I think it much preferable that we all come down to your level, Herr Mathers."

After a moment Mathers responded. "And I think it infinitely more preferable that we ascend to the top, where you are."

The blonde woman again appeared at the top, alongside her companion. There was no mistaking what she held in her hand. It was a Remington Double-Repeating Deringer pistol. Its twin barrels were pointing at him.

"Oh, very well. Come down if you must." Mathers turned and retraced his steps down to the small open area at the bottom of the stairs. The others turned and followed him, in turn followed by the three Germans. They were soon all gathered in the small area there.

"How do we get out of here?" Sarah was not really expecting an answer.

Alec looked about him and then looked upward again.

"I would guess that the ceiling is about ten feet above us. Too high for me to jump up and grasp the edge of the hole. And the walls are rough but not rough enough to give any sort of hand or foothold."

"There is nothing here we can use to get up there." Sarah looked around again, knowing that the area was bare. "We cannot even move the meditation bench over, to stand on. Not that it would be anywhere near high enough."

"Well now, I wonder." Alec walked over to look at the long slab of stone. "Not anywhere near high enough; you are right. But it is a very long bench."

"What do you mean?"

"Let us have a good look at it." He took the lantern and got down on his knees to closely examine the block. "Don't forget that we thought the altar was solid, only to find that it had a lid. Perhaps this is also like that."

"But even if it is, what good will it do us?"

"Just a minute. I have got the beginnings of an idea ... *if* it has a lid."

He ran his fingers all around the top of the block, carefully feeling for any differences on the surface. "It does not feel hopeful," he said.

"Let me try." Sarah knelt beside him and gently ran her fingers around it. "There is enough roughness that you really cannot tell whether there is a lid or if it is just the coarse irregularity of the sides." She sighed.

"Well, let us just assume, for the moment, that there is a lid and let us try to move it." He knelt up and placed his hands on the side of the stone block, close to the top. "Put your hands close to mine. We might be able to pivot it with all of our energies at one point."

She did as he said and they pushed. They strained for a long time before giving up.

"It's no use. I cannot keep it up," said Sarah, dropping down again to sit on the ground against the block. "It must be solid."

"We need something to push against," said Alec. He looked behind him. "The wall of the nearest cell is just too far back. That would help a lot if I could brace myself and push from the wall."

Sarah sat up. "Wait a minute, Alec. We might be able to."

She moved over and sat with her back against the wall, her legs extended in front of her. "Now, you push against my feet."

He saw at once what she meant. He knelt in front of the stone block, edging back till his feet were up against Sarah's; his heels to her toes and his toes to her heels. "Try to keep your legs straight and take the strain," he said. She nodded. He placed his hands on the edge of the block.

"Now!" she cried.

Alec pushed. He found that with Sarah's feet firmly in place behind him, he was able to use them to thrust against and push much more strongly.

"I-I don't know how much more strain I can take!" she cried.

Just then the top of the meditation bench moved.

"Now that is so much better." Herr Krüger smiled around at everyone gathered in the modest space at the foot of the steps, the monocle gleaming in his eye. Madame Arndt still held her Derringer steady, pointing at Mathers.

"I have already told you," said Mathers, annunciating carefully as though speaking to someone unfamiliar with the English language, even though the Germans had proven their fluency. "There was nothing there. The sarcophagus – coffin, if you prefer – held only the remains of the alchemist. There were no papers; no book. All of our hopes were dashed."

"That is so very hard to believe."

"Nonetheless, it is the truth."

"Next you will be asking all of us to empty our pockets!" said Winters, barely holding his anger in check.

"That might not be such a bad idea," said the blonde woman, a slight smile on her overly-cosmetic face.

"Where is the coffin, exactly?" It was the first time the other male – von Knigge – had spoken. His face was unsmiling.

"It is the altar," said Leigh Cranwell. "The top slid back. It was a lid."

Krüger nodded. "That makes sense," he said.

"So what is the next move?" asked Mathers.

"It's this!"

Percy Purdy suddenly dashed forward and attempted to snatch the gun from Rikka Arndt's hand. She half turned to him. There was a loud report and Percy stopped short. He stood for a brief moment stock still, and then fell to the floor.

"Christ in Heaven!" Winters started forward but was pushed to one side by Mathers.

"Percy! Percy, you damned fool!" He dropped to his knees and rolled the young man onto his back. A large hole was evident in the middle of Percy's chest; blood flowing and spreading across his shirt. "Percy!" Mathers' voice was a sob.

Cranwell quickly moved forward and joined Mathers. He soon looked up at the others. "He is dead."

"No!" Mathers grabbed the body and tried to lift it, pulling it to him.

"*Das ist zu viel,*" said Krüger to the woman. "*Warum haben Sie das gethan?*"

She shrugged. "*Er hat mich überrascht. Das thut mir leid.*" She lowered the gun and slid it into her reticule.

Krüger removed his monocle, polished it on a handkerchief, and returned it to his eye. "Well, that is regrettable," he said. "But it is the brashness of youth. We will leave you with your companion." He made to leave the area, pausing only to pick up the lantern that sat beside Mathers, who was rocking Percy in his arms.

Monty Winters moved across to stand in front of the entry to the underground church.

"Just one minute, you dirty Boche!" he said, through clenched teeth. "Where do you think you are going?"

Krüger looked around at the three Golden Dawn members. "Where we are going, and why, is none of your concern, my friend. You look after your leader." He indicated Mathers, who still knelt with Percy's body in his arms. "He needs you at this moment. I would advise taking him up into the sunlight, away from this subterranean sepulcher."

For a long moment no one moved. Then Leigh Cranwell nodded to Winters and the two of them drew Mathers to his feet. They carried the body of Percy up the steep steps, toward the outside world.

The Germans watched them go. Then they turned and went through the small doorway into the nave of Gurat's S. George church.

"I knew it!" Alec was excited. After a pause for them both to get their breath, the two of them pushed the lid back until it fell away from the base.

"Too long, narrow, and short to be another coffin," said Sarah.

"I know ..."

"What? What is it, Alec?" She had moved to go around the far side of the stone box but stopped when she realized that Alec was standing transfixed, gazing down into the dark interior. She moved back beside him, where he now held the lantern high.

"Is – is that what I think it is?" she asked.

For answer Alec handed her the lantern to hold and then got back down on his knees and reached inside. He lifted up an armful of parchment sheets, together with an ancient leather-bound book.

"If I am not mistaken, this is the 'treasure' in the coffin beneath Gurat. This is Nicholas Flamel's notebook and his working papers."

"We still have to get out of here," Sarah said.

"I know."

He had retrieved all of the antique vellum; there was only the one book with it. He had everything stacked neatly on the floor beside the stone container. He looked up at her. "You remember what Mathers said, as he left?"

She shook her head.

"He said 'make use of that meditation bench.' Well, I am going to."

Alec pulled the stone lid upright, to stand on its end. It was narrow so, despite being made of stone, he was able to walk it over into a position beneath the outlet hole. He slowly leaned the top end until it touched the wall. The lid now leaned at a steep angle.

"What was that?" Sarah asked, looking upward.

"What?"

"I thought I heard a sound. I don't know ... like a muffled bang somewhere."

Alec shrugged. "Perhaps a falling rock." He indicated the sloping stone lid. "Now, if I can get up onto the top edge of that – perhaps I can take a run at it, or something – and if I can balance there for just a moment, then I think I can spring upward from there and reach the rim of the hole."

She studied the height of the lid against the wall and the distance from there to the roof.

"Do you really think you can?" She sounded doubtful, he thought.

"*If* I can get up to the top edge," he repeated. "The trouble is, the lid needs to be leaning at a steep angle to get me high enough. A lesser angle would be easier to climb but then I would be left with too much height to make-up in the jump."

"It is very clever," she said.

He smiled. "Only if it works."

He moved back to the far wall and then turned and faced the sloping slab of stone. He took a deep breath and ran forward as fast as he could. He jumped forward to give himself impetus and then tried to continue running up the steep slope. He got three-quarters of the way up the incline before his feet slipped and he fell and rolled down to the bottom again.

"Are you all right, Alec?" Sarah rushed to his side.

"Yes. Yes, thanks. Just a bit winded," he said. He got to his feet. "If at first you don't succeed ..."

On his second try, Alec made it to the top and managed to balance on the narrow edge, tight up against the wall. The roughness of the wall helped in that he was able to find enough texture to hold on and keep his balance. He looked up at the hole, beckoning from above. From where he was perched it didn't seem too far away. Knowing he couldn't maintain his unsteady stance for long, so tight against the surface of the wall, he bent his knees slightly and then leapt upward. The tips of his fingers grasped the edge of the hole. For a moment he hung there, his legs swinging in the air. Then his fingers let go and he crashed to the ground.

"Oh, Alec!" Sarah was there immediately.

He was tempted to stay longer than was necessary, savoring her touch as she pulled his head onto her skirt and brushed his hair out of his eyes. But he knew that he had to keep the momentum going. He gave her hand a squeeze and struggled to his feet.

"Next time!" he said grimly.

Next time he repeated the previous success. He got to the top of the sloping stone lid, bent his knees and leapt, and again managed to grasp the edge of the hole. Once again his legs swung out but he hung on.

"Don't fall!" cried Sarah. She ran forward and pulled on the sloping stone lid. She managed to get it standing upright, on its end. Alec swung his legs over and was able to rest the tip of one of his shoes on the top edge of the lid, so much closer to the hole now that it was upright. It gave him the respite he needed. With effort he started to pull himself upward. He stuck his feet forward till they encountered the wall and he was able to find enough protrusions in the roughness of the surface to assist him in his movement up. Soon he was able to get his elbows and then his chest over the edge. After that it took no time to climb through the hole. He lay panting on the floor of the upper chamber.

"Oh, well done, Alec!" Sarah clapped her hands.

A few minutes later Alec had lowered the ladder and the two of them were finally, once more, able to stand up behind the altar-coffin that housed Nicholas Flamel. Alec's arms cradled the precious documents while Sarah held the lantern. They came out from behind the altar and were surprised to find other people entering the nave from the far doorway at the back.

Both parties – Alec and Sarah and the three Germans – stood for a moment studying each other. Then the Germans advanced.

"So! There are more of you."

"Who are you?" asked Alec.

Krüger waved a dismissive hand. "That is of no consequence, my friend. Let us just say that we have come here, at some inconvenience, to collect that which I believe you hold, so firmly, in your arms. Monsieur Flamel's legacy, I believe?"

"Oh, no!" cried Sarah. "Not after all we have been through. No, Alec. Don't let them have it."

"Don't worry, Sarah. We have earned this. I am not giving it away – not to anyone, for any reason."

The short, fat German snapped his fingers and the tall blonde woman stepped forward. She produced the Remington Deringer from her reticule and leveled it at Alec. "Here is a good reason, *mein junger Freund*," she said.

"Hmm. Yes, you are very persuasive." Alec thought desperately. He wondered what had happened to Mathers and the others. Surely they would have encountered these people when they left? But apparently they had missed one another.

"Place the papers on the altar there and step back," said Krüger. "There is no reason for anyone to get hurt."

Still Alec hesitated.

"Do it!" hissed Rikka.

Alec shrugged. He had no choice. He turned and carefully laid the papers on the slab, as instructed.

"Franz!" Krüger summoned his friend but kept his eyes on Alec.

Von Knigge moved carefully around his two companions and advanced on the altar. As he reached out to take up the vellum, Alec grabbed his thin shoulders and spun him around between himself and the tall woman. "Down, Sarah!" he yelled.

Sarah dived down behind the lectern. A shot rang out and von Knigge gave a cry. He had been hit in the arm. Alec thrust him to one side and joined Sarah behind the stone pillar.

"What now?" Sarah gasped.

"I'm not sure," said Alec. "It was an impulse move!"

There came a click.

"She is out of bullets!" Alec couldn't believe what he heard. "There are supposed to be two shots in that gun. She must have fired one somewhere else." He stood up.

"Nobody move!" A commanding, English-sounding voice rang out.

"Daniel! Daniel Parmington, as I live and breathe!" Alec thought he'd never in his life been so glad to see anyone. He took Sarah's hand and raised her up.

"And Georgina," said another voice, and Daniel's wife appeared beside her husband, in the doorway. Both of them held revolvers: his a Metropolitan Police Webley six-shot and hers a Webley Bulldog No. 2 five-shot. Both Krüger and Rikka raised their hands. Von Knigge clutched his arm and moved out to join his companions.

"What on earth are you two doing here?" asked Alec.

There was a twinkle in Daniel's eye. "We were looking at the almanac and thought that this part of France looked most salubrious at this time of year," he said.

Alec, Sarah, Daniel and Georgina sat around the breakfast table in the dining room of the Hôtel du Commerce, on the Place du Quatre-Septembre in Périgueux. They had enjoyed a good night's rest and a stabilizing breakfast.

"Coming here must have been the best decision you have ever made – from our point of view," said Alec. "But I thought you were tied-in to work at the British Museum?"

"So I was," replied Daniel. He glanced at his wife. "But Georgina's 'woman's intuition' or whatever you want to call it, clicked in. She felt very strongly that you were in some sort of need and then we could not get here fast enough. I forget what excuse I gave them at the B.M. but they were quite decent about it. You may recall, last year Baron Ferdinand de Rothschild bequeathed to the Museum the glittering contents from his Smoking Room at Waddesdon Manor?"

"Yes, I remember *The Times* carrying a number of articles about it," said Alec.

"Well, there are almost three hundred pieces of *objets d'art et de vertu*, including jewellery, plate, enamel, carvings, glass, and maiolica," continued Daniel. "The Baron's will was quite specific that the collection should go into a special room to be named the Waddesdon Bequest Room, quite separate from the rest of the museum. If not, then the bequest would be void. Lot of old fuss and nonsense, if you ask me."

"So with everyone running around and re-arranging things," put in Georgina, "Daniel was able to slip away and not be missed."

"Wonderful!" Sarah's eyes were bright as she clapped her hands together. But then her eyes darkened and she sat forward in her chair. "But, you know, I can't help worrying about the Germans. Silly, isn't it?"

"No, it's not," said Alec reaching out and taking her hand. "They will be all right, I promise you."

"But we made them go down into that horrible little area below the altar and we took away the ladder." She looked hard at Alec. "You and I know only too well what that is like."

He shrugged. "They had a lantern, and we did bandage the arm of that thin one before he descended."

"I must admit, there was probably not too much oil left in the lantern," said Daniel. "I'm sure they were soon in the dark. But then again, we did report it to the authorities as soon as we got here, as you know."

Georgina nodded. "Yes we did. And they said they would get out to Gurat right away. I would not give the Germans any more thought, Sarah."

She tried to smile. "I'm sure you are right. You did put the lid back on the bench down there, Alec, so I doubt they'll even think of getting out the way we did. Not that I can imagine the fat one – or any of them – running up an inclined slab and leaping for the roof the way you managed to do." She smiled at him. Then she looked at the clock on the mantelpiece over the fireplace in the dining room. "Oh, look at the time! I do want to send a telegraph to Inspector Kent and let him know the latest developments." She stood up. "Why don't I walk along to the telegraph office – I saw that there is one just down the road from here – and I'll rejoin you immediately?"

Alec stood also. "I'll come with you."

"No." She put a hand on his arm. "It's all right, Alec. There's no need. You and the Parmingtons have a lot to catch up on. I will be back before you know it."

Alec and the Parmingtons moved out to sit on the terrace and enjoy the sunshine. By the time Alec had gone over the details of their encounters with MacGregor Mathers and his group – the departure from Paris, their travel to Périgueux and then on to Gurat, their imprisonment in the lower level and then their escape – it was already past the luncheon hour. Alec and Daniel both withdrew their pocket watches at the same time, and examined them.

"Sarah's been gone an awfully long time," said Alec.

"Just what I was thinking," agreed Daniel.

"She has probably stopped off to do some shopping," suggested Georgina.

"No. No, that would not be Sarah," said Alec. He got to his feet. "I'm a little concerned. I think I'll check on the telegraph office myself."

"Why don't we all go." It was a statement rather than a question and Daniel and Georgina both got to their feet. The three of them moved out and along the street, the way that Sarah had gone.

The elderly man at the telegraph office – armed with a hearing trumpet and a pair of pince-nez glasses with one of the lenses cracked – remembered a young lady coming in to send a cable to London but had no idea where she had gone from there. He insisted on coming out from behind his counter and looking about the small shop to be sure she wasn't still there. Alec thanked him – three times into the ear trumpet – and left.

"Where could she have gone?"

Alec was obviously greatly worried, noted Daniel. "I could think of one or two possibilities," he said. "But as you said with the shopping idea, they just are not Sarah."

The three of them had started to walk back toward the hotel when Alec suddenly broke away and ran forward, shouting to a cab driver. Daniel and Georgina looked at one another.

"Do we need a hansom?" asked Georgina. Her husband shrugged.

The cab driver seemed loathe to halt but eventually, to Alec's shouts and demands, he pulled his horse over to the side of the road and stopped. As the Parmingtons caught up with Alec, they were surprised to see that there was a man already in the cab.

"Where is Sarah, Cranwell?" Alec was demanding of the occupant.

"I have no idea what they may have done with Miss Wilde," Leigh Cranwell replied, looking extremely uncomfortable. "I wanted no part of it myself, which is why I am leaving."

"Going where?"

"Why back to London, of course. Back to sanity!"

"You must have some idea of what is happening. Where did you leave Mathers?" Alec demanded.

"En route ... somewhere. I have no idea where."

"And he was taking Miss Wilde with him? Why?"

"He and the Reverend Winters. Yes. I have no idea what was in their minds, but I strongly suspected that it was not savory. Which is why I elected to leave."

Alec looked about him hopelessly. Daniel stepped forward.

"You don't know me, Cranwell, but I've heard of you. Now! If you want to proceed to wherever you are going ..."

"I am on my way to the railway station. I am assured that there is a train shortly departing for Bordeaux. I intend to be on it, if you gentlemen will kindly step aside."

"Just one more thing," said Alec. "A clue. Just give us a clue, I beg of you. You say you want no further part of Mathers's abduction of Miss Wilde but, unless you later want to be taken as an accomplice to this act, I suggest you let me have at least some clue as to their whereabouts or their intended destination."

Cranwell consulted his watch and then banged the roof of the cab with his cane. "St. Ursule," he said to Alec. "The convent. That's the last place I know we went. Enquire there."

The cab driver cracked his whip and the horse lurched forward, taking Cranwell on his way. Alec dejectedly looked at the Parmingtons.

"St. Ursule Convent," mused Daniel. "Why would they take her there, I wonder?"

"Unless this Cranwell gentleman was just throwing out a name to be rid of us," suggested Georgina.

"Hmm. Let us hope not." Alec straightened up. "Very well – let us proceed to the convent and see what we can find."

The Lady Superior greeted the trio courteously but without warmth. The convent, on the rue de Bordeaux, seemed a busy place with the interview constantly interrupted by nuns who, to Alec's eyes, looked harried, nervous and servile. For the most part their habits seemed worn and soiled.

"You must excuse us," said Mother Marie, "but we are, as I am sure you noticed, adjacent to the Hospice and much of our work has to do with those in that facility; so much as our coffers allow."

"I will not take any more of your time than needs be," Alec assured her.

"I have seen naught of your young lady," she said. "But from the description you paint of this Monsieur Mathers and his ecclesiastical friend, yes, I have had an encounter with them. They came here late in the evening, two nights ago, bringing with them a young man who was mortally wounded. He had been shot and Monsieur Mathers was unable – or unwilling – to provide me with details of the shooting."

"Were the police notified?" asked Daniel.

It seemed to Alec that the Lady avoided a direct answer.

"The young man was immediately moved across to the hospice and I left word that all enquiries should go there. This would, of course, include any police questions. I do not know where the matter ended since, as you see, we are greatly pressured and have not the luxury, nor the depth of coffers, to indulge in whims and fancies."

"Whims and fancies!" exclaimed Georgina.

"Now if you will excuse me?" The Lady rose and, without waiting for an answer, moved off toward the door.

"Do you know where Mister Mathers and the Reverend Winters were intending to go?" called Alec. "Did they leave an address?"

Mother Marie paused briefly. "It was none of my business to enquire," she said, and swept from the room.

"Well!" Georgina breathed deeply. "She was not as full of Christian charity as one might have expected."

188

"There's more to this than meets the eye." Daniel stroked his walrus mustache and squinted at his surroundings.

"I did notice the emphasis that the good lady placed on the word 'coffers', as she spoke. She mentioned them twice. It's my guess that money might well have changed hands from Mathers to her."

"You may be right."

"So where does this leave us?" asked Georgina.

"On a cold trail, I'm afraid."

They moved out toward the exit. As they were about to leave the convent Alec paused and addressed the young nun who held the door open for them.

"Your pardon, Sister. If I may ask, were you on duty here two nights ago, when two gentlemen brought in a young man who had been shot?"

"Why, yes. Yes, I was."

"And did you see these gentlemen off the premises, as you are with us?"

"Indeed. It is my duty."

Alec smiled his most charming smile at the young nun. "We need to find these gentlemen and have no idea where they might have gone. What can you tell me of where they went when they left here? In which direction did they go?"

The nun glanced hastily behind her and then moved close to Alec. Softly she said, "They had arrived in a hackney carriage and a third gentleman waited in it while the other two bore the injured gentleman inside here. When they left I did happen to overhear the directions given to the driver."

Alec's heart jumped. "Yes? Wonderful. I – we – would be most grateful if you would let us know what was said."

"They directed the carriage to drive to the Hôtel du Périgord, on the place du Palais-de Justice. It is not far from here."

"The Hôtel du Périgord? Thank you, sister. Thank you so much."

"God bless you, sir."

Sarah was furious with herself. How could she have allowed herself to be kidnapped by MacGregor Mathers and the odious Montague Winters? Kidnapped! It was a harsh word but the only appropriate one for what had taken place. She had hardly stepped out of the telegraph office, and had her head down as she closed her reticule, when she was grasped from behind and bundled into a waiting hansom. Who knew what this dubious duo had in mind for her?

She looked about her. She was in the sitting area of a hotel suite. The two men in question were standing by the door, deep in conversation, though she couldn't hear what they were saying. From the dull, and in many areas dusty,

furnishings and décor it was obviously a cheap hotel. She was not surprised, being well acquainted with MacGregor Mathers' parsimonious ways.

There was a knock at the door. Both men were startled.

"Quickly! Take her into the bedroom and make sure she keeps quiet," snapped Mathers.

Before Sarah knew what was happening, the bushy-eyebrowed clergyman had pulled her to her feet and half-dragged her into the next room, kicking the door shut behind them. His large hand closed over her mouth and Sarah found it difficult even to breathe. From the other side of the door she heard voices and thrilled when she thought she could make out Alec's voice. But it was all indistinct and Winters pulled her away from the vicinity of the door and pinned her against the wall beside the small window.

"Say anything – try to scream – and I'll break your neck!" Winters spoke through clenched teeth. Sarah felt truly frightened of the man and believed him capable of carrying out his threat.

There was some arguing going on, by the sound of it, and another man's voice ... possibly Daniel Parmington, she thought? Then Sarah heard the outside door close and heard Mathers' footsteps approaching the bedroom. As the door opened and he came in, Winters released his hand from her mouth. She gulped in a mouthful of air.

"What's happening?" asked the clergyman.

"Surprisingly, that was our Mister Chambers," replied Mathers. "I must give the man credit, he is persistent. The Lord knows how he found out we were staying here."

"But you were going to send a message to him anyway, were you not?" asked Winters.

"Indeed I was. But in my own time." Mathers turned and went back into the sitting area, beckoning for the two of them to follow him.

Winters pushed Sarah down into the chair she had previously occupied and joined Mathers by the door once again.

"I put my proposition to Chambers," said Mathers. "He was only too anxious to comply." He glanced at Sarah. "It would seem he cares more for the welfare of Miss Wilde than he does for the importance and value of that which he holds."

"You are holding me to ransom," accused Sarah. "You want those Flamel documents we found."

Mathers smiled a thin smile. "Let us face it, Miss Wilde. Those documents are of no use to you."

"How would you know?" she snapped.

Winters' eyebrows went up.

"Let me rephrase that," said Mathers. "They are of far more value to me than they are to you."

"I hope Alec refused you!"

"Not at all." Mathers looked smug. "He was only too happy to comply. He is even now returning to his lodging to get the papers and we will then meet – though not here, I hasten to add – and, shall I say, do business."

Sarah's shoulders sagged. So after all they had been through, Mathers was to gain the Flamel material ... and all because she had been incautious enough to let herself fall into the hands of these instruments of the Illuminati. What would Inspector Kent think, she wondered?

Inspector Henry Kent hurried along the corridor and then stopped to tap on the door of his superior.

"Enter!"

Lord Sunbury was seated at his desk behind an open folder of dog-eared papers. He glanced up and waved Kent to a seat.

"Be with you in a moment, Kent."

The Inspector perched himself on the edge of the chair and, from beneath lowered eyebrows, looked about him. He envied his lordship the size and comfort of his office, though admitted to himself that he was happy in his own little space, with all of his own mementoes scattered about him.

Lord Sunbury closed the folder and sat back in his upholstered chair, looking hard at the Inspector. "You said you had a telegraph?"

"Yes, your lordship. Here it is." He half rose and passed the paper across the desk. "Briefly, it says that Miss Wilde and Mister Chambers have found the Flamel documents – ahead of the Mathers group – and are preparing to return home. Er, here to London, that is."

"Quite so." Lord Sunbury studied the cable, sitting forward and steepling his fingers. "It does not give any great details."

"No, your Lordship. These new-fangled telegraphs are damnably – begging your lordship's pardon – extremely expensive and all overseas personnel are instructed to use as much brevity as possible."

"I see." He continued to study the document. "It says 'details follow'."

"Yes, your lordship. That will be by regular post. Miss Wilde is good at that; she always gives a very complete report. It should not be long in coming, though the Frog – the *French* postal service doesn't seem to have the speed of the Royal Mail, sir."

"No. Of course not." He continued to study the cable, though Kent knew it was brief. Finally Lord Sunbury again sat back in his chair. "What will the Golden Dawn people do now, one wonders? I cannot imagine our Mister Mathers giving up too easily."

"No, sir. That would not be like him. We will, of course, keep an eye on him ... him and his cronies. A close eye, sir. Just as soon as he sets foot back on English soil."

"Very well. Oh, and let me know when Miss Wilde's more substantial report arrives. Was there anything else?"

"No m'lord. I just thought you should see the cable right away."

"Quite right, Kent. Quite right." He opened the file folder again, effectively dismissing the Inspector.

"Do you really mean to hand over everything to this Mathers character?" asked Daniel.

The Flamel material was spread out on the floor of Alec's room at the hotel. He and both the Parmingtons were down on their knees examining it. There were sheets of vellum covered in Flamel's spidery handwriting and annotated with hand-colored illustrations, notes and comments. Most of it was difficult to read and would require a great deal of study. Sitting in the midst of the papers was a small book. As he picked it up, Alex at first surmised that its front cover was missing, along with some of the first pages.

"You know, I do believe this is actually the other half of my notebook ... the one that Winters stole," he said, looking closely at it. "That was missing what I thought to be the back cover, but I do believe that these are actually two halves of a whole."

"So, as I said, are you going to hand over everything to Mathers?" Daniel persisted.

Alec shrugged. "I don't see that I have any choice. This is the ransom for Sarah's safe return."

"When do we get her back?" asked Georgina.

"Tomorrow at noon. Near the Cathedral of St. Front. That's at the old Place Marcillac, not too far from the convent. On the west of the cathedral, adjoining it, is a curious tower, said to be the oldest in France. The Vésone tower; one hundred ninety-seven feet tall, Baedeker says. It dates from the eleventh century, apparently. We will meet at the foot of the tower."

"Why there?"

"I insisted it be somewhere public. That was the only place I could think of, since we are really not familiar with Périgueux."

"Not to belabor the point," said Daniel. "But *everything*? Why don't you hang onto the book? They don't know just what is here, do they?"

"No, they don't," Alec admitted. "But I don't know ... I gave my word to hand over all of it."

There was a silence. Then Georgina reached out and patted his hand.

"Sarah is the most important thing," she said.

"Here is a thought," said Daniel. "You might give them all this ... but exchange it for Sarah *and* your original Flamel book. It might be worth a try. I mean, obviously that notebook – or that part of it – didn't contain what they needed or they wouldn't have continued looking for all this other material. So they probably have no further use for it."

"I'd say it would be worth a try," agreed Georgina. "Then you would at least have your book back."

"Hmm. Perhaps you're right."

"We could send a messenger around to them at their hotel, to alert them; so that they bring it with them tomorrow."

It was a dull, overcast day with almost continual drizzle. Alec pulled his top coat closely about him and stepped down from the hansom cab. He had insisted on going alone to the rendezvous, despite protests from Daniel and Georgina. He did not want to run any risk of alarming Mathers and consequently losing Sarah.

Alec looked up at the structure before him. The tower was wide and reminded him, vaguely, of Windsor Castle's Round Tower. The Vésone Tower had once been part of a Gallo-Roman temple dedicated to the town's tutelary goddess. Perhaps he should pray to that goddess, he thought.

He had chosen the Tower thinking it would be busy with people but it seemed that the weather had deterred the tourists. He hurried over to the entranceway; a pair of massive, iron-bound, oak doors, only one of which was open. He followed an elderly couple and a family of three into the structure, paid an admission fee and received a brochure. He was instructed, by an officious, uniformed man with a red face and Kaiser-style mustache, to follow the signs and not to touch anything.

Alec looked around, his eyes adjusting to the dim light. It didn't take him long to spot Mathers, Winters, and Sarah standing together studying an ancient cannon; a pile of cannon balls alongside it. Mathers looked up as he hurried over to the three of them.

"Good day, Mister Chambers.".

"Did you bring the Flamel material?" demanded Winters.

"Monty! Please," said Mathers.

The clergyman grunted and fixed his dark eyes on Alec, his fearsome eyebrows lowered.

"Alec!" Sarah's face lit up and she moved toward him, but Winters grasped her arm and held on to it.

"We do have – business – to take care of, I believe?" said Mathers, smiling.

Alec carried a brown leather Victoria club bag, which he now laid down on the pedestal of the cannon. He opened the top of it enough to allow Mathers and Winters to peer inside. Alec reached in and extracted a sheet of vellum, which he handed to Mathers.

"An example of what is here," he said.

193

"Is this the entirety of the cache?" Mathers asked, looking closely at the parchment.

"It is."

"And it includes the notebook? Or should I say, the second half of the notebook?"

Alec nodded. "And you are returning my original one – the first half, if you will – as agreed?"

Mathers produced the leather-bound book from the pocket of his frock coat.

Alec took it from him and handed Mathers the bag. Then Alec turned to Winters.

"Unhand the lady," he said.

Sarah wrenched her arm free and moved to Alec's side.

"Most charming," sneered the clergyman.

"Come, Monty," said Mathers. Without looking any further at Alec or Sarah, he strode off toward the entrance. Winters, with a contemptuous grunt, followed after him.

Evening

*I*t was a warm August day in London, with the promise of cloudless blue skies for the next several days. One of the new horseless electric cabs, introduced to London streets just two years before, turned off Marylebone Road, glided quietly down Harley Street, and disappeared in the direction of Wigmore Street. Shortly thereafter a more traditional hansom also turned onto Harley Street and deposited its passenger at the door of No. 7 before continuing on its way.

The tall man, with a military-style mustache and military bearing, tapped on the door with his cane and was admitted by a serving man. Having given the servant his top hat, gloves and cane, he was shown into the consulting rooms of Dr. William Wynn Westcott.

"Ah, Mathers! Right on time. Good. Take a seat."

Mathers sat down and looked about him. It was the first time he had been to Dr. Westcott's rooms in Harley Street, despite having known the man for a number of years. Westcott usually summoned him to his club, or picked him up in his carriage while promenading in Hyde Park.

"A beautiful day," Mathers remarked.

"We are not here to discuss the weather," said Westcott. He sat behind a large polished mahogany desk, bare of everything but a single sheet of paper. Mathers tried to make out the armorial bearings on the top of the sheet, but without closer scrutiny was unable to.

The room was richly decorated, as one would expect of a man of Dr. Westcott's caliber. The focus of each of three walls was an ornately framed print of an alchemical illustration. The fourth wall contained a fireplace with a mantel above it on which rested a Louis XVI gilt bronze and marble Raingo Fres clock.

Westcott had been described by his associates as "docile, scholarly, industrious, and addicted to regalia and histrionics." He was unmarried

197

and, so far as anyone knew, had no lady friends, in the ordinarily accepted sense, though he had enjoyed a great many "platonic" friendships with female initiates of the Hermetic Order of the Golden Dawn. He had a receding forehead and a full beard, turning white. He was a head shorter than Mathers but stocky, and possessed deep-set eyes that tended to hold the attention of those he addressed.

In 1881, Dr. Westcott had become Deputy Coroner for Hoxton, and during the early 1890's he was appointed Coroner for the North-East of London. In 1875 he had joined the Masonic Lodge at Crewkerne and in 1878 took a two years' hiatus at Hendon, in order to study Qabalah and other metaphysical subjects. Sometime between 1865 and 1878 he had been admitted to Societas Rosicruciana in Anglia (S.R.I.A.) which was open only to high-grade Freemasons. He became Magus of S.R.I.A. in 1890 and also became Worshipful Master of the Research Lodge Quatuor Comati. Prior to the formation of the Golden Dawn, Westcott had been a member of the Esoteric Section of Madame Helena Blavatski's Theosophical Society. Mathers had also been a Theosophical Society member, though not of the inner Esoteric Section. He was keenly aware of Westcott's background.

"It is now a week into August," said Westcott.

"I am aware ..."

"Please do not interrupt, Samuel. It is now a full week into August. I will admit to being pleasantly surprised that you were able to locate the Flamel tomb – when so many others were not – and to retrieve the all-important book and papers of his experiments. But the days pass. Where exactly do we stand with implementing these experiments?"

Mathers cleared his throat. "I have Leigh Cranwell working on the project day and night. I would go so far as to say that he is making excellent progress ..."

"Meaning what, exactly?"

"He has already produced some gold. A very small amount, without question. But, I hasten to say, it is gold. Pure gold."

"So Flamel's reputation is valid?"

"It would appear so, sir, yes."

"And where do we go from here?"

"I believe that by the end of this month we will have sufficient of the precious metal to advance to the next step ... setting in motion the purchase and transportation of the necessary items for the completion of our mission."

Westcott nodded and, sliding open a drawer in the desk, reached in and removed a Cuban cigar. He snipped the end of it, lit it, and puffed out clouds of smoke. He seemed not to notice Mathers' action of holding a silk handkerchief to his nose and mouth.

"By the end of the month, you say?"

"Indubitably."

"Hmm." Westcott seemed to consider what his visitor had said. He glanced down at the letter on the surface of the desk and then rose to his feet. He walked over to the window, looking out on Harley Street, and stood there reflectively.

"Will that be sufficient time?" he asked.

"I am certain." Mathers also rose and moved to stand beside Westcott.

"One of the joys of this location ... of my rooms here," said Westcott, "is the tranquility and the privacy."

"The privacy?"

Westcott nodded. "Look out at the street, Samuel. Not a soul to be seen. No hawkers, no vagrants, no casual passersby. In a word, no possibility of anyone 'untoward,' let us say, watching who comes and goes here."

Mathers nodded, looking out of the window. "I see what you mean," he said.

A hansom cab pulled up opposite and a white-haired old lady descended. As the cab pulled away she walked, leaning heavily on a cane, to ring the bell of the house. The door opened and she went inside.

"All professional people here," continued Westcott. "Mostly of the medical profession. With occasional patients visiting, as you see."

Mathers nodded.

"Yes. I am at ease here, Samuel."

On entering the house, the white-haired old lady turned into the first room on the right. It was bare of furniture but for a small table in the heavily-curtained window. Two wooden chairs were at the table. In a corner of the room, on a wooden box, rested a lit gas ring bearing a steaming kettle of water. There was a teapot and some cups and saucers beside it on the top of the box. A red-faced, overweight man sat on one of the chairs, looking out of the window as best he could through the thick net curtains.

The woman straightened up, raised her hands, and removed both bonnet and a white-hair wig, revealing red curls beneath.

"How is it going, William?" she asked.

The man glanced back at her, over his shoulder. "Quiet, Sarah, very quiet," he said. "There's just been one visitor who went in about a 'alf hour ago."

She put down the wig and bonnet, slipped a shawl off her shoulders, and took a seat on the other chair.

"Who was the visitor?" she asked. "Anyone we know?"

"You tell me," responded William. "Look! There 'e is now; comin' out."

Sarah sharply drew in her breath when she saw Samuel Mathers step out of the house opposite. He looked left and right, as though hoping to see a cab, and then strode off down the road toward Wigmore Street.

"'Oo's 'e?" William asked.

"That, my friend, is Samuel Lidell MacGregor Mathers. None other."

"G'orn!" He carefully wrote down the details in a notebook on the table.

"You be off now, for your lunch, William," she said. "I can handle this for a while. You must need a break."

He got up and stretched. "Can't say I'm not ready."

When William had left, and she was alone, Sarah looked back through the notebook to see what other activity had taken place. There had been no other visitors that morning.

"Enter!" Lord Sunbury didn't look up immediately when he heard the knock at his door. When he did glance up it was to acknowledge Inspector Kent.

"I have brought a visitor with me, m'lord."

The inspector stepped aside and Alec came into the room.

"Ah! Chambers. Good to see you. Come along in."

Alec and Inspector Kent came into the room and took the seats indicated to them.

"Now what brings you here, Chambers?" Sunbury asked, adjusting his monocle.

"Firstly, my lord, I felt that I should apologize for allowing the Flamel material to fall into the enemy's hands; especially after the effort we all put into getting it." Alec had been worrying about the outcome of their exploits for some time and had finally prevailed upon Inspector Kent to let him speak directly to Lord Sunbury. "I gave you my word that I would get to the Flamel papers before Mister Mathers and his group, and to retrieve them for you. I failed."

"Not at all." Lord Sunbury sat back in his chair, unconsciously reaching out to finger a well-worn pocket Petrarch on a corner of the desk. "You did precisely what had been asked of you ... you located the tomb of Nicholas Flamel and you discovered the cache of papers. If you hadn't found them, they would still be missing, since Mathers had no idea where they were hidden. That they then ended up in his hands is certainly unfortunate but not reprehensible on your part. As I understand it, it was an act of gallantry of yours to save a young lady in distress."

"Well, that is true, my lord," Alec admitted, feeling a little relieved. "Yet when I reflect on your words before I left England, I wonder if that 'gallantry,' as you so kindly put it, should even have been considered by myself bearing in mind the end goal of the Illuminati."

"To my mind, Chambers, gallantry is always to be considered. But you are quite right to bring up the machinations of the Illuminati." He turned to Inspector Kent. "Tell me, inspector, what is the latest on that front?"

"They do seem to be proceeding apace, m'lord. But on the positive side we are keeping up with them, as it were. We know what progress they are making in their gold processing and are carefully observing where they might be going from there."

"Have we yet established the exact mode of assassination they have in mind for our sovereign?"

"Unfortunately no, m'lord. Though it does seem to be something which will involve a number of people. In other words, it's not just a single assassin."

"Hmm. That does open up a number of possibilities."

"May I ask, my lord, what happened to the three Germans we left in Gurat?" asked Alec. "Were they apprehended?"

"Ah!" Lord Sunbury leaned forward and rested his arms on the desk top. "Kent; you may like to answer that."

"Yes, m'lord." The inspector faced Alec. "We had a report from Inspector Jean-Paul Mignet, of France's *La Sûreté Nationale.* He said that there was no sign of anyone in the cellar under the church at Gurat."

"What?" Alec was amazed. "I can't believe they got out of there. Did this French policeman say how they might have got away?"

"We did discuss it, sir," said Kent. "Inspector Mignet said that these three Germans were not unknown to him. In fact, he has been trying to catch up with them for quite some time."

"And what did he say about their escape?"

"The only possibility he could suggest was that the tall thin one might have climbed on the shoulders of the woman ..."

"What?" exclaimed Lord Sunbury.

Inspector Kent couldn't help smiling. "Yes, m'lord. This was quite an Amazon of a woman, if I may say so. By far the action figure of the three. Inspector Mignet acknowledges that."

"How on earth would he get onto her shoulders?" asked Alec.

"Mignet suggests that the shorter fat one allowed him to climb up by way of his back. When up on her shoulders, the man would probably be able to reach the edge of the entryway."

"Good Lord!" Sunbury shook his head in disbelief.

Alec also smiled. "Whatever works, I suppose. I would have loved to have seen it."

"Mignet says there has been no sign of the trio since then," said Kent.

"Hmm." There was a pause.

"There is a particular gentleman we have under surveillance," said Lord Sunbury finally, now addressing Alec. "He has a house in Belgravia.

Mathers's superior, Dr. William Wynn Westcott, has been called there on a number of occasions, presumably for instructions. Are you familiar with Westcott, Chambers?"

"I have heard the name, your lordship. In connection with the Golden Dawn, if I'm not mistaken."

"Precisely. He was one of the founding members of that order but in recent years has stepped back out of the limelight." Lord Sunbury looked hard at Alec. "Have you ever met the man?"

"No, sir."

"As I thought. Good. It occurred to me that here might be an opportunity to make inroads on the organization."

"My lord?"

Lord Sunbury got to his feet and started to pace the floor as he spoke. "The Prime Minster – the Marquess of Salisbury – is a good friend of mine. He is also Secretary of State for Foreign Affairs, as you may or may not know. In that capacity I asked him to do a little background research for me. Among the items he came up with was the fact that our Dr. Westcott is in possession of a library of some size; a library dedicated to alchemical and other occult works. This, it seems, was originally owned by a Kenneth MacKenzie, who died at an early age in 1886. MacKenzie apparently died in mysterious circumstances but we need not concern ourselves with that at this time."

"You say Westcott now has this library?" asked Alec.

Sunbury nodded. "Indeed he has. The library had come down to MacKenzie from one Frederick Hockley, MacKenzie's mentor. Hockley died the year before MacKenzie, by the way."

"Might one wonder where Hockley got the library?" queried Alec.

Sunbury nodded. He stopped pacing and stood with his back to the large window, looking at the two men. He ran a hand over his well-groomed steel-grey hair and then clasped his hands behind his back. "Good question. Apparently he had inherited these rare books from a Sigismund Bacstrom, a Scotsman who founded a magical group in Scotland. Presumably this Bacstrom had amassed the works over a long period of time. Now, ostensibly the library – by the time it had passed into friend Westcott's hands – was supposed to be for the use of members of the Hermetic Order of the Golden Dawn, yet few if any members have ever seen one volume from that collection."

"But it does exist?"

"Undoubtedly. Mathers certainly knows of it and is possibly one of the few who has, in the past at least, had access to it."

"Where, m'lord, does this feature in our investigation and what would be Mister Chambers's part in it?" asked the Inspector.

"I was just coming to that. Thank you for keeping me on track, inspector." Sunbury moved back to the desk and sat down again. He leaned toward Alec. "You have a book shop, Mister Chambers. You are also familiar, as we know, with much of this occult material that is somewhat Greek to the rest of us!"

Kent chuckled. "*Very* much Greek to me, m'lord. Yes, indeed."

"You also frequent estate sales and auctions, as I understand it," Sunbury continued. "I think, therefore, that you could speak on common terms with Dr. Westcott on these matters. Would you not agree?"

Alec stroked his chin. "Well, yes, my lord. I suppose I could. So what do you have in mind? How may I help?"

"I think we can arrange for you to meet Dr. Westcott; to make his acquaintance. I can arrange for a friend to introduce you ... casually, of course. I will leave the details up to you but I would like you to ingratiate yourself there – if that is not too strong a term – to the point where you might be our eyes and ears."

Alec thought for a moment. "But although I have not met him, my lord, I would imagine that he is aware of me, through Mister Mathers."

"Ah, yes." Lord Sunbury nodded thoughtfully. "Yes, I'm sure you're right. However, we have it on Inspector Kent's authority that Mathers did not report anything of your activities in the search for Flamel's tomb. Westcott is not even aware that you traveled to the Continent. Apparently Mathers wanted Dr. Westcott to believe that he did everything on his own initiative, from decoding the enigmatic gravestone to the actual discovery of the Flamel papers."

Alec chuckled. "Yes, I can believe that of him."

"So, although Westcott may know of your bookshop this can only add to his willingness to converse with you on matters metaphysical, surely?"

"But would he not be extremely guarded as to the plans of the Illuminati, my lord?"

"Oh, I'm sure he would be. I would expect nothing less. But once you have gained his trust, there is always the possibility that he might let slip just the smallest item of interest to us. It may be nothing major in and of itself, but enough to give us a clue, a hint, to bigger and better things. What do you say, Mister Chambers?"

"Why yes, of course, my lord. I will be happy to do anything I can. This strikes me as very much a long shot, but if it can produce anything advancing us I shall be more than happy to do it."

"Well done, Chambers. Well done."

"Ah, Westcott!" Sir Geoffrey Burlington-Smythe, two large books tucked under one arm, waved to Wynn Westcott.

The men were at the estate sale of the late Colonel Sir Joshua Tavistock, explorer and collector. Tavistock's collection ranged from South American butterflies to Japanese *shunga* art, by way of African pottery and Middle Eastern mosaics.

"Burlington-Smythe," acknowledged Westcott, dryly. "What've you got there?"

Sir Geoffrey indicated the books under his arm. "These? Oh, just a two-volume set on the history of Freemasonry. Not especially rare but I don't have them so I thought I would avail myself. Find anything interesting yourself?"

Westcott grunted. "Not so far. Tavistock supposedly had a rare gem on Tika spider divination in the Cameroons, but I haven't found it yet. Damnably badly organized, this sale. Can't find anything!"

"You should speak to my young friend here," said Sir Geoffrey.

Alec had been standing respectfully behind him but now moved forward slightly.

Westcott peered at Alec. "You one of the organizers?" he demanded. "I have one or two words to say to you, young fella."

"No, no." Sir Geoffrey waved his free hand. "This is a friend of mine ... Mister Alec Chambers. He knows a thing or two about books."

"Does he now?" Westcott looked more interested.

"Yes, sir," said Alec. "I have a bookshop just off the Charing Cross Road."

Westcott screwed up his eyes and rubbed his chin, as though to nudge his memory. "Chambers? Chambers? Have I been to your shop?"

"No sir, I don't believe so."

"Chambers? Wait a minute." It was as though full memory came back to him and Alec wondered just how full that was. "Yes. Wasn't your shop broken into a month or so back? I think I read about it in *The Times*. Elderly man killed, as I recall. Was that your father?"

"No sir," said Alec. "Though in many ways he was like a father to me. You have a remarkable memory, Dr. Westcott."

"So I've been told. Hmm. Just what is your interest, Mister Chambers?"

"Really anything in the occult line," said Alec. "That is my speciality."

"Ah, yes." Westcott nodded his head slowly and then looked hard at Alec. "Did you not write some small booklet on the alchemists, as I heard?"

"I did, sir. Or about one of them. Not that I sold many books." He chuckled. "It seems there is not a great deal of interest in the subject these days."

"Oh, I don't know. I have a full library on the subject."

"Do you now?" Alec tried to sound as excited as he felt.

Sir Geoffrey put his head back and laughed. "Ah! When two bibliophiles meet, eh? Methinks I shall leave you two alone while I get on with looking for my own treasures. I'll see you later Westcott; Chambers." He wandered off between rows of glass-topped display cabinets.

Westcott turned away and started strolling toward the adjoining room. Alec went with him.

"Do you happen to know Samuel Mathers?" It seemed an innocent question from Westcott, but Alec was certain he was being felt out.

"Oh, yes," he returned breezily. "He often looks in at my shop. Not a really regular customer, but he does like to keep up on anything new I unearth."

Westcott nodded and said nothing.

They moved through the next room of butterflies and moths and were about to turn to a smaller room where many of the books were displayed, when a stooping figure, with unkempt hair and wearing an ill-fitting suit, hailed Westcott.

"Dr. Westcott?" The man had a pronounced German accent. "I am Axel Küstermeier. I was told I might find you here."

The doctor paused a moment and then murmured to Alec "Excuse me, Chambers. I have to speak with this gentleman; I will talk with you later." He left Alec and moved forward to meet the newcomer. Alec turned into the book room.

Aleister Crowley almost bumped into Florence Farr as he emerged from MacGegor Mathers's office. He growled at her and went to move on along the passageway.

"What is the matter with you this morning?" Florence asked.

Crowley stopped and turned to look at her. For a long moment he stood without saying a word, and then he said, "Would you not think that he would be grateful for the way I ran things while he was away? Would you not think that he would be overjoyed even, to find that I had taken things in hand and had run matters smoothly and without rancor on the part of any of the G.D. members? Would you not ...?"

"No, I would not!" Florence snapped.

He looked at her blankly.

"You ran nothing," she said. "One might say that the G.D. continued *in spite of* you!"

"He is complaining about the state of his office." Crowley ignored her comment. "That office which should be mine ... and which *will* be mine in the not too far distant future."

"You think so?"

"Come now, Miss Farr. You are one of our brightest when it comes to divination, are you not? Surely you have seen it in the crystal? The stars, perhaps? Or your speciality, the I-Ching? Things are changing here at the Hermetic Order of the Golden Dawn ... and not necessarily for the better."

He turned and strode off down the passageway.

With a shrug, Florence moved on and entered the Scriba's Office, until recently occupied by Sarah Wilde. There she found Arthur Waite searching for a bottle of glue.

"Things have gone from bad to worse," he said. "I can never find anything I need. Miss Wilde has gone. Moina has gone. Crowley is running rampant. Mathers himself is in a funk, aiding and abetting Leigh Cranwell in some secret project. We haven't had a satisfactory ritual since Mathers got back from his foray across the Continent ... and what was that all about?"

Florence smiled. "I know. It is organized chaos at times. But SRMD has a plan of some sort, I am sure. He will reveal it at the appropriate time."

"But that does not help me find a bottle of glue," sniffed Waite.

Florence reached up to a shelf and brought down a bottle, which she handed to him. "Here, Arthur. Don't worry; things will get sorted out."

He tut-tutted as he wandered out of the room.

Florence tapped lightly on the door adjoining Mathers's office and went in. Mathers was sitting at his desk morosely staring out of the window. He looked up as she entered.

"Good morning," she said brightly. "I am going to be away for the rest of the day so I thought I would look in and see if there was anything of importance I should be made aware of?"

"You are busy this afternoon?"

"Yes. You know we are doing a revival of John Todhunter's *A Sicilian Idyll* at the Garrick. I have got rehearsals."

"Did you not do that a just a few years ago?"

She nodded. "It is being revived. I am playing Priestess Amaryllis again. You remember – she summons the Goddess Selene to wreak revenge on her unfaithful lover."

"Ah, yes. Well, the less said about unfaithful lovers right now, the better. Now, will you be here for the ritual on Wednesday?"

"If it does not run too late, yes, I think so," she said. "But I think there are more important things to be discussed right now."

Mathers looked quizzical.

"The morale of the society is at an all-time low," Florence said.

"I have already spoken to Crowley about that."

"No." She shook her head. "This is not Crowley-inspired ... at least, not entirely. There is general malaise, Samuel. People are not happy with what they see as your cavalier attitude."

"My what?"

"Your attitude. You spend far too much time running back and forth to see Cranwell. What exactly is Leigh doing that is so important, anyway?"

Mathers got to his feet and, turning his back on her, paced over to the window. "Suffice it to say that it *is* important, Florence," he said. "You are aware of my – affiliation with another international organization ..."

"Yes, I am."

"It is important that I come through on certain promises I have made." He turned to face her. "That is all I can say. You understand?"

Florence was silent for a moment. Then she said, "*This* organization – the Hermetic Order of the Golden Dawn – is the one that is important to me, Samuel. I will not see it destroyed in its heyday. I will resign my own part in it before I see that happen."

"I would never accept your resignation," he said.

"You may have no choice."

They stood facing on another for a long moment, and then Florence turned and left the room.

It seemed to Sarah that it had been a long time since she had been to tea with Alec at one of their favorite teashops. She looked around at the other customers enjoying their repast at the scattered tables. A trio of piano, violin and cello played quietly in a corner in a miniature "palm court," comprised of potted palms on wrought iron pedestals. Waitresses moved quietly about the shop. It was very relaxing and Sarah smiled to herself.

"You look pleased," said Alec.

She turned to look at him. He was very handsome, she decided. Though she had actually arrived at that decision quite some time ago; even before their French escapade.

"I *am* pleased," she said. "I don't have to work for that obnoxious Mister Mathers any more, I enjoy my work with Inspector Kent, and I get to have tea with you. What could be better than that?"

Alec laughed. "Obviously you are easily satisfied," he said.

She poured the tea and added the milk and sugar for him. He accepted the cup, his eyes locked on hers.

"And what are you up to?" she asked, offering the plate of delicate sandwiches.

"It has actually been fairly busy at the bookshop just recently," he said, taking a sardine paste sandwich. "Jeremy decided to stay on and help me out, since we've lost poor old Merryfield. And I think Jeremy really enjoyed running things while I was away."

"What does he normally do?"

"I think he was left some sort of a legacy from an ancient aunt, or something. Or so he declares. I don't know how much truth there is to it. He bought a small farm in Surrey, intent on becoming a gentleman farmer, but it does not hold his interest, it seems. Anyway, he really seems to enjoy being at the shop with me."

"You've known him for a long time, haven't you, Alec?"

"Yes. We were at school together."

They enjoyed their tea, and each other's company, and listened to the quiet strains of the trio.

"I hear you're still spying," said Alec suddenly.

She looked up, surprised, but was pleased to see that he was smiling. "You are not too upset, I hope?"

"Not so long as it's not dangerous," he said. "I understand you sit and gaze out of a window for hours on end. How dangerous can that be?"

She laughed. "Boring is a more apt term, I think. Yes, the inspector wants to know just who is visiting Dr. Westcott, when they are there, and for how long. Trying to establish a pattern, I presume."

"Well, we are both onto the same man," said Alec reaching for a petit four. "I have been put in touch with Dr. Westcott myself."

"Actually in touch with him?" She also took one of the little cakes.

Alec nodded. "Yes. Lord Sunbury arranged for a friend of his, who knows Westcott, to introduce me. Casually, you understand? I'm supposed to get to know him as well as possible so that I can pick up any little comments he may let slip."

"So you're a spy too!" she cried.

They both laughed.

"As it happens, I did stumble onto something, quite by chance, the very day I was officially introduced to Doctor Westcott."

"Oh?"

"This unsavory-looking German gentleman introduced himself to Westcott. Gave his name as Axel Küstermeier. He looked as though he had come in off the street; as though he had been sleeping in his clothes for at least a week. I thought Westcott would brush him off or even have him ejected, but no. Westcott was then in a hurry to be rid of *me* and the two of them walked off with their heads together."

"Have you told Inspector Kent?"

He shook his head. "Not yet, no. I did some asking around but have not been able to find out anything about the man, so I think perhaps I had better advise the good inspector. He can then pass-on the name to Lord Sunbury."

Chapter Nineteen

"Your Axel Küstermeier is what we know as an anarchist, Mister Chambers," said Inspector Kent, settling back in his seat and looking about him at the other diners. He dabbed at his mouth with the napkin which he had tucked into the collar at his neck.

"An anarchist?" Sarah's eyebrows went up and she looked at Alec.

"And he's not 'my' Axel Küstermeier, inspector, I hasten to say." Alec smiled at both of his dinner companions. He had invited Inspector Kent and Sarah to have dinner at Overton's, a restaurant opposite Victoria Station that was known for its excellent fish dinners.

"A figure of speech, if you will pardon me, sir," said Kent. He returned to his meal. "This is very good fish, and the sauce is a treat. I can taste lemon juice as well as pepper."

"Oh, do you like it? It's devilled white bait, together with flounder and filleted sole," enthused Alec.

"The inspector is right; this is delicious," said Sarah. "But what is white bait? I've never had it before."

"It's a small fish caught only in the River Thames, or so they claim. They also claim that it has to be cooked within an hour of being caught, though at some restaurants I think that would be in question."

They continued eating in silence, the fish accompanied by brown bread and butter and washed down by a slightly chilled Spanish Amontillado.

"So what more do you know of 'my' Axel Küstermeier?" asked Alec. "As an anarchist, was he involved in any bombing activities that we would know about?"

"I doubt that, sir. He's from Germany – as you so rightly surmised from his accent. It seems he is newly arrived in England, though he speaks our language very well."

"Does he have any sort of a record here?"

"No, sir, he does not. Exactly what brought him we do not know, though Lord Sunbury has some idea, I believe."

"The German recognized Doctor Westcott," said Alec. "Though I gather they had never actually met before."

The inspector finished his fish and reluctantly pushed away the plate. He glanced about him as though to see whether or not there might be more fish offered. Then he leaned in a little toward the others and lowered his voice.

"Lord Sunbury has a request for you, sir. And for you too, Miss Wilde."

"Oh?" They spoke together.

"Let me be absolutely correct on this." The inspector reached into the pocket of his coat and pulled out his dog-eared notebook. He turned pages until he found what he was looking for.

"Ah. Here we are." Kent cleared his throat and then took a sip of wine before continuing. Alec glanced at Sarah and smiled.

"Apparently Lord Sunbury's friend the Prime Minister, and Secretary of State for Foreign Affairs, has been keeping an eye on one Sir Charles Ridley. Sir Charles, it would appear, has been making one or two trips to Germany and it was through his efforts – not to mention his financial support, Lord Sunbury says – that this Küstermeier was brought across the Channel."

The waiter came and cleared away their plates, then returned with dessert, which brought a smile to Inspector Kent's face.

"Ah! Gooseberry Fool. My favorite," he murmured.

"Go on," urged Alec.

"Yes, sir. Sorry. Now where was I? Oh, yes. Exactly why Küstermeier has entered the picture we do not know. But, as Miss Wilde here can attest, he has been visiting Doctor Westcott at his Harley Street office on more than one occasion."

Sarah nodded. "Indeed he has. And what is of special interest is that our Mister Mathers has also been there at the same time."

"A regular meeting then," Alec suggested.

"It seems that way, sir," said Kent.

"So what is this request from Lord Sunbury?"

"Ah! Yes." The inspector read carefully through his notes before looking from one to the other of them. "Lord Sunbury has some concern about this anarchist being brought into the plot against our gracious queen. He asks, therefore, that the two of you – since you were so successful in your recent excursion to France – that the two of you go to Germany ..."

"Go to Germany?" Again Alec and Sarah spoke together.

"To what end?" finished Alec.

"I was about to come to that, sir," said Kent.

"Sorry," said Alec. "I didn't mean to jump in on you."

"That is quite all right, sir. Now." He again studied his notes. "Lord Sunbury says that Axel Küstermeier is returning to Germany in two days time. He would very much like the two of you to follow him – inconspicuously, I need hardly say – and to monitor his movements. Find out, if at all possible, what his business is with Westcott, Ridley, Mathers and all." He sat and awaited their response, his Gooseberry Fool forgotten.

Alec looked hard at Sarah. She returned the look and nodded, barely perceptibly.

"Not to put too fine a point upon it, inspector," Alec said, "but I presume that the expenses will be covered? I am happy to ..."

"Oh, of course, sir. Of course. Lord Sunbury has assured me on that point."

"Thank you." Alec studied his own Gooseberry Fool. Then, with a quick glance at Sarah, nodded his head. "Very well, inspector. You may tell Lord Sunbury that we will do it. You will, of course, give us all the details before we leave?"

"Of course, sir. Of course." Kent looked at Sarah. "And thank you, Miss Wilde. This is certainly over and beyond your regular duties at the Yard, and it will be so noted."

After disembarking the cross-Channel ferry at Calais, Alec managed to get close enough to Küstermeier at the railway booking office to hear his final destination: Stuttgart. They took the train from Calais to Lille and, from there, on through Hurson and Mezieres to Thionville.

"There is no direct route," Alec told Sarah. "So it looks as though we have an eight or nine hour journey ahead of us. Perhaps we can catch some rest."

The journey across France, and skirting Belgium, proved uneventful. They had no difficulty keeping Axel Küstermeier in sight. He seemed self-absorbed and spent much of his time sleeping, reading a worn, red-covered book he kept in his coat pocket, or simply staring out of the window of the train. They changed trains at Thionville and went north, through Treves, to Coblence, where they had to change again.

There was a long wait at Coblence for the southbound train that went, by way of Manheim and Heidelberg, to Stuttgart. Alec had his Baedeker's with him and spent some time studying what Karl Baedeker had to say about Stuttgart. He made a mental note of the most convenient hotels.

"It seems a long way around," remarked Sarah, as the train left Heidelberg.

"Yes," agreed Alec. "The stationmaster at Thionville was saying that they are always talking about putting in a direct line between Strassburg and Stuttgart, which would save a lot, but no sign of it yet."

They left Heidelberg and the line crossed the fertile plain of the Rhine. After Bruschal the train went through a short tunnel and, as they came out the far end, they both admired the ruined castle and the modern château of Count Langenstein. Another, much longer, tunnel eventually took them under the watershed between the Rhine and the Neckar, then across a long and ancient viaduct.

After Ludwigsburg the line climbed in a wide curve to the Forst Tunnel and then on through a series of tunnels and bridges. Finally the mile-long Hochdorfer tunnel opened into a fine view of the distant chain of mountains – the Swabian Jura. Feuerbach village was the last little town they passed before descending through the valley basin into the heart of one of Germany's largest wine-growing regions. The train finally approached the big Stuttgart North Station – the Haupt-Bahnhof.

Alec's German was, as he told Sarah, "Rusty!" but he felt he could make himself understood well enough for most things.

"*Ich bin ein Engländer,*" he said to her with a smile. "I am an Englishman. *Sprechen Sie recht langsam* ... speak very slowly!" They both laughed.

When the train finally came to a halt, there were enough passengers disembarking for them to keep some distance from Küstermeier yet still not lose sight of him.

"Look," said Alec. "He is being met by someone."

Sarah, who had been directing a porter to her luggage, looked up.

A bearded man in a dirty, grey, box-back overcoat had fallen into step alongside Axel Küstermeier. His serge hook-down cap was tight over long, stringy, blond hair. His trousers were stuffed into worn black boots. He had a scruffy, blond mustache.

The porter followed Sarah and Alec as they headed toward the station exit.

"Oh, no," murmured Alec. "The other man has a pony cart waiting. We are going to have to move quickly or we'll lose them. There, Sarah! Let's get that cab."

"My luggage!" she cried.

Alec thrust a one Mark banknote at the porter. "*Tragen Sie dieses Gepäck nach dem Hotel Marquardt,*" he said. He took Sarah's arm and they hurried to the waiting Gurney-style cab. Alec opened the rear door and as they hurriedly got in, Alec told the driver to follow the pony cart, "keeping at a distance."

"Where are we going?" asked Sarah.

"I have no idea, but I didn't want to lose our man or we would never find him. I told the porter to send the luggage to the Marquardt Hotel, which is closest to the station. We can meet up with it when we get there."

She nodded, and then strained to see out of the small window beside the driver.

"It's a good job there is a lot of traffic," she said. "That little two-wheeled cart would probably leave us behind if the road was clear."

"Yes, and make us that much more conspicuous," agreed Alec.

"It is a cute little piebald pony," said Sarah, "but it can keep up a good trot, even when pulling two adult men."

The cart led them away from the Haupt-Bahnhof, south along Konig Strasse. After little more than a mile, it turned left onto Stift Strasse, passing the octagonal-towered Stiftskirche in Stiller Square. The cart made a quick turn to the right and then back to the left onto the narrow Enge Strasse, where it stopped.

Alec banged on the roof of the cab and shouted "*Halten Sie gefälligst!*"

The driver pulled over beside the church and Alec jumped out. Sarah was about to follow but he stopped her.

"No, Sarah. You take the cab back to the hotel and I'll join you later."

"Cannot I come with you?" she protested.

"No. This time let me go alone, on foot. Next time you can be the one to follow and another time we will go together. This way they are less likely to become aware of us. If we always go as a couple, they are more likely to notice us."

Sarah could see the wisdom of that so, reluctantly, she bid him farewell and watched longingly out of the rear window as the cab turned and retraced its passage.

Alec quickly crossed the road toward the house into which the two men had disappeared. It was one of the three-story row houses in the small side street leading off from the square. The ground floor was made up of shops with flats above them. The men had gone through a small door between two of the shops, apparently leading to stairs to the upper levels. Almost immediately another man came out of the closest shop and led away the pony and cart. Alec strolled past the shop and along the short street to its end. Then he turned and strolled back again. He made a mental note of the house number into which Küstermeier had gone.

"*Guten Abend*, Herr Chambers! How nice to see you again."

Alec spun around. His mouth fell open as he found himself facing the tall, blonde, German woman, Rikka Arndt. He had last seen her confined to the lower level of the cavern beneath Gurat's subterranean church.

Leigh Cranwell was not pleased to see MacGregor Mathers.

"Why do you keep hovering over me? I have told you, repeatedly, that this is going to take time."

Mathers did not reply immediately but pushed past Cranwell and advanced on the table full of paraphernalia that filled much of the room.

A strong odor of sulfur, reminding Mathers of rotten eggs, filled the room. He automatically reached into his pocket and extracted a silk kerchief which he held to his nose, as he did whenever anyone smoked a cigarette or cigar.

"You would never make an alchemist," muttered Cranwell.

"Nor would I wish to be one. How are we progressing?"

"*We* are progressing well ... despite continual interruptions!" said Cranwell, going back to his work.

"Tell me," said Mathers, allowing the handkerchief to drop a little but then hastily pressing it back to his nose. "Will this really work?"

"What do you mean, will it work?"

Mathers turned away and spent time examining books on a bookshelf as far away from the table as he could get. "I know what everyone says ... what you say, Leigh. I keep being assured that Nicholas Flamel was the *extraordinaire alchimiste*. He produced gold for years; gold that was examined and acknowledged and utilized."

"So what are you trying to say?" asked Cranwell, his head down over his work.

"I don't know. I – I am just a little uncertain, I suppose."

"A bit late for that, is it not? After all we went through to get Flamel's papers?"

Mathers sighed. "I know. I know. But I have put a lot of my own money – a *great deal* of my own money – into this, gambling upon its success. Can you honestly assure me, Leigh, that by following Flamel's instructions you really will produce gold?"

There was a long silence, which Mathers thought might have been deliberate, just to aggravate him. Then Cranwell spoke.

"You can relax, SRMD. This is the real thing. I can see, as I progress, that this is the way it is supposed to work. Nicolas Flamel was indeed an extraordinary alchemist. Thank the gods he made such detailed notes of his work."

Mathers nodded thoughtfully.

"Good," he said. "Good."

For the next hour or more Mathers hovered over Leigh Cranwell as he worked.

"By the way," Mathers remarked at one point. "That pendant that we found around Flamel's neck ... I found the insignia that was on it in one of the books at the *Bibliotheque Nationale*. Apparently that was the 'membership card,' as it were, of the Brethren of Inner Truth. So Nicholas Flamel was indeed one of that group."

Cranwell grunted and went on with his work. Much later it was he who broke the silence.

"You know," said Cranwell, "the alchemists arrived at the axiom that nature was divided into four main sections: warm, cold, dry and damp. Basically Aristotle's theory. From these four philosophical regions everything was derived. Their doctrine claimed to ..."

"I don't care," interrupted Mathers. "Just get on with it, Leigh. I've bought you retorts, glasses stills, this new Bunsen-Desaga burner, aludels and athanors and God alone knows what else. Now just use all of this apparatus and let me know when you've got results. And remember, please, that time is of the essence."

With that, Mathers picked up his top hat, cane and gloves and left. Leigh Cranwell breathed a sigh of relief.

Sarah settled into a roomy armchair in the lounge of the Marquardt Hotel. She laid out a map of Stuttgart and studied it, her finger tracing a line from the railway station to where Alec had jumped out of the cab. Questioning the Concierge, she learned that the church in Stiller square – the Stiftskirche – was a basilica of the 12th century and had been rebuilt in the Gothic style in 1436. Although she doubted that there was any connection, she found it intriguing that this date was close to that of Nicolas Flamel's death. It was strange, she thought, how things seemed to keep coming back to that alchemist.

The buildings around the church were mixed, with shops, restaurants, offices and flats. Close to the church, the Concierge said, the shops were of a high standard yet just around the corner – where Sarah remembered the pony cart letting off Axel Küstermeier and his friend – there was a big change with a low class of people renting the flats and shops there.

Sarah was immediately concerned, but the Concierge assured her that in daylight hours Alec should come to no harm. The trouble was, Sarah thought, looking out of the window, dusk was fast approaching.

Alec turned away from Rikka Arndt, only to find that one of her male companions – Konrad Krüger – was sitting in a carriage that had pulled into the curbside. He smiled and inclined his head to Alec, stroking his mustache.

"*Guten Abend*," he said.

"Won't you join us?" asked Rikka. She opened her reticule, allowing him to see the black metal of a revolver inside.

Krüger opened the door of the brougham and held it open. Rikka came close behind Alec. He had no choice but to climb into the carriage. He was followed by the woman, who closed the door. At a sign from Krüger, the driver urged the two horses forward and they moved off.

Alec tried to memorize the route they took but quickly lost track as the Germans drew him into conversation.

"We have to thank you for our stay – albeit a brief one – in the Gurat cavern," said Krüger.

"I compliment you on your escape."

The German inclined his head. "It was not difficult," he said.

"And where are you taking me now?" asked Alec, trying to espy any noticeable landmark that they might pass.

"Stuttgart is a complex city," said Rikka. "Have you been here before, Herr Chambers?"

He shook his head. "No."

"Ah!" She smiled. "Now I, you see, spent many years here as a young girl."

Alec had trouble imagining Rikka Arndt as a young girl.

"It is, as I say, a complex city," she continued. "There are fine old trees in the royal but public park. The older ones, I have noticed, now have their ancient limbs supported and their wounded sides wrapped."

Alec thought this might be a clue as to where they were in the city, but when he looked out of the carriage window there was no sign of any park; they drove past tall buildings.

"The Alte Schloss," sighed Rikka, enjoying her reminiscing. "The Schloss-Platz is still untainted by the 'fabriks' of the neighborhood, sending out their foul breath to smoke the turrets and to blight the bloom of the so-beautifully laid-out Schloss -Platz garden."

"Enough!" said Krüger. "Just take a look up the hillsides, Rikka. See the new, modern architecture. Broad streets, not like these narrow, cramped ones. The Wurtemberger is a much more agreeable type than the Prussian."

She waved a dismissive hand at him and muttered under her breath. Alec didn't catch what she said but it brought a frown to Krüger's face. They then rode in silence for a while.

"You never said where you were taking me ... or why," said Alec, breaking the silence.

"That is correct," said Krüger. "We did not. Nor do we intend to." His right eye gleamed behind his monocle.

Alec noticed that the daylight was fading. He worried about Sarah and the fact that she would be worried about him. For a moment he thought of jumping out of the carriage and trying to flee but the two horses that pulled it were keeping up a good pace, plus he had a captor on each side, which would make it difficult to open a door. He contented himself with trying to see where they traveled.

The brougham came to a stop outside a large, detached house on a tree-lined street. There were two more houses before the road ended, running into a cross street. Despite the dim light, Alec was able to make out the names on a sign at the crossing: Augusten Strasse and Paulinen Strasse. They were outside number thirty-one Augusten Strasse.

Krüger led the way, walking swiftly up to the front door. Rikka Arndt slid the black revolver out of her reticule, enough to let Alec see that he should follow the short, fat German. She had apparently replaced her Deringer with a six-shot Reichsrevolver. Larger and heavier than the Deringer, Alec was sure it took up all of the space in Rikka's reticule.

"No heroics, Herr Chambers," she hissed.

He followed Krüger into the house. Behind them the brougham moved off.

The house was empty of furniture and Alec sensed that it had been empty for some time. Krüger led the way through to the back and into a room that had obviously once been the library. There were floor-to-ceiling bookshelves – bare of books – around much of the room. A large fireplace took up half of one wall and a heavily-curtained window another. There were two or three empty wooden packing cases, some partly-filled with straw. Straw also scattered about the room, mingling with scraps of paper and other detritus left from some earlier clearing of the room.

A large and ungainly oil lamp balanced on one of the packing cases. Krüger lit it and turned up the wick. One lone chair stood in the middle of the floor. He indicated it and told Alec to sit.

"What is the matter? Can you not afford furniture?" asked Alec as he took the seat.

Krüger did not smile. Rikka locked the door behind her and then moved around to stand in front of the window draperies. She slid her gun back into her reticule, along with the key.

"Why are you here, Herr Chambers?" asked Krüger. He paced all around Alec, examining him from all sides.

"Do you not know? I thought you had all the answers," Alec replied.

"We will have," said Rikka, fitting a cigarette into a holder she had taken from her reticule. It was a pale mauve Egyptian cigarette, Alec noted. Expensive. She lit it from the oil lamp.

Krüger removed his monocle and polished it on a silk handkerchief from his breast pocket. He returned the handkerchief and fitted the monocle back over his eye.

"We have it on good authority that you came to Stuttgart close on the heels of one Axel Küstermeier, is that not so?"

"You tell me," said Alec. He noted that there had been no mention of Sarah. Perhaps they didn't realize she had accompanied him, he thought. That would be good.

"We have no time for playing games." Rikka drew on her cigarette and blew smoke in Alec's direction. "You are here because Lord Sunbury ordered you here. You are to watch Küstermeier and report back. Am I right?"

"You obviously know everything so why do you even need me here?" Alec got up as though to leave.

"Sit down!" snapped Krüger. "You are going nowhere. The door is locked."

"You are protecting Küstermeier," said Alec. "I can see that. That is why you want me here ... to allow your friend to act without my observation."

"Ha!" Krüger spat out the expletive.

"We are no friends of Herr Küstermeier," said Rikka.

From the tone of her voice, Alec believed her.

"He and his sort are not on our level," she continued.

"*Genug*!" snapped Krüger. "Enough!" He swung away abruptly, and bumped into the packing case bearing the oil lamp. The lamp swayed for a moment and then fell. It shattered on the floor, sending burning oil in all directions and setting fire to the loose straw and paper.

Rikka rushed forward, as though to catch the lamp as it fell. At the same time Krüger tried to save it. They bumped into one another and Rikka slipped and fell. Her dress immediately caught fire and burst into flames. She beat at it with her bare hands.

Alec leapt up from the chair and ran to the window, tearing down the drapes. He turned and tried to beat at the flames that were quickly engulfing the blonde woman. It flashed through his mind that she was not uttering a sound. Most people – women and men – would be screaming in that situation, he thought.

Krüger grabbed the curtain from Alec and tried to help, but the lower end of it caught fire and he dropped it. Rikka tried to regain her feet but slipped on the burning oil and fell again. Now she screamed. The fire spread quickly across the room.

Alec picked up the chair he had been sitting on and ran at the French windows. The legs smashed through some of the panes but the doors themselves did not open. He was aware now of Rikka's increased screaming and smashed repeatedly at the multi-paned doors. Glancing back over his shoulder, Alec saw Krüger on the far side of the room, having grabbed up Rikka's reticule, searching feverishly for the key to the room doors. Alec turned back and slammed the chair into the framework, which finally disintegrated. As he fell through the doors, carried by his own impetus, the air rushed into the room and the fire inside exploded like a bomb. He heard Rikka's scream and then it was cut short. All was silent but for the fierce roaring of what had now become a major fire. All he could do was back away from the heat. He fell to his knees. He was shaking.

The Concierge of the Hotel Marquardt peered over the top of his steel-rimmed spectacles and appraised the figure who had stepped into the hotel foyer. Sarah saw Alec immediately and, with a little cry, sprang up from her seat and hurried forward. Alec stood hatless, without his gloves and cane, and with the torn lapel of his frock coat hanging down, victim of the precipitous travel through the broken French windows.

"Alec! Are you all right?"

He managed a smile. "Yes. Fine, thank you, Sarah. Though I can't say the same for our German friends."

"German friends?" She looked perplexed.

"I will explain everything shortly," said Alec. He turned to where the Concierge hovered uncertainly.

"We need two of your very best rooms, adjoining and with a common sitting area," he said. "Our baggage to be taken up right away, and unpacked."

At the mention of best rooms, the Concierge brightened visibly and signaled the desk clerk. "Take care of this gentleman, Schmitt." He turned back to Alec. "Is there anything else I may do for you, sir?" His eyes ran over Alec's damaged coat.

"Indeed there is," said Alec. "As you see, I have had something of a sartorial accident. First thing in the morning I will need a good tailor to attend me."

"Yes, sir. Of course, sir."

Alec and Sarah went up to their rooms, agreeing to meet in the sitting area when they had both refreshed themselves. Alec arranged for a meal to be sent up.

Bathed and finally able to relax, Alec, in an elegant, blue-grey Venetian cloth house coat, with satin-inlaid collar and cuffs, sat on a silk

tapestry-upholstered parlor-suite sofa. Sarah, looking equally elegant in a deep green, French cashmere tea gown, trimmed with yellow satin ribbon, perched on a side chair. He told her the full story of his kidnapping, although he played-down the details of the fiery demise of the two Germans.

"I am so thankful you survived," Sarah said, her eyes glistening as she studied Alec.

They were interrupted by the waiter knocking on the door and then wheeling-in the dinner they had ordered. When everything had been laid out on the dining table, the accompanying butler finally waved away the waiter and pulled back the chair for Sarah to sit. When they were seated, Alec dismissed the butler.

"We will take care of this ourselves," he said.

With a barely discernable raising of one eyebrow, the butler bowed and retired.

"Now, tell me again," said Sarah. "With all the details. I cannot believe that those terrible people we encountered in France escaped and followed us here."

"Well," said Alec, pouring wine for them both, "It has been some time since we left them in the cave at Gurat but, yes, I was certainly surprised to see them here. I must presume they had some mission that interweaved in some way with ours."

"Yet you say they claimed they were not with that Axel Küstermeier?"

"They spoke of him with some disdain. As though anarchists are beneath them."

"But are they both on the same side?" She helped them both to the sliced pheasant breast and vegetables and offered him the sauce.

Alec shrugged. "It's hard to tell. I would imagine that they are, though only in so far as that they might be useful to one another. I would surmise that the German group – the trio from Gurat – are part of the Illuminati and the anarchists are just that ... anarchists. The Illuminati apparently have some use for anarchists right now."

Sarah ate for a while, her brows furrowed. "What are anarchists known for?" she finally asked, taking up her wine-glass.

"The thing that immediately comes to mind is bombing, I suppose," said Alec. He too sampled the wine.

They both suddenly stopped what they were doing and looked at each other.

"They're going to explode a bomb to kill the queen!" cried Sarah.

"My god! I think you're right!"

By midday Alec had been fitted out in a new frock coat and had bought a top hat, gloves and a cane to replace those lost at the house on Augusten Strasse. He and Sarah had a late breakfast in the hotel dining room; the only people there.

"I have been thinking," said Alec. "Obviously it is now most important that we keep an eye on Axel Küstermeier. But that is not going to be easy."

"Why is that?"

"He and his companions are in a low-class housing unit, where we saw them go from the railway station. I was being fitted for my new coat earlier and thought to myself how inappropriate it would be for visiting such a place."

"You intend to visit him there?"

"Not formally, of course." Alec smiled at her and she responded. "But in order to learn of their plans, it is going to be necessary to get close to them in some way."

"What do you have in mind?"

"My torn coat gave me the idea," he said. "I enquired of the tailor and learned that there is, among the many shops in that area near the Stiftskirche, one establishment that deals in cast-off garments."

"Go on."

"If I buy and wear some old, worn clothes more appropriate for that area, it will be much easier to blend in and get close to these anarchists."

"You are not thinking of joining their group, are you?" Sarah sounded concerned.

Alec shook his head. "No, my German is not good enough for that, I'm afraid. Probably good enough to eavesdrop and learn of their plans, but not to become actively involved with them."

"And how are you intending to eavesdrop?"

"I have been wondering about that. I think the first thing is to visit the building."

"Will you not be questioned as to why you are there?" asked Sarah.

"Probably. Although it looks as though there are a number of flats in that building. I could pretend to be looking for someone ... just as a start; to see the lie of the land, as it were, and to find exactly which flat Küstermeier is in."

Sarah shook her head. "I don't like it, Alec. Suppose they catch you?"

"Catch me at what?" he asked. "I will try my best not to look suspicious ..."

They both laughed.

"I suppose you are right," Sarah said. "I ... I just worry about you, Alec."

Their eyes met and he reached out to touch her hand. A waiter approached their table to replenish their coffee cups and the moment passed.

"So it is settled," said Alec when the waiter had gone. "I will acquire a sacque suit, or some-such, and then reconnoiter the area. If you would be so good as to wait here, I will report back just as soon as I am able."

"Just remember what happened the last time you went off without me," said Sarah, a smile on her face.

"I am not likely to forget," he replied ruefully.

"One of my operatives has reported that Mister Leigh Cranwell has set-up shop in a mews in Chelsea, m'lord," said Inspector Kent.

"I thought he was working out of his home in Notting Hill?"

"So he was, m'lord, but it's my understanding that this undertaking became too large for that."

Lord Sunbury pursed his lips and looked thoughtful. "You think, then, Inspector, that they are having success in this project?"

"I am sure of it, sir. There were a number of complaints from neighbors about foul odors and even, it was said, some small eruptions ..."

"Eruptions?"

"Explosions, m'lord. There were some windows blown out, as I hear it. I believe Cranwell still maintains his residence at Notting Hill but he has been obliged to remove his alchemical experiments."

"I see. Well, keep on top of this, Inspector."

"Oh, I will, sir."

"And keep me informed."

Alec felt uncomfortable and dirty in the clothes he was wearing. He had been assured, when he bought them, that they had all been laundered before sale, but he still felt discomforted. Looking down, he realized that the dirt on the front of the jacket belied the seller's assurances. Trying not to think about that, Alec walked briskly along the pavement toward where Küstermeier and his friend had entered the building.

Alec had changed clothes in his room at the hotel and managed to slip out without encountering the eagle-eyed Concierge. There would have been many unasked questions there, he was sure! He had walked around the corner from the hotel and obtained a cab to take him to Stiller Square. Between two shops on the narrow Enge Strasse, he opened the outer door on to the stairs going to the upper floor flats. The door handle felt gritty. He wiped his hand on his suit jacket. He could feel the over-large hookdown cap, that completed his outfit, slipping down on his head.

A middle-aged woman was coming down the stairs, a small child clutching her hand.

"*Guten Tag*," said Alec. He looked up the stairwell and then back at the woman. "Herr Küstermeier?" he asked.

The woman seemed to think for a moment. "*Sieben und zwanzig,*" she said, and went out of the door.

"Twenty-seven," murmured Alec. "Good."

He climbed the stairs, aware of the dirt and filth on the steps and the almost overpowering stench of boiled cabbage. At each landing there was a wall-mounted single gas-jet with a dull, greasy reflector of ribbed tin fastened to the wall behind it.

On the second floor Alec passed a door that was cracked open allowing a pungent odor of sauerkraut to emerge. The smell fought and eventually joined forces with the odor of the cabbage. Alec moved on.

He came to number twenty-seven and paused, listening at the door. He could hear voices inside but could not make out what was being said. As he straightened up, the next door burst open and a big, burly man, with unkempt hair, bushy beard and shaggy eyebrows, staggered out and made his way toward the stairs. He thrust past Alec and nearly knocked him down. There was a strong smell of beer about the man.

Alec watched him disappear down the stairway and then turned to move on along the passageway. The door from which the man had emerged hung wide. Glancing in, Alec saw that it was a single room with an unmade bed at one end and a kitchen area at the other. There was no one in there.

Alec moved quickly into the room and closed the door. He wasn't sure what he was going to do; just reacting to circumstances. He looked about the room. It was barely furnished. The kitchen sink was filled with unwashed dishes. There was a single small table in the space between the end of the bed and the kitchen sink, with a single wooden chair beside it.

He walked over to the wall between that room and number twenty-seven. Pressing his ear to the wall, Alec could distinguish three male voices; the deepest one being Küstermeier, which he remembered well both from his brief encounter with him and William Westcott, plus overhearing him at the railway booking office in Calais. There was a second man with a high voice and a third who tended to mumble. Through the thin walls Alec could almost make out what they were saying ... but not quite.

He looked about him and then smiled. He recalled an old trick from his childhood. He crossed quickly to the sink and took up an empty beer glass. Moving back to the wall, he placed the open end of the glass flat against the wall and then pressed his ear to the bottom end. The voices became amplified and he could hear everything, as though echoing through a tunnel.

"But that's what I'm saying." It was Küstermeier's voice. "This Doctor Westcott is a man of his word. He has promised that the money will be there waiting for us in exchange for the goods. Payment in gold, no less. A straight exchange. Simple."

"Nothing with these English is simple, Axel. You should know that." It was the high-pitched voice. "It's not easy to get together that much gunpowder. It will be a big risk. One I am not sure we should be taking."

"But look at the reward," cried Axel. "Think of what we can accomplish ... things that are important to us! With that money we can do so much for the movement."

"I agree with Axel," said the third voice.

"Oh, you agree with everything he says!"

"Now that's not fair," whined the same voice.

"Enough!" said Axel. "So it will take a bit of an effort to get it together. But then we have only to see that it is all stock-piled at the coast, ready for loading. We will be paid-off there and they will be responsible for the actual movement across the Channel."

"Who handles the exchange?"

"It matters little to me," said Axel. "I will do it if you like, or you can."

"Huh! No. I want no part of it."

"Let Axel do it," said the mumbler.

"Fine. Does this Herr Doctor know where to meet?"

"Michelet and Macé."

The high voice grunted agreement.

Alec heard a sound, not unlike a roar, from behind him. He spun around to find the hirsute giant framed in the doorway. He glowered at the intruder.

"Er, twenty-nine?" cried Alec, implying that he was looking for that flat.

It seemed to work. "*Nein!*" the bewhiskered man pointed farther along the passageway.

Alec moved forward quickly, ducked under the big man's arm, and scurried off toward the stairs. He was halfway down them when he realized that he still held the empty beer glass and that he had lost his overlarge cap.

"Well done, Samuel. I must admit I have had my doubts along the way."

"My word is always good, sir," Mathers stated, his head high.

"Of course it is. Of course it is. Far be it for me to say otherwise." Doctor Westcott straightened some papers on his desk and then looked up at the tall man standing facing him. "So you have a shipment of gold bars ready to go, have you? And they have all been carefully checked? They are definitely gold?"

"No question. In fact I have already taken the liberty of repaying the moneys it had been necessary for me to put forward up until now, from my own account, so that gold had better be good!"

Westcott chuckled. "Indeed it had. Please extend my congratulations to your minion – what is his name? I can never think of it."

"Leigh Cranwell, sir. Yes, I have had him working day and night to get this finished. He has done yeoman service."

"Right!" Westcott became all business. He slid open the top drawer of his desk and took out a ledger, which he opened and studied. "We are about to enter the next stage, Samuel. Very delicate. You will need to keep your wits about you."

"Yes, sir."

"I shall advise Sir Charles. Be ready to move as soon as I give the word."

Leigh Cranwell felt uneasy, but could not think why. All seemed fine, on the face of it. He had achieved what he had set out to do and was elated just to have had the opportunity. He had worked with Nicholas Flamel's original notes and had followed the instructions to the letter, seeing the miracle of common lead bars become gold ingots. It had been long, hard, tedious work but a labor of love in many ways. Oh, to be sure he had been working under the insufferable Samuel Liddell MacGregor Mathers but, to be honest, he would never have had this opportunity without Mathers.

Cranwell looked at the gold ingots, neatly packed into wooden crates. The top still had to be fastened down on the last one and he moved forward to admire the golden gleam, reflected from the gas sconce on the bare brick wall. He reached out and, with a rag, rubbed at a slight blemish on the top bar. A light tarnish but nothing to worry about, he thought. He placed the lid on the wooden crate and hammered it down.

"But we do not know *where* they will be making the transaction," said Alec. He ran his hands through his hair as he paced up and down the small sitting room.

Sarah, on one of the parlor-suite chairs, smiled at him. "You did wonderfully well," she said. "Listening through the wall was a stroke of genius. I am very impressed."

He stopped pacing and looked at her to see if she was serious. When he saw that she was, he smiled back at her but was conscious of blushing.

"Just the spur of the moment," he mumbled.

"And you have the names of the people they will be meeting," Sarah continued. "What was it? Michelet and something?"

"Macé. Michelet and Macé. But we don't have their first names neither do we know where to find them, other than at some Channel port. We need to pinpoint it, if we are to keep on top of this."

Sarah got to her feet. "Well," she said, "We need to keep up on any possible movements of theirs. It's my turn to do something, I think."

"What are you going to do?"

"Don't worry, Alec," she said. "I am just going to take a turn around Stiller Square – perhaps even down Enge Strasse – just to keep an eye on any activity in that area. Oh, please do not worry ..." She saw his stricken face. "I am not going to dress-up in old frocks or anything like that. I will not enter the building, I promise you. But we do need to take turns watching that place, just in case. You had said so yourself."

He accompanied her to the street and got a cab for her, waving her off. Then he hurried along to the closest telegraph office and sent a wire to advise Inspector Kent of the latest developments.

"Surveillance, as Inspector Kent terms it, can be very wearing on one's feet," said Sarah some three hours later. She collapsed on to the parlor-suite sofa and kicked off her shoes. "I was much happier ensconced in a comfortable window seat across the road from Dr. Westcott's rooms on Harley Street."

Alec pulled his chair a little closer. "Anything to report, Sarah?"

She shook her head. "I was hopeful at one point. The blond-haired man who drove the pony cart and met Küstermeier at the railway station emerged from the building and I was in two minds whether or not to follow him. I finally decided to stay in case Küstermeier himself went anywhere. I'm glad I did."

"He came out of the building?"

"Yes. I followed him as discreetly as I could, but he only went as far as a local greengrocer's and bought some cabbages and other vegetables. Then he went back into the building again. Very disappointing." She sighed.

"Well," said Alec. "At least we know they are not going anywhere today ... unless they take off this evening."

"Or even during the night. I would imagine anarchists are not averse to doing things under cover of darkness."

Alec sighed. "I'm afraid you are right. I suppose we should really set-up a twenty-four hour coverage, just in case." He didn't feel too enthused about the idea.

Sarah shook her head. "No. I have a feeling we do not need to go to that extreme. Call it 'woman's intuition' if you like, but I believe things are going to be very quiet on Enge Strasse for a while."

As it turned out, Sarah was right. She and Alec took it in turns watching the building, but without making it a day and night observation. From time to time one or other of the three men – the third one emerged as a young man barely out of his teens, with bright red hair and the wispy beginnings of a mustache – would set off on an errand but never of any great length.

It was just over a week after their arrival in Stuttgart, and installation at the Hotel Marquardt, that there was any development of any significance.

Sarah had been looking in shop windows till she felt she could describe every article, and its price, in every shop within a block of the Stiftskirche. She looked down at the locket-watch hanging from her dress. Another half-hour, she resolved, and she would return to see what Alec had been doing. As she looked up again she glanced toward the end of Enge Strasse. A piebald pony drawing a pony cart emerged from the street and set off at a brisk pace around Stiller Square. There were three men squeezed into the cart: Axel Küstermeier and his blond friend, with the thin, younger man with the flaming red hair sitting between them. He was wearing a bright blue coat that, to Sarah's mind, clashed with his hair color. But what especially excited Sarah was when she noticed the small and battered suitcase being clutched by Küstermeier. It was the same suitcase he had carried with him from London. She had seen it a dozen times on the rail trip across Europe to Stuttgart. This must be it! Küstermeier must be leaving for his rendezvous. But what should she do?

It didn't take Sarah long to make up her mind. As it happened, a Gurney cab had just dropped off a couple in front of the church. She hailed it and, guessing at Küstermeier's destination, told the driver "Haupt-Bahnhof!" She was certain he would be going to the railway station and she was determined to discover his intended destination.

Ostende was in the Belgium province of West Flanders. It had a population of approximately 41,000, was the second port of the kingdom, and was the country's most fashionable seaside resort. It was situated at the central point along the forty-two mile coastline, facing the North Sea. In the Middle Ages Ostende was strongly fortified and underwent a series of sieges. The last vestiges of its ramparts were finally removed less than thirty-five years ago, in 1865. In recent years a whole new town had been created.

The *digue*, or parade, constructed of solid granite, extended along the shore for almost two miles in a southerly direction from the long jetty, which protected the entrance to the port. Sea bathing was considered unsurpassed and there were always dozens of bathing machines lined along the sandy beach. The royal chalet and a magnificent casino were the most prominent buildings on the sea front. In the rear of the town, a fine park with a race course had been added. Local newspapers carried the news that the following year, to celebrate the new century, extensive works were to begin for the purpose of carrying the harbor back two miles and a series of large docks was already being excavated and extensive quays constructed.

Ostende had a very considerable passenger and provision traffic with England. It was also the starting point of a number of railways along the coast and to the southern towns of Flanders, connecting to Brussels, Cologne and Berlin.

"It reminds me of Brighton," said Sarah, looking about her as the open carriage bore her and Alec along the west part of the embankment. In Stuttgart she had been able to report back to Alec that Küstermeier and the young boy had boarded a train to Ostende. Alec had been pleased and excited and, as quickly as they were able, they had packed and left the hotel to follow the trail.

The carriage passed the Royal Pavilion, impressively sitting atop a section raised above the promenade. The green shutters went well with

the brown siding, thought Sarah, though she expected something more grandiose overall. Farther along the main west part of the embankment spread a line of shops, on the ground level of the impressive four- and five-story houses and hotels. Blue, white, and red-and-white-striped awnings spread down over their fronts to give some shade to passersby. On the beach, dozens of bathing machines were being used, with men and women in horizontally-striped and solid black bathing costumes venturing down their steps into the gently rolling surf. Many people – couples and singles – strolled the flat sandy beach, several of the women sporting parasols. Children flew kites, and tested their skills with diabolos.

"Where are we staying?" Sarah asked.

"This is the height of the summer season," Alec replied. "There are very few vacancies anywhere."

"But we have got rooms somewhere?" She sounded worried.

Alec smiled at her. "We will be living in luxury – though probably for only a short stay – at the very impressive Royal Palace Hotel. In fact, here it is now."

Sarah leaned forward and was startled to see an imposing gatehouse of white stone, topped by a blue-tiled, domed roof with a large golden crown resting at its apex. A curving colonnade stretched off to the right and a wrought iron fence to the left. The road led between the four massive pillars of the gatehouse and she could see an immense five-story building in the distance. Like the gatehouse, it was white-faced with a blue tile roof.

"But ... this must cost the earth," she whispered.

Alec nodded. "I am sure it does. But Lord Sunbury assured me that he would carry all expenses ... and this is the only accommodation available. So just enjoy it, Sarah."

He reached out and took her hand. She did not withdraw it.

Sarah strolled along the pier; white-painted balustrades on either side of a wide wooden walkway. She inhaled the salty sea air, the ozone reminding her of her childhood holidays at Brighton. At the far end of the pier, which opened out into a large semicircle, was a small lighthouse, the Belgium royal standard flying nearby. Four telescopes on stands were at the very end of the pier, to allow visitors to scan the horizon for ships. As Sarah reached the nearest one, a large twin-funneled paddle-steamer passed close by. "No telescope needed to study that," she thought.

Alec had gone enquiring about the town, to see if he could discover any clue to where Messieurs Macé and Michelet might be found. Sarah had wanted to go with him but finally succumbed to the temptation to explore the sea front a little.

She went to one of the available telescopes and swung it around, away from the water, to study the Ostende front. The solid row of buildings, stretching away along the embankment, was most impressive. In the Gothic Revival style, they lent a real majesty to the face of the town. She envied those visitors who had ocean-facing rooms in the many hotels along the front.

The promenade was wide with occasional gas lamps scattered along its length. Steps descended to the near-white sands of the beach. She smiled when she focused in on a family whose two small children had built a sand castle and had stuck a Union Jack in the top of it. A small black and white dog frolicked about the structure, yapping at the children.

As she returned her attention to the buildings behind the beach, she was caught by the magnificence of the famous *Kursaal,* or casino. A high pillar-supported canopy encircled the main building, swinging in a vast circle back from the promenade. Beneath the covering, tables and chairs were set out for refreshments. The casino proper reared up in impressive style, with a connected series of multi-paned windowed arches with doorways leading out onto the upper deck of the canopy. It made her think of the arched openings around Rome's famous Coliseum. A second tier of round-arched windows, standing shoulder to shoulder, surrounded the smaller upper level of the structure, and an elaborate cupola projected up toward the rear of the building.

Sarah swung the telescope around to the far side of the port entrance. The channel used by the commercial cargo ships was quiet but beyond, as background to the forest of cranes and ships' masts, there seemed to be a general bustle around the many buildings and warehouses attached to the docks. Horses and wagons – both empty and loaded – were manipulated about the dock area. She focused on some of the stevedores and other dockworkers.

Sarah was about to abandon the delights of the telescope when something caught her attention. In the middle of a small group of men going through a side door into one of the big warehouses, she saw a slight figure with carrot-red hair and wearing a bright blue jacket. In a second he had disappeared. She gasped. She swung the telescope upward to read the insignia on the side of the building. It was two large letters M; one in red and the other in blue. Beneath them, in small black letters, it said *MICHELET et MACÉ.*

Alec was excited by Sarah's discovery.

"You have saved us a tremendous amount of work," he said. "We may even have had to abandon efforts to find Küstermeier. This is a big town and he could have been anywhere."

"It was pure luck," she said, modestly. "I don't even know why I swung the telescope over to look at the port."

"Well, thinking about it, that was certainly the most logical place to look. Oh, well done, Sarah!"

She smiled back at him and enjoyed the moment.

They were sitting in the hotel restaurant sampling the speciality of the house: crayfish prepared in a buttery, white wine, cream sauce. They had eschewed the offer, by the waiter, to try eels served in a green herb sauce. Eels, they learned, were widely consumed all over Belgium.

"So what is our next move?" Sarah asked.

"I think we need to pay a visit to the M and M warehouse. There may well be evidence of the imminent shipment of gunpowder, or even the arrival of the gold that the Illuminati is paying for it."

"Can we do that openly?" she asked.

"Oh, I think so," said Alec. "What I propose is that we turn up there with me ostensibly enquiring about shipping costs between Belgium and England. While I keep the warehouse official talking, you can wander off – as though you are thoroughly bored with my actions – and see if you can spot anything of interest; anything that might be connected to Küstermeier and the anarchists or the Illuminati."

"I think I can act bored," she said with a smile.

They finished off their meal with the famous Belgium waffles.

The open carriage pulled around a dray that was being loaded with large barrels of fertilizer. The aroma caused Sarah to cover her mouth and nose with a delicate lace handkerchief. Alec directed the carriage driver to take them across to the M and M building. The conveyance maneuvered around freight wagons, trucks, drays and even a noisy steam-driven trolley running on rails. There were a number of vessels tied up at the docks, some being loaded and some unloaded.

The door into the warehouse was at the end closest to the dockside. Alec noted three ships tied-up in the vicinity; one a paddle-wheeled steamboat and the others two-masted sailing ships. He and Sarah got down from the carriage and entered the warehouse. A thin, totally bald, harried-looking man with a bundle of papers under his arm, looked up and raised his eyebrows enquiringly.

"I am Monsieur Arnaud Maes," he said. "Are you looking for someone, or for some cargo?"

"I would like to speak with the person in charge," said Alec imperiously.

"That will be Meneer Niek Peeters," said the man. "He should be in the office." He nodded his head to indicate a windowed area close by, sectioned off from the rest of the open space, and then he moved away, studying the papers he carried.

"Meneer Niek Peeters," said Sarah, in a low voice. "Is he Dutch, do you think?"

"It could be," said Alec. "Belgium is strange in that it has three languages, French, German and Dutch. Here in Flanders the main one is Dutch." He noticed the worried look on Sarah's face. "Don't worry though, just about everyone speaks at least two of the languages and most also speak English."

They could see a short, fat man in a suit inside the office, apparently arguing with another man in working clothes. The workman finally gave a shrug and turned and left. Alec went forward and tapped on the glass. The fat man looked up, took in Alec's top hat and frock coat, and then hurried out.

"Yes, sir? How may I help you?" he asked. He had a ruddy complexion with a strawberry birthmark covering one side of his face and half of his nose. His bushy sideburns and walrus mustache seemed designed to help hide the deformity.

"I am enquiring into the costs of transporting and storing certain consumables," said Alec, as though used to dealing with such warehouse managers. "My company is opening new markets in Belgium and Holland and your facility was recommended to me."

"Why yes, sir. Delighted, sir."

"Really," interrupted Sarah, fanning herself with her lace handkerchief. "I must get outside and take some air. It is far too confining in here."

"Of course, my dear," said Alec. "Just amuse yourself with the sights and sounds of the dockside. I will join you when I have finished my business here." He turned back to the warehouse manager, who was smiling and half-bowing ingratiatingly.

"Now, Meneer Peeters ..."

Sarah strolled away and out of the door, leaving them to discuss whatever it was Alec had decided would keep them busy for a while. She observed one of the sailing ships, its cargo of large cloth bales being unloaded and piled high on the wharf. After a few moments she moved on. She saw that a loaded lorry, drawn by two horses, had pulled on to the dock alongside the steamboat. It was loaded with small barrels and seemed to be preparing to move the containers on to the boat. A man was standing on the quay shouting to the boat crew and telling them to be very careful with the cargo. She moved forward as though in idle curiosity. She was surprised when the man turned back to the lorry and she saw that it was Axel Küstermeier.

He glanced at her but, to her relief, was apparently too busy with what he was doing to take any great notice. However, suddenly the red-haired young man came around the far side of the lorry and, when he saw her, he paused in mid-stride. Sarah looked away and moved closer to the edge of the dock, as though to get a better view of the loading process. Then she casually strolled farther along, toward the rear of the boat. She found that her heart was pounding.

Sarah opened up her parasol and positioned it so that her face was partly obscured from the two men. Küstermeier seemed absorbed in what he was doing and, she saw, the younger man was ordered up into the bed of the lorry to manhandle the barrels. She studied the cargo vessel for several minutes and then, nonchalantly, strolled back to where the carriage was waiting and, as the driver opened the door for her, she climbed in and sat to await Alec.

"I am sure I have seen that woman before, Axel."

"What woman?"

"Why the one who was walking around while we were getting ready to move the gunpowder aboard the ship."

"Seen her where?"

"Back in Stuttart."

Küstermeier laughed.

"No, seriously, Axel. I noticed her because she has red hair like mine ... well, not really like mine. I mean, hers isn't as bright and red as mine is, but still ..."

"So what is this? You think that all redheads are after you? Following you across half of Europe? I don't think so!" And Küstermeier laughed again, long and loud.

"How do you think it went, Alec?" asked Sarah, as they drove away from the docks.

"It seemed to go smoothly," he said. "Though to be honest, I really didn't understand half of what Meneer Peeters said. Talking about bills of lading, and import and exports regulations. Docking fees and warehouse fees. No; much of it was beyond me." He grinned ruefully. "But he did not appear suspicious in any way. We parted on good terms, with my assurances that 'my company' would get back to him." He smiled at her. "And how did your part go?"

Sarah told him of her surprise at meeting Axel Küstermeier but that he didn't seem interested in her. She told him that she suspected that the barrels being loaded onto the boat were barrels of gunpowder destined for the Illuminati's nefarious scheme back in England.

"We have to alert Inspector Kent," Alec said.

Sarah nodded. "Yes. I did get a good description of the steamer, for him. It is painted maroon, with cream funnel and paddle-wheel covers. The inscription on the rear end ..."

"The stern."

"If you say so." She smiled. "The inscription said that it was out of Gravesend; the Royal Terrace Pier."

"Wonderful! Well done, Sarah. Gravesend is where vessels on their way up the Thames take pilots and custom-house officers on board. My guess would be that they intend either to unload the gunpowder there and take it into London by road, or perhaps to transfer it to some local vessel that the officials would not think of as having come from the Continent."

"I cannot wait until we let the Inspector know all this," said Sarah happily.

Cyril Henderson was an enthusiastic yet serious young man, not long out of college. He worked for Inspector Henry Kent and loved his job. He was of medium height and well built, with his dark hair parted very precisely on the left and held down with liberal doses of macassa oil. He had thought seriously about growing a mustache but hesitated for no good reason. He now stood, dressed in a four-button, single-breasted, navy-blue, worsted serge suit. His white shirt had a two-and-one-quarter inch stiff linen collar accented by a deep maroon bow tie. He wore a small-brimmed bowler hat but did not sport a cane.

Cyril stood on a small dock at Tilbury, across the River Thames from Gravesend. He held a pair of Zeiss Porro prism binoculars to his eyes and studied the river craft with great care. He was there on Inspector Kent's orders, entrusted with the task of spotting the vessel with the barrels of gunpowder returning from Ostende. The inspector was certain that the cargo would be transferred to another boat, or even to a land-based vehicle. Cyril was to observe and then follow. He was to be, and to remain, inconspicuous and simply to determine the final destination of the gunpowder.

Cyril was excited, though went to great measures not to show it to the men with him. They were the captain and the deck hand – Cyril thought that was the correct term – who stoked the boiler. They were utilizing the steam launch *Alert*, of the Thames Division of the Marine Police. The launch had a single white funnel with the ship's wheel located immediately in front of it. She had a sharp, steel prow with a yellow lantern pointing ahead. A green lamp hung on the side of the vessel, to indicate that it was a police boat. Cyril was glad to note the big yellow lamp on the bow, since the sun showed signs of starting to slide down the sky and there were indications of fog developing in patches.

"Any sign of her, Mister Henderson?" asked the captain. He was in the uniform of the Metropolitan Police but his weather-beaten face attested to his years working the river.

"Not as yet," replied Cyril. "But patience is the name of the game, they say." He had been standing studying the estuary traffic for almost an hour.

"That they do."

The boiler man, also in police uniform, tugged at a straggly mustache and gazed up at a flock of seagulls wheeling above a nearby fishing boat.

"Should we worry about the possibility of fog?" Cyril asked. No one replied.

Twenty minutes later Cyril straightened up and adjusted the field glasses.

"Hold on, Captain. I think this is it. Yes! Yes, I do believe this is what we have been waiting for."

The three of them watched the maroon and white paddle-wheeler come into view, hugging the banks of the river as though to lay claim to being a local vessel and not one that had come into the estuary from across the Channel.

"There is a number of steam ferries go out from the other pier – the Town Pier – and come across to here; to Tilbury," said the captain. "She's probably hoping to be taken for one such."

The paddle-wheeler worked its way around barges, steamers and merchant vessels, and finally tied-up at a shipyard dock just beyond the Royal Terrace Pier. Cyril kept his glasses trained on it.

"Just three men, so far as I can see," he reported. "And one seems to be shouting across to the captain of that Thames sailing barge that's also tied-up to that dock."

"Aha!" said the captain of the *Alert*. "D'ye think they're going to move the cargo over to that?"

That was precisely what took place. For nearly an hour the three men watched from across the river as the barrels were moved, one by one, to the sailing barge. When the transfer was completed, almost immediately the barge hoisted sail and prepared to pull out into the river.

"Get you to shoveling, McKay. I want a good head of steam built up so we can make a fast run if we need to."

"We will need to hang back so that we are not noticed," said Cyril, anxiously.

"Aye! Have no fear. But they sailing barges can move at a fair pace when the wind's aright, believe me. We just need to be ready to keep abreast, is all."

The barge moved slowly out into the main stream, then seemed to catch the wind and, heeling over a little, pushed up white foam from her bow and set off westward, toward the city. The *Alert* cast off and started moving inconspicuously through the outer river traffic, in the same direction.

There was a lot of traffic on the River Thames and, to make matters worse, the fog was beginning to build. A number of Thames sailing barges plied up and down, their big rust-red sails towering over lesser vessels. Several times Cyril was afraid they had lost track of their prey, but the captain of the *Alert* always seemed to come through, knowing "their" barge from the others. Rowing galleys, paddle boats, barges; a wide variety of vessels seemed to fill the waterway.

A sudden stiff breeze filled the sails of the sailing barge and it leaped forward.

"Stoke that boiler, McKay!" shouted the captain. Cyril, ahead of the funnel and close to the captain, leaned out, trying to get a better view forward.

"Pull in that green lantern," said the captain to Cyril. "No point in alerting them to the presence of a police boat." He then spoke over his shoulder to McKay. "Come on, man! Give me some steam!"

They had reached the first bend of the Isle of Dogs. The breeze still filled the upper sails of the barge but did little to blow out the fog from the pockets around the peninsular. Suddenly Cyril heard the captain curse and saw him spin the wheel. A large merchant vessel suddenly loomed up out of the gathering darkness.

"Get the hell out of my way!" shouted the captain, uselessly.

The *Alert* swung sideways and smashed into the side of the merchantman. Cyril was sent spinning across the deck and into the water. A number of sailors, now leaning over the side of the bigger ship, shouted and cursed. McKay went to get the boathook.

"I think stocks are low," said Jeremy, as he and Alec walked about the book shop in Denmark Place. "We had a steady number of customers while you were away, and I managed to keep them happy."

"Oh, I am sure you did, Jeremy. I really thank you for taking over for me," said Alec. "I just hope I can settle back into the old rut again." He smiled. "I am not a lover of chasing about the Continent, for whatever reason. Especially when pursued by decidedly antagonistic types."

Jeremy chuckled. "Some people would love to have a little adventure in their life." He took off his steel-rimmed spectacles, examined the lenses in the light, and then, seemingly satisfied, replaced them.

"Does that include you?"

"Oh, running your book shop is all the adventure I need, thank you very much."

They went into the back room – once the flat of Edward Merryfield and now a storage area – and started sorting some of the books there.

"I will have to see if there are any forthcoming auctions I should go to," said Alec. "In this business one has to keep up with such things. Little treasures stored away by someone and suddenly becoming available to other collectors, are the life blood of this business."

"Oh, by the way," said Jeremy, "a gentleman was in last week asking for you. A Doctor William Westcott, I think his name was. I have got his card up front in the cash drawer."

"Westcott?" said Alec. "What did he want?"

"He said that he had been introduced to you at some sale a while back and that this was the first chance he had had to look in. He seemed disappointed that you weren't here. He asked if it was true that you were up on alchemy books."

"What did you tell him?"

Jeremy chuckled. "I said yes, you were considered an expert." He suddenly looked worried. "I hope that was all right? I really had no idea what you knew on the subject, just that you had mentioned it in passing. I wanted him to come back."

"That's all right," said Alec. "I had spoken to him briefly and I know Inspector Kent wants me to keep up that contact."

They spent the next hour sorting books and dealing with larger orders. A few customers came into the shop, many of whom said how glad they were to see Alec back. As one of them left, Alec turned to Jeremy

"That was Tommy Lord," he said. "Quite a character. He plays the horses and seems to do well at it."

"Bit of a precarious livelihood, don't you think?" said Jeremy, brushing his hair out of his eyes.

"Absolutely," agreed Alec. "But he did ask me about the Ascot Festival and whether or not I was going."

"Ascot? Wasn't that back in June?"

"That was Royal Ascot," said Alec. "The Ascot Festival is always in early September, for three days. Saturday is usually the best day."

"So are you going?"

"I did think of it. How about you, Jeremy? Would you care to come along?"

"I am not much of a one for horse racing, but a day out might be fun."

"We could make up a party," said Alec, with growing enthusiasm. "Sarah would want to go, I know, and I thought of Daniel and Georgina Parmington. It would be good to see them again."

"Yes, it would," said Jeremy. "I enjoyed working with Daniel on that code thing."

"We lost 'em!"

"How did that happen?" asked Sarah.

The inspector shrugged. "An accident. It was getting dark and a bit foggy and the police launch ran into the side of a merchantman. No real damage done but enough of a scuffle for them to lose track of the barge and its contents. There are always a number of sailing barges out on the river and it's not easy to tell one from the other."

"Have we no idea where they were heading?"

"None at all," said Kent. "All we can say for certain is that they had passed the Isle of Dogs, but that leaves an awful lot of river upstream where they could have gone to roost."

Sarah stood in front of the large map on the wall of the inspector's office. She traced the line of the river with her finger. "A *lot* of places they could be hiding," she agreed.

Inspector Kent sighed. "Ah, well – no use crying over spilled milk, as my old mother always used to say." He had been standing beside her at the map but now turned away and returned to his desk. "I think you had better continue your surveillance of Doctor Westcott's office," he said. "You never know who might turn up there. Now that the gunpowder is in this country, in the London area, things may start to move. It's possible we could see a lot of things develop. We might even get lucky and have someone lead us to where the explosives are."

"It's Friday today," said Sarah. "The doctor is not usually in his office over a weekend. Would you like me to start on Monday?"

"Yes. I think so." He looked at a calendar hanging on the wall next to the map. "Big plans for the weekend?" he asked.

"As a matter of fact, yes," said Sarah brightly. "Alec suggested going to Ascot for the Festival ... or at least one day of it. Some other friends are going to join us. How about it, Inspector? Would you like to come?"

Kent straightened some items on his desk. "No, thank you, Miss Wilde. I don't think so. Somehow horse racing and police work don't seem to mix well, in my mind at least."

"But you should take a break."

"Oh, I will, Miss Wilde. I will. I've got a lot of garden work to be done before the Autumn really sets in."

"The thing of it is, gold does not tarnish."

Leigh Cranwell stood in front of a chest of drawers in his bedroom and spoke to himself. He had got into the habit of doing that after years of living alone. In some way it helped firm-up his thoughts, when he vocalized them.

He looked down at the bar of gold bullion lying on the top of the dresser in front of him. More than half the bar was badly stained. He again took a soft cloth and rubbed at the gold. It made no difference.

"It can have a certain amount of discoloring, I suppose," he said.

When the first gold had been produced, using the Flamel instructions, Samuel Mathers had insisted on having it examined by a jeweler acquaintance. The man had affirmed that it was, indeed, gold.

Several times during the process of transmutation, specimens had been examined. All had come back positive. So why was he now feeling so uncertain? Why was his stomach in turmoil? Leigh Cranwell could not explain it. He should have been jubilant, but he was not.

Mathers had pushed him, no question. Mathers had been on his back the whole time, pressing him to produce. Slow and steady, was Leigh's motto. Better to take plenty of time and be sure the job was done correctly, than to rush it and ...

He picked up the gold bar for the tenth time and looked closely at it. He put it down again. He twisted the ends of his mustache. He sighed. He paced about the small room. He had produced a very large number of these gold bars and they had been taken out of the country, as he understood it, and used to pay for some merchandise. He was not clear on the details but then, it didn't really concern him.

Why had he got involved with this group in the first place, he asked himself? He was a loner. He was not a joiner. But he had heard many reports of this Hermetic Order of the Golden Dawn. *Hermetic.* That was to do with alchemy, and he had always been fascinated by that subject. He had also found that the rituals of the Order brought him a certain peace. Its meditation regimen had certainly been most beneficial, he felt. And there were one or two good people in the group. Old Arthur Edward Waite for one. Not that Waite was really old; he just *seemed* old. A bit stand-offish but very knowledgeable in many fields, it seemed.

Studying books and then putting into practice the various theories advanced by those books, that was what Leigh found so fascinating. Mister Mathers had indeed been very generous in gathering together and providing all of the equipment needed. He had even managed to procure a secluded environment in which Cranwell could work, when the project took a momentary bad turn. He still had a ringing in his ears from the suddenness of the explosion that had blown out the windows.

But the discoloring of the gold bar was troubling. It should not be doing that. Just a day or so before, that same bar had been gleaming ... perfect. Now it was changing. Very disturbing.

It may not have been Royal Ascot but it was still Ascot and Sarah noticed that everyone dressed accordingly. She admired Alec in his elegant, grey, swallow-tail frock coat and grey top hat. Jeremy and Daniel were similarly dressed. Sarah herself wore a gown of green grosgrain silk with wide, brown, skirt reveres. The sleeves of the gown were ornamented with brown cut-velvet decorations. A brown and green bonnet, adorned with three partridge feathers, sat on her carefully coiffed head.

Georgina had a light blue gown of brocaded tulle with pleated yellow canton crepe falling down the front and emphasizing the edges of the sleeves. She wore a taffeta silk hat, the crown and brim draped with alternating folds of silk and velour and trimmed with a large bunch of violets and foliage above and below the brim.

Alec led the way to a private box on the first floor balcony of The Grand Stand. Sarah saw that there were many other boxes, each with up to six people in them. Behind the uncovered stalls of the first floor was a large room known as the Drawing Room, containing free seats for the public. The roof of The Grand Stand held free benches arranged in tiers going all the way up to the clock tower.

They took their seats and made themselves comfortable. Alec explained that it was a triangular right hand course of one mile and six furlongs, which did not mean a great deal to Sarah or Georgina. The men nodded sagely, as though they fully comprehended the significance.

"The showcase race today is the Middlesex Stakes," said Alec, passing out programs to each of them. "There are also two other races of note."

"Is not Lord Rosebery's filly the favorite for the stakes?" asked Daniel, looking at the program.

"His horse Ladas, yes." Alec nodded.

"Lord Arlington's Matchbox is also something of a favorite, I think," said Jeremy, standing and looking around at the bookmakers' boards.

Sarah also stood, to get a better view, and looked about her. The day had dawned overcast and grey but had quickly brightened up, with the sun breaking out even before they had left for Ascot. The Ascot Festival was not only about horse racing but also about family enjoyment. There was something of a carnival atmosphere, with entertainments and activities for the whole family. She could see coconut shies, Punch and Judy booths, donkey rides and a host of other activities.

Georgina moved forward to stand beside Sarah and pointed to a small crowd of women across the track, on the far side.

"I see the suffragettes are here," she said.

"They are making their presence felt everywhere, it seems," said Jeremy, without looking up from his program.

"And quite right too," said Sarah, with feeling. "It is absurd that women are not deemed intelligent enough to vote."

"I wonder why they are here today?" said Georgina.

"The favorite horse belongs to Lord Rosebery. As you know, he was Prime Minister until four years ago, and he was very outspoken against the suffragettes," said Daniel.

The women across the track were holding up placards, obviously having chosen their location the better to preach to the people in The Grand Stand.

"If they are to get any sort of recognition, they will need to do something really outstanding," said Alec. "Something that will bring everything to an abrupt halt."

"The jockeys are mounting up!" cried Daniel. "Not to bring the discussion to a close," he added apologetically. "It was just that I did not want you to miss it."

The jockeys were each given a leg-up and sat astride their mounts ready to parade around the area.

"Ladas is at nine to two and Matchbox at nine to one," reported Jeremy.

"Have we placed a bet?" Sarah asked Alec.

He smiled and nodded. "A modest one," he said. "Just in the spirit of the occasion."

Daniel and Jeremy smiled and nodded.

"Likewise."

"Indeed."

As the horses rode out to the starting line, everyone in all of the boxes came to their feet.

"The horses should reach their post at 1:15pm," said Alec, checking his pocket watch. "They will be off a minute or two after that."

There was a tremendous roar from the crowd as the horses leapt forward. Sarah was immediately caught up in the excitement. She found herself cheering-on Lord Rosebery's horse Ladas, which was the one Alec had bet on. With a thunder of hooves the horses rushed around the track.

The race developed into a tussle between Ladas and Matchbox, as predicted by the touters. For a short while another horse, Kernow, moved up to take the lead but was unable to hold it in the uphill section of the track and fell back. Ladas was two lengths ahead of Matchbox and heading for the finish line when suddenly all was confusion.

From where she stood, it looked to Sarah as though the leading horse had fallen. She could make out the crimson and gold of the jockey's silks as the poor man was thrown and then trampled by the horses coming up behind. But there was something else there. Something – or someone – in a dark blue dress. Sarah quickly made out the words that were buzzing through the crowd.

"A woman!"

"My god! A woman's thrown herself in front of the horse!"

"It's a suffragette!"

"She has committed suicide!"

Alec, Daniel and Jeremy shepherded the two women out of the box and down the rear of The Grand Stand and away from the track. There was commotion all around them. Most families were doing as they were doing and trying to leave. Women were crying and children were wailing, not knowing what was going on. Some few men were irate and berating the suffragettes but the majority were either sympathetic for the woman who was now a martyr for her cause, or were in too much shock to know what to think.

Despite the confusion, and thanks to Alec's persistence, they managed to procure a carriage and to get away from the race track. As they passed through the gates, Alec said, "Well, I did say they'd have to bring everything to a halt in order to bring the focus on to their cause."

"They most certainly did that," said Daniel.

Chapter Twenty-Three

he Reform Club was quiet, with few members present. Samuel MacGregor Mathers and the Reverend Montague Winters sat in the high-backed leather chairs in their usual corner, nursing their usual glasses of whisky.

"Repercussions," said Mathers, gazing morosely into his whisky glass.

"What do you mean, repercussions?"

"Just that, Monty. There are always repercussions."

"To what?"

"It is that damnable alchemical gold."

"But I thought that had been your saving grace?" The clergyman's bushy eyebrows drew together.

"I do have to admit," said Mathers, "that it did save the immediate situation, but Cranwell's bungling has now jeopardized everything, it seems. And so, my dear Monty, there will be repercussions."

Winters' face remained puzzled as he looked at his friend. "Would you care to elucidate?" he asked.

Mathers sighed and drank from his glass. Then he set it down and turned slightly toward the clergyman.

"Cranwell has advised me that there is a problem with the gold. This, after we have used what was produced to pay for certain goods; certain material obtained from a group of people in Germany. These people are not, shall we say, calm and understanding. They are the sort of people who will take matters into their own hands, if and when they discover that the money they were paid was not exactly as it should be."

"Not as it should be?"

"It was gold and now it is turning back into lead!" said Mathers, in exasperation.

Winters' face cleared. "Ah! I see," he said.

"Do you? Do you see, Monty? Do you see the position in which this leaves me?"

The clergyman sipped his drink. "Can you not simply return the ... these 'goods' you mentioned?"

Mathers shook his head. "No. The matter is far more reaching than that." He took up his glass again and drank, then leaned closer to his friend. "You have heard me refer to this organization, the Illuminati?"

"I have. And I am not entirely in the dark, Samuel. I presume that you belong, in some way, to the Illuminati and that you are involved in some plot of theirs. Am I correct?"

Mathers slowly nodded. "You are indeed. I am in a kind of probationary position. My advancement within that organization – which I very much desire, as I'm sure you are aware – is dependent upon this particular venture being successful."

"So you cannot return the merchandise?"

"Precisely. It is needed. It is important. It was not easy to acquire and I am, at the moment, viewed in good stead because of my part in acquiring it."

"Cannot your friend Dr. Westcott help you?"

Mathers sighed. "Dr. Westcott is my link to the Illuminati. He is a moving spirit in that organization and he has – until now, at least – taken me under his wing and given me the opportunity to prove myself. I cannot let him down"

"An enigma indeed."

"It would seem to me," continued Mathers, "that we must proceed on the assumption that the anarchists ..."

Winters' bushy eyebrows shot up.

"Yes, that is what they are, Monty. Anarchists. As I was saying, we must assume that they have not yet discovered the, er, problem with their gold and that they will not discover it until after the event."

"The event?"

"The merchandise to which I referred is gunpowder. The event is the blowing up of ... well, I must not go into details, old friend. I am sure you understand. But you see my quandary?"

It was Winters' turn to slowly nod. "The Illuminati is not a forgiving institute, I take it," he observed.

Mathers gave a short laugh. "Hah! No, they could never be so described." He was silent for a moment. "The Illuminati are intent on creating a new world order, Monty. A new world order. Do you know what that means?"

Winters shrugged. "A lot of organizations have tried to change the world, Samuel. I don't think they are ..."

"Not just 'change the world', Monty," interrupted Mathers. "More like *re-create* the world ... in *their* image."

"Oh!"

"And to do so, it is necessary – obviously when one thinks about it – it is necessary to remove the old world order. To *remove* it, Monty. Completely."

"But ..."

"They have assassinated world leaders, old friend. They have brought about wars. They have introduced death and destruction. They are very, very powerful, Monty."

"And you want to be a part of this?" Winters sounded incredulous. "To my mind, you are playing with fire."

Mathers looked profoundly unhappy. "I think – for once in my life, my friend – I think that I have bitten off rather more than I can chew."

The two men sat in silence for a long while.

"And what of the gold you took for yourself – to pay off your debts?" Winters finally asked.

"Good God!" Mathers blanched. "I had not thought of that." He finished his whisky in one gulp. "That gold went to the bank."

"Then you may be all right," said Winters. "I would imagine it is possible that it has since been recirculated. They may not be able to trace it to you."

"Let us hope that is the case." Mathers signaled the waiter, who hovered some distance away. "You'll have another drink?"

"Oh, yes." Winters was sure on that.

Alec alighted from a hansom cab and approached the door to Dr. Westcott's offices. He gave his card to Westcott's man and was shown into the waiting room. Alec had decided to take the bull by the horns and go to visit Westcott on his own turf. Lord Sunbury wanted any information that could be gleaned and Alec was anxious to oblige.

The man returned and led the way down a short passageway to the main office. Westcott got to his feet as Alec entered and, coming around his large mahogany desk, extended his hand.

"So good to see you, Chambers. You are lucky to catch me in, as it happens. I don't believe you advised me of your coming?"

"My apologies for that, doctor," said Alec, shaking hands. "I happened to be in the neighborhood and, on a whim as it were, decided to see if you might be available. I certainly do not mean to impose."

"Nonsense. No problem. Do please take a seat." Westcott returned to his own seat behind the desk. "I did look in at your shop a few days ago, but you were not there."

"No. I'm afraid I was away. I was sorry to miss you." Alec moved across to the indicated chair but stood for a moment studying a framed print on the wall. "How interesting. Is this an original print?"

"Indeed." The doctor indicated two other framed prints on adjacent walls. "All three of these I obtained at a sale. They were loose leaves from a long discarded volume."

He rose and again came around the desk to stand beside Alec, looking at the print. "These were the only three worth saving, I felt."

The picture Alec was looking at was alchemical in nature. It showed a dark figure standing behind a fiery furnace. A lion stood on hind legs, reared up to the rim of the furnace on one side, with a bear on the other side. Flames, smoke, and black birds rose from the fire.

"From the *Philosophia reformata* of Mylius?" asked Alec.

"From 1622. You are indeed up on your alchemy," replied Westcott, visibly impressed.

Alec gave a dismissive wave of his hand. "Oh, I just happened to know of this particular image," he said. "Pure chance."

"It is, of course, a representation of the black queen at the moment of volatilization, indicated by the black birds ascending. The lion, of course, represents the acid in the process. The stage of blackness is the initial stage, as you know."

Alec turned to look at the other two prints, moving across to the next one to see it closer.

"*Solutio perfecta*," said Westcott. "The conjunction of opposites in the Hermetic vessel." The picture showed a large aludel, or glass vessel, containing a young couple lying in the bottom, engaged in sexual intercourse, with the figure of a baby above them and with seeds sprouting out of the neck of the bottle. "Conception and then birth of the new order; the new form of the base metal," said Westcott.

"And what of this third print?" asked Alec, moving across to the other wall. The picture showed an alchemist approaching a large furnace which spewed forth flames. Behind him was a table with symbolic figures seated at it. A pot holding a blooming rose stood on the table and, in the foreground, a lion was eating a serpent. The word *Senatus* was written on the table.

"An important part of the whole process," said Westcott. "Indeed this is the act that brings about the last picture we looked at; the new birth."

"These are all from the 1622 book?" Alec asked.

Westcott smiled and nodded. He returned to his seat and Alec also sat. "Yes. All from 1622. What a wealth of symbolism just in these three illustrations, would you not agree, Chambers?"

"I most certainly would," said Alec. "Which is much of what makes alchemy so fascinating to me."

For the next hour the two men talked of alchemy and then of books in general. Alec had to admit that he enjoyed his time with the coroner. It was a stimulating discussion and they parted on very good terms, with promises to meet again. But as Alec drove away, he felt disappointed that he had not been able to discover any clues to the doctor's intentions.

"There's a policeman at the door, asking for you," said Jeremy.

Alec looked up from where he was placing books on shelves. Through the glass panes of the shop door he could make out the shape of a large figure in dark blue. With a sigh, he put down the rest of the books and went to the door.

"Yes, Officer? What can I do for you?"

"Mister Alec Chambers?"

"That is correct. Is there a problem?"

"That is not for me to say, sir," said the portly sergeant. He pulled out his notebook and consulted it. "I have a message from a Inspector 'enry Kent. 'e says that if you can be at Scotland Yard by ten o'clock – that is in less than a 'our, sir – then you might like to go with 'im to Battersea Park."

"Battersea Park? Why would I want to go to Battersea Park?"

"That is not for me to say, sir."

"Did the inspector give any sort of a clue; any reason for going there?"

He studied his notebook. "Something about a Thames barge, sir?"

"Ah!" Alec looked around at Jeremy.

"Don't worry," said his friend. "You go off and play with the inspector. I'll mind the store."

Alec grinned. "Thanks, Jeremy. I owe you."

When Alec got to Scotland Yard he found Inspector Kent and Sarah both ready to leave. With them was a smartly dressed young man, his dark hair carefully plastered down with oil. His brown eyes fastened on Alec. Kent introduced him as Cyril Henderson, one of the inspector's detectives.

"This is the young man who attempted to follow the barge upriver from Gravesend," said Kent as they all got into a Clarence brougham, which had a police driver up on the box. "As you may recall, he only lost it after the police launch was bumped into by another vessel."

"They nearly up-ended us," said Cyril, his face serious.

"I hear you got thrown into the river," said Sarah.

Cyril made a face. "Yes, miss. Well ..." He made much of closing the door of the carriage and lowering the window.

Sarah caught Alec's eye and smiled. He returned the smile.

The carriage had soon pulled out of Scotland Yard and was proceeding down Victoria Street.

"Why are we going to Battersea Park, Inspector?" Alec asked. He and Sarah sat facing Kent and Cyril.

"We are not going to Battersea Park itself, sir," replied Kent. "Henderson, here, refused to give up on finding that Thames barge. He finally tracked it down to a wharf just the other side of the park. That is where we are going. I thought you would like to be in on it, sir, along with Miss Wilde, of course."

"Thank you, Inspector. Yes. I would not want to miss it." Alec then addressed himself to the young detective. "How did you manage to trace the barge?"

Cyril looked pleased with himself. "It was just a matter of perseverance, sir. I made numerous enquiries up and down the river as to the whereabouts of a Thames sailing barge that had moved up the waterway from Gravesend on that particular date. I finally managed to find a man who said that he knew the vessel and that it frequently made use of this Battersea wharf."

"Well done," murmured Sarah.

"The barge is at the wharf now, sir," added Kent. "Which is why I thought it might be a good idea to pay it a visit."

They moved along Buckingham Palace Road, Commercial Road, and then down to the Chelsea Embankment. The Clarence drove along Grosvenor Road and finally crossed the river by the Albert Bridge. It was a beautiful sunny day and as they reached the end of the bridge they all looked down longingly at the green fields of Battersea Park.

Approaching the southern bank the inspector said, "If you can look over to the right there, sir, you'll be able to make out the wharf, which is our destination."

They looked and Alec could see a barge sitting at the dock, its sails furled. "That must be our boat," he said.

They got out of the Clarence at the wharf and Inspector Kent led the way forward. A man in a faded, well-worn, pea-jacket was directing two other men to coil lines and otherwise make the barge ship-shape. He looked up at the inspector.

"Was there something I might be helping you with?" He had an old clay pipe in his hands and was tamping down tobacco into the bowl.

Kent introduced himself and then studied the barge. "This your barge?"

"Aye."

"And you are ..?"

"Cap'n Herbert Entwhistle, at your service, sir."

"And would I be right in saying, captain, that you ran this barge upriver, from Gravesend to this wharf, on the evening of August 31?"

Captain Entwhistle studied the tobacco-packed pipe for a moment and then slipped it into a pocket in his jacket. He lifted the grimy, ancient captain's hat he wore and scratched the top of a totally bald head. Then he replaced the cap and ran his hand around the chin-line white beard he sported.

"From Gravesend, you say?" he said, a thoughtful expression on his face.

"That is what I said," returned the inspector. "On the evening of Thursday, August 31."

"You were carrying a cargo of barrels," said Cyril, hoping to help jog the sailor's memory.

"Ah!" Captain Entwhistle seemed to place the cargo. He nodded his head. "Them barrels, you say? Yes. Yes, sir, I did indeed run this very barge upriver on that day and date. Might I ask why you are asking these questions?"

"What happened to the cargo?" asked Kent. He screwed up his eyes and studied the captain. "Did someone pick it up? Or did you set it down some place other than this?"

"No, sir. Here is where I set the cargo. Here is where I was asked, and paid, to bring it."

"And what happened to it?"

"Why bless my soul, sir, I would not know the final destination, now would I?"

"You might," said the inspector. He stood and studied the barge for a while. "You have all the necessary papers for operating this vessel, do you, Captain Entwhistle?"

"Why – why yes, sir. Yes sir, I do." He sounded worried.

Kent nodded. "I'm thinking it might not be a bad idea to take all those papers back to the yard and check them."

"Check them? But they are all in good order, sir, I assure you."

"Oh, I am sure you are right," said the inspector, walking a little along the dock side and studying the barge. "But I have found, in my line of work, Captain, that it always pays to make doubly certain. Regulations are regulations, you know. It shouldn't take more than, what? A week or so, I would imagine."

"A week or so?"

"And, of course you would not be able to operate the vessel until such verification had been successfully concluded."

Alec looked at Sarah. They both smiled, admiring the inspector's *modus operandi.*

"But – but I have contracts! I have to sail later today, with the tide, and go up to Hammersmith. I don't get paid to just sit around and do nothing!"

"Ah!" The inspector nodded his head understandingly and continued to study the barge.

There was a long moment of silence and then the captain shook his head. "All right, inspector," he said, resignedly. "You win. I was not paid no extra for keeping mum. It's all over there." He pointed toward the rear of the wharf, where a number of wooden sheds stood.

"Let's take a walk back there then, shall we?" said Kent.

They all followed Captain Entwhistle as he led the way back and along to the largest of the sheds, on the end.

"This is the one. This is where we stacked the barrels after we unloaded them."

Alec studied the large padlock on the old wooden door. "Are they still inside?" he asked.

The captain shrugged. "I suppose so. I wouldn't really know, sir. My contract ended when I unloaded the barrels. I 'ave been away on other jobs since then."

"Hmm." The inspector looked at the padlock and then at the windowless building. He turned to Cyril. "Henderson! Think you can find a crowbar around here somewhere?"

Alec and Sarah helped Cyril look. Eventually, seeing the way things were going, Captain Entwhistle volunteered a crowbar from his barge. He even had one of his own men bring it to the shed. Inspector Kent gave a nod to the man and the captain did the same. The sailor attacked the lock and in no time had wrenched its bolts out of the rotting wood that was the door. He stood back and the inspector moved forward.

"All right. Henderson, you go in first."

Cyril pushed open the battered door and entered the building, with Inspector Kent, Alec, Sarah and the Captain right behind him.

Inside, the large shed was mostly empty but, in a pile in the center, were sixteen wooden barrels. They were all empty.

"There's plenty of dust on the floor," said Alec, bending down to study the planking. "I would say that the barrels were opened here and the contents transferred to some other containers."

"Something not so conspicuous, I imagine, sir," said the inspector. "What would you know of that, Captain Entwhistle?"

"Me? Why nothing, sir. Nothing! I assure you. We – me and my men – we unloaded the barrels from the barge and we stacked them in here. Then we left, sir. I don't know anything about what happened after that." He dug into his pocket and pulled out his pipe.

Inspector Kent looked at the pipe, then up into the captain's face. "I wouldn't light that if I were you," he said.

"What? Why ever not?"

"Look about you. Look at the air."

A beam of sunlight was streaming in through the opened door. In the beam, particles of dust were obvious, gleaming and glimmering in the light.

"I don't . . ." began the captain.

"Gunpowder!" said Alec. "Gunpowder dust. It's only particles ... but it is still gunpowder."

"That is what was in them barrels?" The captain's mouth gaped.

Kent nodded. "Oh, yes. They were full of the stuff."

"Dear God! I would never have agreed to move them if I'd known."

They all moved back outside and Cyril pulled the door closed and stuck the padlock roughly into the holes from which it had been wrenched. "That will hold until we can get a squad of men over here," he said. "We need to examine those kegs for any other clues, right Inspector?"

"Right, Henderson. Now, let's get out of here. Captain Entwhistle, I don't think I will need to speak to you again but, if I do, I will look for you here. Right?"

"Right you are, sir," said the captain. Alec thought he looked relieved to be able to go back to his barge.

The Clarence carriage got back up onto the bridge and started across, toward Chelsea on the far side. Suddenly an explosion came from behind, rocking the carriage on its springs. The driver stopped and they all climbed out. Thick black smoke billowed up from the rear of the wharf they had left. The big shed had disappeared and those adjacent to it were in flames.

"Captain Entwhistle had to have his smoke, I presume," said the inspector, dryly. "Henderson, you had better hoof it back there and see if there is anything you can do. I imagine we will no longer have to worry about examining the barrels for clues, though."

Chapter Twenty-Four

It was early evening when a hansom cab traveled the length of Fleet Street and then made its way along Cheapside. By the time it reached the west end of Commercial Road it was quite dark. The two figures in the cab were silent for most of the ride. As gas lights were turned on by the lamplighters, and mist began to rise from the river, MacGregor Mathers peered out of the window.

"Where the devil are we?"

Monty Winters looked out his side. "Approaching Limehouse, I do believe."

"Thank God for that! I don't know if this will be worth the abominable ride to get here."

"Oh, it will, Samuel. It will." Winters chuckled.

The hansom turned toward the river and finally stopped not far from Limehouse Pier. The two men alighted and Mathers paid the driver who, without a word, cracked his whip and quickly drove away, disappearing into the night.

Limehouse Reach was reckoned to be the end of the London Pool, which started at London Bridge. All around were the London Docks, where ships from around the world came to discharge their goods. Large custom sheds and bonded warehouses held the incoming produce. There were bulky stacks of hides, heaps of bales, and long rows of casks. Below ground were great cellars for the storage of seemingly inexhaustible quantities of wines and oils. In "The Kiln" adulterated tobacco, tea, and a wide variety of confiscated goods were burned. The tall chimney from the kiln was locally referred to as "the Queen's Tobacco Pipe."

The moon was nearly full but clouds fought to hide it. Narrow Street ran along the north side of the river, following its curve. Off from Narrow was a small street named Ropemakers. Winters led the way to this narrow, cobblestone alley. Loud drunken shouts issued from a nearby public house, where laughter, music from a concertina, and occasional shrieks added to the noise. A number of raggedly-dressed children huddled on the street outside the pub's entrance, some standing on tiptoe to try to see in the windows, others sitting bundled on the ground.

"The newspapers and popular fiction portray this Limehouse area as one of nothing but opium dens, sordidness and debauchery," said Winters, looking around to get his bearings. "But it is not as black as it is painted."

Mathers eyed the shabbily dressed characters along the street, only vaguely visible in the gaslight and through the encroaching mist. An overly painted young woman, with a badly scarred face, advanced on him and asked if he had a cigarette. She batted her lashes at him and pursed her scarlet lips. He waved her away.

"I am not sure whether I want it to be as black as painted or not," he said.

Winters laughed. "Oh, you do, Samuel. You do. I know you."

They passed a gin-shop and then a slop-shop and came to a flight of stone steps leading downward. The steps were old; their centers worn down by countless feet. At the bottom of the steps was another ill-lit cobblestone alley.

"Come on, Samuel," said Winters, and proceeded to descend to the lower level. Mathers looked up at the jagged chimney stacks on the houses all around him. Beyond them, in a brief glimmer of moonlight, he made out the masts of tall ships at the docks. He turned away and followed his friend.

"Sun Wen has a fine establishment," said Winters, "with first class opium. That will keep me happy."

"And me?"

"Ah!" said Winters, enigmatically. "Sun Wen has a young pot boy who is most obliging. I think you will like him. For a shilling or two, he will see that you are more than happy."

Mathers grunted.

They made their way past individuals and groups of people, till they came to a small cottage with a bare gas flame flaring on its outside wall. None of the windows seemed to be illuminated though Mathers, when he looked closely, saw that in fact there were very low lights burning inside the establishment. Winters went up to the door and knocked with a series of knocks in a particular pattern. After a long wait, during which Mathers wondered if anyone was home, a window in the upper half of the door opened and a wizened Chinese face looked out. It scrutinized the two of them for a moment and then broke into a grin.

"Ah! Mister Winters, sir! Greetings! So you return to our little heaven on earth? So happy!"

The clergyman did not return the smile. "Get the door open, Sun Wen, and let's get to it," he said.

There was a noise behind the Chinaman and as he opened the door a trio of burly men pushed past him on their way out. None of them seemed steady on his feet and Mathers moved to one side to give them plenty of room to pass.

The last man – and the largest of the three – suddenly stopped and stared at Mathers.

"Well, damn me!" he said. A smile slowly broke across his grizzled face. "If it ain't Mister bleedin' MacGregor God-awful Mathers!"

The other men stopped and, standing swaying, looked back at Mathers.

"I beg your pardon?" said Mathers.

"Ho! You beg my pardon, do you? 'ere! Look at this face. Remember me? You should do."

The face was ruddy and topped by a dirty cloth cap. Brown-grey whiskers traveled down his cheeks to end in a scraggly beard. There was a jagged scar on his left cheek. Mathers gave a sudden gasp of recognition and took a step backwards.

"No trouble!" cried Sun Wen. "No trouble!"

"You were supposed to have left the country," Mathers said. "I gave you money and a passage on a boat to France."

"And you fink I'd leave this 'ere old country where I was born and raised? Ho! You got another fink comin' is all I can say."

"No trouble!"

"I gave you money for ... for what you did, and I paid passage for you to the Continent."

"'The Continong'," mimicked the man. "Fuck the Continong, Mister Mathers. And you too."

"Here, I say!" said Winters, stepping forward.

"This, Monty, is the gentleman who took care of Chambers's man a few months back." Mathers drew himself up to his full height; a little taller than the man he faced. "Apparently he would rather face the gallows than avail himself of the route I provided for him."

"Oh, Jack Wilson ain't goin' to no gallows," said the man. "There's only one man can tie me to that killin', and that's *you*, Grog-blossom!"

The other two men had moved back, to stand one on either side of Jack Wilson. Both, Mathers thought, though bleary eyed, looked capable of causing him harm.

Suddenly Jack Wilson produced a large knife, its blade springing out of the handle with a loud click.

"I say! Steady!" said Winters.

Mathers suddenly slid his hand down his walking cane, to grasp it more firmly, and then brought the large silver head of it down hard across his opponent's hand. Wilson dropped the knife with a howl, but both of his companions produced similar evil-looking blades and leapt forward.

259

"No trouble!" shouted the Chinaman.

Winters swung his cane forward and, with a quick tug, slid a sword blade out of it. "Come on, you Cock Robins!" he cried, and lunged at the closest man. The sword blade pierced the man in the forearm. He let out a howl and, with his free hand, grasped the blade and snapped it off.

"Shit!" said Winters.

A shrill police whistle sounded, blown by Sun Wen. The Chinaman had closed the lower half of the door but blew the whistle as hard as he could.

"Look out, Monty!" cried Mathers.

The third man leapt forward and sank his knife blade into the clergyman's stomach. Winters gave a gasp and sank to the ground.

An answering police whistle sounded from the top of the steps Mathers and Winters had earlier descended.

"Run!" shouted Wilson and, without seeing whether or not his companions were with him, he turned and made off toward the river. The other two followed right behind him.

Alec and Jeremy were checking a delivery of books newly arrived from publishers.

"Some good books here," said Jeremy. "Here's an unusual one – *Aradia, Gospel of the Witches of Italy.*"

"Let me see." Alec peered over his shoulder. "Ah! Just published by David Nutt, I see. They're down the Strand."

"Who wrote it?"

Alec read from the book's title page. "Charles Godfrey Leland. He's an American, I understand, although he has been living in London for the last thirty years or so. I believe he is the President of the English Gypsy-Lore Society. This book is probably something connected with that."

"And what is this?" Jeremy carefully unwrapped a smaller volume. He opened it.

"Ah! It's a new printing of *The Nursery Alice.*" He read, "*A Special Edition, to be read by Children aged from Nought to Five.* I see it has got a new cover."

"Yes. It is one by E. Gertrude Thomson. I have been waiting for this to come in. It sells very well, of course."

"*Alice's Adventures in Wonderland* has always been popular," agreed Jeremy. "It has been a favorite of mine since I was a child."

Alec took a copy of the book and sat down in a chair, idly turning the pages.

"Beautiful illustrations," he murmured. "Just look at this picture of the White Rabbit."

"I love Bill the Lizard," said Jeremy, settling in another chair and similarly flipping through the pages. "Here. At the start of Chapter Five." The two men spent some time going through the children's book and reliving their early enjoyment of it.

Suddenly Alec stopped. He lowered the book and stared at Jeremy.

"What?"

"The Red Queen," said Alec. "My God, I've just realized something."

"What?"

"The Red Queen ... the Black Queen."

"There is no Black Queen." Jeremy pulled off his spectacles, shook his mop of hair and replaced the glasses.

"Not here. No," said Alec. He was excited. "But in alchemy there is. This picture of the Red Queen suddenly reminded me. Wait a minute."

He got up and went to one of the book shelves, running his finger along the line of books. "I am sure we have a copy here somewhere." He finally stopped and pulled a book from the shelf. He quickly flipped through the pages. "This is a collection of alchemical illustrations," he said. "I am almost certain what I want is included in this ... ah, yes! Here it is."

Jeremy hurried to his side.

"The Black Queen," said Alec. "From the *Philosophia reformata* of 1622. Jeremy, I am sorry. I have got to see Inspector Kent right away."

Inspector Kent preceded Alec and Sarah going into Lord Sunbury's office. Sunbury seemed pleased to see them.

"Excellent job by your team in tracing that Thames barge, Kent," he said, once they were all seated. "Too bad the evidence exploded. But at least we have another piece of the puzzle in place."

"And now, your lordship, I believe we – that is, Mister Chambers here – has a very important piece."

"Indeed?"

Suddenly Alec felt unsure of himself. What if he was wrong? Perhaps he had rushed into this without properly examining everything? Then his eyes caught Sarah's. She smiled at him and nodded.

"It is just an idea," he started, but quickly found himself gaining confidence as he explained his thought processes. "When I visited Doctor Westcott we spent some time discussing three alchemical prints he had framed and on his walls. I thought it strange that he had these particular ones; they didn't seem especially significant to me, at the time."

"And now?" urged Sunbury.

"Now I think they are vitally significant. Let me explain, your lordship." He stood and placed both the *Alice* book and the alchemical book on Lord Sunbury's desk.

"I was looking at the Red Queen, here in the *Alice* book, and it passed through my mind that the way Gertrude Thomson has drawn her, she bears a certain resemblance to Her Majesty."

Sunbury looked at the picture. "You had better not let Her Majesty hear you say that," he said with a smile. "But you are right, Chambers. There is indeed a resemblance. Go on."

"For some reason – perhaps just because they are both queens – I thought of the alchemical picture in Westcott's office. The Black Queen. Who is the 'Black Queen'?"

"I see," said Sunbury. "Yes, of course. Her Majesty has been in mourning for years. She is, and I believe has been referred to as, the Black Queen."

"Precisely," said Alec. "Now, following on that, if that one particular print of Westcott's symbolizes Her Majesty, than may not the other two prints also be related? May not they be some sort of indication of the plot that the Illuminati is brewing?"

"Hmm." Sunbury sat back and thoughtfully stroked his beard. "Can you enlarge on that?"

"Yes. I think I can," said Alec, with growing excitement. He turned through pages of the alchemical book until he came to another illustration. It was the one of the aludel, with the figures inside it. "Here is the second of Westcott's prints. The *Solutio perfecta.*"

F.   SOLVTIO PERFECTA   III.

"The Perfect Solution," murmured Sunbury. "And that could be both 'solution' in the sense of liquid and also solution in the sense of the answer to a problem."

"Exactly," said Alec. "The birth depicted in the aludel is the birth of the New World Order ... the Illuminati! The Black Queen – Her Majesty – is, then, representative of the Old Order; the one to be eliminated."

"And the third print?" cried Sarah. "Oh, sorry! I am talking out of turn." She blushed. "I just got carried away, I'm afraid."

They all laughed.

"I think we are all feeling something of that excitement," said Lord Sunbury. He turned back to Alec. "Miss Wilde is right. What of the third print?"

"That," said Alec, "is the key to the whole plot." He turned pages to find the picture he wanted. "Here it is."

"The alchemist approaches the furnace," he continued. "Note the flames gushing upward. Almost like an explosion in a tower, wouldn't you say? And behind him, we have the lion of England, and a group sitting at a table."

"What is that written on the table, sir?" Inspector Kent, unable to restrain himself, was on his feet looking over Alec's shoulder.

Alec smiled grimly. "It says *Senatus*. That means 'Council of Elders' or 'Senate'. I would put it another way ... the House of Lords."

Chapter Twenty-Five

"You are saying, then, Chambers – and let me get this absolutely right – that you think the Illuminati's plot is to blow up the House of Lords with Her Majesty in it? In other words, another damnable Guy Fawkes-style gunpowder plot?"

"We know they obtained the gunpowder, m'lord," said Inspector Kent. "We have long suspected that it was an assassination conspiracy aimed at the queen ..."

"And here is indication that it will take place at ... well, obviously at the State Opening of Parliament," finished Alec.

"Good Lord! That's Wednesday November the first; less than a month away," said Sunbury.

"But don't the Beefeaters always make a search of the basement of the Houses of Parliament, as a precaution?" asked Sarah.

"Have done every year since Mister Fawkes's attempt," said the inspector. "It has become all part of the ceremony of the State Opening."

"I think a *preliminary* search is called for," suggested Alec. "They are not going to place their gunpowder anywhere obvious. The search by the detachment of the Yeomen of the Guard is more ceremonial than anything, these days. We need a proper search."

"I agree, sir," said Kent.

"Absolutely. My thinking also," said Sunbury. "Kent – you can organize that? Perhaps Mister Chambers here would be kind enough to accompany you?" He looked directly at Alec. "I agree, absolutely, with your assumptions, Chambers, and I thank you, on behalf of Her Majesty, for your vigilance."

Alec was at a loss for words and busied himself picking up the books he had brought with him.

"May I go along as well?" Sarah's bright eyes moved from Lord Sunbury to Inspector Kent and back again. She held her breath.

"I do think it would be to our advantage to have an extra pair of eyes, m'lord," said Kent.

Lord Sunbury nodded. "Yes. Of course. By all means."

As Alec, Sarah and Inspector Kent left Lord Sunbury's office, the inspector turned to Alec.

"Oh, by the way, sir. You will be pleased to know that we have apprehended the scoundrel who killed your man Merryfield."

"You have?" Alec stopped and looked at he inspector. "How did you get him? Where was he?"

"He was involved in another murder, sir. As a matter of fact, the murder of the bushy-eyebrowed clergyman whom you may remember as having broken into your house some months back. The Reverend Montague Winters; though you may recall my telling you, sir, that he was no longer legally of the clergy."

"Winters is dead?" asked Sarah.

"He is, Miss Wilde. He was set upon by a gang, in Limehouse, and stabbed. I'm afraid he succumbed to his wounds. He was at a known opium establishment at the time."

"Opium?" Sarah nodded. "I can believe that of him."

"So who was it that actually killed Merryfield, inspector?" asked Alec.

"One Jack Wilson, sir. Oh, a nasty piece of work with a known history of violence. He was an accomplice to the murder of Winters, it seems."

"It is a brutal kind of justice," said Alec, as they walked on.

The cellars of the Houses of Parliament were dark and dusty.

"Are these the same cellars that Guy Fawkes used?" Sarah looked about her as she moved through the ill-lit basement, an oil lamp in her hand.

"No," said Alec. "Almost everything was burned in the great fire of 1834. It was then rebuilt, cellars included."

"But these are the cellars that are underneath the buildings today," said Inspector Kent. "So these are the ones we need to search. If the Illuminati really do plan to blow up parliament and Her Majesty, then it is most likely here that they will put the gunpowder."

The three of them moved slowly through the many interconnecting cellars. Boxes of dusty files, cloth-covered oil paintings, books, scrolls; the minutia of government was scattered throughout.

"Guy Fawkes was Spanish, was he not?" asked Sarah, of no one in particular.

"Actually he was English," replied Alec. "He was born in York and was a pupil of the Free School of St. Peters there. Apparently he left England in the 1590s and went to Flanders where he enlisted in the Spanish army. He earned quite a name for himself under a Colonel Bostock at the Battle of Nieuport in 1600."

"But he did go to Spain, sir, didn't he?" asked the inspector.

"Oh, yes." Alec nodded. "He was sent to advice King Phillip II concerning the true position of the Romanists in England. It was while he was there that he became reacquainted with Christopher Wright, one of his old schoolmates. The two of them tried to gain Spanish support for an invasion of England, when Elizabeth died."

"I take it they did not get the support," said Sarah.

Alec shook his head. "No, the Kingdom of Spain was in far too much debt and fighting too many wars to assist Catholics in Britain. But word must have got about. Guy Fawkes came in contact with those planning a conspiracy against the crown, in England. In May of 1604 Fawkes joined Thomas Percy and three others. They met at the Duck and Drake Inn in the Strand, here in London. There they all signed an oath to proceed with the gunpowder plot. It was masterminded by John Catesby."

"But it was November 1605 when they tried to blow up King James," said Kent. "Any idea what took them so long?"

Alec chuckled humorlessly. "Something like that takes a lot of planning, inspector, I am sure. Also, it seems they were not the smartest of conspirators! Fawkes and the others started out by trying to dig a tunnel under the building. It seems that this proved difficult, partly because they had no way to dispose of the dirt and debris and partly because they went in the wrong direction! So they ended up renting a cellar beneath the House of Lords. By March of 1605 they had hidden 1800 pounds, or 36 barrels, of gunpowder in the cellar."

"That sounds like a lot," said Sarah.

"It is," said Kent. He turned to Alec, caught up in the story. "So what happened then, sir?"

"Well, it was a lot of gunpowder but some was poor quality. Still, there was enough to have done the job."

"Did someone break the oath?" asked Sarah.

Alec nodded. "In effect. One of the conspirators wrote a warning letter to Lord Monteagle, advising him not to attend the State Opening of Parliament. Monteagle received it on October 26. The conspirators became aware of the letter the next day but after Fawkes had confirmed that nothing had been touched in the cellar, they resolved to continue with the plot."

"Is that when the authorities found them?" asked Inspector Kent.

"By Sunday November 3," continued Alec, "the conspirators felt that they were safe and made plans for leaving London immediately after the explosion. The next day the Lord Chamberlain, with Lord Monteagle and John Whynniard, searched the buildings. Guy Fawkes went for one last check of the gunpowder and they found him standing by a large pile of faggots. All seemed innocent so they left. However, they all felt that Fawkes himself looked suspicious. They again searched the cellars a little after midnight, and that was when they discovered the gunpowder underneath the wood. Guy Fawkes was immediately arrested."

"Did they get the others?" asked Sarah, breathlessly.

"Oh, yes, Miss Wilde," said the inspector. "That I do know. All of them were eventually caught and justice was done."

"Well, let us just hope that justice can be done here," said Alec. They had covered the entire area under Parliament and found nothing suspicious.

"Lord Sunbury should be waiting for us upstairs," said Kent. "We had best go and report to him."

"I would suggest that we trace the path that Her Majesty will tread," said Lord Sunbury. "If there is nothing in the cellars, then there must surely be gunpowder secreted on this level."

Alec, Sarah and the inspector, accompanied by the Steward of the Houses of Parliament, Sir Gregory Ford, moved to the outer courtyard of the House of Lords, outside the Sovereign's Entrance to the Victoria Tower.

"Here is where Her Majesty will arrive, in the Irish State Coach," said Sunbury.

"At precisely 11:15am," interjected Sir Gregory. "We have to follow a most exact timetable; every minute is accounted for."

"Precisely," said Lord Sunbury. "Her Majesty leaves Buckingham Palace at exactly eleven of the clock and travels the Royal Route accompanied by the Household Cavalry. She is greeted here at the Victoria Tower by the Earl Marshall and the Lord Great Chamberlain – the Duke of Norfolk and the Marquess of Lincolnshire, respectively. Together they enter the Tower, here, and proceed to the Queen's Robing Room."

Ford led the way up the Norman Staircase and into the tower proper. They stood for a moment in the Norman Porch, a small square hall with Gothic groined vaulting and borne by a finely clustered central pillar.

"There are one thousand one hundred rooms, one hundred staircases and three miles of corridors in the palace," said the Steward.

"Happily we need concentrate only on this one corner," said Lord Sunbury, with a smile.

"That is the Guard Room, on the right," said Sir Gregory. "Obviously we do not need to check in there."

"On the contrary," said Lord Sunbury. "I think we need to check everywhere, regardless."

"I agree," said Inspector Kent.

"Very well."

Alec thought that the Steward sounded annoyed, but Sir Gregory obediently led the way and opened the door into the Guard Room. Two off-duty guards sprang to their feet and came to attention. Sir Gregory ignored them.

"As you see," he said to the others, "there is little here other than the necessities for those patrolling the corridors and entrances of the House."

They all looked around the large room and then retreated outside again.

"Over here, opposite the Guard Room, is Printers Court," said Lord Sunbury.

It was a wide and long court with doors opening off of it. Oil paintings covered the walls, above dark wainscoting. The Steward detailed the rooms as the Housekeeper's office, a Cabinet room and the Deputy Speaker's office. Backed onto the Court, at the far end, were the rooms and offices of the Yeoman Usher, the Proxy Room and the Dress Room. Satisfied that there was nothing suspicious in that area, the five of them withdrew again to the foyer.

"Her Majesty will proceed through this doorway," said Sir Gregory, pointing ahead, "to go to the Queen's Robing Room. This vast area to the left is the Royal, or Victoria, Gallery. As you see, it is hung with many historic oil paintings, but there is nowhere to hide explosives."

The room was over one hundred feet long and two stories high, hung with chandeliers. The floor, or pavement, was fine mosaic work. The ceiling was paneled and richly gilt. The walls were covered with portraits of past monarchs and overshadowed by huge depictions of the Battle of Waterloo and of the death of Nelson at Trafalgar, both by the artist Daniel Maclise.

"What is this used for?" asked Sarah, in a hushed voice.

"Banquets are occasionally held here," said Sir Gregory. "And visiting Heads of State will sometimes address both the Lords and the Commons in here."

"Then let us examine the Robing Room," said Lord Sunbury.

Alec and Sarah were both taken aback at the grandeur and opulence of the Queen's Robing Room. It was a large square room, forty-five feet in length, ornamented principally in red and gold. Paintings on the walls depicted the legend of King Arthur, as interpreted by William Dyce who had been commissioned to decorate the room. Other allegorical paintings complemented the main ones.

At one end of the room, on a three-step dais, sat a throne with a foot-stool before it. High above it was an elaborate canopy and behind it a great representation of the coat of arms of Great Britain. The ceiling was an intricate maze of decorative work and a huge, imposing and elaborate fireplace sat along the wall opposite the many tall, mullioned windows. Above the fireplace the three virtues were illustrated as Courtesy, Religion, and

Generosity. Hospitality and Mercy were displayed on the north wall. The fine dado paneling had carvings by Henry Hugh Armstead, depicting Arthurian legends. Queen Victoria's monogram was in evidence about the room.

"This is where Her Majesty will don the parliamentary robe and the Imperial State Crown," said Sunbury. "From here she will lead the procession through the Royal Gallery to the Chamber of the House of Lords."

"Well I think it safe to say that there would be no gunpowder in here," said Sarah, brightly.

"Where now?" asked Alec.

Sir Gregory led the way out of the Queen's Robing Room and around to the small rooms along the south wall of the palace.

"There are just small offices from here," he said. "The waiting room, the Clerk's office, Lord Great Chamberlain's room, his dressing room, and a writing room."

"We shall just look into the first two, I think," said Sunbury. "Then I imagine we have seen all that we can associate in any way with a potential disaster."

"I agree, m'lord," said Inspector Kent.

The small room on the far side of the Robing Room was empty; stripped of its furnishings and paintings. The window was boarded up and there were workmen's tools lying about.

"As you see," said the Steward. "They are repairing the window – replacing some sort of damage, I believe."

"What is this room normally used for?" asked Alec.

"It is the waiting room," said Lord Sunbury. "For the use of constituents who come to speak with their parliamentary representative."

"Can it be locked?" asked the inspector."

"Most assuredly. Whenever the men are not working in here."

"Good. Please make sure that is done, sir." Kent addressed himself to the Steward, who made a note in a folder he carried with him.

"And the room on the far side of this one?" asked Alec.

"The Clerk's Office, Mister Chambers. Always kept locked when not in use. There are many important files in there."

They stood at the end of the Victoria Gallery.

"That covers this whole corner of the tower," said Lord Sunbury. "From here Her Majesty leaves the Robing Room and proceeds down the Victoria Gallery and into the Peers' Chamber. So, either we have missed the cache of gunpowder – unlikely, to my mind – or else it has not yet been put in its place."

"There is another possibility," said Sir Gregory.

Sunbury raised his eyebrows.

"That there is no conspiracy," continued the Steward. "I ask you, Lord Sunbury. How likely is it ... really?"

270

Sunbury looked past Sir Gregory at the inspector. Alec could have sworn he saw the slightest hint of a wink, but couldn't be sure.

"You may very well be right, Sir Gregory. You may well be right. But," Sunbury sighed, "we cannot be too sure now, can we?"

The policeman on duty watched the carriages departing the House of Lords. The session was over, apparently, and he considered whether or not he should show initiative and close the great wrought-iron gates and lock them. But who knew whether or not some lord – some peer of the realm – might have late business to do in his office?

"You lock them gates at eleven of the clock, Constable Sykes, and not a moment before," the sergeant had said, as he always said at the start of every shift. But no one ever came around to check.

Constable Sykes squinted up at Big Ben. Not even eight of the clock yet. That meant another three hours, probably for no good reason. He swore to himself. He thought of his cozy little room in Lambeth, just behind the hospital. Mrs. Wiggs would have a pot of stew going, as she always did. That would taste good. Or even just a nice cup of tea would slip down uncommonly well.

He shook himself. What was he thinking? He tucked his thumbs into his black varnished belt and walked, with his accustomed swagger, across the courtyard and back, his brass-buttoned coat tails swinging. Back and forth, whistling tunelessly and filling his mind with thoughts of becoming a sergeant himself one day. Why not? It was quite possible, if he continued to fulfill his duties so well.

A half hour later Constable Sykes had stopped walking and whistling and stood with his hands gripping the railings of the gate, gazing out at the little traffic that moved around Westminster Square and off down Victoria Street. It had started to rain; dark clouds threatening to bring a downpour. He had wandered around to exchange complaints with the constable at the other gate, down near the bridge, but the man could talk about nothing but his wife and kids. Constable Sykes, a confirmed bachelor, had no interest in that.

He whistled through his teeth again; this time a recognizable tune. *I dreamt that I dwelt in marble halls.* What made him think of that? Now he could not stop thinking of it! Perhaps it had something to do with being on duty at the Palace of Westminster. He hunched up his shoulders and wondered if he could shelter under the entrance to the Victoria Tower.

The clip-clop of hooves drew his attention. A coal cart, pulled by two large but ancient shire horses, came slowly along Abingdon Street, from the direction of Lambeth Bridge. A bit late to be making deliveries, he thought. The cart turned into the courtyard and stopped. Constable Sykes, mildly curious, moved forward.

An old man, with a dirty-faced boy beside him, peered down at the policeman. Both had empty coal sacks over their heads to keep off the rain.

"This 'ere the 'ouse o' Lords?"

Constable Sykes took off his tall pot hat, scratched his head, and replaced it. He made a performance of turning and looking up at the big clock face and then all around at the Palace of Westminster. Then he turned back to the coalman.

"Well o' course it's the bloomin' 'ouse of Lords!" he said. "What a barmy question! So, what do you want? Bit late to be delivering coal, ain't it?"

The old man sniffed and then produced a dirty, coal-besmirched handkerchief and noisily blew his nose.

"Bin a long day," he said. "Don't want no never-mind from the likes o' you, even if you are a copper. Winters comin' and these 'ere lords want their comfort."

Constable Sykes strolled around the cart, eyeing the big coal sacks, each filled to the brim.

"You know where you go with them?" he asked.

The old man gave his nose another blow and then pocketed the handkerchief. "Ought to by now," he said. "You want to give me a 'and unloadin'?"

"Get out of 'ere!" said Sykes. "I've got my own work to do."

The old man chuckled at his joke; the boy beside him also laughing. With a crack of the whip, the two big horses were made to get moving again and Constable Sykes watched as the coal cart disappeared around the side of the palace.

Suddenly the skies opened up and the rain came down in torrents. Constable Sykes scrambled for shelter.

Samuel Mathers looked about him as he and William Westcott followed the white-haired retainer into the grand house in Belgrave Square. Mathers stared at the green onyx marble staircase and at the *caiyatydes*, the sculpted female figures supporting entablatures on their heads with columns rising above. His eyes were drawn to the circular lantern light above the hallway and to the bronze figures on the stairway. Elaborately framed oil paintings decked the walls above the dark wood wainscoting.

In the room to which they were led, Mathers took in the gilded, painted-timber, coffered ceiling above and the thick Turkey carpet beneath his feet. His eyes could not avoid the huge painting of the Spanish Armada and the portrait of Sir Francis Drake over the white marble fireplace.

As they entered, a man rose from a green leather, winged armchair before the fireplace and advanced on Westcott with his hand extended.

"William! So kind of you to come," he said, and shook the doctor's hand as though they were long lost friends. He then turned to Mathers. "And you must be MacGregor Mathers. I have heard so much about you from my good friend here."

Mathers drew himself up to his full height, though he found he was still an inch or two shorter than the man who had greeted them. "My pleasure, Sir Charles," he said.

Sir Charles Ridley – dressed impeccably in a dark grey, swallow-tailed, frock coat and striped trousers, with a gold-highlighted waistcoat and maroon cravat – ushered them to two of the several chairs about the room and had the butler bring them drinks and cigars. Mathers settled back and lit his smoke, with a feeling of accomplishment. He felt that he had at long last reached that status to which he was most entitled. He looked about him and felt satisfied.

"So, the big day approaches," said Sir Charles, drawing on his cigar.

"Indeed." Westcott sagely nodded his head.

"And we have you to thank for much of this." Mathers found that Sir Charles was looking at him and raising his glass in a half toast.

"Well, er, yes, Sir Charles. I suppose ..."

"Mathers did his part." Wetscott sounded somewhat reluctant to match his host's enthusiasm, Mathers thought.

"Of course he did. Of course." Ridley sipped his drink before continuing. "And from what I understand, we now have the means to produce sufficient gold to accommodate our many and diverse strategies. Once this immediate play is carried off, then we may introduce numerous varied courses of action."

Suddenly Mathers felt uncomfortable. "Gold?" he asked, querulously.

Sir Charles Ridley locked eyes with Mathers. "Gold," he said firmly. "It is my understanding that you were instrumental in producing the gold that was necessary for this present exercise?"

Mathers noticed that Westcott said nothing. He sat and sipped his drink, drew on his cigar, and let the conversation flow around him.

"Has not Doctor Westcott informed you?" asked Mathers, in an attempt to shift the focus from himself.

Westcott remained silent. Sir Charles kept his eyes on Mathers. "Informed me?" he said.

"Yes. The gold we produced ..." he swallowed. "The gold we produced, apparently it was not – not – stable."

"Not stable?"

"No, sir. It – it ... over a period of time, it changed back to that raw material from whence it came."

"After how long a period of time?"

"In fact, Sir Charles, quite a short time."

There followed a long silence, during which Mathers became conscious of the ticking of a tall case clock that stood in a corner near the door by which they had entered.

"Did you not acquire the working notes of the alchemist Nicholas Flamel? I thought that was the object of the exercise of sending you across the Channel and about the Continent."

"Yes! Yes, Sir Charles." Mathers suddenly felt hot. He could feel sweat trickling down his armpits. "Yes, we did indeed acquire that material and we followed those notes to the letter. However ..."

"However?"

"It would seem that, perhaps, there was too much pressure ... the time limit ... We did produce some gold, I must say." He finished in a rush.

Sir Charles put down his glass and rose to his feet. He moved across to stand by the fireplace. He removed his pocket watch and checked it against the time indicated on the grandfather clock, then returned the watch to his waistcoat pocket. Mathers sat ... and sweated.

"The Illuminati," said Sir Charles, "is a world-altering entity. What is to happen in three days time will have repercussions around the globe. Not since the 'encouragement', let us say, that brought about the French Revolution – the French have never fully recovered from that – has there been anything quite to equal what will take place on November the first."

"I must admit that Mathers did produce gold sufficient for this coming event," volunteered Westcott, finally joining in the conversation. "If I might be allowed, Sir Charles, there is every possibility that the problems encountered in the alchemical process can be overcome when there is not the time constrictions that we had here."

Sir Charles seemed to consider that. Mathers silently thanked Westcott for his words.

"That is true," Mathers blurted. "We can refine the process, I have no doubt."

"And what of the gold you used to buy the gunpowder?" Ridley moved back to stand by his chair, and again took up his glass. "Have you heard nothing of those from whom you made the purchase?"

"I have heard that the anarchists have been making enquiries regarding my whereabouts."

Sir Charles waved a dismissive hand. "They can be taken care of," he said. "Though it may not be immediately, since we are so involved in this present action. Do you have somewhere you may lie low?"

Mathers nodded. "I had already thought about that. My wife is in Paris. I think I might persuade her to let me secrete myself there for a while."

"Good. Good. And what of your Golden Dawn?"

Mathers glanced at Westcott. "Aleister – Aleister Crowley – has been pushing hard for a long time. I may let him take over, temporarily, for a while. See what sort of a job he does. Let us hope that he does not run it into the ground."

Ridley puffed on his cigar and walked about the room. He spoke generally, but Mathers realized that many of his remarks were being directed at him.

"With the – regrettable – death of Her Majesty, Albert Edward would ascend the throne. We all know that he is a weakling; a playboy much given to gambling and fornication. This is good for us and, indeed, one of the *raisons d'être* for the assassination. The Marquess of Salisbury is in his third term as Prime Minister. We have tried to put pressure on him before but he may have to go the same route as our beloved monarch. Certainly it would be advantageous to the Illuminati if the country should suddenly find itself in a state of chaos."

"I imagine it will do precisely that when the House of Lords explodes," volunteered Westcott.

Sir Charles Ridley nodded. He looked hard at Mathers. "You wish, as I understand it, to be a part of our organization?"

"Indeed I do, Sir Charles." Mathers rose to his feet, not quite knowing why but feeling the action appropriate.

Ridley again nodded. "We can use foot soldiers," he said. "This has been something of a test to date. I think we may be able to make use of you in the Illuminati."

Mathers stood tall and felt glad.

Cyril Henderson scratched his head.

"I don't know that we have the time, right now sir, to get involved in a theft like this," he said.

Sir Gregory Ford, Steward of the Houses of Parliament, sniffed.

"I fail to understand what the timing of this has to do with anything," he said stiffly. "A theft is a theft. Is it not the job of the Metropolitan Police to investigate such an occurrence?"

"Indeed it is, sir," said Cyril, trying to look sympathetic. "But as you know – only too well, I am sure – tomorrow is the State Opening and our men are stretched thin preparing for that event. We will be only too happy to look into ..."

"It is November the first tomorrow," said Sir Gregory. "This is England. London. It is not the warmest place in the world."

"Yes, sir, I know ..."

"The members of Parliament – and most especially Her Imperial Majesty, when she deigns to visit here tomorrow – would like to be warm and comfortable."

"Yes, sir ..."

"The theft of the palace's coal, I would have thought, should be a priority."

Cyril sighed. "Yes, sir," he said resignedly. He pulled out his notebook and studied what he had already recorded. "You say that there was a delivery just four days ago, and that none of that coal can now be found?"

"That is correct. The constable on gate duty witnessed its arrival and then had the coalman sign on his way out."

"You have that signature, of course, sir?"

"Of course." The Steward produced a creased piece of paper and handed it to Cyril, who studied it carefully.

"Is this the usual coal merchant?" he asked.

"It is."

Cyril studied the wavy signature at the bottom of the delivery note.

"It says, John Johnson," he said.

"That is correct."

Cyril studied it a while longer, then he looked up, slowly, at the Steward.

"Are you familiar with the name John Johnson, sir?"

"No, of course I am not," said Sir Gregory irritably. "Why would I be? It does not mean anything to me."

"No sir," murmured Cyril. "Nor to most people. But John Johnson was the name used by Guy Fawkes when he was pretending to be a servant, just before the Gunpowder Plot!"

Chapter Twenty-Six

he crowd outside Buckingham Palace broke into shouts and cheers as the big, black, wrought-iron gates opened and the one-hundred-strong Guard of Honor marched out, in their scarlet and gold uniforms, followed by a military band. Behind them came the Household Cavalry and various elements of Household Division, who trotted out of the palace forecourt and onto the tree-lined roadway that ran from Buckingham Palace to Trafalgar Square. This stretch had been dubbed "The Mall" from the French *Palle Maille*, a game King Charles II had been fond of playing up and down that muddy stretch of road. The Mall followed the north side of St. James's Park for half a mile, and had eventually been popularized as a promenade by Charles II. At Trafalgar Square it met up with Whitehall, which ran past the Admiralty, the Horse Guards, and the Treasury, toward Westminster Square and the Houses of Parliament.

The first of the carriages came through the gates to greater cheers. This and the next carriages carried the Robes of State, the Imperial State Crown, and the Sword of State and Cap of Maintenance. It was 11:00 am on the morning of Wednesday November 1, 1899.

The cheers swelled to a roar as the Irish State Coach finally made its appearance; dark blue and black with elaborate gold decorations topped by a gold crown and pulled by four pure white horses. The interior was covered in blue damask. The royal coat of arms was on the doors. Inside sat Her Imperial Majesty Queen Victoria, Queen of the United Kingdom of Great Britain and Ireland, Empress of India. She nodded, smiled, and occasionally raised a hand to acknowledge her loyal subjects. The drive to the Victoria Tower at the Houses of Parliament would take exactly fifteen minutes.

Inspector Kent ran his finger around the stiff white celluloid collar that threatened to cut off his air supply. He did not care to be so formally dressed and knew that buying a new, unforgiving collar was a mistake. He had an old, slightly frayed, linen one that would have looked fine, he knew. He wished he had worn it.

Cyril Henderson had reported to him that the Yeomen of the Guard had passed through the basement of the Houses of Parliament and found nothing untoward. They had subsequently sent word to Her Majesty that all was well and had been served well-earned refreshments. Inspector Kent was not altogether surprised that they had found nothing. In his mind he ran through the upper rooms they had inspected.

"Henderson!"

"Yes, Inspector?"

"Did you personally check the upper rooms; those around the Queen's Robing Room?"

"Oh, yes, sir. Never fear. All 'unnecessary' rooms locked until after the ceremony."

"That waiting room?"

"The one where they were working, and replacing the window? *Double*-locked. I did it myself – put a padlock on it, alongside the regular lock that the Steward took care of."

Kent grunted. "Good."

"The Clerk's Office, next to it ... they would not let me put a padlock on that but it *is* locked, sir."

"Good." The inspector had a last look around and then turned to descend the stairs to the Tower entrance. "Come on, Henderson. Maybe the Steward was right. Maybe there is no plot."

The procession turned around the corner of Trafalgar Square and onto Whitehall. The adoring crowd was heavy. Street Liners guarded the whole route, presenting arms as the Royal Coach passed. Policemen were scattered along the route also, between the Street Liners. They, too, came to attention and saluted the royal personage. Slowly but inexorably the Queen moved on toward the Palace of Westminster.

Just past Downing Street, and the new Public Offices – the Home Office, Foreign Office, Colonial Office and India Office – the street had been widened, presenting a greatly enhanced view of Westminster Abbey.

Alec and Sarah stood in the crowd opposite the Treasury, in front of Montague House, the mansion of the Duke of Buccleuch. They had left Inspector Kent at the House of Lords and were slowly working their way up Whitehall, to meet the oncoming State Coach.

"I am certain the gunpowder is in there somewhere," said Alec. "I cannot understand why we didn't discover it, but I am certain it's there."

"I agree," said Sarah. "So what do we do?"

"This whole ceremony is so precisely timed," said Alec. "The Illuminati knows that. Wherever the gunpowder is, they will have a fuse that is carefully set to bring about the explosion at exactly the time when the Queen is in the Robing Room."

"Why there?"

"It cannot be in the Lords' Chamber itself – we know the Yeomen of the Guard did a thorough search there, along with the cellars. The queen goes to the Robing Room when she arrives at the palace and then she will spend five to ten minutes in there. That has to be when they will act."

"I am sure you are right," agreed Sarah. "But how do we stop her? Queen Victoria is not one to upset the ritual of a State Ceremony just as a precaution; even against assassination."

The crowd suddenly shouted and pressed forward. It became impossible for Sarah to make herself heard to Alec. She found herself separated from him. She saw the Irish State Coach approaching, its four white horses moving rapidly. She had to do something. Visions of the queen being blown to pieces; of the Illuminati coming to power in England ... in the world; visions of dark clouds covering the skies ... And then, suddenly, her thoughts flew back to the day at Ascot, when the suffragette had thrown herself in front of Lord Rosebery's horse. What was it Daniel had said? "That most certainly brought everything to a halt!"

Sarah didn't stop to think. She ducked down and thrust herself through the crowd. She pushed under the outstretched arm of a policeman and ran out into the road. The State Coach was there; almost upon her. Without another thought, Sarah threw herself in front of the matched white horses.

"A doctor? Is there a doctor in the crowd?"

"Stand back! Stand back!"

"Watch the 'orses now! They bin scared enough!"

Alec forced his way through the crowd. The coachman had climbed down from his box and the police had tried to form a barrier around the side of the State Coach to protect the queen. Alec could see Sarah on the ground between the great hooves of the leading horses. He evaded the outstretched hand of a burly police sergeant and ducked under the belly of the near-side horse.

"Sarah! Sarah, darling! Speak to me. Are you all right?"

Down on his knees, he slipped an arm under her head. His heart skipped as he saw her eyelids flutter and then she was looking up at him.

"Did – did we stop it?" she asked, in a faint voice.

He almost laughed. He hugged her to him, his eyes filled with tears.

" *You* stopped it! You did it," he cried.

Suddenly he was aware that everything had gone quiet. He looked up and saw the queen had descended from the carriage and was peering around the front of the horse, looking down at Sarah.

"Is she one of those suffragette ladies?" The voice was querulous.

Sarah struggled up into a sitting position.

"No, your majesty. Though I must admit to having been inspired by one."

The queen turned to the police sergeant. "Get her out of there," she said.

Sarah had been incredibly lucky in that she had managed to grasp the shaft between the two horses and to hang onto it to keep from falling beneath their hooves. She had then fallen to the ground as they slowed.

Alec apologized to the queen and tried to explain the reason for stopping the coach. She turned away and was assisted back into the carriage.

"We had to delay your majesty," he said desperately. He glanced up at Big Ben. Delay her they had, for a good ten minutes, apparently. "It was a matter of life or death," he added. " *Your* life or death, your majesty."

At that moment a loud explosion came from the direction of the Houses of Parliament. Everyone looked up to see thick black smoke billowing up from the far side of the Victoria Tower.

After Dark

Chapter Twenty-Seven

"There was only one place for them to stack the gunpowder," said Inspector Kent. "That was in the Waiting Room; the room next to the Queen's Robing Room. And that, of course, would have been the most effective place to detonate it."

"But we looked in that room and it was empty," said Sarah. "You even had it locked."

Kent smiled. "Locked the door, yes, Miss Wilde. But the window, if you remember, was being replaced. It was not yet firmly set in place. They removed the window, stacked the gunpowder inside the room, and then replaced the window. The gunpowder had been placed inside coal sacks, with bits of coal on top of each to hide it. With the door locked, no one thought to look inside that room again."

Inspector Kent, Lord Sunbury, Alec and Sarah stood surveying the damage in the Victoria Tower.

"The would-be assassins did not plan this as well as they might," said Lord Sunbury. "First of all, we were lucky in that the powder they had was not of the best quality, plus much of it had got wet and did not explode. We have found one or two full sacks, still soaking wet. Secondly, the explosion, when it did come, blew out the window thus absorbing most of the impact. The wall between the waiting room and the next door office, as you can see, also took much of the blast, since it was basically just a thin partition wall."

"What about the Robing Room itself, my lord?" asked Alec. "That, after all, was their primary target."

Sunbury nodded. "Indeed it was," he said. "But even had Her Majesty been in that room, I think she would have fared better than the Illuminati intended. The wall did suffer cracks but, as I have said, the main force went elsewhere. One or two oil paintings fell from the wall in the room but otherwise it survived very well."

"Was anyone hurt?" asked Sarah.

"Unfortunately some over-zealous spectators had trespassed," said Kent. "They worked their way around, hoping to catch a glimpse of Her Majesty. They were hit by flying glass and some small fragments from the wall. No one seriously injured, however."

"Thank heaven," said Sarah.

"Thank heaven indeed, that you yourself were not hurt," said Lord Sunbury to her. "What you did, to delay Her Majesty, was incredibly brave."

Sarah blushed. "I – I did not stop to think," she murmured.

"Nonetheless," his lordship continued, "Her Majesty was impressed and extremely grateful."

"I hope she was," said Alec. His eyes locked on to Sarah. "I was afraid we might have lost her ... Sarah, that is, not the queen!"

"To that end," continued Lord Sunbury, "I must advise you that Her Majesty summons you two – Mister Chambers and Miss Wilde – to an audience at Buckingham Palace at ten o'clock on Friday morning. Two days from now."

"Oh!" was all Alec could say.

"What shall I wear?" whispered Sarah.

"You might also like to know, sir," said the inspector, addressing Alec, "that there have been some swift actions on the part of the Yard. It appears that Sir Charles Ridley was the main Illuminati agent for this assassination attempt. To pay for his sins he, and a couple of cohorts, are now on their way to residence in the Tower of London. He will be charged with treason, which is a hanging offense, as I am sure you are aware, sir."

"And Doctor Westcott?" Alec asked.

"Ah!" The inspector rubbed his chin. "Now there I am afraid he managed to fly the coop, as it were, sir. Disappeared without a trace, as they say. But we have high hopes of tracking him down."

"What of Samuel Mathers?" asked Sarah.

"Ah, yes, miss. Mister Mathers, I am afraid, made a very quick exit across the Channel to join his wife in Paris. Not a problem, of course. We have an extradition agreement with that country."

"So who is running the Golden Dawn?" asked Sarah.

The inspector pulled out his well-worn notebook and consulted it. "A Mister Aleister Crowley, it would appear," he said. He looked surprised when Sarah laughed.

It was a small gathering at Alec's rooms in Westmoreland Terrace, a week after the assassination attempt. Mrs. Jenkins had presented an excellent dinner and now, as they relaxed away from the table, Gordon moved among the guests ensuring that wine glasses were kept filled.

Lord Sunbury had sent his apologies for being unable to attend, due to a government meeting, but Alec was pleased to see all of his other friends there: Sarah, Inspector Kent, Daniel and Georgina, and Jeremy.

"All right, Alec," said Jeremy, when they were all settled and relaxed. "Now you have to tell us about your audience with the queen. All the details, if you would be so kind."

Alec looked at Sarah and they both smiled. She wore a pale green *mousseline de soie* gown and elbow-length white gloves. A single strand of pearls was around her neck and her deep red hair was piled up on top of her head. He thought that he had never seen her look so beautiful, nor so happy.

"Well, as you all know by now, Her Majesty did me the honor of knighting me."

"*Sir* Alec Chambers," sighed Jeremy. "There will be no keeping up with you now, my friend."

Alec chuckled. "I am still just myself, Jeremy. Titles will never change that."

"But start at the beginning, do," said Daniel. "Did you apprise Her Majesty of all the dark doings of the Illuminati? Our chase across Europe, for example?"

"Oh, yes. The queen seemed most interested in the Nicholas Flamel material, and the cipher and everything. She was fascinated by the coded gravestone and especially by the Gurat underground church. I told her of how Sarah was kidnapped, when they could get the notebook no other way."

"And I told her of Alec's escape from the burning house in Stuttgart," added Sarah. "Then our trip to Belgium and the way the gunpowder was eventually carried up the Thames in a sailing barge."

"You two most certainly did cover a lot of ground, if I may say so, Miss Wilde," said the inspector, sipping his wine.

"All in the line of duty," said Sarah.

"I would say you went over and above that," commented Georgina. "How long were you with Her Majesty?"

"More than two hours," said Sarah. "We even had tea with her!"

They all smiled.

"But what I do not understand," persisted Georgina, "is why you, Sarah, did not receive recognition. Not to downplay Alec's knighthood, but it was you who threw yourself in front of the Queen's carriage."

Alec and Sarah exchanged looks.

"She would not accept any recognition," said Alec, spreading his hands in despair.

"I told Her Majesty that I would be getting my recognition very soon ... in another way," said Sarah.

"What on earth do you mean?"

Alec rose and crossed to where Sarah sat. He took her hand and turned to his friends. "Sarah and I are to be married," he said.

There were congratulations from them all. Hudson was sent for champagne and they all toasted the happy couple.

"So when you marry Alec – *Sir* Alec – you will become *Lady* Sarah Chambers," sighed Georgina. "Now I see it. Now I'm happy!"

"Well I am not," snorted Daniel. "I think the Queen got off extremely cheaply, if you ask me."

"Now, Daniel," soothed Alec. "There is still more to tell." He turned to Sarah and inclined his head. She smiled and looked around at all of their friends.

"When Her Majesty discovered that both my parents are deceased," she said, "she insisted that she would provide my dowry ... an incredibly generous dowry at that."

"Bravo!" Daniel put down his champagne glass and applauded. "Now that is more like it."

Just then the front door bell was heard to ring and Hudson went to answer it. Shortly afterward he showed Lord Sunbury into the room.

"Many apologies for my lateness in joining you," he said. "The cabinet meeting wound up earlier than expected so I thought I would rush over and see if I could catch some of the festivities."

"Delighted to have you join us," said Alec.

"They have just broken the news of their engagement, my lord," said Jeremy. "Also, of the Queen's generosity."

"Bravo," said Sunbury. "Yes, and fully deserved, if I may say so."

Hudson brought him a glass of champagne and topped off the glasses of the others. Sunbury stood for a moment smiling around at them all.

"What?" asked Sarah, her eyes twinkling. "Your lordship looks a little like the cat that ate the canary."

"Indeed," he said. "For I am the bearer of more news. But let us be comfortable. I hate standing!"

They laughed and sat down again. As though to draw out their expectations, Lord Sunbury drank some champagne and then complimented Alec on the vintage.

Jeremy started tapping his foot, though Alec thought it was probably an unconscious movement.

Lord Sunbury cleared his throat. "As you know, Sir Charles Ridley, for his sins, ended up in the Tower. His goods and holdings are, then, surrendered to the Crown. It seems that you two ..." here he smiled at Alec and Sarah, "... have really touched the heart of our beloved sovereign by saving her from probable assassination. In her infinite wisdom, then, she has made up her mind to make you a wedding gift ..."

"What!" Sarah couldn't help interrupting. "But she has already been more than generous."

"None the less, she has asked me to advice you that, as a wedding gift, she is presenting you with the house – a rather fine house, I have to say – in Belgrave Square, lately owned by the traitor Sir Charles Ridley."

There was a long silence.

"Well done!" Daniel came to his feet and clapped his hands. The others quickly joined him.

"How wonderful!"

"So richly deserved."

"What a way to start your married life," said Georgina.

"Gracious! That will be an enormous change from my rented rooms in Bloomsbury," said Sarah.

"Oh! One more thing," said Inspector Kent. He fumbled in the tail pocket of his frock coat.

"What now?" asked Sarah. Her eyes went to Alec, who shrugged his shoulders.

The inspector brought out a small, carefully wrapped package and handed it to Alec. As he took it, Alec's eyes lit up.

"I think I know," he said.

Kent smiled. "Yes. You might call it a wedding gift from the Illuminati. It is the other half of the Nicholas Flamel notebook. We ..." he inclined his head towards Lord Sunbury, who smiled and nodded. "We thought that the two halves should be brought back together and kept that way."

"That is wonderful. Thank you," said Alec.

"All the other material – the loose pages of Flamel's notes – have been presented to the British Museum," said Daniel.

"I could not think of a more complete and happier ending," said the inspector.

"Oh, I think I can," said Sarah, moving across to the inspector. "One more thing. As you have heard, my father is deceased. So, inspector, would you please give me away at our wedding?"

The inspector almost dropped his champagne glass. His face turned red and he beamed around at everyone. "It would be an honor, miss – er, Lady Sarah – Miss Wilde."

Appendix

Trithemius Code

	1	2	3	4	5	6	7
A	Jesus	Immortal	Producing	Angels	Gives	Grant	Eternal
B	God	Omnipotent	Saving	Archangels	Delivers	Requiring (needy)	Perpetual
C	Savior	Compassionate	Illuminating	Saints	Attributes	Faithful	Infinite
D	King	Ineffable	Conferring	Spheres	Increases	Attendants	Angelic
E	Pastor	Universal	Moderating	Heavens	Presents	Righteous	Immortal
F	Author	Almighty	Expressing	Sea	Renders	Penitents	Enduring
G	Redemptor	Magnificent	Governing	Earth	Remits	Good	Incomprehensible
H	Prince	Puissant	Disposing (of)	World	Renders	Supplicants	Incorruptible
I	Maker	Just	Dominating	Man	Envoys	Hopeful	Durable
J	Creator	Sempiternal	Dominator (of)	Men	Envoys	Hopeful	Durable
K	Conservator	Celestial	Creating	Sun	Transmits	Patient	Permanent
L	Governor	Divine	Cognizing	Moon	Administers	Afflicted	Ineffable
M	Emperor	Excellent	Gilding	All	Permits	All	Celestial
N	Moderator	Triumphant	Blessing	Hierarchies	Inspires	Tormented	Divine
O	Rector	Just	Constituting	Bodies	Retribution	Perturbed	Interminable
P	Judge	Clement	Confirming	Spirits	Orders	Desolated	Perfect
Q	Illustrator	Peaceful	Conducting	Souls	Contributes	Mortals	Sincere
R	Illuminator	Pacific	Sanctifying	Times	Frees	Humans	Pure
S	Consolator	Invisible	Honoring	Humanity	Confers	Languishing	Glorious
T	Sire	Eternal	Ministering (to)	Ages	Manifests	Repentant	Supernatural
U	Dominator	Invincible	Exorcising	Eternity	Reveals	Catholics	Invincible
V	Dominator	Invincible	Exorcising	Eternity	Reveals	Catholics	Invincible
W	Dominator	Invincible	Exorcising	Eternity	Reveals	Catholics	Invincible
X	Creator	Benign	Elevating	Firmaments	Maintains	In the World	Peaceful
Y	Psalmist	Pitiable	Sustaining	Stars	Admits	Sinners	Happy
Z	Sovereign	Incomprehensible	Vivifying	Air	Agitates	Charitable	Excellent
&	Protector	Excellent	Ordering	Cosmos	Develops	Virtuous	Uplifting

Trithemius Code

	8	9	10	11	12	13	14
A	Life	(Together with His) Saints	In Heavens	Majesty	Incomprehensible	Sincerely	Preached
B	Joy	Servants	Ever and Ever	Goodness	God	Really	Announced
C	Joyousness	Loved	Without end	Kindliness	Creator	Saintly	Published
D	Glory	Saved	In one Infinity	Sapience	Favor	Evangelically	Revealed
E	Consolation	Beatified	Perpetuity	Charity	Jesus	Devotedly	Denounced
F	Felicity	Elected	Sempiternity	Power	Transformator	Intelligibly	Acclaimed
G	Beatitude	Confessors	Enduring	Infinity	Dominator	Evidently	Exulted
H	Jubilation	Apostles	Incessantly	Sublimity	Preservator	Publicly	Summoned
I	Tranquility	Evangelists	Irreversibly	Benignity	Immortal	Faithfully	Interpreted
J	Tranquility	Evangelists	Irreversibly	Benignity	Immortal	Faithfully	Interpreted
K	Amenity	Martyrs	Eternally	Commiseration	Supreme	Ardently	Reported
L	Recreation	Angels	In Glory	Excellence	Mighty	Constantly	Narrated
M	Clarity	Archangels	In the Light	Pity	Omnipotent	Sagely	Served
N	Union	Dominions	In Paradise	Clemency	Ineffable	Carefully	Praised
O	Peace	Proselytes	Always	Mercy	Redemptor	Virtuously	Recited
P	Light	Disciples	In Divinity	Divinity	Sempiternal	Catholically	Pronounced
Q	Glorification	Deified	In Deity	Deity	Governor	Cordially	Repeated
R	Benediction	Ministers	In Felicity	Omnipotent	Rector	Reverently	Treated
S	Security	Sanctified	In His Reign	Virtue	Sovereign	Theologically	Speculated
T	Favors	Predestined	In His Kingdom	Love	Invincible	Justly	Collated
U	Fruition	Preferred	In Beatitude	Perfection	Puissant	Divinely	Spread
V	Fruition	Preferred	In Beatitude	Perfection	Puissant	Divinely	Spread
W	Fruition	Preferred	In Beatitude	Perfection	Puissant	Divinely	Spread
X	Happiness	Prophets	In His Vision	Force	Merciful	Learnedly	Cognized
Y	Light	Patriarchs	In His Magnificence	Magnificence	All Powerful	Entirely	Recognized
Z	Exultation	Cherubs	To the Throne	Grandeur	Magnificent	Studiously	Contemplated
&	Pleasures	Professors	In all Eternity	Favor	Sanctified	Spiritually	Produced

291

LaVergne, TN USA
06 December 2010

207447LV00004BA/6/P